Unwrapped Sky

BOOKS BY RJURIK DAVIDSON

Unwrapped Sky
The Stars Askew (forthcoming)

The Library of Forgotten Books (collection)

Unwrapped Sky

Rjurik Davidson

A TOM DOHERTY ASSOCIATES BOOK

NEW YORK

UNWRAPPED SKY

Edited by James Frenkel

Map by Ellisa Mitchell

A Tor Book
Published by Tom Doherty Associates, LLC
175 Fifth Avenue
New York, NY 10010

www.tor-forge.com

Tor® is a registered trademark of Tom Doherty Associates, LLC.

The Library of Congress Cataloging-in-Publication Data
is available upon request.

ISBN 978-0-7653-2988-2 (hardcover)
ISBN 978-1-4299-4838-8 (e-book)

Tor books may be purchased for educational, business, or promotional use.
For information on bulk purchases, please contact Macmillan Corporate
and Premium Sales Department at 1-800-221-7945, extension 5442,
or write specialmarkets@macmillan.com.

First Edition: April 2014

Printed in the United States of America

0 9 8 7 6 5 4 3 2 1

For Maryellen, Alastair, and Francesca

ACKNOWLEDGMENTS

My editors, James Frenkel and Liz Gorinsky; all my family; Tessa Kum; Scott Westerfeld; the guys at Serapeum: Andrew Macrae, Keith Stephenson, Peter Hickman; Brendan Duffy; Matthew Chrulew; Ben Peek; the ClarionSouth Class of 2005; the Supanova crit group; my comrades at *Overland* journal: Jeff Sparrow, Jacinda Woodhead, and Alex Skutenko; and Leena Kärkkäinen.

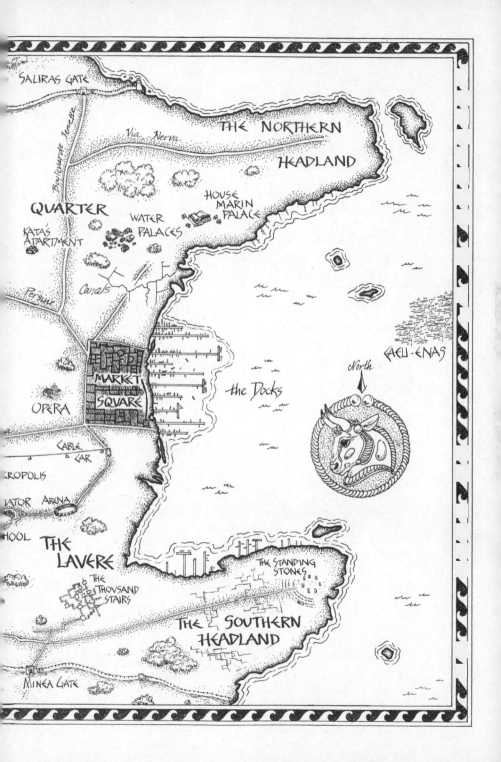

Behold what quiet settles on the world.
Night wraps the sky in tribute from the stars.
In hours like this, one rises to address
The ages, history, and all creation.

—Vladimir Mayakovsky, "Past One O'Clock"

PART I

ENDINGS

The God Aya was ever rebellious. When others lazed away their days in the pleasure garden, he could be found digging curiously at the things that lay beneath the ground, or performing one-man shows to entertain himself.

"Sit down!" Alerion yelled.

"No!" Aya danced a little dance, something like a jig. There was a twinkle in his eyes.

Alerion sighed and rolled over to sun himself once again. He splashed water on his face. "You'll be the ruin of us."

But Aya did not hear, for he was already building a great palace from crystals he had found deep beneath the earth. The palace glinted in the sun and when Aya laughed, the sound echoed through its many passageways like a stream tinkling over stones.

That was the way of it: the other gods, happy and passive; Aya, searching always for something new, building and creating, restless. The joy Aya took in his many ventures upset the other gods; deep within, they wished to subdue him. This was before the War and the Cataclysm, yet their causes were to be found in the gods' resentment toward their restless comrade.

As Aya admired his palace, he did not notice Alerion's brooding eyes settling on him.

—from The Legend of Aya

ONE

For the first time in ten years the minotaurs came to the city of Caeli-Amur from the winding road that led through the foothills to the north. There were three hundred or more of them. From the city they appeared as tiny figures—refugees perhaps. But as they approached, the size of their massive bodies, the magnificence of their horned bull heads, the shape of their serrated short-swords, became apparent. The minotaurs had come for the Festival of the Bull. When the week was over, they would descend from the white cliffs on which the city perched and board the ships that would carry them out over the Sunken City and home to their island of Aya.

The citizens watched the minotaurs silently, from their balconies or the city's white walls. Some of the elderly leaned toward each other and whispered: "So few? There are so few of them." Many of the children, especially from the factory districts, ran out to meet the magnificent creatures, laughing and calling to them until they drew close and the power and size of the minotaurs quieted them. Gliders swung out over the creatures and watched them from above, safe on the cool currents of air that swept in from the sea. Finally, when the minotaurs arrived at the city, some, who still held to the old ways, fell onto their knees in supplication. The minotaurs were still worshipped as gods by a few, though to harm them was considered a crime by all.

The orderly line broke apart when the minotaurs entered the city and spread out like tributaries into a delta: some climbed their way down to the water palaces and steam baths that ran along the peninsula at the northeast side of Caeli-Amur. Others caught the sooty street-trams through the windy streets along the cliffs, or took the cable car that ran from the massive machine tower near the piers to the top of the cliffs. Those minotaurs seeking knowledge ventured to Caeli-Amur's famous cafés, where philosopher-assassins debated in the afternoon, drinking coffee and eating fruit. By nightfall, the minotaurs could be found in the liquor palaces and beer halls.

In one such drinking tavern called the Ruins, long after the sun had descended over the mountains to the west, Kata eyed a group of minotaurs. They dominated the place, which, perched on the edge of the factory district close to the city's northern gate, was typical of workers' establishments of the area. The proprietor of the Ruins had decorated the hot and dirty hall with a bar along one wall with fragments of ancient technology scavenged from the old places. In one corner, a lamp was cleverly constructed from a ragged half of a broken metallic sphere; the remnants of its insides—an intricate latticework of fine metals—were blackened and twisted. Strange angular implements hung on the walls: here what seemed to be a bulging glove ending in protuberances of unknown function, there a shield-sized fragment of a larger curved structure, geometric shapes cut into it. Had these pieces functioned in any way, the Houses would long ago have confiscated them. But as they were ruined, they remained weirdly beautiful decorations reminding the patrons of the long-lost glories of the world.

Usually filled with gray-eyed factory workers—the older ones keen to deaden their aching bodies with cheap beer, the young ones filled with rage and likely to end up fists flying in the surrounding alleys—the wooden stools and tables were as rough and worn as its clients. This evening, the men sat frightened and quiet in the corners, or slunk past the minotaurs, hoping not to brush against them. Minotaurs were quick to anger, especially when they were filled with beer or hot-liquor.

Kata knew she would have to approach; she needed two of them. But first things first, she thought as she took a drink of the bitter liquid from the flask at her waist. She kept her face still, though she wanted to grimace. The medicine tasted earthy and pungent, like dirt and ul-tree roots mixed together.

She watched and scratched distractedly at the metal sheaths

that rubbed against her skin beneath her shirt. Realizing what she was doing, she stopped. The shirt was dark and loose, and she wore a skirt that reached her knees. Together they showed off her shoulder-length hair, which was black as the minotaurs' eyes. Beneath her clothes Kata was lithe and unusually muscular; she was an athlete, of sorts.

A group of four minotaurs sat laughing at the front of the room, telling one another jokes about labyrinths and reminiscing about the Numerian Wars. She remembered the Festival of the Bull a decade earlier, when she was living on the streets after her mother's death, but had forgotten the sheer physical *presence* of the minotaurs. Their shoulders and chests were like the statues of Caeli-Amur's heroes that stood in the water-parks to the south of the city, where waterfalls and canals flowed gently through manicured gardens. The statues were seven, eight feet of white marble, muscles sculpted beneath their stone cloaks. But it was the minotaurs' heads, those most valuable of trophies, that emanated majesty: the flaring nostrils, the wiry and perfumed hide, and most especially, the deep and dark eyes, mesmerizing and inhuman. Kata was afraid to look into the eyes, but she would have to.

To one side along the bar sat a slightly smaller minotaur with a dark hide. He did not speak but seemed to be brooding.

That one, she thought.

She slid down the bar and stood next to him.

"Why are you watching us?" he asked.

She could not look him in the eye; she felt guilty. "How far is it to Aya, across the sea?"

"Five days, if the wind is good."

"Why don't you use steamers? You could be sure to arrive in time."

"Tradition. Anyway, I do not trust steamers. What if they break on the open sea? What if those wheels along their sides fall off? Give me the wind any day. It cannot be conquered but offers its gifts freely. It is a trusty partner, at times."

She looked up into his left eye and then away from its glistening darkness. Its inky magnificence horrified her.

"What have you here, Aemilius?" The booming voice came from

another minotaur. She forced herself to look up at the massive head towering over her. She held his eye for a moment before looking away.

"You know," he said, stepping toward her so his chest came close to her face, "there was a time when a minotaur could stay wherever he liked during the Festival of the Bull."

The smaller one sat impassively. "Those days are gone, Cyriacus."

Kata stood up and placed her hand against Cyriacus's chest, which was like a solid wall close to her face. He must have been almost seven feet tall. His presence was magnetic, his strength palpable. She pushed against him. He didn't move. She pushed harder, and he took a step backwards. "It's rude to stand so close to someone you do not know," she said.

Cyriacus laughed and turned. "Hey, Dexion. We have a spirited one here."

Aemilius leaned into her and said, "It is not wise to play with minotaurs. They are unpredictable and dangerous."

"I can hold my own," she replied. He nodded, turned, and walked away, leaving her with Cyriacus.

"Have a drink," the minotaur said, handing her his own tankard.

She took a swig of the liquor, which burned her throat. She held back the cough. "Anlusian hot-wine," she said, feeling her lips and mouth burn with the spices, the vapor rushing into her nose, making her eyes water.

"Yes. These new liquors fire the belly and the mind."

"I live close to here," she said. "I have more wine there, and it is free."

He stood close to her again, and she felt the heat of his breath on her face. She forced herself to look up into his deep black eyes and put her hand against his chest again. This time she did not push him away.

The edge of the factory district was filled with families and older workers who had managed to escape living in the center of that industrial quarter. Here the apartment blocks rose to four and five stories and were built from bricks and concrete. Not crammed together like those in the center or the district or the slums close to the Arena, yet without the vastness of the Arantine where the elite of House Arbor built their mansions, Kata's neighborhood was reflected its citizens' status. Here they could breathe the fresh air that drifted from the sea, only occasionally punctuated by billows of smoke.

As Kata and Cyriacus walked along the narrow street where her apartment was located, the little street-child Henri ran next to them, "Kata, Kata! Yensa fudge, Yensa fudge?" Offering them a pouch of the toxic hallucinogen, he was unmoved by the minotaur. Kata liked that about the boy, whose face looked pure, despite the streaks of grime across it. She'd known a hundred like him: their innocent faces shrouded violent and animalistic instincts, the kind you needed to survive on the streets. Even now his eyes were wide as saucers, a sure sign he had eaten his own fudge.

She pushed the boy away. "Not now."

The boy scurried around them to Cyriacus's side. "Yensa fudge? Yensa fudge?"

The minotaur swung his arm out and the boy flew into the gutter, his eyes blinking rapidly. Kata looked back at him and shook her head quickly, as if to say, stop it.

Leaving the boy coughing behind them, Kata and Cyriacus climbed up the stairs that ran along the side of the building. Kata's apartment was on the third floor of her building.

The key rattled in the lock, and the door swung open. Kata lit the lamp by the door. It was her windowless parlor, a kitchen off to one side. More stairs led up to her bedroom and a balcony that overlooked the eastern parts of the city, the Opera House and the docks.

Kata walked over to the table and leaned against it. Cyriacus slammed the door behind him—it shuddered on its hinges. He strode toward her, grasped her by the waist, lifted her like a doll, and sat her on the table, leaning in so she could smell the hot spices of the Anlusian wine and his hide, scented with pungent ginger and clove perfume. She touched the side of his face, feeling the thick, wiry hair. But still she could not look him in the eyes. Quickly she took her hands from his face so she would be ready.

Cyriacus stepped in and pulled her closer by the hips, so their bodies were hard against each other, Kata's legs splayed around his trunklike thighs, her skirt riding up her legs. She placed her hands on the table behind her as he slowly and carefully unbuttoned her shirt with thick, powerful fingers. He looked down to see the waistband that held the sheaths behind her back.

"What?" he said, laughing. "A knife belt? What would a little—?"

But Kata had already drawn both long-daggers. She plunged them into his ribs. Cyriacus let out a deafening roar and threw the table away from him. Kata flew through the air backwards, the table rolling and spinning beneath her. She struck the wall and fell to the floor, the table crashing against her shins. She felt no pain yet, just the rush of adrenaline.

Cyriacus stared down at the two daggers, his head shifting from left to right in disbelief. Only the handles were visible, one jutting from each side. Blood coursed in deep red streams down his waist and onto his thighs. He snorted, looked up at her, and said, "You've killed me."

Kata struggled to her feet and stared back at him. She was horrified by the scene: everything was wrong. Though she had killed before, it had always been in the wars between the Houses. She had felled three men with her knives, watching them collapse in seconds before her. It was war and she felt no remorse. Now she could hardly bear the sight of this magnificent creature at the end of its life.

Astonishingly, Cyriacus came at her. She turned and ran to the stairs that led up to her bedroom, thumping footsteps close behind her. She pushed herself, taking the steps three at a time, her heart rattling in her chest. If she could make it to her bedside table, she might stand a chance.

She burst into the room and dived across the bed, reaching for her bolt-thrower on the small table. From the corner of her eye she saw him charge into the room. She turned, raised the bulky weapon, and fired a bolt. Blood spurted from his abdomen like pollen from an open flower.

He staggered back and came at her again. His nose flared and a rumbling sound—either in anger or pain, she couldn't tell—came from his chest and throat.

She threw open the doors and ran onto the balcony, reloading the thrower. No man could withstand such physical punishment, yet Cyriacus still came at her, immense and godlike. She heard the final click of the thrower and raised it, but it was too late. He was on her, his force crushing her against the balcony wall. A cry escaped her lips. So, she thought, this is how it ends—I was wrong to commit this blasphemy.

His breath steamed from his nostrils; his long, thick tongue lolled from his mouth. "I will crack your neck like a rabbit's," he said, grasping the top of her head in one huge hand. "I will take you with me, woman, to the land of light."

"Please," she said, her voice broken with fear and resignation.

Cyriacus looked at her in puzzlement, blinked slowly, his hands losing their strength, and crashed to the floor like a cliff into the sea.

Kata left him there, changed her clothes, and walked out into the night. Henri was gone: off to peddle his fudge elsewhere; the Festival of the Bull would be good for business. He'd be back: the streets around her apartment were his turf. He slept somewhere in the neighborhood, perhaps in a dry drain or a nook beneath one of the apartments.

She cut through the factory district. It was full of dirt and grime, the smoke from the underground machines pumping out even at night. She had never forgotten her mother's last words as she lay in the factory infirmary, her face a splotchy red-white, the contagion eating away at her insides: "Do whatever you must to survive, Kata. The gods know there's nothing else to do." And then blood had come to mother's lips and dribbled down her chin, her chest had thrust forward unnaturally, an awful odor was loosed in the room, and she had died. The next day Kata was on the street. She cried that first day—never again.

After her mother died, Kata had grown up in these streets, running with the urchin gangs, selling trinkets, stealing, doing odds and ends for House Technis, running messages, setting up robberies and murders. She had been a pinch-faced girl, scrawny but sly. Like the other children, she had dreamed of joining the ranks of dispossessed philosopher-assassins who lived moment to moment in Caeli-Amur, debating in the cafés in the afternoon, lounging in the liquor halls in the evening, forever at the beck and call of the Houses. She had one more minotaur to kill and she would be free.

Now Kata climbed up through the city toward the mountaintop and along the edges of the factory district. She kept away from the larger streets where the city was alive with news of the minotaurs' arrival, and after half an hour arrived at House Technis. She slid through a side gate in the outer wall that surrounded the complex of palaces and administration buildings, gardens and ponds.

She came to the enormous palace, like the monstrous invention of a child's fantasy, the ancient building swamped by layer after layer of extension, new wings and towers that had been added, regardless of architectural taste or style. It appeared as if blocks had simply been piled crazily one upon the other without design. Even now, as Kata glanced up at the towering structure, builders were working on the west wing.

Kata passed along the labyrinthine corridors that, having also been built at different times, were forced to accommodate themselves to the planless structure to which they had been added. Pneumatiques whizzed and whirred overhead on hundreds of tiny wires. Along the walls, pipes rattled and shuddered and heaved: some carrying small barrels filled with instructions, others of unknown purpose. In the background, the constant thump of steam engines could be heard, as the building shifted the rooms deep inside its mobile southeastern wing around each other, according to some preplanned sequence. She had never been inside that particular technological marvel, but had heard that it was easy to lose yourself as each room rose, fell, or spun before locking temporarily into its new location.

She slipped past a constant stream of house agents rushing to and fro, some carrying boxes, others pushing carts filled with delicate new technologies from the New-Men in Anlusia, yet others dragging bound and hooded seditionist prisoners to the dungeon. The place was a cacophony of voices yelling to each other all manner of things: what directions to Subofficiate Aruki's office, about the latest strike to break out in what was becoming a wave of industrial unrest, about favors offered or claimed in return. Guards leaned against the walls beside their bolt-throwers, short-swords dangling from belts. Others played dice in a little alcove.

Kata passed through small grottoes; a large room filled with sec-retaries lined in rows, each busily shuffling papers; another where cramped offices, enclosed by five-foot walls, stood like little build-ings in the vastness of the room. Pneumatics zipped in and out of the little offices as if running on a vast network of spiderwebs.

She found Officiate Rudé, a wiry little half-Anlusian adminis-trator, in his office. Like most Anlusians, he had a youthful visage for someone so late in life: it was his quick and energetic move-ments, his slim and boyish body. He told her to wait as he signed a number of papers.

"Strikes, strikes, strikes." He rubbed his face with his hands. "Why should the workers be so belligerent now, when things are changing so fast?"

"Perhaps it's because things are uncertain that they think they can seize their opportunity." Kata was aware that as winter had broken and spring set in, a wave of strikes has broken out in the city. The first few—the weavers who worked for House Arbor and the fishermen employed by House Marin—had been threatened into returning to work. Later, subofficiates were replaced, sedi-tionists thrown into the dungeons, adjustments made to the facto-ries' operations. But that had not stopped more spot-strikes from breaking out like little fires on a smoldering summer's day.

"Well, the House has had enough. The time for kindnesses is over." Rudé looked up from his forms. "Let's get to work then, shall we?"

Things were set in motion. Rudé accompanied her with two work-men back to the apartment in the carriage that would secretly carry away the minotaur. She took them to the balcony but avoided the sight of the minotaur's body.

Rudé took a sharp intake of breath and ran his hands through his fire-red hair speckled slightly with white. "Majestical," he said. "Fascinating. I should have liked to talk to him. . . . I didn't think you would do it."

"I told you I would," said Kata.

"I knew you were hard, but even so."

She stole a glance at the creature. It lay at odd angles against the balcony wall.

"Get to work," Rudé ordered.

The workmen opened their cases and took from them mechanical saws and jagged knives with wicked blades.

"And be careful of the horns. They're the most valuable pieces. And the hide," said Rudé.

"You people . . . ," Kata said.

"Remember, you asked for this job." Rudé looked away from the minotaur across the city.

Kata could not bear the high whine of the saw or the wet thump of the minotaur's flesh, so she walked down the stairs.

As Rudé followed her, he called back: "Don't damage the eyes. Our thaumaturgists need those eyes for their preparations. Don't get anything in the eyes." He followed Kata into the room and said, "One more, Kata, and your debt will be repaid. Think about that. Think about how hard you've worked. Just one more minotaur."

"Even if I repay the debt, I'll never be free of you. None of us ever will. It doesn't matter which House, you're all the same."

Rudé threw his head back and laughed. "Kata, remember, without us you'd still be on the street. Remember whom this building belongs to." Technis had bought many of the buildings in the area, as if they weren't content with their other forms of control but craved power over the citizens' everyday lives.

From above, she could still hear the sickening sound of meat and bone being cut to pieces. When they left, she suddenly felt an aching in her legs and back. She looked down at her blood-covered shins, pieces of skin scraped into ridges near her ankles. The adrenaline had long ago left her and now all she could feel was pain.

TWO

Two nights after the death of Cyriacus, Kata watched the Sun Parade, celebrating the moment four hundred years earlier when the sun had broken through the fog and Saliras's forces had been routed by the minotaurs and the Caeli-Amurians together. Caeli-Amur was a city of festivals. Festival of the Sun, Aya's Day, the Stars Descent, Celebration of the Dancing Goat, Alerion's Day, the Twilight Observance—rare was the month when there was no celebration to be had.

The parade descended from Via Gracchia on the top of the cliffs toward the Market Square by the piers. Figures walked with hideous masks: distorted faces that looked as if they had melted in great heat; goats with gigantic eyes and too-thin faces; and, of course, bulls. Others played thin, high-pitched flutes or circular drums that fit beneath their arms and could be squeezed to change the pitch. All were dressed outrageously in oranges, reds, yellows. Crowds watched from the side of the road, clapping at the leering masks. Scattered among them were the minotaurs.

Kata glanced at the crowd. On the other side of the road stood the smaller and darker minotaur she had met at the bar. She emptied the acrid medicine from her flask, gagging as she swallowed it. It was the last of the preparation. When she had finished the job, she would be able to afford more. She had spent most of her remaining money at the markets, buying deadly herbs. From these she had prepared poison, mixing it with the flagon of wine, which she then placed in her cupboard. She could not risk another fight: Who would have believed anyone could be as strong as Cyriacus, to take so much physical punishment?

She had poison enough for ten men. That should be enough.

She scuttled gingerly through a break in the parade, dodging the drummers and dancers. Her shins were still scabby and bruised.

"Hello," she said to the minotaur.

"Ah," he said, "the woman who can hold her own. And did you?"

She smiled. His eyes did not seem so terrible this time; they seemed to be laughing. "I always hold my own."

"I see. I'm Aemilius."

"Kata," she said. "You're not marching in the parade."

He shrugged and looked to the sky. "Look at the moon. Can you see Aya's handprints, side by side, from when he threw it into the sky?"

"It's bright, isn't it?"

"So bright that on a clear and calm night like this, you can see the Sunken City through the crystal water."

"No." Kata frowned in disbelief. She knew that Caeli-Enas, Caeli-Amur's sister city, was deep beneath the ocean. But she had always assumed that it was lost in the murky depths.

"I swear. Would you like to see?"

She hesitated. She should take this chance. It was falling into her lap. "Yes."

They marched together up to the great steam tower—full of thumping and clattering from the engine at its base—that powered the cable car from the top of the cliff to the piers. There were too many people on the streets, and the walk would have been a long one.

They entered a doorway in the tower's base and climbed wide stone stairs up to a wide entrance chamber with a platform opening out to the air on one side. A bustle of white-haired people with pointy beards or shawls or aging, curved backs stood around, whispering to each other excitedly. To view the city and the Sun Parade from the cable car was popular among the older citizens. The youth lined the streets or marched in the parade itself.

Kata and Aemilius watched as a cable car swung around the rear of the tower and reemerged at the open side of the chamber. They stepped into the car, which filled with people around them. There was no conductor—the cable car had always been free in

Caeli-Amur, a remnant from ancient days perhaps. The workers who kept it going were supported by donations from the citizens. Some civic spirit still lived on in the city.

As they swung over the city, looking at the parade winding below like a cascade of lights, Kata noticed the passengers in the carriage kept away from Aemilius. She recognized their wide-eyed apprehension.

"You realize the effect you have on those around you," she whispered to him.

"Of course." Aemilius did not look about: to do so would be undignified.

"You have a strange bearing; you hold yourself apart somehow."

"And you," he said. "You do also."

She looked away from him, down at the street-trams caught in the traffic below. The streets were like rivers of yellow and flickering lights. She could think of nothing more to say.

They reached the docks, nine piers jutting into a glassy, silent ocean. Clippers and cutters floated between monolithic steamers, the new and the old side by side. The piers were quiet: there were no signs of the Xsanthian dockworkers and only a few boatmen moved around carrying rope or boxes of tools. The moon hovered above, lighting a section of the water in one silvery molten band. Aemilius paid a boatman and took a small rowboat.

"It's too far," she said. "We need a steamer."

"It's not too far. Get in."

She hesitated, then stepped onto the dark wooden planks of the boat.

Aemilius rowed away from the city, over the glassy ocean, the oars making satisfying creaks against the wooden oarlocks and subtle splashes as they entered the water. The two of them were silent as they left the city far behind, though they could still hear the laughter and the pipes and drums of the festival floating over the water.

"Look," said Aemilius after some time.

Kata peered over the edge of the boat and put her hand to her chest in astonishment. "You can see it, you can really see it."

Beneath them Caeli-Enas shimmered silvery white. Buildings and boulevards came suddenly into focus and then blurred again as the water moved quietly beneath them. Perched on its sunken hill, the great white dome and marble pillars of a statuesque building emerged briefly into view. Over four hundred years that city had slept beneath the ocean and with it, the last secrets of the ancients. A sense of wonder awakened in Kata. For the first time in years, she felt that the world was a large place filled with possibility.

"Most of the city was white marble," said Aemilius. "I walked those streets when I was young. I watched white-caparisoned horses pull crow-black carriages. I watched street-officers lighting gas lamps on hot summer nights as lovers drifted through the wide streets."

"How old are you?" asked Kata.

"Five hundred and twelve."

Kata drew a long, quiet breath. So old. Eventually she said, "There is a sadness about you."

"Look," he said. "Can you see something moving down there? They say there are still sea serpents with heads like houses, bodies big as Numerian caravans."

"There are," she said. "I've seen them. They come closer to land during the winter." She caught a glimpse of something snaking through the Sunken City's streets. It seemed to warp in and out of existence. A chill ran down her spine. Should the creature surface, their rowboat would capsize and the serpent would swallow them whole.

"Perhaps we should head back," she said.

Again, Kata led a minotaur up the cobblestoned alleyway to her house. Again the creature came in without encouragement, looking around her parlor with interest. He stopped at the bookshelf that held the few philosophical classics she could afford: Marka's *Unintentional Action* and Ugesio's *Morality and Madness*, the two most popular texts.

"You taught yourself philosophy?" he said.

"A little."

"This book *Unintentional Action,* what does it argue?" Aemilius said.

"Ah, one of the new philosophers. Marka argues we only have the illusion of choice, the illusion of free will. He says that we are controlled by our past, by our surroundings, that we are forced into certain actions." The streets where Kata lived as a child, the death of her mother, flashed into her mind, as did her desperate and ongoing desire to escape them, to escape the memory of them.

"And what do you think?" Aemilius asked.

"I think he's right. We are all forced to do things we'd rather not, to compromise."

"But is it not possible that our very knowledge of those forces allows us *some* measure of freedom?"

Kata pressed her lips. "I don't know. Sometimes I don't even know where I am."

"The ancients said that everything has its place," said Aemilius. "Everything finds its place."

"Those days have passed."

"Perhaps."

"Would you like a drink?" She felt a knot in her stomach and tried to swallow, her throat dry with fear. Nausea built up in her body. Her little finger twitched, then was still. Oh no, she thought, not now. She fought the rising sickness back.

"Yes," he said.

She walked to her small kitchen, took the flagon of wine, two cups, and placed them on the bench. She stared at them.

"You have no windows in this room?"

"It's hemmed in on all sides. Above, there is a balcony."

"It is a sparse house. Not much comfort here."

"As much comfort as I need. I fought for this place. I struggled for it. Even now it is not yet mine." She stared at the flagon. She should pour the cups, but she could not. Nausea rose again in her body. Oh no, she thought. Quickly. She unstopped the flagon but set it down again on the bench before she dropped it. Her legs gave way beneath her and her body shook violently, as if her legs and arms were driven by an engine. She gurgled as the fit came on. Aemilius was above her, grasping her shoulder.

"Kata, can you hear me?" He grasped her hand. "Squeeze my hand. Try to squeeze my hand."

Though her body shook and spasmed, she was aware of his presence above her. He held her hand and her shoulder and he comforted her. Though his voice faded away, as if down a long corridor, she was not entirely alone.

When the fit was over, she felt as if she had been wrung like a wet piece of clothing, twisted and distorted and empty. Aemilius carried her upstairs to her bed and laid her down.

"You will be all right now," he said. "But you must sleep."

Kata closed her eyes and opened them again. Aemilius was sniffing the air and looking around curiously.

Exhausted, Kata drifted off to the sight of him sitting above her, his deep eyes impassive, occasionally closing as he looked down on her. When she woke he was gone.

The following afternoon, Rudé let himself in to Kata's apartment as she lay on her cushions in the corner of the parlor, still exhausted from the fit. It took her a day to recover, at least, and now that she had run out of the preparation that eased her condition, her body would remain tired and drawn.

"This is my house," she said to Rudé, lifting her head with effort. "You can't just come in here."

"But I can," he said, holding up his key, straightening his sharp-lined clothes. "And I will."

"I need money, for medicine."

"Do you now? The agreement was *two* minotaurs. Not one."

"I need an advance."

"I see. Well, don't ever claim that House Technis is not generous, that it doesn't look after its own." He carefully placed a pile of ten florens on the table, stacked like a little tower. "By the end of the Festival, yes?"

"Yes."

There was a knock on the door. Rudé, his wiry little body always full of quick movements, darted against the wall for protection. Officiates lived in fear, even though the vicious war between

House Arbor and House Technis had recently fallen into a lull. It was rare to find them out on the streets, meeting their agents and assassins face-to-face, which was mostly the province of the sub-officiates. It was a measure of the mission's importance that Rudé should oversee it himself. Unlike the Directors, who were surrounded by aides of all kinds, officiates needed to organize their own protection, if they felt it warranted.

"Get the door," Rudé said, pulling out a long-knife from underneath his jacket.

Kata pushed herself to her feet and wearily opened the door. Aemilius stood towering behind it.

Exhausted, she hesitated. She couldn't think of a way to stop the minotaur from entering and meeting Rudé. In any case, she was pleased to see him. His presence calmed her, as if he were a cool rock against which she could lean, close her eyes, and rest her face. Guilt washed through her now. For he had been nothing but gentle and caring, and she had been—no, it was best not to think about her deception. These thoughts rushing though her head, contradictory feelings swirling within her, Kata finally said, "Come in."

"I came to see if you were feeling better."

"I am, thank you."

"Well, look," said Rudé, smiling slightly, the knife hidden. "A minotaur. Fantastic . . . Let me see. But you're a little small for a minotaur, aren't you?"

"Is greatness measured by size?" asked Aemilius.

Rudé approached Aemilius, looking even smaller as he came close to the minotaur. "Incredible."

"A friend of yours?" Aemilius asked Kata.

"Oh," said Rudé, "I've known Kata since she was just a girl. I've seen her . . . grow up."

In those days, Rudé had kept in touch with the children on the streets of the factory district. "Hello, Kata," he had always greeted her ebulliently. "No smile for me today?" Sometimes he had taken out a little toy, a windup bird or a mechanical man, and given it to one of the children. The urchins had prized the toys above all others, for they were made with rare technical skill. Powered by springs and wires, the birds would fly and the men would march. Some were even powered by thaumaturgy. The children had never seen anything like them. Rudé had taken special interest in Kata. Her sheer strength of will seemed to impress him. She was the quickest messenger, the most determined servant. "My little Kata," he had said. When she was fourteen, he said, "I know a philosopher-assassin who might be interested in taking on a pupil." Kata had leaped for the chance: to be a philosopher-assassin, that was the dream of all the children. It was their only escape from the factory district. And so she met Sarrat the Numerian and escaped the grimy factories and the filthy alleyways that surrounded them.

Now, as Rudé obliquely mentioned those days, Aemilius nodded, as if thinking.

"I'd better go," said Rudé, grinning quickly. "There are things to do! But I should very much like to see you again, minotaur. I should very much like to talk to you."

"Perhaps you shall," said Aemilius as Rudé closed the door behind him. "Strange," he said to Kata, "is he a New-Man, with all that quick energy?"

"Yes, he is half-Anlusian," said Kata, swaying slightly on her feet. "You can see it in his actions, his movements . . . his ambition."

"I have never been to Anlusia, but I should very much like to see it. They say the New-Men are voracious, insatiable, that they take everything they can and destroy it to rebuild it. They say their city is constantly growing, constantly changing—even more than Caeli-Amur!"

"But is that any way to live? Isn't that just distracting yourself from who you are, by concentrating solely on what you do, what you have?" She pursed her lips: she sounded just like Sarrat, who held to the Cajian philosophy of asceticism. It was a philosophy she'd rejected, and even now she thought of the time she'd spent on the streets, of her desire to own her house. She was no ascetic.

"Of course. And for that reason I should like to see it. To watch the New-Men build their technical wonders, only to throw them away."

Kata shuffled to the kitchen. The flagon was where she left it. "Would you like some wine? We didn't have a chance last night."

"No. I have someone to meet. Thank you, though."

Kata relseased the tension that had been building up in her body. She was not well enough today. She returned the flagon to the cupboard and walked him to the door.

"Rest," Aemilius said.

"I will."

She closed the door behind him and collapsed onto the cushions in the corner. She would kill him, or perhaps another minotaur, tomorrow. But even as she thought it, her mind was filled with doubt.

THREE

In the mornings, the streets around Caeli-Amur's Factory Quarter bustled with grime-streaked workers, their brown clothes camouflaged in the fog and smoke that later dissipated in the morning sun. The workers descended quickly down the cobblestoned streets and alleyways, disappearing in and out of the haze on their way to the early shifts. At times the lines of figures coalesced into groups, taking a brief moment for greetings, then separated once more. Other lines—the night shift—straggled in the opposite direction, their soot-stained faces grim in the morning light. Everywhere surrounding them were the street urchins, dashing about on unknown business, running in gangs, smiling their disarming smiles, their hands slipping into unsuspecting pockets and emerging with half-empty purses. The mornings in the Factory Quarter were the happiest, the most filled with promise, as if things might be getting better, achieving a fairer balance. At night things were different, when the smoke merged with a sea of roiling fog, when the pitter-patter of children's feet was enough to terrify the passerby, and a disarming smile was likely to mean a rapid, knife-filled death.

Subofficiate Boris Autec hustled along the streets, stopping every now and then to catch his breath. His round body was no longer used to all this walking: it seemed bloated like a bladder and his once youthful face had now settled into heavy middle age. But his heart was beating quickly for other reasons. He was about to visit the Tram Factory, with its welders and fitters, its hammering and sawing, its sparks that danced on the floor like miniature symbols of life. The Tram Factory: he knew it, had once loved and hated it. Now he was afraid.

Boris reached into the bag that swung over his hip, drew out a flask, unscrewed the lid, and took a swig. The Anlusian hot-wine burned his mouth and throat while his eyes watered. After a few minutes, his body surged with energy. His armpits grew damp, his jaws clenched, he licked his lips—he felt alive. The hot-wine kept you awake like strong coffee and filled the body with unnatural strength, the mind with thoughts of invincibility. He reached again for the flask.

When Boris reached the factory, he stood by the open double doors and watched. A row of freight-trams stood along one wall, their walled trays gray and grim: if you wanted to haul something heavy around Caeli-Amur, this was the way to do it. Along another wall stood passenger trams used for ferrying Caeli-Amur's population. These were alive with solar hues: reds and yellows and oranges. The city was not just growing but changing; demand was high for transport that could move the population quickly and efficiently. In one corner a boiler, firebox, and valve gear sat like the insides of a creature. Around it were scattered pieces of trams: wheel sets, axleboxes, blastpipes.

The tramworkers knew he was there, but went about their business without acknowledging him: the young ones still filled with fresh vitality; the old with that haunted look, the *drained* look.

As Boris strode in boldly, his chest jutting forward like a peacock's, a heavy man emerged from behind one of the passenger trams, its silver fittings sparkling. The man shrugged his hunched shoulders and closed his heavy-lidded eyes slowly. "So they sent you."

Boris clenched his teeth. "Mathias, your hair has gone gray."

"It happens to workers."

"It happens to us all," said Boris.

"Come on then." Mathias turned and walked across to a tram at the far end of the factory. Its windows were blackened around the edges when they should have been silver framed; its insides ruined by fire. The red and gold paint on its walls was blistered and discolored.

Boris nodded, aware of the other workers standing in groups, staring from behind. "Pick one or two—those most responsible— and I'll be able to save the rest."

"How can we know what happened? Most likely we calculated the binding formulae incorrectly. The engine exploded as a result."

"Come on, Mathias, we both know that's not true."

"Oh, but you know it *could* be. You know that we are not taught properly, not trained in the right calculations, that we are *squeezed* until we end up like Mad Mister Alter, or just *give out* like the Numerian Bachara. You remember him, don't you?"

Bachara had slowed down like a windup toy, growing ever bonier until one day he just stopped in the factory, his eyes and teeth strangely white in his black face. He hadn't collapsed like the dead usually do. Rather, he seemed in some state of suspended animation, never to return to this life. Boris remembered the horror of the Numerian's eyes. He imagined something flickering in there, as if Bachara was aware of the horror of his own predicament.

"You know it's nothing to do with your training." Boris crossed his arms, sweat sticky on his skin. He licked his lips, which seemed thick and bloated. "You know I'm on your side, but the House won't tolerate sabotage. Please, let me help."

Mathias's heavy eyelids blinked slowly. "There was a time when once you would never have asked this of me."

Boris's mouth seemed terribly dry. He swallowed uncomfortably. "Make sure you fix the tram. Make sure there are no more accidents."

One of the workers said something behind him and laughed.

"It will happen again," Mathias said. "It will keep happening."

"Remember when we were friends?" Boris's voice was soft now, both sad and accusatory.

"Before you chose . . . before you moved up."

With impossible strength fueled by the hot-wine, Boris clasped Mathias by his tunic and threw him against the tram's wall. The tram shuddered and clouds of black smoke billowed from its ruined insides. Mathias gasped, his head rocking forward from the force, his jaw opening in shock. Boris held the heavy worker a foot from the ground. The hot-wine filled him and coursed through his body. He took one hand away and grabbed Mathias by the jaw. "What was I supposed to do? I had a sick wife and a child!"

"We all have troubles: sick wives, sick families, sick grandparents."

"Not like Remmie, you didn't! She was taken by those things and little Saidra looked on with these great sad eyes, wondering what was happening to her mother." Even now the image of his wife's death and his little daughter came to mind. Everything had been for the love of his family.

Mathias looked away from him, guilty. "Be careful whose side you take Boris, the world is changing faster than you can imagine."

Boris walked slowly up through the city, out of the factory district, along the Via Persine that ran from the Market Square by the docks, to the north of the crumbling white cliffs, all the way to House Technis Complex. The whole place was the very image of industry. People were acting; events were occurring; Technis was on the march. And Boris was a part of it. As there was no direct route to the offices Boris sought—the Palace having been cobbled together without a plan—he climbed up and down stairs and finally to a door on which hung a little plaque: OFFICIATE RUDÉ.

Inside, Rudé sat behind a desk, a collection of fountain pens angling toward him, two neatly piled papers beside them. His hand moved quickly between the papers, shifting pages from pile to pile, even as he wrote. On one side of the desk sat a strange contraption, all metal arms and wooden trays.

Boris stepped forward and waited for Rudé to stop writing.

"Watch this." Rudé placed a sheet of paper in one of the machine's trays. He pulled a lever near the base of the contraption. The tray tipped, the paper disappeared, there was a tearing sound, and strips of shredded paper emerged from the back of the machine, curling into a little pile.

The officiate grinned brilliantly, looking like a child with a toy.

Boris stared in disbelief. "What—?"

"I made it myself. Watch this." Rudé put a pile of papers in another tray, pulled another lever at the base and the papers were shuffled into some kind of order, landing in a series of pockets that poked out of one side. There was a grinding sound. Bits of paper were crumpled within the mechanism and the whole thing shuddered to a halt.

Rudé grinned again, ran his hand through his hair, and shrugged. "So—the Tram Factory."

"Sabotage."

Rudé joined his hands. "At this time! As if the Festival of the Bull and the House's thaumaturgists pressing down on me like a clamp aren't enough! What do you suggest?"

Boris shifted in his seat uncomfortably, like a restless child, before settling himself again. "We should teach them the thuamaturgists' protection charms. These are good men, but they're frustrated. Too many are destroyed by the binding formulae we teach them. They cannot protect themselves. The Other Side leaches into them, warps them, or drives thems mad, little by little."

"Nobody can control thaumaturgy! Not even the greatest thaumaturgists in the world can stop the Other Side from leaking through. Not even the Sortileges of Varenis. Yes, we could train them in the protection charms, but what for? So they can live another few years? No, we won't train these workers as true thaumaturgists. We don't place such power in the hands of those who haven't come through the *proper processes*. Buy them off. We don't want this to go higher," said the New-Man. "The Elo-Talern have of late started to take an interest in such events. For more than ten years they have left us be, but now they have reawoken."

Boris shifted uncomfortably. Like all, he knew the myths of the Elo-Talern—those creatures hovered over Caeli-Amur like shadows on a wall. The gods had warred and broken the world beneath them in a cataclysm of terrible proportions: the seas boiled, the skies burned, and the earth was torn apart. Seeing this, the grieving Aediles of Caeli-Amur despaired. After Aya was thrown down and the other gods had left the world in grief, the Aediles called out to the universe for a new force to bring order to the city. They spent their nights invoking powerful equations until they summoned the Elo-Talern. Perhaps these creatures had risen from a vast sunless empire deep beneath the ground, or from the Other Side beyond the walls of death, or had descended from the skies.

They brought order to the city and with that order came untold horrors that the Aediles had not foreseen. In their sorrow, the Aediles retired from the world and were never seen again. So the myths went.

Boris had caught half-imagined glimpses of the Elo-Talern's silhouettes at the Opera, tall and thin, watching from their boxes like decadent princes. All he heard of them were tales of terror. A toothless old man once grabbed Boris by the arm in a liquor hall. "Not two years ago I was a young man. And look at me now. I am only twenty-three years old." The old man then leaned back and stared into his mug: "The Elo-Talern—they came to me in my sleep and they sucked away my youth." The old man began to cry.

The spring air in Caeli Amur was warm that night, as if the world were gesturing toward a hot summer to follow. The wind whispered through Boris's open window and caressed his cheek as he sat waiting and thinking at his table. Outside the city was dark; clouds had rolled in, wrapping the sky into one great swathe of darkness. A bottle of hot-wine stood on the wooden table like a lone sentry in the desert. He ran his finger along the fissures and breaks of the wood. When had these cracks appeared? He couldn't remember. The table was unfixable now, but it had a kind of beauty of its own. Around him, it seemed as if shadowy shapes moved, flickering figures at the edges of his vision. Yet when he turned, they would be gone. Tired, that's what he was. Tired.

The sound of three blows to his door startled him. Taking his bolt-thrower from where it leaned against the wall, he wound the lever on its side and listened to the clicking that indicated the internal mechanism was tightening. Holding the bolt-thrower behind him, he walked quietly to the door and quickly pulled it open. A dark shape with hunched shoulders loomed before him.

"Mathias," Boris said.

Neither man moved. To do so would be to start everything again: the raking over history, the recriminations, the disappointments. Behind Mathias stood his wife, Corette, her face and hips broader than he recalled. She had the hard countenance of a woman from the Factory Quarter, her face set against the world. Behind them walked a young man, perhaps seventeen years old, whose dark hair seemed to throw his entire face into dark shadow.

Eventually, Boris returned to the table and gently placed his bolt-thrower beside the bottle of hot-wine. He sat down.

Mathias closed the door behind his wife and the young man. "I wasn't sure if you still lived here."

"All the Technis officiates are in this area."

"I thought you might have moved closer to the Complex."

"I have a view of the sea."

"The things you acquire when you're prepared to compromise." Mathias stood by the table awkwardly, Corette and the young man observing from a few steps behind. Clearly they were there for support more than to participate in the conversation.

Family, thought Boris, how wonderful it had been to have one. Around his house he still kept Remmie's possessions. In the bedroom, a cupboard filled with her dresses. Not long ago, he had taken them out, laid them on the bed. Some had been moth-eaten and he had cried out at the sight of the ruinous little holes. Not knowing what to do, he eventually hung them back in the cupboard.

"Sit down while you're insulting me." Boris gestured to the chairs that circled the table.

The three of them sat, their dusty clothes and grimy faces out of place in the little house, which though simple, was no worker's cottage. There were three bedrooms, and the lower floor opened out into a small courtyard dominated by an empty pool. In the courtyard's center stood a statue of Alerion, gazing imperiously out toward the sea, though a high wall, topped with hundreds of blades, blocked the ground-floor view. Boris had installed these defenses when his family moved in: in those days the House Wars were raging, and subofficiates could expect death to come at any time.

"It's been what, fifteen years?" said Boris.

"Since you threw me out?"

Boris smiled, but there was a touch of sadness in the down-turned corners of his mouth. "You showed no understanding."

"I was young." Mathias brooded at the tabletop, looking up only irregularly.

"No. It's part of your nature. We were friends, but as soon as Remmie was ill, you simply disappeared—and Saidra just a little child. What did I know of raising children?"

Mathias passed his hand over the wooden table, feeling the grain as if he would find answers there. He stared at it, lips pursed and silent. Finally he said: "What is she doing now, Saidra?"

"She dances and sings at the Opera." Boris's face came alive. "You should see her, Mathias, you should see the way she moves on the stage!" He pictured his daughter on the stage. Often he watched her from the crowd, looking only at her movements, fancying he could distinguish her voice among the chorus. How proud he was of her.

Mathias smiled. "I remember the way she danced as a child."

Boris grasped the bottle on the table and took a swig before passing it to Mathias. "Perhaps you could come one day with me to the Opera, to see her. She never comes here."

After Remmie died, Boris had looked after Saidra as best he could. As a child, she had been so delightful: twirling and dancing in their little apartment for him, twisting and smiling with the great openness and clear eyes of a child. He had washed her clothes, put the food on the table. He had even tried to help her with her love of music. But Boris had no talent for it: Saidra had inherited that from Remmie. Still, he ensured she had an excellent teacher, a retired castrato who taught her with a little baton in each hand, one for counting out the beat, and one for striking her on the knuckles when she made a mistake. Boris had left the factory and become a subofficiate to help pay for Remmie's treatments. After she died, he had remained in the position for love of Saidra. He would make sure that his child had the best life she could.

"This is Rikard." Corette spoke in her gruff voice, gesturing to the young dark-haired man. "Our son. We were trying to interest him in the Festival of the Sun, but he finds it a meaningless tradition, and the minotaurs just men with the head of bulls."

Rikard looked at Boris through narrow eyes that glimmered. There was something distant and brooding about the boy.

Boris spoke to Mathias as he examined Rikard: "He looks like you, when you were young. He has the same hard, fiery eyes. Almost old enough to start in the factory."

"By the gods no," said Mathias, turning to his son. "Study: that's what he needs to do. You're too bright for the factories, aren't you?"

Rikard looked back and raised his eyebrows ever so slightly, at which his parents both burst out laughing. The tension that had hovered over the conversation dissipated. "Have a drink." Boris passed the hot-wine to Mathias, who put the bottle to his mouth and sputtered, his eyes watering. "What is this stuff? It burns!"

"Hot-wine," said Boris laughing. "The best."

Mathias took another draft and shuddered involuntarily. "Water! Water!" Already there were beads of sweat on his face. He rushed to the kitchen and put his mouth beneath the water-pump, his arm moving the lever furiously.

"The water will just spread the heat around," said Boris.

Rikard turned the bottle over and examined its intricate Anlusian stamp, an image of a little machine.

Corrette swatted his hands and glowered at him. "Rikard!"

"Be careful," Boris said to Mathias. "Your strength will have increased. You may break things."

Returning to the table, Mathias picked up the bolt-thrower, holding it in one hand.

Boris tensed as Mathias slowly pointed the thing at him, looking down the barrel with one eye closed. "Have you come to kill me?"

"Of course not." Mathias put down the bolt-thrower. "It has no bow."

"No. It's one of the new models. It works somehow by pressurized air and springs. But it's deadly nonetheless."

"Remember how we used to hunt spear-birds in the hills? And the sun would beat down on that rocky landscape and the nights would suddenly become cold?"

"We could search for two, three days, without seeing a bird," said Boris. He remembered how unexpectedly, as they climbed close to the great wide sky itself, he and Mathias would disturb a nest and the female spear-birds would come circling down in their death pattern. They would have to crouch back-to-back and hold off from shooting the bolt-throwers until the spiral had become close enough for them to feel the wind from their leathery wings.

"We would bring them down so they writhed on the ground like great flapping tents," said Mathias.

"We were young then, weren't we?" Boris turned his head: something dark had shifted in the room's corner. But when he turned, it was gone.

Mathias leaned forward. "How can you forget, Boris? How can you pretend not to see how things are for us in the factory? Yes, you never suffered like the others from the thaumaturgy. You left too soon. You never had visions or felt sick as the binding charms settled. But let me tell you—for me things are not so good. At times I feel a great chasm open up close to me, and I see into other universes. Strange fish-things swim there in the air, and there are voices that don't go away."

Something stirred in Boris he would have preferred to remain untouched, something he thought he had disposed of long ago. To find it awakening inside him was like seeing something dead burst from the earth and shake away all the dirt and rotten leaves from its fur, to cough out dirt from its blackened teeth, to look up with wild and desperate eyes.

"You'll help us, won't you?" said Mathias. "You won't turn your back on us, will you?"

Boris gulped at the wine until there was but a little left in the bottle. He looked away, out into the blackness. Down there, somewhere, lay the sea, deep and cold, and beneath that the Sunken City. He spoke flatly: "When Remmie was dying she would cough all sorts of things from her lungs. Little creatures they were, wriggling, all surrounded by phlegm and mucus. When she finally died, these things came out of her nose and her mouth and even from behind her eyes."

"You are a good man," said Corette. "I know that you are."

Boris continued to look out into the distance, his heart pounding violently from the wine.

"There's talk of a strike," said Mathias.

"It'll be a provocation," said Boris. "You know Technis: Everything must run smoothly, efficiently. There must be no disruption to the schedules. The Directorate of Varenis has ordered fifteen for their Minasi district. Technis can't lose face before the Directorate. I'm thinking of what's best for you. I'm thinking of what's best for *all of us*. The House will not tolerate—"

"It's a question of what *we* tolerate." Mathias's voice struggled out, his face slightly flushed.

Boris nodded slowly. "Hold off on the strike and let me come to the factory. I'll compile a report and we can see if we can improve things for the tramworkers. I'll do my best, I promise."

"I knew you were a good man," said Corette. "But, Boris, you look unwell."

"It's the damned hot-wine," said Boris. "It drains you like a leech. Anyway, don't mother me, Corette."

"I'm *not* concerned. Not for a representative of House Technis."

"Always the generous one."

She grinned. "I've worked the textile mills for fifteen years. I don't need more worry."

And so they sat and talked: Corette, coldhearted and friendly at the same time; Mathias, with his rough and short sentences. Rikard remained quiet, but Boris felt the boy's restrained intelligence and watchfulness. It was as if Rikard was sizing up Boris's every words, his slight gestures, and storing them away for some future task. Boris found it unnerving.

When it was time for Boris's visitors to leave, he showed them through the door. As they stepped into the street, he pulled Mathias back and whispered quietly in his ear: "Can you see them? Can you see the shadows? They're all around us. They're watching us, even as we speak. I can hear them, whispering to me."

Mathias's eyebrows came together in puzzlment. He touched Boris on the arm. "Sleep now."

"Come again, if you'd like," called Boris, but his voice dissipated in the darkness and his house seemed empty. Mathias had been his first visitor in—how long?—years. As he returned to the table he felt, for the first time in as long as he could recall, he remembered what it was like to have friends. But the danger of it, the risk, was masked by the hot-wine, which kept him close to the state he had searched for over the years. It deadened his pain, just as it deadened his joy.

FOUR

In the following days, Boris returned to the factory. He watched closely as the workers finished a new tram from carefully arranged pieces of wood and steel. Boris found himself unexpectedly looking forward to the precision of the workers, the marvelous way the vehicle was constructed, the sparks that danced across the floor as the whirring machines spun against metal. Each time he looked forward to the sound of Mathias's laugh, or his words of encouragement to the younger workers, or the way his hunched and heavy frame sprang to life in the confines of the factory.

But he noticed also the little moments where charms and incantations were needed. Sometimes the workers would emerge from these trances ashen-faced and distraught. When the steam engine was almost complete, Mathias took it on himself to perform the binding charm so that the engine could withstand the intense pressures within. As others watched on, he spoke the formulae, drawing the ideograms in the air. The engine gleamed with a sickly green light that seemed to settle on the metal like a shroud and become absorbed. Mathias staggered and his legs gave way. A burly worker caught him before his knees struck the ground, but he called out like a man suffering hallucinations. "The air. They're in the air!" An eerie green glow had settled also on him, and his face was slick with an unnatural sheen. "Swimming, swimming." Boris's skin crawled at the sight and he averted his eyes. That night his dreams were haunted by enormous creatures that rolled menacingly in black waters.

Eventually, the tram was completed, gleaming and new and ready, sitting on the tracks, a golden mechanical marvel. The workers stood around and Boris felt in them, despite everything, a sense of pride in their work.

"Beautiful, isn't she?" Mathias drew his hand across his forehead, a dark smudge appearing beneath.

"May as well start her up," said Boris.

One of the workers leaped into the driver's carriage that sat up front, while two others stoked the fire.

"It's getting hot already and summer's not yet upon us," said Mathias. The doorway to the street was nothing but a sheet of brilliance.

Boris nodded, watching the workers fire up the tram. A puff of soot burst from the funnel.

The worker in the driver's carriage leaned out the window, "She's not movin'."

"Why not?" asked Mathias.

The worker just shrugged and turned back to the levers in the carriage. He leaned out again. "Dunno."

"Fire her up some more." Mathias turned back to Boris. "So when are you taking me to this Opera of yours?"

"Tomorrow, or the next day. Whenever you'd like."

"Still not moving," said the driver.

"Why don't you—?" began Mathias. The rest of his words were inaudible.

An explosion tore the air apart. The tram burst along its side, pieces of metal flying through the air followed by an immense spray of water and steam. Someone screamed, but Boris was on his knees, his hands over his face. He stood up. Mathias was already running toward the wreck of the tram, twisted like a wet shirt. Mathias turned and his mouth opened, but Boris could barely hear him. His head seemed swathed in bandages, the sounds deadened. He staggered forward as great clouds of steam rose from the factory floor.

Mathias dragged the driver's body from the ruins of the carriage and placed him on the ground. Mathias stopped and looked at the great flaps of the driver's skin that hung from his hands. Even more sloughed from the driver's body like the skin of some overripe fruit.

Other workers were screaming in the corner of the factory, one staggering around, holding his face. Blood and yellow stuff dribbled between his fingers. Others stood motionless, overcome by the horror.

Finally, Boris staggered toward Mathias, who now kneeled by the body.

"S-sabotage," Boris struggled to get the word out.

Mathias looked up at him, his worn face twisted. His voice came as if from far away. "Damn you ... damn you ... This is no sabotage! The binding formula was wrong, or the pressure of the steam was too great. *You*—you don't train us. You use us like parts in a machine, ready to be replaced when we are worn out."

Boris reached down and touched the blistered body tenderly. His hand came away wet with red liquid. "You are right," he said. "I will see justice done. I will take your demands to the House. Let's do this right, together."

That night—the night of the Sun Parade—Boris laid his head on the top of the table, the empty bottle of hot-wine sitting in front of him like a broken promise. He yearned for another bottle, yet knew that it would lead him to his ruin. It was a full day since he had drunk his last bottle, and he could barely move. It was as if every ounce of strength had been drained, as if sand had been rubbed into his eyes, as if some rodent gnawed away at his stomach. But he would wait out this temporary suffering, which would pass, along with the desire for hot-wine.

A glorious moon hovered in the sky, lighting up the flat sea with molten-silver light. The sounds of the Sun Parade drifted in from outside: pipes rising and falling, drums banging, people laughing. He should have been out there, circling around the minotaurs with the rest of the population, following the parade to where it finally ended in the arms of the Northern Headland, where the water palaces and steam baths would be thrown open to whoever wished.

Boris slept fitfully at the table for half an hour, but his dreams were filled with great sluglike creatures, big as stream-trams, that slithered around him, their voices echoing strange chants until finally one slithered on top of him, and he thought, I'll die. I'll die, now, beneath the weight of these creatures—the Elo-Talern. When he woke, shadows seemed to flicker across the room. Yes, he thought, they're here again, hulking shapes in the corner of the room. He blinked. Something hissed softly behind him. He turned, afraid. Nothing was there.

In the morning, the desire for hot-wine was like a hungry creature swimming around his insides. Everything seemed at a distance, as if painted in a shade of white. He needed more wine; he needed it *now*. In the back of his mind, he vaguely remembered his decision not to buy any more wine, but this seemed like the decision of another person, someone long ago and far away. In any case, he would stop later, once he had solved the tramworkers' problems, once things were easier, once Mathias and he had rebuilt their friendship on firm ground.

Rudé had suggested Boris meet him in Market Square. It was time, the officiate had told him, that he met the hot-wine supplier. There Boris would be able to put the tramworkers' case to Rudé. He steeled himself, pictured himself doing it, saying, "We must teach them the protection charms. We must change with the changing world." Anxiety rushed into him and he pushed the image from his mind. It would be fine.

The Opera overlooked Market Square, which opened out to the piers. The first thing that struck Boris was the smell of the market: fish intermingled with the spicy meats sold by Numerian street vendors. He picked his way through the bustle, careful not to knock over any of the glass cases that housed schools of fish so small that they seemed to be just puffs of orange smoke swirling in the water. He deftly avoided Xsathian dockworkers, huge and still writhing octopi thrown over their shoulders. Finally, past the center of the market, where contortionists bent themselves through impossibly small hoops and puppeteers put on tragedies and comedies, he found Rudé, drinking strong black coffee and playing chess with another New-Man, a cadaverous little figure who smoked a fetid-smelling weed. Only half-Anlusian, Rudé was the larger of the two, though both shared the darting movements of New-Men.

"Here." Boris passed a pouch of coins to the officiate.

Rudé took a handful from the bag and passed it to his kinsman. To Boris, he said: "Quadi will give you the wine."

The New-Man took a puff of his rank-smelling cigarette, then ground the stub out on the cobblestones. A final waft of noxious smoke caused Boris to cover his nose momentarily. Sweet mercy, he thought to himself, it smells like something died. How anyone could smoke such stuff was beyond him.

Meanwhile, Quadi opened a square leather case that sat beside him, full of neatly stacked bottles. He passed five to Boris, who placed four of them gingerly in the bag that hung from his shoulder. The fifth he uncorked and gulped hungrily. Even as he swallowed, he fancied his strength returning, as the wine's energies coursed into him.

Smiling, Quadi's teeth were frighteningly large and white in his skeletal face. "Your people are not built to drink these."

"Why not?" Boris slowly placed the bottle into the bag with the others.

"Some say you will see into the Other Side, see the shapes of the dead as they move around us, see the plane of death and its pathways moving off at oblique angles to our own."

A black-skinned Numerian, a great golden ring through his nose, passed close by, leading a line of long-necked creatures that looked like exotic goats. One of the things stopped. The Numerian pulled the rope and the beast bared its teeth, bleated angrily, and followed. Perhaps they were headed to one of House Arbor's famous balls where the entertainments were diverse: jugglers and illusionists; mime artists and contortionists; castrati choirs and thaumaturgical musicians; and, of course, exotic creatures from across the sea.

"These will be the last. I tire of this stuff." Boris pressed his hands together, wrapped his fingers around each other. "Officiate, I'd like to talk to you about the tramworkers."

"Yes, and I would like to talk to you about them also." Rudé jumped to his feet with the rapidity of a small mammal. "Come on."

"Our game!" Quadi laughed, holding the chessboard in the air.

"I'll remember the positions of the pieces. Don't think you can escape!"

Boris and Rudé took the stream-tram back up along the Via Persine toward the House Technis Complex. The tram chuffed and lurched and rattled as citizens held on to the handles and poles. The conductor, decked out in a Technis uniform of plain gray that made him look like a prison guard—Technis was not known for its aesthetics—checked their passes.

Boris asked Rudé, "Why is he so thin, that Anlusian, Quadi?"

"You know we don't like to be called Anlusians," said Rudé. "We prefer to be called men from Ariki. Or just Ariki-Akians."

Anlusia had been the name given the land of the New-Men by Hardarra the explorer, who had discovered this strange new race of people after the cataclysm. He had returned from his journey filled with stories about the New-Men's technologies. The city of Tir-Aki, he claimed, was a great steam-driven thing, a mammoth mechnical beast of pipes and engines and constantly moving parts—a gigantic version of the Technis Palace's southeast wing.

A group of marchers from the Sun Parade sat against a wall, their long masks still hiding their faces, bottles beside them. They must have been up all night. A minotaur stood on one corner, surrounded by laughing children who playfully touched the creature before running away. At a distance stood several young women. They seemed shy, as if they were building up the courage to talk to the creature. Boris could not understand the obsession the people seemed to have with the creatures. Yes, they were ancient; yes, like all such creatures they were touched by thaumaturgy—but in the end they were simply living creatures. Rikard was right: as far as Boris could see, they were just men with the heads of bulls. Even as he thought this, some part of Boris realized he was, for some reason, denying the truth of things.

Boris turned back to Rudé. "Is Quadi unwell?"

"He's come here to die."

"That weed he smokes would be enough to kill any man," Boris said.

Rudé smiled and continued. "They come here, far from Tir-Aki, or Nara-Aki. Far from their homes, far from the restless and re-lentless growth of their people. Like my mother."

Boris thought he saw Saidra nestled into one of the tram's seats, reading. When the young woman looked up, he realized it was not his daughter, even if she shared the same round-faced prettiness, the same large contemplative eyes. Seeing his glance, she closed the pamphlet she was reading and slipped it into her bag. Yet he glimpsed its title: *The Conquest of Pain*. Was it simply a philosophical tract from one of the philiosopher-assassins' man-darins, or was it a seditionist tract? It had become hard to tell these days, though no doubt the Houses' officiates had drafted a policy explaining the distinction. He cared little for the subject anyway; he had never been a philosopher; he preferred to think of himself as a man of action.

"Their homeland makes them ill?" Boris continued to study the woman, who, uncomfortable under his gaze, looked out the window.

"My mother would have known. Perhaps Quadi can explain it to you better. I think they cannot find meaning in such an exis-tence. They are emptied by it. So they leave and find another city to die, the way a cat lies hidden beneath a tree."

Boris laughed. "Meaning!"

"Some people need it."

Boris looked up toward the Factory Quarter, where smoke and soot hovered in the air. "It's a hard thing to find." He waited, let the thought settle. "I think we should change our attitude toward the tramworkers. I think—"

Rudé touched him on the arm. "The Elo-Talern want to see you. For long they have taken no interest in such things. Why this sudden attention, I cannot say. But something is changing in the city. They want to hear from someone close to the street, close to the factory."

"But . . ." Boris looked down at his shoes. Cracks from age and dryness ran along their sides. "I've never."

"You'll be fine," said Rudé, but his cheerful demeanor was gone.

When they stepped from the tram, Boris glanced back at the

young woman, who glared out the window at him. She was like Saidra in more ways than one.

Once in the Technis Complex, Boris and Rudé passed along a gloomy winding corridor, where the number of agents thinned out. Here the walls shuddered with steam-pipes powering some unknown sections of the Palace. The pipes diverged from each other, rejoined and curled, wrapped around each other like snakes. Wheels and handles were spaced randomly along them, presumably to control the flows of steam and liquid. Gas lamps hung from the roof, but these succeeded only in illuminating the rusty dilapidation of the corridor.

They came to a sign, which read, ZONE RESTRICTED TO OFFICIATES. KEEP OUT. The corridor continued into the mountain behind Cacli-Amur, but there were no lamps to light the way and the pipes gave way to an older and simple architecture of smooth walls. Rudé lit a lamp stored in a niche and they continued on.

With each step, Boris wondered what all this meant. For fifteen years, his routine as subofficiate had been the same: Take messages and parcels between officiates, visit factories and report back. Now he was finding himself in places of influence. He could use them to change things for the better. The higher he climbed, the more influence he'd have. The thought brought on the rush of feelings once more: excitement that burst into him like a fountain; anxiety that clamped him like a vise.

They came to an accordion-style grille door and stepped into an elevator that shuddered and groaned as it took them higher. Boris glanced quickly at Rudé, who seemed unconcerned by the clattering sounds of machinery that echoed around them. They had entered a part of the Palace of unknown age. The elevator was clearly a recent construction, built perhaps in the last thirty or so years. But gone were the even newer technologies such as the pipes.

The elevator trembled to a halt and Rudé pulled open the door. Boris followed the New-Man down a dry and dusty corridor, bracing himself against a cold wind. Other smooth-walled corridors led away to his left and right, and disappeared into darkness. Occasionally, open doorways showed empty halls and galleries, which Boris imagined had once been the scene of great parties and balls, but were now only ghostly shells, the hollow reminders of long-dead dancers. The walls were set with evenly spaced symmetrical shapes—triangles, squares, hexagons, octagons—whose austere beauty seemed to add to the cold wind. Elsewhere along the wall, alcoves were filled with crumbling humanoid statuettes with trunks that writhed from their faces, or insect creatures with long mandibles, or many-eyed humans operating strange machinery. Boris shuddered: What strange histories did they describe?

Rudé smiled briefly at Boris, but his eyes were without joy.

The corridors wound on, now up winding staircases, now across bridges that spanned empty and echoing ballrooms. All the time, strange implements made of hooks and cogs and wheels and blades and springs and a hundred unknown components hung unused and forgotten on the walls.

Now Boris's anxiety intensified and became a shadowy fear that seemed to shift around his chest and gut and his vital organs. The strangeness of this place, and the knowledge that the Elo-Talern lived somewhere in this decaying world, haunted his thoughts.

Finally, they came to colossal double doors covered with ornate, spiraled bands of metal in intricate patterns. Ideograms, although inscribed in the door, seemed impossibly to *hover in front of them*, as if belonging to a different plane of existence.

Rudé touched the doors and they groaned open of their own accord. A great throne, set on a dais, stood toward the end of the hall, in front of another set of double doors. Pillars ran on both sides of the hall. Behind them lay only darkness and a kind of subtle swirling fog caused by the cold. Boris could not be sure how large the room was, and his mind played tricks on him: Dark shapes flickered around them, shadows that disappeared when his roving eyes tried to fix them.

As Boris and Rudé stood in the middle of the room, the fog hung almost imperceptibly around them, a spectral presence that gave the surroundings an otherworldly feel. Perhaps somewhere in those long dark halls they had crossed a threshold and ventured into some liminal space, some borderland of life and death, far from the world of sun and laughter far away.

"Will—?" Boris began, but his desire to speak faltered and the word echoed eerily around the room, leaving the silence humming unnaturally.

"Do—?" he began again.

"Wait," said Rudé softly.

The doors behind the throne groaned. They came apart with terrible slowness. For what seemed an eternity, nothing came through them. Then, finally, a shape emerged. Boris grabbed his flask. Without taking his eyes from the Elo-Talern, he unscrewed the lid.

The Elo-Talern took three or four steps on spindly legs, improbable muscles and tendons flexing and bulging in strange and disturbing places.

As she walked, Boris heard a cracking and groaning, like a broken wooden machine. Unnerved, almost afraid to keep looking, he searched for the source of the sound, which seemed to be coming from her joints. Boris was horrified to see that they bent both ways, so that her knees doubled back after they straightened, just as her elbows swung in both directions. Her head turned imperiously on its long neck and stared at Boris.

Boris closed his eyes and felt the tension in his muscles. When he opened his eyes she had moved again. She collapsed her long body onto the throne, where she leaned in a languid pose, one spidery leg thrown out, the other with its foot to the floor. As she rested there, she flickered out of existence, replaced briefly by a decaying creature—cadaverous cheekbones and blackened teeth—resembling her, yet not quite her. She flickered back into existence, and the smell of rotten leaves wafted past Boris to mingle with the dampness of the building.

"So." Behind her whispery voice came a sound, like dry paper rustling. "Tell me about these . . . troubles." To make herself comfortable, she shifted her torso, which was too long for the rest of her, as if a whole midsection including extra vertebrae had been added.

Rudé turned to Boris, whose legs began to tremble. Nobody said anything.

"Boris," said Rudé.

"There's been . . . sabotage . . . at the Tram Factory. . . ." Boris looked at that terrible face, the jutting forehead, the cheekbones impossibly high and sharply defined so the withered mouth was far below and miniscule. "One of the workers has been planting explosives. . . ." Boris searched for the words. He tried to think of ways he could put the tramworkers' grievances diplomatically, so that the Elo-Talern would see their plight, yet know that he was there to help the House. Nausea gripped him and he swallowed uncomfortably. "There's a mood out there . . . there's all sorts . . ."

Rudé stepped forward: "Not just in the Tram Factory. There are little groups and circles springing up everywhere: on the docks; in the textile mills; in the Quaedian. There are pamphlets and broadsheets filled with mad radical ideas circulating."

Again she flickered and her face became skeletal and rotten before flickering back to life. She leaned forward, and her neck seemed to stretch out and elongate. *Crack. Crack. Crack.* Before anything could be said, she began: "What sort of men are they, these tramworkers?"

"Stubborn, strong, and . . . honest. They talk much about justice these days. It's not the first time . . . a long while ago . . . but that talk died away . . ." Images of Mathias flashed into Boris's mind. Again the words eluded him. "They are changed by the thaumaturgy we force them to use. They are squeezed like fruit until they are dry. Perhaps we should train them properly, in the correct formulae, so that they might be protected."

The Elo-Talern laughed; it sounded like the raven's call. "Don't they understand that we cannot return to the world before the cataclysm? Those days are gone. In any case, we would threaten ourselves by releasing such knowledge. There are other paths for those who want to learn the Art. Paths for people who seek to better themselves. They can join the House Thaumaturgists. Compare what they are doing to your own situation, Boris. Were you not once a tramworker? And look what *you've* done for yourself."

Boris's eyes darted left and right. He found no answer.

Once more she slouched back into the throne: "Are you not happy with the way Technis treats *you*? No—these tramworkers have chosen their life and now they must deal with the consequences of their choice, just as you have chosen yours. If there is a strike, we shall act quickly. Are you capable, Subofficiate Autec? Isn't this what you've lived your life for? A defining moment? Think of the rewards when you succeed. You could begin to achieve those things you've always wanted to achieve. To have the things you want to have. *What is it you want, Boris?*"

Boris sweated under her gaze. His mind would not produce the thoughts he wanted, nor would his mouth form the words. All that would come to his mind was the image of Mathias with his heavy-lidded eyes, his slumped posture.

"I'll discuss with my colleagues." The Elo-Talern moved her hand in circles. "The workers want a new life, do they? We'll give them a different life, or the Furies will."

She stood with the sound of popping. Boris closed his eyes once more. When he opened them she was gone. Boris had failed. Now all he could think about was escape from that room.

FIVE

The Artists' Quarter of Caeli-Amur was one of the oldest. Called the Quaedian, its cramped streets were too narrow for carriages or trams. Packed along the alleyways were boutiques full of curiosities, and bookstores, the walls of which were hidden by piles of books and manuscripts, parchments and ancient bas-reliefs. Surrounding the nearby piazzas, eateries offered Caeli-Amur's famous spiced soups, and red wines from the foothills to the south. Above the eateries, tiny bars with wrought iron balconies overlooked the streets. In the afternoon, students and artists drank the exorbitantly priced flower-drafts and flame-liquors in the glass cabinets behind the bar. As evening closed in, the students leaned from the balconies and teased the passersby.

Maximilian thought of it as *his* quarter. He had made himself at home, come to know the rhythms of the universities, filled with students who yearned for forbidden knowledge: the kind only available in the cataloged libraries of the Houses.

When news spread of the printing press protests, Maximilian found himself—against Kamron and the Veterans' policies—standing at the open doors of one of Arbor's workshops in the Quaedian. A mass of printers were busily breaking the presses, which published Arbor's publications. Beneath the high-arched roof, the air was filled with a sense of danger and exhilaration. Light cut in through high narrow windows in the factory, where thirty presses, each standing at seven feet high and long, stood in rows. The printers were laughing as they jammed metal bars into the screw mechanisms, or struck levers and sheets of type with hammers. Others were scattering cast metal parts and type over the ground. He saw three of the gray-uniformed men, close to the door, heave over one of the screw-presses, which crashed onto the floor with a boom. Others were smashing bottles of ink, which splattered blackly against a far wall.

Around Maximilian, a crowd of onlookers watched curiously. What did it mean that the workers were breaking their own machines? Like the other houses, Arbor's finances seemed in order. Indeed, Caeli-Amur was a bustling and growing city. Old buildings were relentlessly torn down, new ones thrown up in their place; the sound of hammering and sawing echoed through the city. Meanwhile, the demand for books and broadsheets had grown rapidly. The printers had become ever more efficient, pumping out masses of printed matter every day, and yet their working conditions had not improved. And now, only days before, Arbor had announced that they would introduce steam-driven presses, replacing their workers with new technology, just as Technis had done in their printworks a year earlier. Here was the printworkers response.

Maximilian shook his head. If only the seditionists had a way of contacting the disenchanted workers more efficiently, rather than the slow process of individual recruitment that they used. But Kamron had been clear: Their strategy was to wait, grow incrementally until some time in the future.

Like many seditionists, Max had been converted by one of Kamron's pamphlets. He had come to Caeli-Amur from his hometown to the north, for he knew that it was in the cities that history was made. Anyone with an interest in thaumaturgy must eventually venture to Caeli-Amur, or Varenis, or another of the world's great cities. He had roamed between the bars and cafés of the Quaedian, learning scraps from the apprentices, filled with dreams of greatness. He had made friends with an intellectual from one of the universities, Odile, who smuggled him a pamphlet called *Thaumaturgy and History*. One evening Max had taken it to the dingy garret he shared with two others. He still remembered the shock as he had read the first page, how Kamron's words had turned his world on an angle, so that everything looked strange and new.

The pamphlet had ranged over the history of the world and thaumaturgy's place within it. The world had suffered a fall, and seditionism, it argued, was a regenerative philosophy. Seditionism recognized that the natural state of affairs had been replaced by a transitional period of recovery, through which they were now living, from the cataclysm almost a thousand years before. In this historical moment, all things were fragmented: thaumaturgy from everyday life, the heart from the head, freedom from responsibility, power from the people, the people from themselves. The Houses, Kamron argued, were the ultimate expression of this broken whole. The task was to regain the lost unity, to heal the broken parts. Max had spent the whole night reading, and then rereading, the pamphlet.

By dawn he was an avowed seditionist. Odile laughed at him and quoted an ancient aphorism: "Impetuosity leads only to regret." She was an intellectual, not a seditionist, she said. The two could not coexist. Max protested. A true intellectual *needed to be* a seditionist.

Max had found Kamron through a series of intricate steps, following whispered rumors and half leads, until eventually he met the soft-faced Iniria in a secret room. Her slow-moving calmness had been the opposite to everything he'd expected of a seditionist. But later he realized it had helped him accept her directions: she blindfolded him and led him to the hideout. That was before Ejan had taken control of the initiations and turned them into brutal and testing affairs.

Max had imagined that the seditionists must be a group of hundreds, so it was with some shock that he realized there were only eighteen of them, and Kamron was not at the head of an army fighting for freedom. But it was of no matter. Now, however, Max felt a desire to build that army, and here at the printing works seemed to be the very soldiers he sought.

Beside him, the tall and willowy Odile ran her hand through her short-cropped blond hair as they watched the printers now setting alight the paper stocks that were piled up against one of the factory's bluestone walls. The smoke billowed toward the roof.

"Not just here—the tramworkers, too," said Odile. "There's been sabotage at their factory."

Max nodded. "The Xsanthians have been unhappy down at the

docks." Max had visited the strange fish-men where they lived in the darkness beneath the wharf that very morning. House Marin kept them like slaves; they spent their days diving for pearls and shellfish, or loading and unloading ships.

"Guards!" someone called out, and the crowd scurried in all directions away from the printworks.

"Take care," Odile said. She touched his arm briefly, then was gone.

Max, too, turned away. Everything, he knew, must be subordinated to the long-term interests of seditionism. Now was too dangerous a moment to connect with the printers, and he had already disregarded Kamron's strictures by contacting the Xsanthians. Still, he thought of Nkando and felt the pain in his chest. Nkando—he pictured the dark skin of her face, the thickness of her lips, the way her head tilted up when she looked at him—he had turned his back on her, too. The memory burned in him and he pushed it away.

Max walked quickly toward the foot of the cliffs but stopped while he was still within view of the factory. Blue-uniformed Arbor guards trotted up toward the printworks, long pikes in hand. They rushed into the building, and there were the sounds of violent struggle: the clash of metal on metal, belligerent rough-voiced calls, screams of pain. Max emmited a low sound of frustration that only he could hear, then turned, and walked away.

As Max walked closer to the cliffs, so that their white faces loomed high above him, he was aware of the shadowy figure, a presence slipping through the remaining pedestrians, now close, now farther behind, like a ball being dragged on a string.

The streets were even narrower here: three- and four-story buildings pushed up close to each other, the shops and bars miniature little things, able to only fit ten or so people. Iron balconies faced each other across the narrow spaces. The bars were busily being cleaned after last night's Sun Parade. Great piles of rubbish—abandoned cloaks, minotaur hand puppets, empty bottles of Ayan flower-drafts, the last scraps of traditional goat stew—filled stinking barrels pushed up against the walls. In no time, rodents would begin picking through them, attracted by the fetid odor that wafted along the alleys.

Stopping to glance in one of these bars, Max sensed the figure hovering behind. He walked on a little, pretended to look in boxes of books standing outside a bookstore. He ran his hands through his curly brown hair, feeling the locks with his fingers, and glanced at his pursuer: a suited man, unremarkable in every way, a man dressed to be unseen. Max was of two minds. He should hide, lose himself among the winding streets. That's what Kamron had always argued: lie low, hide, wait. But Max was filled with the desire to strike back, to uncover his pursuer, to act.

Maximilian moved on, nearing the place where the houses ran up against the cliffs like an incoming sea. The streets doubled back on themselves or opened out into small squares, hidden away, some no larger than a small room. Staircases led to arched walkways that ran high above street level, a second network above the first.

There were fewer people on the street here: mysterious pedestrians, faces hidden beneath their cloaks, students scurrying, he assumed, to meet their friends, elderly men or women carrying bread, bottles of milk, cartons of tomatoes.

In this little maze, Max flitted from street to alleyway until, coming to one of the squares, he pressed himself into a corner, drew several forms in the air with his hands—small mathematical ideograms—and uttered a couple of equations beneath his breath. He entwined the two together just so. Thaumaturgy had its own language of numbers and symbols. Like any language, it possessed a grammar. Its elements—its calculations and processes—had to come one after the other at the appropriate time.

Around him, the world seemed to light up. The walls, the paint that adorned them, the cobblestones—everything pulsed with radiant power, bursting with a previously unseen life, immanent with meaning. He considered beginning one of the protection incantations that would protect him from the harmful effects of the thaumaturgy, but he didn't have time. His pursuer would turn the corner at any moment.

As he waited, his uncertainty grew: his heart hammering on his ribs, his mouth dry, his hands sweaty. From the alleyway he heard the sound of footsteps, a soft *pat-pat-pat* on the cobblestones. Maintaining his illusion, he drew his knife, long and thin.

The sound rang out in the quiet stone walls. He held the blade with one hand to kill the sound, and clenched his teeth. The footsteps came closer now, *pat-pat-pat,* and Max tensed, ready to spring.

A lone figure walked through the archway. Max remained rooted to the spot, unable to leap, his heart rattling like a broken engine within him. The figure passed though the tiny square, not six feet from him. He exhaled: it was only a servant woman with an apron, holding a small basket of oranges in her hands. Max leaned back, his back hard against cold stone.

Before long he again heard the sound of footsteps approaching. On the opposite side of the square, the woman passed through the archway. The second set of footsteps stopped, close to the archway out of sight. Max tensed again; his heart raced.

The suited man looked around the corner of the archway. Around his eyes were lines of worry. When he opened his mouth, perhaps in fear, Max could see a couple of teeth were missing, the others yellowed. He looked straight at Max, but did not see the invisible seditionist in the corner. The illusionist's charm was effective. The man quickly looked away toward the opposite corner of the square.

Max leaped and slammed into the man with his shoulder. Someone let out a gurgling cry and Max realized it came from his own throat. The world lost its immanence as the thaumaturgy shimmered away. He crashed to the ground with the twisting body beneath him. Somehow he pushed the man down and straddled him, his knife pressed against the man's neck.

"No!" The man's eyes widened in fear.

Max looked down at that face, now twitching and shuddering, as if undergoing some kind of fit.

"Please." The man shuddered again.

"Why shouldn't I?" Max clutched the knife madly, driven on by some unknown force within him, his heart thumping now with exhilaration.

The man looked at him, "Because . . ." The man's face gave one last tremble and froze in a final spasm. He let out a wail and started to cry. "I'm only, I'm only . . ."

"What?" asked Max. "You're only . . . you're only . . . . Which House?"

"Technis," said the man.

"What do they know about me?"

"I've got children. A family. My daughter's name is Camille. She's four."

"Shut up."

"My name is Pi . . . P . . . Pierre."

"Shut up."

"I'm—"

Max struck the man's cheek with the back of his hand. His wrist hit bone. Pain shot up to his elbow. "What do they know?"

"I don't know. They just pay me to keep an eye on things at the docks. I was supposed to follow anyone approaching the Xsanthians. I . . . I'm supposed to find out where the radical groups are hiding."

Max prepared to kill the man. He pressed the blade against the House agent's skin. The man tried to elongate his neck to escape the blade, but it was no use.

"I won't work for them anymore!" said Pierre. "I have a child. Her name is Camille."

I'll kill him, thought Max. I should not let a Technis agent know me, recognize me. Max hesitated. He had never killed a man, and now the very notion seemed surreal and impossible. He lost a sense of all his reasons, of the world itself and his place in it. He stared at the knife, gleaming against the man's neck. But he couldn't do it. The man's name was Pierre. He had a child.

The blow struck him on the side of the head, hard. Max's body went limp and he collapsed to the cobblestones, face first. Instinctively, he curled into a ball as a second blow glanced off his shoulder. Then he was kicked hard in the leg. He felt the foot sink into his soft flesh. Pierre was already up, and Max caught sight of his leather boot, the sole coming away from its heel.

"You scum. You seditionist scum. I don't have no daughter. You believed that?" Pierre laughed. "I don't have no children."

A vicious foot come down on Max's ribs. He groaned.

A second voice said, "You're supposed to follow them secretly, you fool."

"Not so secretly so you lose sight of them. Where were you, huh? We were supposed to be working together, and you just disappear," said Pierre.

A foot struck Max's head and he lost all strength. He slumped down and his head fell sideways on the cobblestones. A properly placed blow could kill him now.

Pierre held the knife to Max's throat. He felt the tip, sharp and cold, and felt his own helplessness. Max lifted his head and shuffled to one side on his stomach, but Pierre followed him, the knife breaking his skin.

"What are you? A cockroach?" said Pierre.

"Don't kill him," said the second voice. "We're just supposed to follow them."

"Come on then," said Pierre. He stood up, kicked Max one final time, knocked the breath out of him.

"Let's get back to the factory," said the second voice. "No use that one anyway."

"You think the captain will let us off for the rest of the day?" said Pierre.

The two kept chattering as they walked away, leaving Max crumpled on the ground.

Some minutes later, Max struggled to his feet. He checked himself; everything was all right. He had bruises, especially on his right side, a cut on his head, the lightness of concussion perhaps.

He brushed himself off and walked onwards, at first leaning forward and holding his side. Then he straightened up and walked with more purpose. This was just the beginning, he knew. The worst of it was yet to strike.

Ten minutes later, the sickness hit him, as it always did after he used the Art without a protection incantation: first the waves of lethargy as all strength was stripped from him. He found a little alcove where he leaned back against the wall and again pressed himself against the cool stonework, feeling its rough edges against him. What use was it, this thaumaturgy, if it struck you down like an invalid? That was the price of power: nothing spent, nothing received, though sometimes, for no reason, the sickness was worse than at others. He knew this was only the beginning. He had seen the Houses' skilled workers—engineers, tramworkers, mechanics—with strange growths on their faces and bodies, who died young or ran mad in the streets. For those who stood unprotected, unable to control the powers, it was worst. It was said that the ancient Prism of Alerion, in which the god's very soul was encased, would enable the thaumaturgical arts to be used without penalty. But the Prism had been lost in the dark years after the cataclysm. Now the only defense was to be found in charms of protection, deflection, and control. But even the Houses' thaumaturgists, who knew those formulae and could control the forces as one did a dangerous animal, often ended knobbly and warped, as if their bodies were made of wax that had been heated just a little. Others seemed physically unaffected, but their personalities had changed deep within. It was the fate of all who used the Art—it would be his fate also.

SIX

Satisfied that he was no longer being followed, Maximilian climbed the rising pathways to the top of the cliffs, where scores of cafés overlooked the low part of the city. On the other side of them ran Via Gracchia, one of Caeli-Amur's wide thoroughfares, where carts and carriages competed with steam-trams. Halfway along Via Gracchia, to the south, stood the steam tower, powering the cable car, which swung through the air toward the docks. Yet farther along, the via ended in the Arantine, where Arbor's mansions sat on their stately and cobblestoned streets. Max rarely passed in that direction: it lay beyond the realm of workers and factories and universities, where he felt most alive, where he felt the pulsing vitality of the people whom he loved. But the Arantine lurked in his mind like an unexpressed thought. One day the seditionists would march into the neighborhood not as outsiders but as victors.

Max continued up toward the towering, sheer-faced peak of the mountain. His body ached from the beating, and he still felt the Art's unnatural sickening somewhere deep inside him. But he continued on. The pain and the illness would pass. Around him, picturesque white houses nestled one above the other, clinging to the ever-steeper incline as if at any moment they might slip and tumble down. The higher he walked, the more the houses thinned out and were interspersed by small cliffs and thick tough vegetation. In a wide space between two houses, Max stopped and scanned the streets around him for pursuers. He then turned and scrambled up a rough path into a dry brushland. There he entered what might have been a dry and barren sewer outlet, ten feet in diameter. Yet its perfect circularity, the grooves that ran along its walls, hinted at another, lost purpose. Entering the tunnel still excited him, even after these last years. There was a mystery to the tunnel and the darkness beyond that fired his imagination, as if below the crust of the earth lived a world of possibility.

Within seconds he was in the dark, the spring sunlight a sheet of white at the end of the tunnel; with each step the darkness became more profound. After twenty paces, he reached an alcove where twenty or so lamps hung on the wall. He lit one with a match and passed farther into the tunnel. After some time, the path widened and he passed through a gigantic open door. Here the floor and walls became rough, as if excavation deeper into the mountain had been hastily abandoned. Max continued through the tunnel, rising and falling, widening and narrowing. At places the rocky passage was dry and dusty, at others water dripped from the roof and along the walls. Having passed through the memorized sequence of turns, Max turned and walked directly into the rock wall and passed through it, as if it were not there at all.

Max came to a T-intersection where the walls were flat and again consciously constructed. Perhaps those who built the underground complex had here accidentally broken through to the cave tunnel. Light warmed the walls, and farther down, a heavy door with a wheel mechanism that gave way to a dark cavernous hall—the Communal Cavern. At its center a number of figures moved around the strange combination of banks of levers and tables set with glossy surfaces—technology whose use had been long lost and which now lay dead and cold. Wood-fired ovens glowed in the gloom; people sat in reclining chairs and couches. Along one side of the cavern stood four black pillars, fifteen feet tall, like giant sentries overlooking the space. He inhaled the smell of woodsmoke and dampness, a comforting scent that reminded Max of his safely hidden hopes.

Out of the shadows stepped a figure. "Max, there you are."

"Kamron." Max's arms hung leadenly by his side, a sign of his repressed shame and disappointment. The older man had been waiting for him and obviously knew that Max had been out in the city.

"You're hurt. You were caught." Kamron squinted at him.

"It was nothing, just a scuffle," said Max. It would hurt more tomorrow, he knew.

"Come with me, son." Kamron, walking stiffly and unevenly, led him away. One of Kamron's legs was longer than the other; one knee straightened a little more easily. Max knew that beneath those clothes, he was bent and misshapen, like a bag into which odd-shaped vegetables had been forced.

Max followed Kamron along the side of the cavern. Here the walls were marked with flat and shiny surfaces; streams of wires jutted from the wall and fell toward the ground like frozen waterfalls.

They entered Kamron's room, with its hundred miniature glittering lights that danced across the walls. Having achieved a new configuration, they would freeze, little clusters of light in a new and beautiful arrangement. Then they'd burst once more into motion, one of the few of the old technologies that functioned in the seditionist base. Mostly the lights were gone, the levers jammed and broken, the pads blackened, the glass melted.

Kamron sat slowly in one of the semicircle of chairs arranged in the center of the room. He gestured to another seat for Max. "So how goes the printworkers' struggle?"

Max sat in silence. How did Kamron know that he had attended the demonstration? Picking up on the tension, the lights darted rapidly across the walls and suddenly froze in anticipation. He drew a breath and tensed. The words tumbled out. "They smashed their own presses, because they have no other ideas of how to fight. It's *our* fault because we've just left them to work things out for themselves." He waited for a minute. "I'm sorry I didn't tell you I was going to observe them."

Kamron brought his hands up to his face, his fingers softly dabbing his eyelids. Kamron's movements were always slow and gentle. Max could not tell if he had internalized a state of grace, or was simply old. His voice was low, gentle, pursuasive. "Max. The art of politics is the art of knowing what to do next, and what *not* to do."

Max summoned his courage. "Things are changing in Caeli-Amur. The Xsanthians are ready to strike on the docks."

Kamron stood up, walked across to the shelves, and up picked one of books. "Eldra's *Decline of the Old World*. I found this book deep in the basement of an old music instructor; it had been his grandfather's. He had no idea of its worth, and was happy for me to take it. Imagine that: your work, left in the basement—perhaps the *only* remaining copy. He argues that the conflict between the gods was about more than just their personalities. It was between those who wanted only to play and dance—Aya and his followers—and the rest who wanted things to be orderly. After the war, the citizens of the Old World, sick of these conflicts, drove the gods away. And when the gods left us: that was the cataclysm, the moment that civilization fell. You should read it."

"The time of reading is over." Max looked directly into the old man's eyes. The lights increased in intensity, illuminating parts of Kamron's craggy face, throwing other parts into darkness.

Kamron laughed uneasily. "You are ready to fight. And you *should* be. It's only natural. But, Max: look at us. There are thirty of us—only thirty. It took us fifteen years to build up what we have, to accumulate our scant knowledge of thaumaturgy, to create this library. How can our knowledge compete with that of the Houses, with all their history? With all their resources? We cannot get involved in struggles that will only be defeated."

"We could be a hundred in a week," said Max.

Kamron ignored him. "Slow preparation. The machines—that is what you should put your focus on. Work out what they are, what they do."

The machines lay in their vast hall, not far from the Communal Cavern, silent and dead, like the metal bones of huge creatures that had shuffled into one final formation and died. Max wanted to say, "Those machines are useless, broken," but found himself nodding instead.

"Haven't I led the group through dangerous times?" Kamron said.

Max looked down at his own feet. When Kamron had first taken him as an apprentice, Maximilian thought that they would conquer the world.

"Patience," Kamron had said four years earlier, when the group numbered only eighteen. He had sat quietly in the vast dark communal hall, illuminated by only a couple of candles that lit a sphere around them. "Almost all knowledge is hidden in the House Libraries."

"Why don't we infiltrate them?" said Maximilian.

"They would discover you. If they didn't discover you, you would be changed by them. You would think that you were using them, but your environment would start to shape you. Moment by moment, you would find that you would see things differently, the way *they* see them."

"They would not see me." Maximilian spoke a few words, drew the ideograms in the air, and shimmered out of existence.

Kamron laughed. "You have talent for illusion. Perhaps it is your calling."

Maximilian emerged back into the world. "No, I will master all the forms of thaumaturgy."

"Nobody can understand all the forms. Not even the Sortileges of Varenis." When parents didn't scare their children with images of the Elo-Talern, they spoke about the Sortileges. Almost no one knew what they looked like: some said that they were huge men, with rolls of fat rippling down their sides, others that they were changed in ways that none could describe, their faces hidden by deathmasks, their power radiating from them like heat. They ruled the city of Varenis, two weeks' march north through the hills, like priest-gods. They were said to each have mastered one of the forms and had paid a price greater than could be imagined.

"According to the Histories, the gods mastered all the forms," Max said. The great goal of thaumaturgy for centuries had been this—unification: the notion that one can step back and create a grand unifying theory, one that connected all the rambling, disparate, fragmented thaumaturgical forms from Alchemy to Illusion to Transformation. The concept stirred Maximilian's imagination.

"Are you a god?" Kamron's soft voice hovered in the little bubble of light. "If you had mastery of all the forms, what would you become?"

Maximilian felt drained from the use of his illusion. He placed his hands on his knees to hold himself up, held the nausea at bay. Next time he would remember to use the protection incantation.

Now, four years later, Max looked at Kamron's knobby hands. Some knuckles stood up like mountains and others looked worn away; he looked at Kamron's body, bent forward in the midsection, bent backwards at the chest higher up; he looked at the neck, shifted sideways so Kamron's head looked forever like it might slip off the shoulders altogether—all these effects of a life's work in thaumaturgy. Kamron had been careful to use the Art only when he must. Even with the charms of deflection and protection, this is what he'd become.

Kamron spoke in low, slow tones. "Max, you're forbidden from visiting the Xsanthians. You're forbidden from seeking out strikes."

Max stared at Kamron. He was shaken, aghast. The injustice of it cut at him. In any case, Kamron had no right to command him. But Kamron had built the group, and its members obeyed him. He was a hero, in Max's eyes.

Max looked down at the floor. "You've been a good leader. You've given us everything. I'm sorry to have questioned you." But even as he spoke, Max knew he was not speaking the truth. He was outgrowing Kamron. The older man was no longer a mentor. It was time for Max to strike out on his own, and yet how could he betray this man who had been like a father to him? But Max would. He would visit the Xsanthians and urge them to strike. He would explain his views to the Veterans. He would assert his independence. They had no right to refuse him.

Kamron leaned over and ruffled Max's curly brown hair. "You are such a dreamer! A romantic! Oh, if only I were young again."

The lights dimmed slightly and moved in gentle waves along the walls, throwing soft silvery light on the two seditionists.

Later in the afternoon, Max sat with Omar and Giselle in the Hall of Machines. In the darkness, intricate black metal constructions sat like a cohort of fearsome crouching creatures and gigantic skeletal birds. In two directions the metal shapes disappeared into the shadows. In another direction a light indicated a distant corridor, lit by a strange purple mist that seemed never to dissipate. A five minutes' walk along that corridor lay the Communal Cavern.

The three seditionists sat before a machine, a complex conglomeration of pylons and plates—a great metal scaffolding. Deep within, wires and tubes entwined crisscrossed in a complex lattice. Fingerlike vises were attached to its machinelike arms. How long it had sat there, silent as a corpse, none of them could tell. Like all the technology buried beneath the mountain, the machines dated from the time of the ancients.

Giselle riffled through one of several books that lay upon a table, illuminated by a lamp, as Max and Omar pushed and prodded at the machine's arms.

"It's hopeless." Giselle looked up with her sharp eyes. She ran her hands through her red hair, causing it to form a curly cloud around her head. "I don't know why Kamron has us work on these things. The Histories have almost nothing useful to add. Listen to what Karmilla says in her *Narratives*, 'And when Alerion was tired of Aya's gibes, he gathered around him the gods and they turned on Aya with all their instruments and machines, and Aya, who felt that machines were not a way to happiness, was forced to flee before them. And wherever he traveled—to the clouds and beneath the sea—they pursued him. They dug through the earth like moles, they flew through the sky like birds, and Aya, who had never been afraid, was now afraid.'" Giselle looked up from the book. "I mean, it's the usual stuff: machines for flying, machines for digging. Just legends, nothing more than legends."

Max and Omar still poked and prodded at the machine.

"Hey!" said Giselle. "Are you listening to me?"

Omar looked over and grinned, the small man's teeth exceptionally white against his olive skin. "Were you saying something?"

"I think I heard a sound from over there," said Max, still examining the machine. "Over in that area." He waved his arms in the general direction of Giselle. Max and Omar had been friends for ten years. They met as teenagers on the Dyrian coast, to the north of Caeli-Amur, where officiates mingled with tourists from Varenis; where Directors and officiates lazed in the summer in their grand villas on the coast. Omar's family was descended from the original inhabitants of the region. His parents farmed oysters. Max's parents had run one of Dyria's pleasure villas, complete with baths and library. Max had spied Omar in the library, reading voraciously the Histories, and the two had become friends, so close that they now had developed almost a language of their own. Then they had both become friends with Nkando. But Nkando was long gone, and whenever Omar talked of her, Max remained silent.

Finally, Max had left for the opportunities of the city. Omar had followed a year later when Max was already a confirmed seditionist. It did not take long for Max to convert him.

Giselle put her hands on her hips and pursed her lips in half-amused annoyance. She started reading again. "'Like all the gods, Aya's essence had been replicated in the Great Library of Caeli-Enas, where knowledge was contained in a million books and by other stranger and more exotic means. Such knowledge could be drunk like an elixir, so that in but the passing of a moment one could absorb great histories, geographies of faraway worlds, all the secrets of the universe, one could taste the spirits of long-dead souls. Even the secrets of the Magi could be absorbed from the Library, in the time it took to close one's eyes. All one needed was the code to give to the librarian.'"

Max stood up and looked into the darkness with the thought of the Great Library of Caeli-Enas, sunk so close to them beneath the sea, so impossible to reach. To absorb knowledge in an instant, thought Max. Something more rapid and efficient than reading, could that be possible? The secrets of the Magi: *Something that would forever change the relationship between the seditionists and the Houses.* Even now he could picture himself standing tall before the House thaumaturgists. How they would tremble at his mastery. Then, at the head at the seditionist army, he would lead the wave of demonstrations, one after another in the coming months, until the House structure fell. But he stopped these thoughts. Seditionism was not a place for individual glory. He felt guilty at his ambitions and resolved to refocus his attention on the good of the group: when he returned, he would put himself at the disposal of the seditionists. He would be theirs to command. Now, however,

was the time to focus on the machine. He reached into a gap between the metal plates on its great torso. A soft hum emanated
from it and he and Omar leaped back.

"What did you do?" Omar's voice bleated.

"There was a lever in there," said Max softly.

The machine glowed from within with an unnatural green
light. The humming increased and it lurched into motion, shuddering and shaking from side to side. Ten or so arms of some sort
unfolded from the scaffolding and it hoisted itself up on two legs.
The machine let out a deep groan, as if it had experienced epochs
of sadness. Then it shook again, the entire mechanism shifting
internally, and it elongated, like a long-necked animal reaching up
for leafy foliage. The groan increased, like the call of a wounded
beast. Raising one metal claw, the machine dug away at itself as if
something deep within its mechanical insides hurt.

Max and Omar both took a number of steps backwards.

A deep red glow appeared in the insides of the machine. Max
retreated farther from the rush of heat.

The pylon-arms of the machine opened out again, reattached
themselves to other parts of the machine. What had previously
been the socket now became a metallic hand. An elongated octa-
gon, which might have been a head, began to shake and, with a
whine of rage and frustration, the machine collapsed in upon itself, the glow petering out with the smell of something burning.
The darkness enclosed again.

"Do you want to try the lever again?" said Giselle.

Max glared at her.

"You know that Ejan thinks we should pursue another course
also," said Giselle slowly. "We must make life unbearable for the
Houses: break their locks, ruin their carriage wheels," said Giselle.
"Even . . ."

Omar looked at Giselle dubiously. "Even what?"

Giselle now approached the machine also. She touched the
metal on one of its long arms. The machine hummed. She stood
back. "Even strike at their personnel—assassinate the Directors and
their officiates."

"You can't shoot a system." Max turned back to the machine;

he was torn between the fact it had moved and the debate with Giselle. "I know you support Ejan, but don't you find him over-zealous? Striking physically against the Houses: as if sedition were only military action! It implies the final test between us and the Houses, but before the citizens support us. It's madness."

"More mad than hiding here in this hole?" Giselle turned to look at him. "Anyway, you misunderstand. You're seeing things upside down. One doesn't *attract* support before fighting, one fights to attract support. It's a way of showing that things cannot continue as usual, of showing that resistance is possible. Anyway, perhaps you should be worrying about Kamron?"

Max ignored her comment. "And when does Ejan plan to begin this campaign of his?"

"We've already begun. We've struck Technis's Tram Factory."

Max could hardly believe it, and some part of him was jealous. Ejan had the conviction to act without the approval of the Veterans. "Kamron will banish him. Kamron will banish all of you."

Giselle took Max's arm and turned him away from the machine. "You know that together your circle and Ejan's circle form the majority of the group. Together you can change its direction."

Maximilian had a group of six followers to whom he was teaching the basics of thaumaturgy. Together with Omar, there were eight of them. With Ejan's group of ten, they were more than half of the thirty seditionists. He shook the idea off. "I would not make such a deal. We stand for completely opposite things. It would tear the group apart."

Omar stepped between them. "Sorry to interrupt you, but you realize that this machine moved."

Turning his mind from the debate, Max pulled over the step-ladder, climbed up, reached up and pressed the machine on what looked like a breastplate. The machine quickly dropped down in to a kind of squat. Beams of light shot from between its metal exoskeleton. From somewhere inside came strange voices speaking in an unknown language. Fragments of sentences, "Il Guilmar. Il Timar. Il Endus. Il Panadus!"

A gap the size of a man opened up in the machine's insides and a platform emerged beneath it. Its base was a dark metal. The walls of the cavity were formed by imbricated plates of metal, punctured by thousands of microscopic holes. Complex twines of tubing and wires emerged from the spaces between the plates, while various protuberances seemed randomly scattered. Finally, hidden high up within the machine hung something that looked like an inverted flower with its petals opened, like a helmet sectioned into four. From the walls there was a complex series of open clamps that might close over an operator's forearms. Similar clamps, which when closed might form a boot of sorts, emerged from the rear of the cavity close to the base-plate.

"I'll climb in," said Omar.

"No, let me," said Max. "I'll just step inside and see if anything happens. Then I'll step out again."

Ignoring Max, Omar stepped up to the machine, which still hummed gently. He put both hands on the platform and pulled himself up, placed both feet onto it, and his head and torso disappeared in the darkness. "Hmm," he said, "nothing's happening." He turned around and added, "Oh."

The platform rose as the machine straightened itself like a soldier standing to attention. The boots begin to close over Omar's feet.

"Look at this . . . ," said Omar.

"What is it?" said Giselle.

"Oh my—," began Omar but he stopped, groaned slowly, and then screamed hideously, like a man being tortured. His voice came out then garbled. "Needles!"

"Omar! Omar!" Max and Giselle ran around the machine.

The screaming continued "No! No!" The smell of something rotten wafted from the machine and the thing took two jerky steps forward, knocking over the stepladder. Omar's wail gave way to the broken high whine of someone whose voice could no longer contain the power of the cry.

Max grabbed the stepladder and placed it in front of the machine. He scrambled up, off balance, tried to press the breastplate, but fell down to the floor. Again he scrambled up the ladder, hoping the thing would not move. He reached up, pressed the breastplate, and the machine dropped to the ground. The platform descended, the boots opened, the vises that had clamped around Omar's legs gave way. Moaning, Omar slid from the insides of the thing, blood coming from spots along his arms and legs. He raised his hands to his face, a face that had been burned so that it was swollen-red and blotchy. His hair, once thick and black, was burned away in several places.

Max grasped Omar as he slid out. "Take his legs."

Together they carried him toward the Communal Cavern, Max holding him beneath the armpits, Giselle carrying his feet. All the time Omar groaned and muttered strange words and stared out into space, his eyes were focusing on another world. Along the long corridor lit with purple mist they carried him. In the Communal Cavern, other seditionists rushed about asking, "What happened?" Max made a bed on which Omar could lie while Giselle prepared poultices. Omar's eyes fluttered open and roved around until some time later they fixed on Max as he sat beside him. "You should have seen it, Max. You should have seen the visions. The world. The voices, I can still hear the voices," said Omar. "Il Panadus. It Tenerebris . . . ," he said. "The voices of the angels . . ."

When Kamron squatted beside Omar, Max squinted at the old man. "This is your fault."

SEVEN

With the money Rudé had given her the previous day, Kata walked slowly to Via Persine, where she caught a tram to the market. In her mind, she ran over the previous day's events: her fit; Rudé's arrival, followed by Aemilius's; the way Rudé had looked at Aemelius in awe. After their departures, she spent the remaining hours resting, as Aemilius had suggested, and her strength had slowly returned. She thought of the flagon of poison she had stored in her kitchen. The memory of it all filled her with doubt and dread.

At the market she bought a bag of medicine from the old peasant woman. She now had enough to last her a couple of months. As a child, the fits had come unexpectedly, and after her mother died, she had often found herself lying in some gutter in the factory district. Once, she had regained consciousness to find a group of boys standing around her. One of them had pulled her dress up and they were all busy staring at her nakedness. Instinctively she kicked out, and the boys had run away laughing. She felt dirty for the rest of the day.

About six years ago, a young apothecary had seen her having a fit in one of the cafés, and he'd kneeled down beside her. She still remembered the softness in his eyes and the gentle way he spoke. He told her to try the preparation made of roots and leaves from the south, and it had staved off the fits. For years she hoped he would return and sweep her away somewhere and look after her. Though he hadn't, she remembered him still.

Now the old woman at the market sold the preparation, along with many others: for aches of the joints, to help with agues and fevers, to heal broken limbs. Looking up at her, the old woman's grin smoothed out her wrinkly face. "Ah, you're a good-looking girl."

Kata smiled weakly. She had never considered herself good-looking. Yes, she had long black hair and intense eyes, but she had always thought her brooding countenance precluded words such as "pretty," "beautiful," or "good-looking."

Behind her, a group of blue-uniformed Marin guards rushed past toward the docks, tridents in hand, nets hanging from their shoulders.

The old woman nodded toward them. "It's been nothing but trouble down there on the docks since the minotaurs arrived. Holy, they call those beasts. Inhuman is what I'd call them."

Kata peered toward the great steamers that sat on the piers, but could make out nothing but the guards gathered around some disturbance. Some of the guards held their nets in hand, ready to throw. "It's been nothing but trouble since before they arrived," she said.

The woman pursed her lips, raised the eyebrows that jutted from her forehead like spindly bushes. "But things are going awry now, what with all these talks of strikes. Arbor's printworkers yesterday, broken by the House, but not before they smashed up their presses."

Kata smiled weakly again. "Perhaps things will settle. Perhaps it's this heat."

The old woman looked up at the hazy sky. There was no wind, and the air seemed the hang heavily around them. "Ah, I haven't seen days like this since before the House Wars started. It's in the air; you can feel it. Birds fly directionless; the morning sun had been glowing a furnace red; specters have been seen in the ruins of the Ancient Forum —portents."

As Kata mixed the preparation and drank it, the old woman watched her curiously. Kata's limbs relaxed a little, letting go of the tension that threatened to tip over into a fit. She had failed the day before with Aemilius: she had let him go. Now she must make amends with another minotaur. She looked down at the old woman, who grinned and said again, "You're a good-looking girl."

Kata left the market and searched for a minotaur, but every time she found one, something stood in her way. First there were too many of them, gathered near the steam baths on the northern peninsula of the city, with no way of isolating one. Another simply ignored her when she approached him in the high-art café called Anthalas, filled with odd-shaped sculptures and instalations designed for the twin black cats that had made it their home. A third, telling stories of the Numerian Wars and Saliras's assault on the city, was surrounded by wide-eyed young women whose hands · reached out to touch him. Yet others laughed and played games with sticks and bone dice with old men and women. The citizens had grown more comfortable with the presence of the minotaurs.

With each failure she felt the sickly feeling of dread creeping into her. Desperation made everything seem out of focus. Her eyes flitted from one person to another.

Slowly she made her way up the white cliffs on foot. She passed a building whose walls were plastered with a patchwork of posters calling for an end to the Houses. The style was in modern reds and blacks: strong straight-lined figures of workers, standing in front of a cubist representation of the House Technis Complex. The posters were marked with A CALL TO ARMS. Beside the posters someone had scrawled, *I'll end your house.*

Finally, she scaled the winding stairs that hugged the city's northernmost cliff, which stood by itself close to the mountaintop. The path was like a mountain goat trail, dangerously doubling back on itself, at places so steep as to be almost a ladder. Eventually she reached the Artists' Square that jutted from the cliff like a great sandy disk. Painters with their easels were dotted between tables where men with braided hair and spectacles drank green tea. There she found Aemilius playing chess with another minotaur.

Kata sat next to them and looked over the city below. It was beautiful, despite the smoke that rose constantly from the factories or the slums in the Lavere Quarter far to the south. The city was silent; only the sound of the artists' voices could be heard, rustling on the wind.

"This is Kata, Dexion," said Aemilius.

"You have a new friend already?" said Dexion, whose hair was light and sandy. His hands were smooth and young looking.

"I do," said Aemilius, looking at Kata.

"You old ones, you never surprise me with your cunning," said Dexion.

"No," said Aemilius, "nothing like that."

"Oh no. Nothing like that," said Dexion, laughing also. "Actually, I remember seeing her with Cyriacus. You know, no one's seen him in days. There are rumors, rumors of abductions, of a black market."

"Rumors don't stand for the truth. He'll be around," said Aemilius, looking across to Kata.

Kata felt her stomach tense but kept her face impassive.

Dexion nodded and said, "I'll leave you two to your friendship then."

"But our game?"

"Next time," said Dexion.

"You're only leaving because I have the upper hand."

But Dexion was already walking away across the square, looking around happily. Vitality and enthusiasm radiated from him.

"The city is beautiful from the square," she said.

"Look at the smoke though, poisoning the air."

"I grew up on the streets around those factories. I learned to love the dirty alleyways, the grime-covered walls."

"Yes," he said, "there's energy in the new technologies. Many possibilities. Many choices."

"They bring new conflicts also," said Kata. "The Factory Quarter is filled with damaged workers. Some are broken, but some are not. There's talk of revolt."

They sat in the afternoon sun, watching the painters around them try to capture the scene just so, in their very own ways, and talked. Aemilius had been born on Aya, he explained. Like all minotaurs, he had burst forth from rock, full of mighty rage, clamoring for knowledge and adventure. He had sailed on sleek longboats, traveled the deserts of Numeria, studied now-lost texts such as Sumi's *Necromancy and Agency* in the ancient Library of the Sunken City. "But I never ventured to the lower levels, where the memories of the ancients are stored. There you could talk with those very memories, and they would stand before you in physical form."

Kata tried to keep the conversation focused on Aemilius, but eventually he asked her about herself.

"My mother died of the contagion when I was a child," she replied. "She had worked in the factories for House Technis. I remember her hands were knobby from the spinning wheels. When you held one, you could feel the calluses, the lumps where there had been breaks. But you know what the Cajiun philosophers say, 'One must pass straight through pain—to attempt to avoid it is to warp your life, to cripple yourself.' "

"It intrigues me that you would know such philosophy. I thought it was out of fashion," said Aemilius.

"It is, among the House philosophers. But many citizens still contemplate it. Some of the philosopher-assassins keep Cajiunism alive. Many who still live in the margins or who, like me, grew up on the streets."

Kata's mentor Sarrat had been a Cajiun philosopher from Numeria. Some said it was the perfect philosophy for those who lived in the deserts deep inland. Sarrat was the calmest man she had ever met; he seemed to live in a perpetual inner silence. Pain, patience, compassion: these were the principles the Cajiuns lived by. But he was perfectly capable of bursting into action, his long black body leaping and spinning through the air. He had taught her this Cajiun style of fighting, based on constant movement, and the philosophy that went along with it. "One must kill as quickly and painlessly as possible," he said after he had adopted her from the streets in an act of charity. His apartment was bare and free of books. Real philosophy could be taught through *practice*, he insisted. Sarrat smiled gently when a year later she brought in a copy of Quelos's tome, *Fear and the Emotions: A Discourse*. Kata had said to him, "I'm not sure I'm a Cajiun philosopher. I haven't the patience or the temperament." Sarrat had sat still, legs crossed, in the center of the room. "Perhaps not."

Now Aemilius looked over at her curiously before taking her

hand in his own rough fingers. "And you have raised yourself up. Look at you now: a real citizen of the city, free, capable."

"Come," she said, "let's go."

She took him back down the staircase, the wind picking up to buffet away their talk. And then down through the streets that grew in size, where children laughed and ran barefoot between houses and old men sat silently on stools by the front doors of their square, blocklike cottages.

Kata led him ultimately to her house. She took him inside and walked to the kitchen. She opened the cupboard door and glanced at the flagon. She left it there and walked back out of the kitchen. Aemilius stood before her, majestic. She reached out and placed her hand on his chest. It did not ripple with muscles as Cyriacus's had, but his body was powerful nonetheless. Kata leaned in and rested her head against his chest, reaching up to touch his hairy face, the bristles wiry and oiled beneath her hand. The smell of sweat and perfume intoxicated her, and she felt calm as his arms closed around her. She shut her eyes and felt his chest rising and falling beneath her cheek. Pushing back, she looked up into his onyx eyes, noticing for the first time the soft and dark eyelashes that interlaced beautifully as he blinked.

"Come upstairs," she said.

"No."

"Why not?"

"I have to leave at the end of the week."

"I don't care. Come upstairs." She turned and pulled him by the hand. He came, hesitantly, behind her, as if she were leading a child into the dark.

The next morning they lay in her bed, watching the light as it slowly shifted in intensity across the wall. In the afternoon, when he left to buy fruit from the markets, she locked the cupboard in her bedroom that held her bolt-thrower. When he returned, they ate the fruit naked at the table.

"Look at this," he said, running his fingers along the roughened edge of the table that had been scraped when she killed Cyriacus.

"Scraped when I brought it through the door."

"I hope you didn't fall and give yourself those bruises," he said.

"No. Those came from Cyriacus."

"Ha!" He threw his head back.

"What?"

"I knew. I smelled his blood on the balcony. What happened?"

"We fought. I struck him and he left."

"He left? Just like that? Don't lie to me. I know what he tried to do. The young minotaurs, they let pain make their decisions for them."

"It's not what you think. He didn't—"

"I'm sorry for whatever happened. I'm sorry you had to go through that."

She crossed her arms and clenched her teeth.

Aemilius reached over and placed his hand over hers. "You are distant."

"To be close to someone is . . . dangerous."

After he left, Kata lay desolate on the cushions, cursing House Technis and their hold over her. She had volunteered so readily, a chance to cancel all her debts at once. But now . . . She had to kill another minotaur. It was sacrilege, of course, which is why they had agents like her perform the task. If necessary, they could deny all responsibility.

She could not fail. She had two days.

EIGHT

In the House Technis Complex, Kata sat before a polished redwood desk on which sat a elaborate mechanical contraption beside a pile of papers. She looked out of the window to the hanging gardens with their red round fruit, their tinkling waterfalls and marble fountains. Soft purple flowers floated on the breeze. She smelled pollen. Technis's gardens attempted to replicate Arbor's, but they could never compete with the exotic and deadly flora—the tear-flowers, frost-reeds, *Toxicodendron didion*—that surrounded the Arbor palace. Technis was not an originator but instead a relentless and efficient imitator.

The door opened. Rudé entered and sat down in the red leather chair behind the desk. "Well?"

"I want to change the agreement."

"We can't. We have customers waiting for the different parts of the body. And the House's thaumaturgists are waiting for the eyes, the liver and kidneys, and the skin."

"Perhaps you could get someone else to do it."

"Yes. I suppose we could. But it's a bit late now. Anyway, I've already given you an advance."

"That was hardly worth the price of the first minotaur."

"Yes, but let's see. You still owe us for half your apartment. Now, we could repossess that . . . but you don't want to go back on the street, do you? Anyway, look at it this way, Kata: It's time for you to show some loyalty. Loyalty will get you far in this world."

The mention of the street struck fear deep into Kata. She could never go back to the street. All those years of struggle, of dragging her way up from poverty, from hopelessness, from a world of cold in winter, heat in summer, relentlessly shifting sleeping places from gutter to empty basement to factory storeyard, running with street urchins, some kindly, others vicious-tempered and dissolute. She would rather die than find herself with no apartment, thrown back into the street.

She rose to her feet and leaned over the desk at him. "Everyone finds their proper place, you know, Rudé. One day you'll find yours."

"Fine," he said, as if Kata had not spoken at all. "I'll come to collect the body at the end of the Festival tomorrow night. I trust you'll be obliging."

She clenched her teeth and took a breath. She glanced at Rudé for a moment. There was nothing for her to say. Not yet.

Kata met Aemilius in La Tazia, a tiny coffeehouse specializing in exotic fruits, nestled dangerously high on the south side of the cliffs where white apartment buildings and eateries were piled upon one another like children's blocks. The coffee there was dark and imported, the cigars rolled across the sea in Ambibia. The owner was a wasted old man called Pezhi, who coughed up black phlegm between bouts of wheezy laughter. Nearing death, Pezhi found everything hilarious.

When Kata and Aemilius entered, Pehzi was talking to a fat philosopher-assassin with a shaved head and two bolt-throwers dangling from the back of his belt—Fat Nik, who had spent years in Varenis and who claimed to have met the Sortileges. As they spoke, Pehzi scratched a long-haired white cat behind its ear. It closed its blue eyes. The cafés and bars along Via Gracchia were filled with cats lounging languorously on high mantelpieces or curled up on chairs, as if they owned the places.

In one corner, two young women played chess, their backs against the wall. Kata took Aemilius out onto the tiny semicircular balcony where a small table allowed them to look over the city and the sea. Kata looked at the peninsula with its steam baths and liquor palaces on the far side of the piers. She would not look at Aemilius.

"I shall not see you again," she said.

"I see."

Pehzi stepped out onto the balcony holding a tray. He placed the coffees on the table. "Waterberry pastries?"

"No."

Pezhi nodded, laughed to himself about something, and left them alone.

Eventually Kata said, "You're leaving the day after tomorrow. You'll sail across the sea to Aya. That's that."

"I see."

"Is that all you can say? 'I see'? What about me? Why are you so—?"

He closed his eyes for a moment, opened them again and reached out to her. "You don't have to feel alone."

"Oh, but I do," she said. "I do have to feel alone."

He lifted her up in both hands and held her close. She could hear his heart beating in his chest, and felt the warmth radiating into her cheek.

"Look over there," he said. "Can you see how the color of the sea changes as it passes over the Sunken City? There are many who still lie on those marble streets, with skeletal horses and crumbling carriages around them. They are the only ones who should feel alone. But we—you and I—we are alive."

"Come back with me," she said. "Come back to my house and never leave. Never go to Aya."

Later, when he was asleep in her bed, she watched as his eyes moved beneath their lids in sleep. Sometimes he groaned and half lifted an arm, as if there was something to fend off in his dreams. She did not sleep that night, but lay awake thinking of how they would spend their last day together. And what she would tell Rudé.

Perhaps there was a chance to convince Aemilius to stay; they would not have to live in Caeli-Amur. They could escape the city and find somewhere quiet. But in her heart she knew it to be a dream, for he was a child of Aya. But she would struggle for it, just as she had for everything in her life.

In the morning she left him asleep. As she walked along the alleyway, little Henri scampered after her, in his hands a dirty pouch of Yensa fudge.

"What's he like, Kata?" His giant eyes, their pupils like black saucers, stared up at her. He reminded Kata of so many of the street urchins. First they sold their drugs or preparations bought from a criminal or one of the Collegia in the Lavere Quarter. Then they slowly sampled them. By the time they were teenagers, their bodies would be emaciated, their eyes forever wide and staring, their teeth rotten. Their deaths would not be far away. This, she knew, would be the fate of Henri.

"Go away."

"Aww, come on, tell us something. Does he know how to *do it*?" Henri grinned lasciviously.

Kata stopped walking, raised her hand to slap the boy. Henri danced away, and said, "Let me know when you want some fudge. Best Yensa fudge in the district!" He scampered off.

Kata wandered through the Factory Quarter, drawing in the soot and grime that rose from those square gray buildings or from the chimneys that led from the underground factories. The workers wandered to and fro like cogs in a machine—each with his little role to play in a greater logic. Just like her, she thought. She walked and walked, for how long she couldn't tell. Hours perhaps. But she found no answers on the streets. She thought of visiting Sarrat. But she didn't wish to hear Cajiun platitudes about patience, simplicity. Eventually she turned around. She had nowhere to go but home. There she would convince Aemilius to run away with her. Again a voice in her head laughed cynically. There was no room for dreams.

When Kata returned to her house she found Aemilius and Rudé sitting at the table eating olives and melon. Three flagons of wine stood on the table before them. She stood in the doorway, aghast.

"We've brought sustenance," said Aemilius.

"Ah," said Rudé, "the woman of secrets returns. I must say, I expected I'd find a minotaur here, but I thought you might be here also." Rudé grinned, his teeth red with wine.

Kata walked to the table and looked at the flagons. They were empty. "Yes," said Aemilius, "I brought Anlusian hot-wine also."

She released her breath.

"So," said Rudé, rubbing his stomach gently. "We'll have to find some more work for you, as you've clearly failed at your last task."

"Are you in an enterprise together?" asked Aemilius, throwing a slice of green melon into his mouth.

Kata turned away from them and saw the empty cupboard.

"What's the matter?" asked Aemilius.

Thinking the question was directed at him, Rudé, who was now looking white, said, "That hot-wine doesn't agree with me. I think I need some air."

"I'll show you the balcony," said Kata, leading him toward the stairs.

"I know where it is."

"Even so."

She led him up the stairs; he doubled over when he reached the balcony. "Oh," he groaned. "That wine. The one we took from your cupboard, was it—?"

Before he could finish speaking, Rudé dropped to his knees on the balcony and vomit came streaming and red from his mouth, dribbling down his shirt, onto the floor.

"The wine, did you drink it all?" she asked.

"We shared it," he said. "Why?" He slumped onto his side.

"It was poisoned."

"No."

"Yes."

"Help me." Rudé fell forward onto his hands, breathing quickly and shallowly, drool coming in long lines from his mouth.

"No. There is nothing that can be done."

"You bitch. You filthy—"

She leaned in over him: "You're nothing, Rudé."

"I fought to be where I am. Like you, I struggled."

"No, you did exactly what the House wanted. You're an appendage."

Only a gurgle came from his white-frothed lips.

She ran back to the stairs, descended as quickly as she could, and found Aemilius standing by the table, steadying himself with one hand.

"No," she said.

"What?"

She stood there, the room between them, looking at his towering presence.

"You," he said. "You didn't."

"I'm sorry."

"So it's true, you murdered Cyriacus." He staggered backwards, unsteady on his feet. "I would have done . . . whatever I could. I would have . . . helped you."

"You wouldn't have. You would have left for Aya with the others. You would have sailed off, leaving me here, alone."

There was froth around his mouth, and his magnificent eyes had lost their edge. They were clouded, as if a white substance were billowing into them.

He collapsed to the floor, his legs, once so powerful, at awkward angles beneath him. "I fought in the Numerian Wars. I defended Caeli-Amur when Saliras's fleet of a thousand ships appeared from the winter's fog."

She sat next to him. "It wasn't meant to be this way. If only you hadn't drunk the wine."

He snarled, a sudden burst of energy lighting his face. "This is how the city repays me. There is no justice."

She took his massive head in her lap and looked down on him. "I'm sorry." She refused to cry.

He looked up at her, his words slurring as he spoke. "The New-Men will take this city, break it down and rebuild it. Then you'll know what it's like to be overtaken, to be obsolete." Finally he lost consciousness, quietly dying in her arms.

When the new officiate arrived at Kata's apartment, a round and middle-aged man with a cold, efficient manner, he surveyed the scene. "You shall have to pay for Rudé's death, you know. There must be payment."

She closed her eyes and tried to block out the sound of the saw as the Technis workmen cut up Aemilius. Still, she did not cry. In her heart she knew it was time to leave Caeli-Amur—she had struggled enough.

When the men were gone, Kata stood on the balcony, watching

over Caeli-Amur. She stood there, motionless. The night stars shone down over the water until dawn broke over the horizon and the sea changed from blue to green with little crests of white.

In the morning the minotaurs stepped down to the piers, one by one, their hulking bodies small against the ships. So, after a week, the Festival of the Bull was ending. From her balcony, Kata watched them leave, these godlike creatures, powerful and mysterious. When the last of the minotaurs embarked, the ships hoisted their sails and made their way over the Sunken City and out to sea.

NINE

For Boris, the Festival of the Bull had been exhausting. Not only the troubles at the Tram Factory, but also the untimely demise of Rudé, the day before, had disturbed him. Even now, as Boris stood in the shadows of the towering Opera building, insects hovering around him in the evening air, the image of Rudé dead on the assassin's floor fixed in his mind. When they had cut up the minotaur, for some reason Boris had felt defeated. In the morning the minotaurs had left, but they seemed to have sparked something in the city. There had been discontent before, but now the air possessed a new vitality and charge. People glanced at each other with greater intent, conversations were rushed and whispered, citizens walked tensely, as if about to break into a run.

Boris met Mathias in front of the towering Opera building, its great dome rising above them, tapering at the top with a circular balcony far above on which stood a mysterious statue. Boris smiled discreetly at the sight of Mathias, dressed in a faded brown suit. Around the tramworker, who stood like a student undergoing an examination, walked black-dressed gentlemen, their beards trimmed just so, and white- or red-gowned ladies from the upper echelons of the Houses. Mathias's eyes darted around, wide and a little fearful.

They filed into the stately building, across the wide marble entrance hall. High above a hundred balls of light circled around the domed roof. Like head-sized little suns, their swirling colors shifted from scarlet to orange to gold and back again. At times individual globes broke away from the others and floated toward the ground before rising once more. Every time he entered the hall, Boris looked in wonderment at the globes; this time he had to take Mathias by the arm to ensure the tramworker didn't walk into anyone else, so entranced was he by the lights.

They walked up a staircase, and into the stalls at the rear of the Opera. Boris allowed Mathias to take in the opulent surroundings: the burgundy curtains, the glittering candles hanging on the chandeliers, the statues of Caeli-Amur's heroes: great stone rulers with flowing robes, towering minotaurs defending the city from Saliras's fleet, augurers peering into the future from their rocky outcrops.

House Technis traditionally sat at the rear of the stalls, while the seats at the front belonged to House Marin. House Arbor, befitting its traditional power, dominated the ground floor seating near the stage. But things were changing now, and officiates from Technis were demanding better positions.

Boris directed Mathias to their seats, and the tramworker was silent as he surveyed the scene.

"Impressive, no?" said Boris. Attending the Opera always awed him: the power of the ancients, inherited now by the Houses. The very place itself seemed to radiate might and influence. It washed over him, bathed him, permeated him. He was a part of it now, close to the center of things.

Mathias looked up at the roof, from which hung oddly angled geometrical shapes that reflected and magnified the music. "What wonderful workers they were in the old days."

Boris's vision of the building shifted with Mathias's comments. He hadn't thought of it before, but Mathias was right, workers had built the place. Boris imagined, long ago, the builders on mighty networks of scaffolding, far above. Somehow the thought took away from the majesty of the place. He preferred to think of it as eternal.

Trumpets sounded. The opera was about to begin. Boris glanced to his right and in the shadowy darkness of the boxes he caught a glimpse of a decaying face leaning forward into the light and then retreating again into darkness. The Elo-Talern sat ever watchful, shadowy figures behind the scenes—seeing but remaining unseen, as they always did in this city. Like cruel and negligent parents they allowed the Houses to make their own dangerous or deadly mistakes. For years indeed, as Rudé himself had said, the Elo-Talern had retreated from the affairs of the city. But in the minds of the citizens, the Elo-Talern always threatened to assert their authority. Perhaps they were beginning to assert it now?

The curtain rose and Mathias sat motionless, engrossed as the chorus opened in complex harmony. Soaring strings and booming drums joined them. Finally strange electronic music—deep shuddering mechanical sounds—engulfed the theater, and green globes of light hovered around the performers as they moved across the stage. The stage itself seemed to shift, for the floor was not one solid piece, but a complex mechanical construction of interlocking ones. The boxes detached themselves from the walls and shifted above the action like clouds on the air, allowing the Elo-Talern and the other notables to adjust the angle of their view.

Mathias grasped Boris's arm. "The ancients. Their technology."

Boris leaned close to Mathias. "Can you see her, third from the left? It's Saidra."

"She looks just like her mother, when she was young."

Boris nodded vigorously. "She's beautiful. We were all beautiful back then, too, weren't we?"

"Age has a beauty all of its own," said Mathias.

"I can't see it," said Boris.

"Do you see Saidra often?"

"No." Boris searched for the words, but shame silenced him. Eventually he settled for: "The young are restless, impatient. They have explosive emotions."

"And they're full of life," Mathias kept his eye on the stage as he spoke. "Not unlike the tramworkers."

Mention of the tramworkers filled Boris with a rush of guilt. He had failed to convince the Elo-Talern of the tramworkers' cause, and that failure burned deeply within him. He wanted to chart a path in which all views were taken into account, all voices heard, all feelings acknowledged. But these thoughts were cut short.

"Look! Look!" Boris clenched his fists in excitement. "The new Siren has taken the stage."

They were silent then, as she strode across the stage, her green eyes, enormous and inhuman, like emeralds in the sun.

Her proportions seemed impossible: her hips too wide and voluptuous, her waist too narrow. When she opened her mouth, her jaw dropped down too far, like a serpent's as it swallows its prey. The sound came more powerfully than any human voice. At times it sounded like the low hum of an engine, at other times the high lonely cry of a whale calling to its lost calf. She broke into quarter tones and trills reminiscent of the exotic music of Numeria. Around her neck sat a golden torc.

Half the audience, men and women alike, sat forward as one. Some even stood, only to be dragged down by those around them. Boris felt something stir within his stomach, a nameless emotion he hadn't felt for years. He wanted to call out, to act, to come to his feet. He had not seen this Siren before. What was her name? He hadn't taken the time to find out.

Before long, she added a second, higher note to accompany the first, and the two melodies rose from her throat to intermingle with each other. One climbed and the other fell, intermingled in complex harmonies. At times one was clear and powerful, the other a tremulous vibrato that hovered first a fraction above the first note, then below. But as they entwined themselves, distinguishing one from the other became impossible.

Boris knew the story: the tragedy of Sarina and Karmal. It would end with the wax earplugs melting in his ears and he—hearing the sadness of her song—throwing himself onto the rocks in an effort to reach her. Boris did not care for the plot. He was happy just to sit there, to watch the Siren with the clinging green dress that shifted itself around her, changing its form as if it were composed of small constantly moving segments, perhaps driven by some incantation or charm. Looking at her he felt as if he were coming back to life after a long and dreamless sleep.

After the performance had concluded, Boris took Mathias through the vast building's labyrinthine corridors, lit by yellow beads that hung from the roof in intricate geometric constellations. Like complex fernleaves, the constellation's smaller component parts were reproductions of the larger formations of which they were part.

The aesthetics of these ancient buildings unnerved Boris: there was something abstract and cold about them, something weird and otherworldly. They made him feel insignificant, a speck in an immense universe of angles and planes, a geometry that he could not fathom.

As they approached the cast's changing rooms, an uneasy feeling rose within him: as if from far away he could feel his heartbeat rattle. He swallowed. They pushed past people hurrying along busy winding corridors. A guard stood in front of the door to the cast's rooms.

"I'm subofficiate Autec," said Boris to the guard. "Saidra Autec's father."

The guard opened the door, "Saidra, your father."

There was silence from within the room followed by the mumble of voices. "Tell him to wait."

Boris and Mathias stood there uncomfortably.

The door opened and Boris opened his mouth. But he closed it again, like a beached fish, dying on the sand.

The Siren passed by them, her dress curling up over her shoulder and narrowing over her breasts as she walked. From nearby, her features seemed slightly changed. Where at a distance her immense eyes and lips had seemed strangely beautiful, now they were unnatural and alien: too large for a human, they evoked a sense of something deeply *wrong*. As if he had seen someone with a terminal illness, he felt fear and repulsion rise in him. She passed them without a look and walked down the corridor to an elevator.

Saidra opened the door. Her hair was braided and she wore an evening dress in the style that was fashionable—hoops creating an internal structure so that it billowed out in places, one shoulder strapless—carefully arranged to look as if it had just been thrown on. She had her mother's deep-set eyes, which made her look perpetually tired, and detracted from what would have been a beautiful round face. "What do you want?"

"I've come to see you," said Boris.

"Why?" An almost imperceptible sneer appeared on her face. Something had changed all those years ago. After she had reached her teens, they fought regularly, and she had said such cruel things. One day she had stood before him, veins bulging on her forehead as she thinned her lips: "I wish it were you who had died."

"This is Mathias. Do you remember him?" Boris said.

Saidra's expression softened. "From the factory."

Mathias nodded and they stood in silence, each waiting for the other to speak.

"Oh, you may as well come to the soirée." She walked past them, turned. "Come on then."

They followed her to the elevator. It rose with the quiet sound of rushing air, not at all like the elevator that clunked and shuddered in the Technis Complex. This was ancient technology, smooth and sleek.

The doors opened to a vast domed room; once again Boris felt distanced from the ancient aesthetic. Though it was a hall, four great platforms hovered in the air, on which stood chattering figures, suited and dressed, sipping Ayan flower-liquor from tall thin flutes. Much like the boxes in the Opera, these platforms moved gently. Smaller platforms detached themselves from the larger ones and carried several guests from one group to another. At the far end of the room, great windows opened out onto a view of the Market Square, the docks and the sea beyond.

Saidra stepped onto one of the smaller platforms sitting on the ground nearby. Boris and Mathias followed and gripped the handrail. The platform rose in the air toward one of the large ones, where a collection of officiates and administrators chattered, their deadly vendettas unspoken beneath their civilized discourse. They laughed falsely at one another's jokes, all the time eyeing others' wives or husbands, their own lovers or favorites.

When the three of them stepped into the assembly, a waiter offered them flutes from a great silver platter.

"So what are you doing here?" Saidra asked Mathias.

"Boris brought me. He thought I might enjoy it. He wanted to show me your performance."

"He wanted to show off his influence to you."

"Saidra!" said Boris.

"Father, all you've cared about is your status. All you've ever cared about is whether my success would bring *you* glory."

Boris pursed his lips and turned away from her. He pulled his flask from his pocket and took a long draft. To hell with Saidra, he thought: to hell with the both of us.

As Boris replaced the flask, he spied the Siren across the platform with a coterie of finely suited men around her: Eduard from House Arbor, with his lanky frame among them, Strazny from Marin, the little hunchback, several more he didn't recognize.

The surge of strength coursed through Boris's body and he was overtaken by a light-headed confidence. He liked that about the hot-liquor, the way it emptied the world of consequences and meanings, leaving only the remnants of them, like empty shells.

Taking no notice of Saidra and Mathias, he crossed the floor to the Siren. When he arrived he could hear Strazny's compliments. The Siren's face was blank with boredom.

Charged with his unnatural daring, Boris reached over to her, took her hand, and pulled her away. "Excuse me, gentlemen, but the star has a previous engagement."

Now the Siren's face changed. The huge eyes lit up with interest, her lips parted revealing her bright white teeth.

He led her to the cold metal railing. The platform had drifted high in the room. From their vantage point, Boris could see onto the Market Square below; there a group of gymnasts performed before a small crowd: tumbling and spinning, flipping and rolling. Just like us, Boris thought.

"A previous engagement, I see." The Siren's voice was quiet and husky; though she spoke in one tone, the soft reverberations of her second voice could be heard beneath the first. This seemed to be her natural method of speaking: one voice predominating, the other silent or deep in the background. The golden torc around her neck was made of fine, intertwined spirals. Two bloodstones were set where it joined at the front of her neck. No doubt they had been bound with the proper protection, though the bloodstone's metallization cancer would not affect the Siren in any case. Ancient creatures were immune to the affliction, just as they were immune to thaumaturgy's deleterious effects.

Her inhuman features again struck Boris; again he felt the mixture of attraction and repulsion. "Well, you looked like you needed rescuing."

She smiled, again revealing brilliant white teeth. One of her front ones was pushed back and half-hidden by the others. "And you're the man to rescue me, I see."

"Well, someone had to. I'm Boris."

"Paxaea. So you are an officiate?"

"Subofficiate."

She nodded and looked away, her face falling once more into disappointed boredom.

Panicking, Boris said the first things that came into his head, "I had to meet you. You are so beautiful. No, not like the others. There's something in my heart. I'm not like those other man. I'm not—"

"You're just a cliché aren't you?" she said. She closed her eyes: first a thin nictating membrane closed horizontally, a thin milky layer through which the eye could still be seen, and then the main eyelids.

Boris was struck silent, his mind blank. He wrestled for the right thing to say, the thing that would unlock her. "What can I say that will make you think otherwise?"

Boris stared through the window to the square below. A contortionist had squeezed his head and arm through a small wooden frame. In order to do so, he'd dislocated his shoulder. His arm now jutted up at an unnatural angle. Around him, the remnants of the Opera audience spilled out into the night.

Boris was disoriented. Why was he alone on one of the smaller platforms, drifting so close to the windows? He tried to reconstruct it in his memory. He had been talking to Paxaea the Siren, and she had said something to him; she had spoken using both her tones something emphatic. It had been strange, eerie to hear those two notes speaking in unison. What had she said? He looked back to the where Paxaea was again surrounded by the other sycophantic officiates.

She had used her voice, her power of suggestion. He could have her punished for it, taught a lesson. But he wouldn't do that to her. He would charm her, open himself to her. He wanted to rush back and grab her by the arm, to turn her and make her understand. He touched a pad on the front of the platform, which drifted slowly back toward the group. He would walk to the Siren the moment he arrived. But as he stepped into the assembly, he couldn't make himself do it. He felt ashamed that she had sent him away to begin with.

Defeated, Boris walked back to Saidra and Mathias.

"Your mother would have wanted the best for you. All parents do, ultimately," said Mathias.

"Not all parents," said Saidra.

"All parents," repeated Mathias.

"We'd better go." Boris grabbed Mathias by the arm.

Mathias shook him off and, leaning in gently, kissed Saidra on her cheek. "Take care of yourself," said Mathias.

"Good-bye, father." Saidra turned away, leaving Boris standing awkwardly.

As they drifted back toward the ground, Mathias said, "Your daughter loves you yet."

"You are wrong." A bitter taste rose in Boris's mouth. Defeat hovered around him, wherever he looked.

"No. It is you who are wrong."

TEN

Boris and Mathias left the Opera, slipping through the bustle of society ladies and stiff-suited gentlemen, down into the Market Square, where the performers were now sitting in what seemed to be an exhausted circle, counting their florens. Boris still felt the sting of Saidra's words, the Siren's rejection of him. Family, love—this was where they had led him.

Boris said, "Let's stay away from the boulevards; let's climb the cliffs."

They passed through the narrow streets and squares of the Quaedian, past the manuscript shops and the ornament vendors. Boris had never liked the area: it was filled with students and intellectuals, artists and bohemians. In one of their ill-fated attempts at reconciliation, he had once gone with Saidra to one of the little galleries that dotted the area. The exhibition contained works with an avant-garde theme: a retro-ancient installation stood in one corner, all geometric angles and shapes. A woman and man had come out and begun chanting nonsense words in a repetitive manner. It was all gibberish as far as Boris was concerned. Saidra seemed to like it, but they both instinctively understood that it was one more instance of the size of the gulf that had opened between then.

When Boris and Mathias reached the cliff, they began up one of the narrow stairs.

Halfway up, they sat on a little ledge. High in the sky to the south, a cable car swung on its wire as it descended from the cliffs toward the cyclopean tower near the south side of Market Square. Beneath its path lay Caeli-Amur's necropolis, a black canvas with shadowy forms, and beyond that, even darker, the ruins of the Ancient Forum, where Aya and Alerion had fought in single combat, breaking the buildings around them, shattering the little squares, throwing the colonnades and arches to the ground. Now, as always, a spectral fog hovered over the ruins, a cemetery of its own.

"The strike will begin tomorrow." Mathis said flatly. "At first I thought to stop it. I thought that these young ones, they were too impulsive. But then I realized, no, it is I who is too slow to act. If not now, when?"

Boris chose his words carefully. "Mathias, you are my friend. The House will mobilize its guards to crush you and I will not be able to stop them. I would not lose you to this." He thought of the words that the Elo-Talern had used: "The workers want a new life, do they? We'll give them a different life, or the Furies will."

"I know you will help us, help the House to see that we have rightful grievances." Mathias rubbed his face with his hands.

"I will. But it will take time," said Boris. "Patience. We will move in small steps, make change in increments. A realistic assessment of what's possible. You were right the first time: You must halt this strike, then we can show the House that you have acted in good faith."

"Good faith!" said Mathias. "Look! Look!" he pulled open his shirt to reveal a strange pattern on his skin. Boris looked closer and grimaced. Scales were growing on Mathias's skin, and at points dotted around his chest little lumps, like eyes, seemed to be emerging. "I have used too much uncontrolled thaumaturgy. Now another universe enters me and I am being remade. Boris, make them see!"

A second cable car climbed slowly out of the darkness to the south of the Opera and was silhouetted against the sky. Clouds moved high above, now blacking out the stars, now revealing them in their milky glory. For a moment things were bright and clear; a moment later they were dark and troubled.

After a while Mathias spoke. "Think of what Remmie would say."

"Don't use guilt against me, Mathias. Anyway, she's part of my past."

"We all stand on our past, Boris. Without our past, who are we?"

"Come on." Boris climbed the staircase again. His mind whirred with thoughts: he stood between the House and the workers but could not see a way to halt the conflict. Both sides were implacable; that was the problem.

When they reached the top of the cliff, Boris looked down at the city below, a thousand twinkling lights, the suggestions of buildings in the darkness, like the obscure outlines of everything in his life, half-hidden in shadow and difficult to see.

Mathias reached out and grabbed his arm and looked feverishly at him. "Take me to the Technis Complex. Let me talk to them. Look at me!"

Boris looked at his friend's chest and repressed a shudder. "Delay the strike. I will take you tomorrow to see an officiate. Together we will make a case."

He pulled out his bottle of hot-wine and took a swig.

The following day, Mathias appeared strangely small in the Technis Complex, though he held himself with a certain calm. Boris, fueled by hot-wine, tired to his bones, and yet possessing a frantic energy, led him through the corridors, filled as usual with a thousand scurrying people: workmen carrying ladders and toolboxes, officiates yelling orders, the occasional thaumaturgist, suited and reserved, gloves covering his warped hands, his facial features all a little askew, or else possessing a strange sheen, or more unnerving still, appearing eerily and suggestively normal.

Rudé's office was empty: the machine gone, the plaque removed from the door. Boris had hoped another officiate had taken up the office. Or if no one had replaced Rudé, then he had planned to find the laughing officiate Ijem, or the grim Olevski.

Instead, on the table lay an envelope addressed to Boris Autec. Boris broke the seal. The letter read: "Subofficiate Autec, when you are ready, press the black pad on the wall behind the desk. We shall meet." It was signed, "Elo-Drusa, of the Elo-Talern."

Boris stood, rooted to the spot. He could skip the officiates and bring Mathias directly to the Elo-Talern. It would be a bold move, and yet it lay before them like an open road. Together they could convince her; she would see the justice of the tramworkers claims. But he hesitated, for the situation unnerved him. He didn't want to bring her and Mathias together. Better for him to make Mathias's case, for he could interpret it, soften it if necessary. But no, it was time to say things plainly.

Boris's hand hovered over the black pad. He pressed it, heard a clunk. "Come on. The Elo-Talern has summoned us."

As they entered the elevator, Boris could see the shapes and shadows everywhere. He gripped his flask tightly in one hand.

As they passed along the cold corridors, Mathias asked, "What is this place?"

"The older reaches of the ancient palace. From before House Technis took it over."

"And these statues, what are they? And these strange implements?" said Mathias.

"Ancient technology: forgotten, or hidden." Again things moved at the edge of Boris's vision, like shadow-beasts circling their prey.

When they reached the great throne room doors, Boris halted for a minute. He tried to prepare himself for what would occur within, but he could not imagine what that might be. How would Mathias act? How would the Elo-Talern react?

"What?" asked Mathias.

Boris looked up at the other man, who returned the glance. They stood there, like images of each other, two rounded, heavy men, face-to-face.

Boris straightened his suit, turned, and entered the hall. Coldness engulfed him. Ghostly mist hung thickly in the air, obscuring everything.

On the throne, the Elo-Talern waited, her long and bony body sprawled out languorously. She sat up in the throne and her torso elongated to the sound of cracking. For some reason she began to laugh, a hacking and alien sound like wooden planks breaking. She clapped her hands together several times and then let out a sigh.

Boris could sense Mathias tense. They walked through the damp clammy air, their feet clapping on the marble floors.

Elo-Drusa said, "So, this is one of the tramworkers, come to beg forgiveness? Tell me, little man, what injustices have you undergone? Have you been forced to work too long? Do you have children to feed? Is there a *sick wife*?"

Shocked by her tone, Boris's eyes remained wide and unmoving.

Mathias stepped forward and with his hunched shoulders straightened unnaturally said: "Who are you, to sit up here and tell us how to live our lives?"

Boris struggled to find words, but none came.

"I admire the young." The Elo-Talern leaned back on the throne. With a series of small crackles, she stretched her arm out languidly. "So much feeling."

"Boris," said Mathias, "tell her."

Boris looked to the floor. Tension gripped his body like a vise. He could hardly bear this confrontation. His certainty had deserted him and he stood frozen, an animal under a hunter's gaze.

The Elo-Talern blinked slowly. "I've met a thousand like you. I've seen you come and go, for . . . years. Go back to your home, live your little life, and be happy. Take what life gives you."

Mathias's voice hardened. "I have taken as much of that life as I can, and I will take it no longer."

"Well, you know what that means." She leaned forward, her mouth tiny and pinched beneath the vaulting forehead and cavernous eyes.

"But I fear that you don't," said Mathias. "But you will come to know it."

She laughed her raven laugh. "Subofficiate Autec. Take this amusing man back to his factory and set him to work."

Boris struggled once more to speak. Failing to conjure any words, he turned and took two steps before realizing that Mathias hadn't moved. "Mathias."

Mathias turned, his eyes falling darkly on Boris, who averted his gaze. Together they stepped from the hall and passed silently through the labyrinthine corridors. Mathias strode furiously, his body tense with repressed energy.

Boris was filled with a deep and sickening feeling of failure. "I couldn't speak," said Boris. "I wanted to, but I couldn't say anything. I just froze."

"I thought I could count on you."

"We'll find a compromise. It can be worked out by talking."

Mathias stopped walking, turned and faced him. "Boris. Does your word mean nothing?"

Angry now, and filled with regret, Boris felt a burning in his throat. "You've always been rash, hotheaded."

When they returned to the bustling corridors of the Complex, Mathias turned to Boris. "You were always weak. You always blew in whatever direction the wind was strongest. Don't come back to the factory. It's no place for you."

Boris reached out to touch Mathias's arm, but the tramworker turned away. Anger rose in Boris again. "We must be realistic! We can't demand an entirely different world! Think of what we risk. Think of our families!"

"You have no family," Mathias, some feet away, turned back and spat out. "You were right. Your daughter loathes you."

"It's not true," said Boris. "Everything I did was for her."

But Mathias had already marched away.

Early the following morning, word of the strike came from the Tram Factory. Boris put his head in his hands. The standing order against strikes would be enacted, the House guards would be mobilized, the thaumaturgists roused and, he shuddered, the Furies would be loosed.

Boris sprang into action. He took a swig of hot-wine to strengthen his resolve and rushed from the Technis Complex. He would personally convince the tramworkers to return to work. Even if some like Mathias refused to listen, his words would move the rest of them. The conflict would be avoided. Then, slow patient work to make the tramworkers' conditions more bearable. Regulations could be drawn up, compromises reached—the gradual path to progress.

Boris arrived at the factory after the fog had lifted, yet clouds still rolled overhead, blocking out the late spring sun. There were no signs of House guards, and he breathed a sigh of relief. About eighty tramworkers stood at the front of the factory, hands in pockets, grinning and whispering. They had the air of brattish children, who had broken a rule and were waiting to see their parents' response. Indeed, they had an air of joviality far out of tune with the potential consequences, even if against the wall were lined old bolt-throwers, aged things powered by external bows, and rusted swords and pikes. Even more wretchedly, knives or pitchforks leaned over a pile of stones dug from the cobblestoned streets. Had they no notion of what Technis might unleash upon them? Boris realized that so far, the Houses had only arrested strikers, thrown them into their dark dungeons, a fate bad enough. He hurried down the cobblestoned road, through the onlookers who stood and whispered to one another at a safe distance.

Mathias strode toward him and called out, "There's no work today, *Subofficiate*. Tell your masters that we will no longer work under these conditions."

The words cut at Boris, yet he continued walking toward them.

"Are you deaf as well as a lackey?" yelled Mathias. The strikers laughed.

Boris finally reached the group, puffing and panting. He pushed through a few of the younger workers to reach Mathias, who had retreated into the group.

Boris leaned toward Mathias, who eyed him coldly. "Please. We can still avoid this madness."

Mathias turned his back to the man from House Technis.

Around Boris the tramworkers circled, and farther away citizens, the old with their smocks and clogs, the young gathered in twos and threes, eyed the scene with interest from the surrounding streets. Boris took out his flask. Inside lay what he needed, what he wanted. Hot-wine, which burned his throat; hot-wine, which made him fast and strong; hot-wine, which made everything sharper in focus, as if before he had looked through watery eyes. He gulped it down.

"Listen," he turned to a young worker, whose lantern-jawed face sneered at him. "We can make improvements, we—"

The worker pushed him and he took a step backwards. Another pushed him from behind and his head was thrown back by the force. As he turned to glare at the white-haired man grinning at him, another pushed him, and yet another. In an instant he was jostled to and fro, rough hands pushing him again and again.

"Wait. No!" Boris pushed back and a skinny reedlike youth was tossed with impossible strength into another.

Boris opened his mouth to speak, but was halted by screams of fear from women and men. He listened to them: the thaumaturgists had come with the Furies.

They were yet out of sight, and against an almost overwhelming impulse, Boris forced himself to run toward the sounds. Up the narrow, cobblestoned street he ran. As it rose up toward Boulevarde Karlotte and farther on the Technis Complex, it curved out of sight. Boris rushed on.

The Furies came down the narrow streets into view. Their keepers, the black-suited thaumaturgists, held whips in their hands, though the whips were the least of their controls.

At the sight of the creatures, Boris fell back against the wall and closed his eyes. He felt sick. He wanted to run. He started to shiver. He opened his eyes again, but did not look straight at them, instead aware of their black shapes roiling and whirling against the gray stones. Occasionally wiry limbs, bloodied torsos, fanged heads would emerge into view, as if the swirling blackness was a cloud, which shrank back to reveal the Furies' true forms. The screams of the nearby citizens were high-pitched and desperate—the screams of those who were not aware of anything but the horror. The creatures rushed forward, stopped suddenly, seemed to recompose themselves into new configurations, and moved forward again. Those citizens who had lingered, hoping to see the confrontation, scrambled away through the side streets, falling in their fear, picking themselves up, never looking back.

The tramworkers backed away; their lighthearted air gone. Mathias turned to his coworkers: "They're just beasts. We've still got these." He raised a weathered wooden bolt-thrower. Others lifted theirs, or grabbed their pitifully inadequate weapons.

Boris pressed himself farther against the wall as the creatures passed him. The guard next to him broke into a low humming moan.

Then came the lead thaumaturgist, dressed in his black suit, his face covered with a bone-white mask carved in the shape of a horse's skull. Death seemed to radiate around him, as if he were from the Other Side itself. Alone, he would have been fearful, a ghastly figure fully seven feet tall. Beside the Furies, he was terrible to behold.

Desperation gripped Boris. This was his final chance to affect events, his final moment to halt the bloodbath to come. Forcing up onto his shaking legs, Boris stepped forward. "Wait."

The thaumaturgist turned the horse-skull mask toward Boris and the other thaumaturgists halted beside him.

"I'm Subofficiate Boris Autec. There's been a mistake."

The thaumaturgist stood still, the mask appeared as if it were caught in some awful rictus. If any emotions passed the thaumaturgist's face, they were hidden. The man's reply was strong and confident. "If you were an officiate, then you would be able to give such an order. But, Autec, you are only a *subofficiate*. Our orders outrank yours."

The thaumaturgist walked on. Boris grabbed him by the arm. "Wait."

Something struck Boris savagely in the face. He dropped to his knees. Time and events seemed scrambled. His cheek throbbed. He looked up, and a horse-skull mask leered down at him menacingly.

Still on his knees, Boris turned to look at the tramworkers, just as a hail of stones rained down around him. The tramworkers formed an unsteady line, stepping forward, shuffling backwards. They loosed another hail of rocks that rattled onto the cobblestones like stony rain. Boris looked at their ruddy faces, most of them youthful. He looked at Mathias with his hunched shoulders, his drooping eyes. To Boris, it seemed as if he were looking back in time, at his own past.

The Furies rushed down the street like great black roiling smoke. Bolts flew through the air and disappeared into the darknesses. The creatures stopped briefly, flooded forward again. The line of tramworkers broke, but too late, for the Furies were already on them and the streets rang with hideous screams. The blackness engulfed the workers, like waves crashing over them. Boris stared at the sky overhead, huge lumbering clouds coming in from the sea.

The screams seemed to last an eternity: horrible, wailing things as men tried to hold desperately on to the remains of their lives. Boris closed his eyes but could not shut out the sounds.

When it was over and the thaumaturgists gone, Boris walked quietly down the street, dodging corpses that lay shrunken, as if their vitality had been sucked by a mountain's high cold winds. He felt a wetness on his face and realized that he was crying. He came to a body lying facedown. With effort he turned it over, but it was not Mathias. He continued on: here a young man, nothing but a blackened lump of meat, but still groaning; there a man silently looking at the ragged stump of his hand; and bodies—bodies everywhere. Finally, he saw a man leaning against a wall, his shirt torn from his body, strange scalelike patterns over his chest, where the eyes of fish shifted wildly.

"Why? Why didn't you listen to me?" Boris's voice broke. "Damn you, damn you."

Mathias was crushed and bloodied. His chest heaved and rattled. "Keep an eye on Corette, and Rikard, will you?"

Boris looked down the street at the bodies thrown about like so much litter. He looked back at Mathias who blinked once, twice. Then slowly, like the changing of the tide, the life drained from his eyes.

Boris spent the afternoon light-headed and empty. He drank hot-wine like water as he wandered the streets of Caeli-Amur. But wherever he passed, he felt an outsider. The Factory Quarter seemed filled with savage darting eyes, the Quaedian with figures unfriendly and aloof, his own apartment sat in empty streets. Nowhere did he feel at home.

Eventually he pressed the pad in Rudé's office and walked slowly to the throne room where the Elo-Talern was waiting, as always.

"So the strike is finished."

Boris stared at the creature in front of him, numb from events, ruined by lack of sleep and food. "No," he said. "No. It has just begun."

"But the Furies?"

"They ruined them, as you promised." Boris's words sounded hollow in his own ears, empty of all meaning or significance. "But maybe not this factory, maybe not this season or next, but soon the strikes will spring up like brush fires in the summer."

"We shall destroy them, also."

"You cannot destroy a fire: you can only put it out."

"And you, Boris Autec, shall let us know where they are, and you shall put them out."

"I will," said Boris bitterly. What else was there for him to do? The tramworkers had brought the House's punishment upon themselves. But even as he thought this, Boris felt the churning of guilt and shame.

"I admired the way which you tried to stand up for the tramworkers. We need people like you in the House. Not just sycophants who say yes to those above and kick those who are beneath them. It may not seem like it, but I value your humanity. The way you are so torn, trying always to do the right thing! Congratulations, you are now an officiate. You are Rudé's replacement, you shall have your own subofficiates to direct."

Boris laughed despairingly. "The tramworkers: let me give them some of what they asked for, whoever is left."

Elo-Drusa nodded. "Some have been arrested. But the new tramworkers, yes, give them as much as you deem necessary."

Boris laughed again. At least now he would have more influence, more ability to change things for the better. He would not let events like the morning's massacre happen again. With his new influence would come rewards. The words of the Elo-Talern returned to him: *What is it that you want?* He thought, tonight, he might attend the Opera, and he might get seats closer to the front. It would take his mind off the day's terrible events. It was only fair.

When he left, he wandered along the corridors, past the alien statues and strange mechanical tools and as he walked, images of raven black hair and emerald green eyes filled his mind.

After the opera, Boris returned to his house thinking of the Siren Paxaea. He had watched her tonight, and dreamed of placing his hands on those luxurious hips, his mouth on those lips. The Elo-Talern had promised him what he wanted.

He threw the window open and looked out over Caeli-Amur and beyond, to the sea. A wind was picking up and there was the distant rumbling of thunder. The stars were hidden behind dark clouds, massive shapes moving across the sky. The air was hot and humid. Soon it would rain, he thought: one of those torrential spring downpours that would feed the thousands of yellow wild-flowers that spring up on the rocky hills around the city. He dis-liked those storms; he remembered how they drenched him to the bone as he hunted spear-birds when he was young. With Mathias. He pushed the man's memory from his mind. He pushed away the grief, the despair, the horror, even as it flooded back. Why did Mathias have to die? Because the tramworker had been stubborn, had refused to compromise. But still shame filled Boris, though he could not be sure why.

Boris closed the window and turned his back.

He would visit Quadi tomorrow, down at the markets; he would secure a supply of Anlusian hot-wine. With hot-wine anything was possible. He opened the bottle that sat waiting for him in his kitchen and poured it savagely into his mouth. Around him, in the corners of the room, shadows flickered like shifting intimations of death. *I'm not afraid of you*, he thought. *I'm Boris Autec.* He took more gulps of wine. His mouth no longer burned from the taste—he had grown used to it. He laughed out loud to nobody. He laughed at the shadows, which rippled and shifted around him. He laughed at the future.

ELEVEN

Maximilian sat cross-legged and alone in the Communal Cavern. He felt the floor beneath him, hard beneath his thin straw mattress. A lamp glowed warmly on the floor beside him, while in the constant gloom of the seditionist hideout, Omar groaned in a half-conscious state, calling out words in a strange language, whether they were cries of help or warning or perhaps the names of forgotten cities on long lost maps, no one could tell. At other times he called the names of the gods, as if imploring them to intervene. Every now and then, he called out the name Nkando. Guilt and worry had gripped Max from the moment Omar had been burned. *I should have stepped into the machine*, Max thought. *It should have been me calling out Nkando's name.* But no, he was not at fault. Omar's terrible accident had been caused by Kamron's policy of waiting and patient preparation.

The evening stretched into night as Max ruminated. The problem with the people's struggles against the Houses was their disparate nature. The factories went on strike when they individually chose, the Collegia whined and complained, the citizens whispered in the streets and squares, the university students circulated forbidden pamphlets, the seditionist groups printed their broadsheets (each with their own eccentricities) and the philosopher-assassins languished bitterly in the cafés. If somehow the seditionists could unite each of these groups into a enormous tidal wave of opposition, then they could change things forever. Images flooded into his mind of a beautiful world where each of these groups was given its rightful say, where, rather than fractured parts of a broken society, they would work organically together. No one should starve, no one should be broken on the wheels of production;

everyone deserved a life which they freely chose. He would begin
with the Xsanthians.

Max examined his fellow seditionists, who sat in their three
little groups, talking quietly. Giselle lounged splay-legged like some
philosopher-assassin with Ejan's little group, their voices low and
incomprehensible in a far corner. The Veterans—Iniria, Antoine,
Elena, Josiane, and Kamron—sat on a set of reclining chairs on the
other side of the brazier. The six seditionists of Max's own little
circle were scattered here and there.

Max placed his empty bowl on the ground and walked toward
the Veterans, who looked up at him kindly. As the most senior of
the group—hence the title Veteran—they possessed an unchallenged
authority. Though at times the group would discuss questions at a
meeting of the entire collective, the Veterans' opinions held sway.
They had risked so much over the years, forsaking family, friends,
lives. When they spoke, the rest of the seditionists listened. Fore-
most among them was Kamron.

Max considered the best way to speak his mind, but decorum
be damned, there was no point in circling around the question.
"I'm going to go back to see the Xsanthians."

They sat in silence, looking at him with puzzlement.

"Always the dreamer," said Iniria softly, her chest rising and
falling slowly as she breathed. She always spoke to calm things, to
make things right. She was Kamron's first weapon of conciliation.
Born among the intelligentsia in Varenis, she had grown up in a
world that produced meandering discourses that separated and
rejoined like crisscrossing paths in the woods.

"There's no point being stuck in here," Max said, looking around.
"In this darkness. If there's any point to us at all, it's to get out
there, among the people."

"Tritons are scarcely people." Josiane, who sat on the floor to
the side of the reclining chairs, used the derogatory term for Xsanthians as she rolled the links of her weighted chain in her hands.
Max had never seen her use the weapon, but it looked brutal. Josiane had been a philosopher-assassin during the House Wars that
had officially ended five years earlier, though unofficially they still
burned at a low intensity. Josiane had come to seditionism late, and

now her short-cropped hair was graying, though she remained as dangerous as a viper sitting on a path. Before she encountered Kamron's writings, she had been an ascetic, living a life without possessions, denying herself pleasures. Now, she had attached herself to Kamron like a bodyguard.

"Anyone who fights against the Houses is a friend of ours," said Max.

"That kind of logic simply doesn't hold," said Josiane. "Just because House Technis is rising doesn't mean that we support House Arbor against it."

"Xsanthians are hardly one of the Houses. The whole House system is what we oppose. The analogy is false."

"Tritons are not even *human*," repeated Josaine, the fire of polemic now in her eyes. "They don't *think* like us. They have a strange intelligence, an odd collective consciousness. If they don't think or feel as individuals, how they could have individual rights?"

"They are forced to work for House Marin. And if you were to see them, torn from their coral homes beneath the water, forced to work like slaves, then your heart wouldn't be so hard." Emotion now flooded into Max. "The work is grueling, and they are controlled by thaumaturgical collars. The slightest disobedience and these collars can be tightened so that the Xsanthians fall to their knees, gasping for air. We should oppose the subjection of anyone, no matter who they are. I'm going to see them tomorrow. I am not asking your permission, I am telling you."

"Now, let's calm down," said Kamron. "Think about it, Max. With all these strikes, the Houses are increasing their surveillance. You'll be followed, and you'll lead them back here, and we'll all end up in the House dungeons. We cannot let you threaten everything we've spent our lives building. So should you contact them again, don't come back."

The silence hung in the air. At first Max stared at Kamron, this father figure to him, this man who he respected—no, loved. Now Kamron had escalated things to a breaking point and Max felt betrayed. Kamron had the support of the majority of the group, and now he was threatening to exile Max. Anger flooded into

Max; he struggled to contain it. He didn't deserve this. He wasn't ready to leave the seditionist group . . . or was he? He was confused. Max searched for a way out of the confrontation. Eventually he nodded. "I understand. You're right." He looked at the Veterans as they looked at him. He turned and walked back to Omar, feeling animosity at his back.

As he curled up on his mattress in the half light of the brazier, Max thought to himself: He would visit the Xsanthians, regardless of what the Veterans said; he would be his own man. He would do it secretly, and should they discover him, they would have to throw him onto the streets.

Now that he had decided, he let his mind wander. He imagined Caeli-Enas, the Sunken City, and its Great Library. There knowledge could be drunk like an elixir, knowledge that could forever change the relationship between citizens and the Houses. He fell asleep thinking of how he might reach it.

That night he dreamed of Nkando crying. She stood on the pier, surrounded by crates and boxes. He tried to run to her along the beach, but his feet kept sticking in the sand. He looked down, he realized that his legs had been eaten by sand-crabs and were now just bloody stumps. When he looked up, Nkando and the cutter were gone, leaving only gray waves crashing over a windswept pier.

In the morning, when Maximilian awoke, he kept his eyes closed and, lying on his thin mattress, the threadbare brown blanket over him, thought of Nkando. He had met her at the library in his parents' pleasure villa on the Dyrian coast. He had been thirteen years old, in the stage of uncomfortable adolescence, when his thoughts, emotions, and body were growing in spurts and dashes. He had felt constantly out of tune with himself.

He had spent a morning swimming with Omar in the crystal-blue waters the region was famous for. Then he had ventured to the library, as he loved to do, restlessly reading whatever he could find: natural history, myths, studies of ancient creatures, botany.

On this afternoon, Max looked up from the history of the Numerian Wars to see her, a vision as if invoked from his book.

About his own age, she walked along the shelves, small and round, white eyes and smooth black skin, apparently puzzled by the referencing system.

Eventually, she turned to him politely, spoke softly in a thick Numerian accent. "Excuse me, sir."

Max smiled and she lowered her eyes shyly.

She asked him to help her, and he had helped her find the books. Then, in return, he had her talk of her home country, of its wondrous creatures—lions, elephants, monkeys—of its jungles and waterfalls. But also of its strange customs: the dance of a thousand virgins before the King; the odd philosophies and animal cults.

"And what do you do here?" asked Max.

"I am owned by Master Etrusca. We're staying on Poppaea's floating villa."

The floating villas drifted along the Dyrian coastline, allowing their guests to disembark in each bay as they saw fit. Guests of the Poppaea villa were welcome to use the library and the baths in Max's parents' villa. Nkando was a slave girl, then, something rare now in polite society, though tolerated. Slavery had mostly been eradicated by the reform of Arisyme, some two hundred years earlier, which the Houses had agreed upon. Now only merchants, members of the Collegia in Caeli-Amur, or on a vaster scale, city-states in Numeria, possessed slaves.

Each day, Nkando would return and each day Max would meet her, sometimes with Omar. One day, she hobbled in, her legs moving stiffly as if they would not bend at the knees. Placing her hands on the table, she lowered herself into a seat.

Max and Omar pressed her, and she burst into tears. "He beats me, with a cane." Her voice was low and filled with shame. She raised her head defiantly. A fire leaped into her eyes. "I fight him, though. I hurt him back."

Omar put a hand on Max's arm to calm him. But emotions rushed in Max nevertheless: a sickness, rage and an unknown feeling he later realized was the first stirrings of love. With each day it grew until it practically consumed his senses. It was Nkando's gentle shyness that had reached into him, her hidden feistiness that wouldn't let him go.

They plotted for Nkando's escape. Max and Omar would pool their savings and rent her a room in a rooming house, hide her until Etrusca left Dyria and headed back with his fleet to Numeria. Nkando was filled with hope. But on the appointed day, she did not return at all. Instead came a tall man, thick-lipped with not so much a beard as tufts of orangey brown hair sprouting from chin and cheeks. Two long red scratches ran down his cheek.

The man slipped into the seat next to Max and Omar. "So, you are the boys. Nkando has told me a great deal about you. Well, at first she didn't want to speak, but eventually, she was eager to." He grinned lasciviously. "She's quite the tiger, you know. But even a tiger can be tamed. It's a pity that I'm about to take a cutter back to Numeria, else I would have had you punished also."

Anger exploded in Max's body. His visioned blurred with white and he lost all sense of hearing. Without awareness he was on his feet and leaping at Etrusca. A flat palm struck straight into Max's face. Max's head snapped back, his legs whipped beneath him and he was knocked horizontal, then he struck the ground. He was overwhelmed by a vast black tide that washed over him.

He regained consciousness to the sound of Omar's voice. "Max. Max."

Etrusca was gone as Max stood shakily to his feet. With Omar, he ran to the coastline. Sitting out in the bay were two floating villas. On one of the many piers at the end of the beach, seamen loaded a cutter with a few crates and boxes of local produce. Standing motionless beside them was a small black figure. Max and Omar ran toward the pier, but Etrusca emerged from the cutter, grabbed the slave-girl by the hair and dragged her aboard. By the time Max and Omar stood on the wet planks of the pier, the cutter had cast off and was sailing on rough gray waters to sea.

Max had called out, screamed in an unnaturally powerful voice. A voice that carried across the ocean. A voice louder than any human voice should be.

Omar stared at him, eyes wide with disbelief.

That had been the first evidence that Max had a talent for the thaumaturgical arts. Of course he couldn't repeat the feat; it was one of those rare and mysterious instances where talent for the art had spontaneously broken through, without formulae or equations—something that the theories of thaumaturgy could not explain.

Max had been filled with black despair and the injustice of the world, at the power some had over others. He now saw it wherever he looked, in the relations of holidaying officiates and their servants, in House Marin's attitude to the workers on their oyster farms and fisheries. At first he had concluded that this was a consequence of humanity's evil soul. He had wanted to tear all forms of society to the ground, burn them away, purify them with destruction. But when he had read Kamron's pamphlet, he had made sense of the injustices of the world. This was a period of transition, Kamron argued. Once the world recovered from the cataclysm, then the Nkandos of the world would be freed. Future generations would look back at this time as a strange aberration, a barbaric consequence of catastrophe, in which people themselves were part of that barbarism. This vision moved him in ways he had never experienced, and it had led him to here, years later, to the seditionist hideout. Max shook himself from his reverie; he opened his eyes and prepared for the day.

As the hours passed, Max became aware of Josiane's eyes fixing on him. To avoid suspicion, he would have to wait a few days before he visited the Xsanthians again. In any case, the day was set aside for Max to train his apprentices. He gathered with them—Oewen and Ariana, Gilli and Philippe, Clemence and Usula—in the square room they used for training. The chamber was one of a series that ran along one side of the cavern, each one a polyhedron. The first, a triangular prism, a trilateral pyramid (or tetrahedron), was used for storage. Max's group used the second, a square-shaped room. Then next, an eight-sided octahedron-shaped room was Kamron's. The fourth, a twelve sided-dodecahedron, Ejan claimed for his group. The fifth (its twenty sides forming an icosahedron) was free to be used by whoever liked. The strange symmetrical purity of the rooms seemed to be something the ancients valued. It awakened Max's imagination and reminded him of thaumaturgy itself, for though that science was asymmetrical—its different disciplines worked in different ways—its base was fundamentally mathe-matical.

When Max entered their square room, the others had already arrived. Clemence walked past the shelves that stored basic thau-maturgical tomes, scrolls and parchments, chemical compounds, lead and mercury, precious stones—hematite and lazurite, onyx—and most impressive, a vial of ground bloodstone that came from Varenis's prison-mines on the western side of the Etolian range. Exposure to the bloodstone could lead to a terrible cancerlike disease that made one's body slowly change color. First, the veins would glow a luminous dark red. Then the eyes would transform into a scarlet color, as if bathed in radiant blood. After this, one would begin to cough out red liquid like a tuberculosis victim, though the liquid itself would crystalize into bloodstone. Then, as the brain roved in strange mineral thoughts, the body itself would harden into slightly malleable bloodstone and freeze into a carmine statue of exquisite beauty. The final result was a statue resembling a melted wax duplicate of the afflicted person.

They would not use the bloodstone today.

They gathered into a little circle on the floor, to continue their studies in illusionary transmutation. Like all thaumaturgy, it was composed of two interwoven techniques: formulae spoken and written in the air. A third, material, element was often added at some point in the sequence. Often this acted as a catalyst or helped intensify the charm. At other times—with particularly powerful spells—it was essential.

Thaumaturgy, then, was closely related to chymistry, biology, physics. Indeed, at times the parallels were plain. But to perform it was an art, perhaps the closest analogy was music. One learned the formulae—just as one learned the relationships of chords in mu-sic, one practiced them, memorized them—but to perform was to forget them, to enact them instinctually. Still, some had a greater natural aptitude for the Art than others. Like mathematics or per-forming music, everyone possessed some talent, but while some struggled, others excelled.

Illusionism was Maximillian's strength, and together they re-examined the equations for a simple illusion and discussed the principles behind them. Then they emptied their minds of all extraneous thoughts and feelings, calmed themselves. Finally, it was Oewen's turn to perform the illusion.

Oewen brushed his light beard with one hand. His face calmed itself, then tensed once more. There was something small and mouselike about him. He recited the formulae and drew an ideogram in the air. In the center of the circle a bowl shimmered. For a moment it transformed into a small chair; then it mutated back into a bowl.

Oewen held both hands in the air. "I can't do it."

Max nodded vigorously. "You can!"

A look of guilt touched Oewen's face. "I don't want to do this any longer. I don't have the talent for it."

"We all have the talent for it!" Max let his head fall back and looked at the roof. "We can all do it. Perhaps you'd be better at one of the other forms—biologism or chymistry."

"Perhaps I'd be better at harvesting crops."

"Patience." Kamron stood in the doorway and looked eagerly around the room, assessing. "Neither of you have patience."

Max pursed his lips. Was Kamron monitoring him and the group? Was he checking to ensure Max was still in the hideout, hadn't gone to visit the Xsanthians? Still, Kamron was right, he was impulsive, frustrated when things didn't happen quickly. But then again, without impatience, they would never achieve anything. People had to be driven for a greater vision, for the good of everyone. Even Oewen. Even Max himself.

Kamron walked into the room. He squatted next to Oewen. "How do you feel?"

"Sick."

"Would you like to try again?"

"No."

"I understand. But speak the formulae more slowly. Once it is done, *then* draw the ideogram. I have little talent for illusionism so I cannot show you, and perhaps you don't either. But I know that you're rushing to get it over with. You're slipping out of your trance rather than staying in it." Kamron calmly clasped his hands in front of him. He had the air of a monk, his soft honeyed tones expressions of everything soft and passive about him. Max watched him: this old warped man whose features were slightly awry, the embodiment of the cost of thaumaturgy, an art rent by contradiction. The mode employed for illusionism was thus: first the spoken formulae, then the ideograms. No additional materials were needed, unlike in the art of chymistry. Illusionism reversed the order used in some of the other forms. Why? Why did they not obey the same laws? Why were the logics of their formulae in contradiction? That was the first great question of the Art. The second was to avoid the cost: the universe's slow distortion of the thaumaturgist. There were charms of protection to ameliorate this price. These two great problems rose like the sun and the moon over thaumaturgical theory. A thought flashed into Max's mind: Was there an underlying logic that unified the two?

"I'll try," said Oewen. Again he spoke the formulae, this time vocalizing clearly and definitely. He drew the ideogram in strong lines. The bowl shimmered, transformed into the chair, and remained fixed.

Oewen smiled weakly as he maintained his concentration. He then released it and it returned to its original form.

Kamron stood up again. "We cannot tell what talent we have. We can only try." When he reached the door he looked directly at Maximilian. "With patience." He was not speaking only about thaumaturgy, Max knew.

After he left, Max nodded to Oewen. "He's right. I'm sorry I pressed you."

Oewen smiled weakly again. "It's all right. I want to learn. We need to turn thaumaturgy from an art of power and oppression to one of liberation."

Max smiled and touched Oewen on the arm. "Quite so."

TWELVE

Several mornings later, Max awoke before the others. In the early hours, the darkness seemed blacker in the Communal Cavern, and not just because the brazier had burned down and the lamps were guttered. It was as if the minute motes of light that floated down the tunnels had not yet made their way in from the outside. Max slipped from his bed. The sounds of sleeping came to him through the darkness: the muffled sound of several limbs shifting beneath bedcothes, the soft snoring of someone across the cavern.

Max was already dressed. He grasped the lamp beside his bed, but did not light it. He could not afford to wake anyone, least of all Josiane. She could move silently through the dark and he feared hearing her voice next to him: "Oh, and where are you going?"

Once outside, he would be free to move about the city, as he liked. When he returned, no one would have proof of his real movements.

The lamp rattled as Max lifted it. He froze. No one stirred. He padded softly through the darkness, fearful he might tread on some unseen object lying on the floor. He reached the corridor, passed through it in the blackness and finally lit the lamp when he reached the main tunnel to the outside. He stepped out into the open air as the golden sun was breaking over the water, lighting it with streaks of white and yellow. Already he could feel the sun's heat on his face. It would be another hot day.

When he reached Market Square, Maximilian watched the bustling activity on the long piers. Seamen padded along the wooden planks of the piers to sleek-lined cutters. Squat steamers maneuvered heavily into place, carrying liquor or machinery from the north. The wharves were an image of brilliant colors—reds and blues of painted boats and colored sails, and the sun catching the sparkling water as it slapped against the boats. The smell of rotten fish wafted over the piers.

Max walked to a stone staircase that led down beneath the boardwalk. A tough-looking man with the rolling gait of a seaman bent over several boxes of minotaur-puppets. A FOR SALE sign leaned up against one of them. The man looked suspiciously up at Max, but turned away disinterestedly.

Descending beneath the boardwalk, Max came to a vast series of dank and dark platforms, connected by walkways that ran all the way north to the water palaces and the House Marin compound. Along the way, they connected with tunnels and subterranean canals, which occasionally broke to the surface into the waterways of that neighborhood.

Here the waters lapped below and the salty smell of brine hung in the air. Brooding seamen guarded storage crates scattered among the walkways. In the darkness, tramps shifted on mountainous empires of rags. Max passed a group of five men carrying cages with long exotic lizards, which made deep guttural sounds. Far away he could hear a man yelling, "It's my kingdom. I am the King. It's mine!"

Treading through the gloom, Max was careful not to slip on the wet planks. A few minutes' walk from the stairs, the platforms gave way to a vast opening, like some subterranean sea baths, and there, slipping in and out of the water in the darkness, were the shadowy forms of the Xsanthians. One of them watched warily from where it sat on the side of the pool, its great big eye on the side of its head unblinking, the scales glistening in the dim light. Max's chest tightened with tension. Their bipedal form intimated humanity, but their great glassy eyes in the side of their great fish heads suggested something altogether alien.

"I've come for Santhor," said Max.

The Xsanthian cocked its head and stared at him. Max stared back into the massive fishy eye. In an instant, Max realized that the eye had no lid, and it was forever open, staring coldly out into the world.

"Sssanthor. He come." The Xsanthian hopped onto its two

webbed feet, dived into the water, and disappeared beneath the surface.

Max waited in the half dark as forms moved beneath the waters in front of him. Three heads burst through the surface in unison, turned with perfect synchronicity and gazed blankly at him with their glassy left eyes. Again in unison, they plunged beneath the waters.

A little while later, another head popped from the water; it was not the Xsanthian Santhor, but the head of a gaunt-looking Anlusian who wore large goggles. He grasped the side of the boardwalk and tried to pull himself out. "Lend a hand, will you?"

Max grabbed him by the arms and the New-Man scrambled out of the water. Great streams of water fell from a strange cylinder on his back. It seemed to be some kind of fan, and attached to the New-Man's chest was a small sputtering engine. A series of pistons and axles wrapped around the New-Man's sides to drive the fan and propel the wearer powerfully beneath the waters. But the New-Man himself was skeletal, his wiry muscles taut beneath his skin.

"Amazing," the New-Man said. "These Xsanthians. Nothing like them back in Ariki-Aki. Do you know that they have three-hundred-and-sixty-degree vision? Have you ever thought what that might be like? I might try to emulate it somehow. A series of mirrors perhaps." He turned his hands from one angle to another to indicate the image in his mind. Turning a knob, he stopped the engine and the fan on his back slowed to a spluttering stop.

"Interested in the Xsanthians, are you?" The New-Man grinned, white teeth flashing. He had the refreshing air of a man free from constraint and fear.

Maximilian found himself saying, "I'd like to help them."

The New-Man introduced himself as Quadi. "Mainly I work at the market, trade in hot-wine, gadgets from Ariki-Aki and Tir-Aki. And you?"

At that moment, a Xsanthian head emerged from the water and, with a kick of its powerful legs and only the softest touch against the edge of the platform with one hand, leaped smoothly onto the walkway. In the other, the creature held a still-flapping fish. It tore off the fish's head, the backbone slipping from the fish's tail like a knife from its scabbard and disappearing into his mouth.

Max stepped back and the Xsanthian stood before him, water coursing from its scales. Immediately, Max's instinct was to step farther back. His heart skipped a beat, adrenaline course though his veins, his muscles tightened. Fear washed over him.

"Santhor."

"Maxsssimilian." The Xsanthian scratched at the black metal collar on its neck with one of the claws at the end of a webbed hand. It seemed to make a grimace but Max couldn't be sure; all he could see were what looked like a thousand teeth, white and razor sharp. Santhor then threw the rest of the fish into its mouth.

Maximilian looked at the Anlusian beside him.

Quadi laughed. "I know when I'm not wanted!" He unclipped his diving machine, held it with one spidery hand, and walked away into the darkness.

To Santhor, Max said, "Have you discussed it?"

"We will protessst, we mussst protesst, but how? Look." The Xsanthian pointed to the collar that clamped around his neck. "How fight these?"

"There are debates happening openly at the universities and the gymnasia and lycées. There are strikes in the Factory Quarter. There are broadsheets circulating. If you were to protest, I could organize for others to support you. We could coordinate it with others who are fighting. All together. Then I could show—" Max hesitated. "We could convince people that together we have power."

The Xsanthian stared impassively. "I go tomorrow to coral fields. Not sure when back. Look: get rid of collars, we fight."

Max nodded, "I will. I'll discover a way to remove the collars."

He could perceive no emotion in the glassy eye of the Xsanthian. It was like the surface of ice: glistening, wet, impenetrable.

On his way back, Max passed through the now-bustling market looking for something to buy as a cover for his actions. He passed by great stalls filled with oranges and grapes, fishmongers selling huge tuna, crabs, and octopi. Around the stalls, elderly women elbowed others aside; students searched through clothes racks for bargains;

and Arbor ladies, followed by entire entourages of bodyguards and servants, purchased great piles of silks. A physician, having traveled from the south, offered his ministrations, though one look at his scalpels, forceps, and clamps was enough to make Max wince.

Max looked through manuscript stalls, though he knew he would not find anything there, only old histories of small towns that dotted the coast, or contemporary romances set in a mythical Caeli-Amur that never existed. Sometimes he would find small piles of abandoned broadsheets with radical names like *A Call to Arms* or *Visions of the People,* filled with semi-factual articles about the Houses. It was a policy of the Veterans that they should be left alone, not only because they might be watched by House agents, but because the groups who produced them were often filled with crazed or mystical ideas. Many were the romantic scrawlings of university students, as likely as not to end up mad in the torture cells of the Houses or to recant quickly and join the ranks of the Houses before they were caught. Others however combined deeper philosophies—apocalypticism, gratificationism, matriarchism . . . with seditionism.

In the middle of Market Square, standing by a stall with two of his followers, the glacial Ejan, his white-blond hair and his pale skin distinct in the city, surveyed the scene. Ejan exuded a sense of calm like the mountains after a storm, beautiful and out of reach. Though he knew that Ejan was a dedicated seditionist, Max had never grown to trust him. There was something altogether too calculating and cold about the northerner.

On the stall sat ointments and preparations, knitted blankets and shawls, spectacles and spyglasses: Ejan and his followers constructed these in their workshop. Their sale brought in much of the group's income. Quite a lucrative amount; Max worried about the seditionists' reliance upon it.

Ejan had joined the group shortly after Maximilian. He had been on the run from House Marin guards for some unknown crime. Moving from rooming house to rooming house in the Quaedian, he had sent the word around that he was looking for seditionists. Kamron had sent Maximilian to meet Ejan and Max had bribed his way into Ejan's empty room, nothing but a small cell with cracked floorboards, paint falling in strips from the wall, a cot pushed against the wall. Several books detailing the construction of weapons and war machines sat in a pile on one corner.

When Ejan returned to the rooming house, Maximilian was sitting on the rough wooden floor. Ejan entered the room cagily, his eyes circling around to see if Maximilian was the only intruder. He held one hand behind his back.

Maximilian remained calm. "I'm not here to capture you. I'm with Kamron Andrenikis."

Once Ejan felt more at ease, his hand moved from behind his back, revealing a long jagged-edged knife.

Ejan explained that he came from one of the great ice-halls in Njagar in the north. He was the eldest son of a chieftain who ruled that ancient fortress built of ice. As heir, he was groomed to rule: taught to fight, to be decisive under conditions of stress, to endure loneliness. But he had rebelled against his father's domineering personality. With each of the young Ejan's insubordinations, the Njagar chief had disciplined him more, as if what the boy lacked was sufficient regimen. Yet the more the father directed the son, the more the son rebelled, until one day, the father, furious at Ejan's refusal to oversee the logistics of a snow-giant hunting party, took the young man by the arm, intent on flogging him. But Ejan struck preemptively, hitting his father with all his force in the jaw. The hulking chief, taken by surprise, collapsed to the ground, blood coursing from his mouth.

Knowing that he had crossed a line, Ejan had hurriedly packed his few possessions, taken his horse and ridden south, heading ultimately for Varenis, which he found enormous and sprawling. There he read seditionist literature, which gave him a sense of direction. Continuing on to Caeli-Amur, he decided to find Kamron Andrenikis.

"I'm here to become Andrenikis's captain."

"But we have no captains. We have no leaders." Maximilian was repelled by the northerner's sense of entitlement. Yet, he knew that it was a sense that he shared. Didn't he too feel that he was destined for great things?

Ejan smiled coldly. "And who are you?"

"Just a seditionist in the group, like all the others."

"I shall not be like all the others."

Max, troubled by the northerner's demeanor, nevertheless covertly led him into the hideout. When he took the blindfold from the man's eyes, Ejan smiled again coldly. "Well, it looks like we're already equals."

Now, as he studied Ejan and his lieutenants behind the stall in Market Square, Max contemplated how he could use the northerner. Ejan had begun to understand that things were changing in Caeli-Amur, but his response was that of a soldier, not a seditionist. Max was repelled by the idea that the seditionists should fight militarily against the Houses, break their locks, ruin their carriage wheels, as Giselle had explained it. On the other hand, if he could convince Ejan that they should turn the group outward, join with the strikers, unite the disorganized struggles, and actually become involved in creating history, rather than looking at it from the outside, then together they could convince Kamron and the other Veterans also.

Max approached the stall and picked up a preparation for pain relief. "Ejan, how is business?"

Ejan stood still and examined Max. "Business is always good. But there are other businesses, other actions, we should discuss. I have been hoping you and your group might participate."

Max picked up a pince-nez and examined it. "Interesting, for I was hoping your group might help in my own activities. Strikes are occurring across the city. We need to unify them, participate in them, bring them together like tributaries into one great river."

"You understand," said Ejan, "that the tramworkers' strike was a result of our activities. We sabotaged the factory. It produced a crisis. It sparked events."

Max looked up into Ejan's piercing blue eyes and expressionless face. "The tramworkers were broken by House Technis. Their thaumaturgists summoned the Furies against them. You sparked their deaths. Anyway, should the Veterans discover your actions, well, things would not go well for you. Mine is a better way."

Out of the bustling crowds of the market shuffled a hunched-over man, rags hanging from his limbs like long gray fronds from some long dead plant. Clear fluid weeped from a great open sore on the side of his face and neck, a small third arm grew from his body—signs of a wastelander, mutated from the chemicals running in poisonous rivers and gathering in the steaming ponds in the northeast. The wastelands were growing, ever encroaching on the terrain around them, changing not only the land, but also the people, animals, flora. There strange creatures moved among odd sentient plants; everything was warped and mutated with cancerous growths. No wonder the wastelanders were flooding into the city.

The people in the crowd shrank away from the wastelander, but the man barely seemed to notice. He staggered toward Ejan and Max.

As the outcast approached, Ejan remained motionless, like a statue of himself. "Don't think that I haven't thought of your arguments, Max: We cannot fight the Houses' thaumaturgy, our strength lies in the citizens, we must prepare slowly. To me they all sound like Kamron's words. Wait and prepare and hide in our little hole like little frightened rabbits. But, Max, you see the citizens through the lens of your own romanticism. They are too complacent and only act when they are personally under threat. We must be the catalyst for their actions. We must force events, provoke confrontations, so that the citizens take sides. Anyway, you know yourself that we need weapons to defend ourselves. The crushing of the tramwokers is proof of that. We don't need less military might, we need more!"

Max clenched his fists in frustration. The smashing of the tramworkers strike *was* proof that without a way of combating the House thaumaturgists, the seditionists had little hope of helping the citizens, but military might without the involvement of the people was worse. "Of course, but that is not what I'm talking about. I'm taking about small violent actions against the Houses—sabotage is idiotic. Don't make me take action against you."

"You would tell Kamron?"

Max did not respond. This man was further from his own views than Kamron, who at least believed the people would one day awaken, even if only in some far-off future time.

The wastelander now arrived beside Max. He picked up an ointment from the stall. "Will this help me with my ailments?" He pointed to his face. As the wastelander spoke, Max noticed a second row of teeth intersecting with the first, as if another body was emerging within him, floating to his surface like a corpse to the top of a pond.

"I'm not sure it's quite strong enough," Ejan said.

The man nodded, placed the ointment down and examined the other medicines seriously. "Hmm, maybe one of these teas."

Ejan stepped around the back of the stall and leaned in close to Max. "So it seems we are enemies. Oh, and Kamron would not like your activities either."

Max looked at Ejan, who stepped even closer, so close that their faces almost touched.

"House agents police us everywhere," said Ejan. "I just didn't think you would join them."

The wastelander picked up a mirror from the stall and examined himself. "Still good-looking," he said to no one in particular. He shrugged and walked toward a line of mules pulling a cart led by several Numerians. Two lions, bodies rippling with muscles, stared sullenly at the wastelander from a cage mounted on the cart.

"If you had not sabotaged the Tram Factory, the workers would still be alive, still able to fight. It is you who will be doing the Houses' work." Max turned and walked away before Ejan could respond. The exchange had disturbed him more than he could express. If Ejan would threaten a fellow seditionist and consider him an agent of the Houses, then what other actions would he be prepared to take?

Maximilian returned to the hideout frustrated. The Veterans, Xsanthians, Ejan—not one of them had helped him. Max, his mind on these problems, didn't notice the figure waiting for him at the hideout's entrance until it was too late. Something wrapped around his ankle and he hit the ground. Dust billowed around him as he looked up.

Josiane stood above him, outlined against the tunnel entrance. Her weighted chain swung malevolently in one hand. "Kamron told you: Don't come back if you see the Xsanthians."

"I was visiting Ejan's stall at the market."

"I've killed more important men for lesser things," said Josiane.

"You've been a hired killer. You've killed for nothing."

"Money is not nothing."

"It is to me," said Max.

"But then you're only an idle dreamer. You have no idea of the reality."

"We're all dreamers. Who among us isn't?" As he spoke, Maximilian knew that he had elided two different things. For all the seditionists were romantics, yet he was a kind all to himself. He knew his reputation was for grand schemes, bold visions, wild fancies. It was true: Sometimes he got carried away. But better that than to be mired into accepting the status quo.

"I'm not," Josiane shifted on her feet.

"And that is your weakness. That's why you cannot see the changes happening before your eyes. You have no imagination."

Josiane was silent; he had struck her at a vulnerable place. Eventually she said, "When the group has returned tonight, then Kamron will decide your fate."

Max waited for her to disappear into the tunnel. Sometime later, he sat for a while on his thin mattress in the darkness. Around him seditionists whispered, and he knew that they were discussing his banishment. He struggled to think through the situation. Kamron would convince the other Veterans to banish him. They would put this position at a meeting and the entire group would grudgingly accept their authority. Even Max's own supporters might accept the Veterans' arguments. Ejan's supporters would certainly accept them. Without Max, Ejan would become the most influential new seditionist in the group. There seemed no escape. Now all Max could do was wait for the evening, when his fate would be sealed.

Disgusted with the situation, Max walked through the corridor with its purple mist, and into that cavernous crypt, where the machines, like squatting metal creatures, sat silent and melancholy. He passed between the columns of machines to the far side of the cavern. Here stood great round doors: gigantic, as if built for giants. Like so much of this ancient technology, they were sometimes smooth, but elsewhere there were wheels and cogs and levers attached to them. Before they had worked on the machines, Kamron had instructed Maximilian and Omar to attempt to open these doors. But no matter what they tried, the doors lay silent and closed.

Max pressed his hands against the doors. Cold and silent, he lay his cheek against their surface. He thought he could hear a hum from somewhere behind them. But then it was gone.

When he returned to the Communal Cavern, Max packed his possessions. He considered what he might do once he was back in the city itself. He would return to living in a garret. Exile. The thought filled him with despair.

The seditionist group sat in an open space to one side of the communal area, looking quietly at one another, tense, expectant. About a year and a half earlier, the group had begun to have meetings in this space, speakers standing before the six black pillars and facing the group. They had begun tentatively at first, as they learned the dynamics of a group discussion. Usually, the Veterans would speak first. Others would agree, reiterating the points already made, often suggesting minor adjustment. Over the last year, the seditionists had gained confidence, and slowly a variety of opinions had begun to be expressed. But never had the Veterans been directly contradicted.

Now, as Max looked over the ragged bunch of thirty gaunt-faced seditionists in their ragtag clothing, he sensed that no one would speak for him.

Instead, Josiane took to her feet before the six pillars. Her weighted chain hung from her belt as she walked in front of the group. She began like a lawyer, her years as a philosopher-assassin evident. "Despite a warning there is one in this group that continues to endanger us. There is one who, despite Kamron's entreaties, has contacted the Xsanthians, whom we cannot trust. There is one who—"

Maximilian stood up, aware of the intrigued eyes of the seditionists shifting to him. He stood to one side, close to the kitchen area in the center of the hall. "Enough of these theatrics. Of course we should respect Kamron and everything he's done for us. He built this group and dedicated his life to the struggle against the Houses." Max looked over at Kamron's pained eyes and felt a sudden flash of doubt. Could they not all work together?

Before Max could continue, Josiane spoke again. "You see. He has no respect for the Veterans. He endangers us. Even now squads from Arbor, or Marin, or Technis might burst into our hideout, might take us by storm, might drag us to their dungeons and feed us to their beasts or their machines. We all feel frustrated. We all feel angry. We all feel that we should do more. But when we are strong: that is the time to reach out, to fight."

Kamron himself stood up slowly on the side of the group opposite from Max. "I've spent my life dedicated to change. To changing the Houses' control of everyone's lives. I never felt isolated from the rest of the citizens. Though why we call them citizens I don't know: Citizens have rights, citizens have a voice. Well before the rise of the Houses that was true. But in any case, I love the people, for I know in their hearts stirs a yearning for the liberation we fight for. But already we have seen the result of openly fighting the Houses. Only yesterday the Furies were loosed on the tramworkers. By the time it was over, the workers' bodies were nothing but charred corpses, their very life force drunk into the Other Side by the creatures. That is what awaits us if we turn outward. To me you are my children. What parent would sacrifice his children?"

Max looked around the circle. Karma and Eli, Aldrus and Philippe—they all looked at Kamron with respect. And didn't he deserve it? Max's eyes roved over the crowd. How could he have thought that he knew better than this grand old man who had fought the Houses for thirty years? Wasn't Kamron's argument the more compelling? Hadn't the tramworkers been rent asunder when they tried to fight? Despair took him. Yes, he was arrogant as they all claimed. And yet there also were some of his circle: Oewen and Ariana, arm in arm, their faces sad, hoping for something.

Farther back in the shadows he caught a glimpse of Ejan's face, the light illuminating one side of it like a shadow puppet. Max considered that face, the coldness of it. Ejan was a man with a drive that Max understood. They both were prepared to act for the cause, sacrifice for the cause.

Max looked at the Veterans: at Josiane with her quick movements, at Iniria with her soft eyes, at Kamron with his kindly old face. When he spoke, his voice rang out, louder and more certain than it had been. He felt that the force of history itself was coursing into him, that the future was seeking a voice and that that voice was his. "Old man. You have given this group much. But it is bigger than you. The cause is bigger than your concerns. The group feel it too. It is time for you to step aside with dignity, for we have reached a new stage, a new phase, as has the world outside. Yes, the tramworkers were crushed, and the printers before them, but these are just the beginning. There are small molecular processes occurring among the citizens, and we would be fools to sit in here alone playing with these ancient machines. No! We will not do that, will we, Ejan?"

Max looked at Ejan, who now stood at the rear of the group, icy and frightening. Behind him the cavern was shadowed in darkness. His movements were slow and calm as he walked across to where Max stood. He put his arm around Max's shoulders. "We will not."

Silence reigned as the meaning of events dawned on the seditionists. Together Ejan and Max's circles were the majority of the group. Kamron blinked in confusion; Iniria smiled a soft confused smile; Josiane's face was cold and impassive.

There was no need for a vote, but Ejan insisted on one anyway.

When it was done, Kamron stood and silently walked away, leaving Max and Ejan looking over the group.

Late in the evening, Maximilian squatted beside Omar, who lay on his makeshift bed close to the center of the room. "We have done it, Omar. We can do what we want. We are free of Kamron and his old ways. I made alliance with Ejan."

Omar opened his eyes and they were clear, for the first time. "Max, I know it—I know the code for the librarian. I know—" He threw his arm out toward the ceiling. It was a dramatic gesture. "I know things that I didn't know before."

"You know the code," Max whispered. "How? What is it?"

"I have knowledge, things I never dreamed of, strange . . .

from the machine. I don't know how. Leave those machines alone, Max, there's no way for you to control them. You must have ancient knowledge to do so."

Max nodded. "Tell me this code."

Omar recited a long series of zeros and ones. It continued for several minutes.

"That's it? Numbers?"

"I don't understand it either, it's a different language. Baycetoo it's called. Let me write it down."

Max fetched a notebook from his possessions and passed it to Omar, who lodged a pen in his blistered hands. They shook as he wrote and he groaned occasionally as he steadied them. Every now and then he stopped, looking out into the darkness, his eyes darting around as he remembered. "Zeros and ones," he said. When he was done he added, "Max, you never recognize your mistakes. Listen to me. Ejan supports no one. Only himself."

"Removing Kamron and the Veterans was a historical necessity. They belonged to an earlier time, a time of preparation. That's how history moves, Omar. People have their moment and then are bypassed." Max took hold of the notebook. Omar still held on to it.

"History . . . is that all you think of?" said Omar.

Max was troubled. He tugged the notebook from Omar's hand and stood up, "I'll talk to you when you're in a better mood. We'll talk more about these things you know."

But later Omar had lapsed again into a state of semiconsciousness, and again he spoke in strange words about long-forgotten destinations, and about a journey through a wilderness where he was harried by unknown creatures that threatened him from all sides.

Late into the night, Max sat alone in the semidarkness near his bed. Kamron had retired to his room, ashen-faced, as if he had foreseen his own death. Max wanted to go to him, to make some kind of compromise, but harsh necessities forbade him. Events marched ruthlessly on. Kamron's time was over. That did not mean he had not been important. Just because something is temporary does not mean it had no value. In fact, a temporary thing, Kamron's life work—the collecting of his books, the establishment of the hideout, the accumulation of rebels around him—was all the more valuable when its time was over. It was a precious and fragile thing, thought Max. Still, Max was more than troubled. A heavy blanket of guilt covered him and he couldn't shake it off. Was he really so certain?

Still hurt by Omar's words, Max sat in the dark, staring out at his empire of freedom. In his mind, a plan was slowly developing. He would learn as much about Caeli-Enas as possible. He would learn as much water magic as he could. Then he would employ the Xsanthians to help him reach the vast store of knowledge held in the Great Library beneath the sea.

Max felt a shape slip beside him. He tensed as he turned to see Josiane squatting low. But she stopped and looked out into the darkness with him, as if the two of them were looking into the future, unknown and dark and full of possibility.

"I'm at your service. What do we do now?" she said.

Max could feel the barely suppressed energy in her body. He examined her. How strange that she would switch sides so easily. She was not one to be trusted. But she would serve for a while.

Max looked her straight in the eyes. "Now we contact the other groups and bring in new seditionists. Now we grow like a creature in the dark, ready to emerge fully formed against the Houses. Now we accumulate knowledge—knowledge of thaumaturgy. Now we travel to the only place where such stores are hidden—the Sunken City." In his hands, he held the notebook with the precious code.

PART II

BEGINNINGS

If prior to the cataclysm each part of society lived in harmony with the others, what was thaumaturgy's place in this? Was it dispersed through-out society in the manner in which creativity is in ours—everyone can be said to have a modicum of it? Or was it specialized, as we segregate the professions (e.g., apothecaries)?

Once post-cataclysmic fragmentation occurred, thaumaturgy underwent its own separation. Where once the Magi were able to deploy the Art as a unified practice, where matter could be dealt with at the level of complexity required, now it broke into its various streams (illusionism, transmutae, weaving, chymistry, etc.). No longer could practictioners work the deep structure of things. Instead each stream operated according to its own logic, its own laws—laws which were often in direct conflict with the laws of the others. A thaumaturgist might interweave one stream with another, but to operate all of the logics at once was impossible. The thaumaturgist would lose control of the forces and instead become controlled by them. Death was usually the result. In those days, the secret of unification was forever lost. The Magi were no more.

—from *Thaumaturgy and History* by Kamron Andrenikis

THIRTEEN

For days after Aemilius's death, Kata lay in her bed, memories washing over her like a vast ocean. She felt as if she were drowning. She wished she was drowning. Her arms and legs felt leaden and she didn't have the strength to leave her bed. There was blood on her hands that would never be washed away, damned spots of it all over her like a rash. The things she might have done with Aemilius, the places they might have seen. It had all been a delusion they had engaged in together, to both their loss. She tossed and turned in her bed. Thoughts came at her like bolts thrown by a mechanized thrower. One after the other: barbed and cruel.

Her door was thrown open in her parlor below, followed by the sound of footsteps coming up the stairs. She turned in her bed, throwing her limbs out and staring disconsolately. The same gray officiate that had organized the clean up after Rudé's death entered the room.

He looked down at her. "Sick?"

"Sick of you."

He looked impassively. "I'm Rudé's replacement, Boris Autec. I have a task that will help you repay your debts to the House, not least for the death of my predecessor."

"Rudé's death was of his own making. How was I to know he would drink the poisoned wine?"

Autec opened the doors onto the balcony, and looked out over the city. "Accident, conscious design, what does it matter? It's the effect of your actions that the universe finally weighs up, isn't it?"

"The universe doesn't weigh anything," said Kata, staring at the wall. "It's yourself that you have to make peace with, if you can."

"Well, in any case, it is time we put an end to these seditionist groups that are spreading these radical ideas. They lead the citizens astray with wild notions, manipulate the impressionable, use legitimate grievances for their own malign ends."

Kata expected to feel dread at the thought of more deception and lies, but found nothing inside. She was an empty vessel, an empty bottle of poisoned wine. She didn't care anymore, one way or the other. "You don't understand. There's nothing left of me. Why don't you have me sweep the floors of the Complex? Something menial, something meaningless?"

"Because you're better than that. It certainly *looks* as if you fed both my predecessor and the minotaur the poison together. But I know it wasn't *entirely* your fault that Rudé died. It was more a matter of disregard than design. Help me capture these seditionists and not only will you be forgiven, but you can have whatever you want. *What is it you want, Kata?* A villa in the country perhaps?"

Kata looked up at the officiate. She felt a flicker inside her. It was as if he understood her deepest desires. A villa in the country: not one of the pleasure palaces along the Dyrian coast where the House officials retired, but beyond the summer villas of Arbor, to the south perhaps, or in the western mountains. A tiny dash of hope flickered in her, like a candle far away in the distance.

"A villa," she said. "I will hand you these seditionists and you will give me a villa."

Autec came over and sat on the bed. He placed his hand on hers. "We do difficult jobs. We don't always choose our actions. We cannot always predict their outcomes. It hurts us, sometimes. And yet we do them because of duty, because—what else could we do? It hurts sensitive souls like ours."

Autec's face looked strained. Though he appeared soft and round, there was sheen to his skin, and a lightly yellow tinge to his eyes. He did not look well. He stood again and walked to the balcony. Looking out over the city he said, "Things wash away, don't they?"

That afternoon Kata listlessly raised herself from her bed and began to prepare. She was broken, but if she was not going to kill herself, then she only had one path she could follow: the path she had always followed. She would do as Technis demanded and earn herself a villa in the country, away from Caeli-Amur. She would always be wounded by Aemilius's death, but this at least might bring some solace, and some independence. One had to survive.

She washed herself in the communal bathhouse, pouring cold water over herself with a bucket. She strapped her knives to her body, dressed herself in her shirt and loose-fitting pants. Finally, she left her apartment and walked to the Technis Complex.

In the Library deep beneath the Technis Palace, a vast hall with lines of catalogs, books, and filing cabinets, she researched the seditionists and their theories. At first she constantly heard the sound of a saw in her head. But as the days passed, she concentrated more, and the sickening feeling became a slow ache. She studied the various radical theories: their internecine differences, their debates, their philosophical lineages. She intuitively understood the subterranean anger at the Houses that lay beneath the theories: Didn't the Houses control everything, didn't they destroy everything? But the idealism also repelled her. The Houses were in control and always would be. And what kind of crazed ideas did these groups have? Many believed in simple reforms: better conditions for workers, for thaumaturgy to be placed at the will of the people, for a return to the days when Caeli-Amur was ruled by a senate. But at their most extreme, these notions of equality merged with visions of worlds where everyone lived in great warrens without personal space, where thaumaturgy created direct mind-to-mind communication which would eliminate the need for speech altogether. For Kata, the latter ideas only served to further discredit the former.

Kata helped create an issue of a radical broadsheet that she called *The New Tomorrow*. She chose an apocalyptic theory for its overarching outlook: she was attracted to the visions of disintegration and prophecies of doom contained in such doctrines. She composed articles about the influx of wastelanders into the city, strange radical poems composed of couplets, calls to action. Though the broadsheet was only four pages long, she held it in her hand as if it were genuine. She had it printed in the House's private printing room, a vast dusty room filled with the cacophony of machines that whirred and clunked and poured out the House's internal documents like water from a waterfall.

During the daytime she felt that things were fine, but when she returned home at night, there was the faintest smell of blood in the air. She wandered around the apartment sniffing but the smell disappeared, only to return when she turned her mind to other things. As she drifted off to sleep, Aemilius would flash into her mind, accompanied by the sounds of sawing. She would awake with a start, her heart beating rapidly, and step onto the balcony and look out over the city to calm herself. Each morning she forced herself to walk the long streets to House Technis. During these days, even little Henri avoided her, his vital eyes examining her from the end of the street before looking away for more likely customers.

Later in the week, Kata visited the University of Caeli-Amur. Nestled on the northern edge of the Quaedian, between the cliffs and the incline on which Via Persine climbed, it was a rambling structure of closely packed towers and villas. At more than ten stories high, it rose above the surrounding area, a little city of its own. Walkways crisscrossed the university's many buildings like a complex of spiderwebs between the many branches of thick brush. Classes were held in wide halls or atria, nestled among the ivy-covered towers. In the midst of these buildings perched on the incline, a library overlooked the sporting fields where students threw javelins and discuses, wrestled and boxed.

Many of the university's windows were stained glass: blues and reds and golds, depicting scenes of the ancients. But in the oldest parts of the university, other windows were thaumaturgically charged. These showed images of long-past scenes, which one might have seen through the window ten years or twenty or even hundreds of years earlier. One moment, the viewer would look through the glass onto the present-day Caeli-Amur. A moment later, that image would dissolve into the city 150 years before. On the field lying below, the viewer might see long-dead student lovers, hand-in-hand, turn and kiss each other, or the ancient Arcadi and Semerillion sects battling in strange combat rites against each other. Sometimes the sun would glitter on white ancient buildings; at others the city would be pitch black and barely distinguishable from the present day. Some claimed to have seen murders performed long ago, others images of the youthful gods themselves in the days before the cataclysm. It was a common pastime of students to organize window-viewing parties where they would congregate with flower-drafts and fruit and watch as images of the past appeared and dissolved.

As Kata passed along an ancient and extended corridor, she glimpsed through the windows to her left—organized so that their images synchronized with each other—a long-gone Caeli-Amur in the twilight. The Quaedian lay below, its buildings cleaner, simpler, spacious and regal. No trams ran along the streets toward Market Square, though the Opera overlooked the city, impressive as always. A festival seemed to be taking place on the fields below, as a thousand figures held candles, perhaps in memorial. Kata gazed through the windows and wondered at the changes that history had wrought upon the city. For below the world seemed quieter and more peaceful, a long-lost wonderland without machines chugging and pumping and grinding their gears. No soot or smoke drifted across the sky. Kata felt a wash of melancholy flood into her at the sight of this vanished past. She then turned away and continued on, for she was not safe here.

The university was officially autonomous from the Houses; in reality, it was part of their entire structure. In the days before the House Wars, the Classics were studied, but as the Houses' grip tightened on the city and its institutions, the study of Philosophy, the Histories, the Ancients and Ancient Species, and all their concomitant subjects, had been increasingly replaced by elementary thaumaturgy. Now the university conveyed those with special affinity for the Art from the streets into the Houses.

However, students had started to openly discuss seditionism, to pass banned manuscripts among themselves, to debate history and politics. The university had become a place for not only Houses to recruit, it seemed. Even as the Houses arrested overzealous student seditionists, others took their place.

Deep in the center of the buildings stood a large garden surrounded by cloisters. Violet and amber crystalline orchids from the deserts of Karrak grew in intricate arrangements, protected by thaumaturgy. In a corner, Kata dropped her broadsheets. There she had found copies of *A Call to Arms,* filled mostly with avant-garde seditionist poems and images of the sort found in the little galleries of the Quaedian. The seclusion of the cloisters, their multiple entry points, allowed for secretive meetings and easy escape.

When Kata returned the following day, the broadsheets she had left were gone. For three days, she worked feverishly on a new issue. When it was done, she returned to the university. As she dropped the second bundle in the corner, Kata was aware of a figure shifting quickly behind her. To remain passive was against every instinct she possessed, but she had to play the part of the young seditionist, not a philosopher-assassin. A hand was at her throat quickly, and she was dragged into a nearby alcove.

A woman's voice in her ear whispered, "It's dangerous to distribute radical broadsheets."

"Some things have to be done."

"An idealist."

"A realist."

The hand let go of her throat and she turned. A middle-aged woman with pale blue eyes, her hair closely cropped, stepped back smoothly. "If you keep handing out broadsheets in that pathetic manner one of the Houses will trap you and you will disappear. You're new at this, aren't you?"

"No," said Kata haughtily.

"Would you consider joining another group, one that has been around for many years? One with much experience?" The woman looked out of the alcove. A couple of blue-robed professors deep in debate approached. The woman pressed Kata into the alcove wall, where they remained silent while the professors passed.

"Why would I want to meet your group?" whispered Kata.

"Strength in numbers, for one," the woman said. "And we can teach you the things we have learned over twenty years."

Kata baited the woman. "I don't believe you know so much."

"We know enough not to drop our broadsheets clumsily in full view."

"It was hardly full view."

"And yet here I am."

Kata allowed a little tentativeness into her voice. "All right, I'd like to meet your group."

"How many of you are there?"

"I will not say, not until I have seen the size of yours."

A second later a cloth was over her mouth and she inhaled pungent fumes. She struggled, but her arms were clamped tightly; she kicked out behind her, connected with something and heard a groan. She tried to wriggle from the grasp but the strength had leached from her limbs. Her lungs burned. The cloth slipped away from her face, then clamped once more against her mouth. She tasted blood on the inside of her bottom lip as whiteness rose in front of her eyes. She gave one more struggle; then her legs gave way beneath her.

When Kata came to, she was in the dark. Her neck throbbed where it joined with her skull and her limbs ached. She ran one hand across the cold stone ground, heard the rattle of chains and then her wrist caught—she was bound. Her ankles were shackled also. She found that she could get herself onto her hands and knees, but because her ankles and wrists were chained to each other, she could not stand. She strained to see in the darkness, but could not make out anything. Her heart now leaped as she realized she had no idea where she was. Perhaps one of the other Houses had abducted her and left her to rot in one of their labyrinthine dungeons, before she could reveal herself to them.

Kata again tried to stand, but could only manage a backbreaking crouch. She crawled at an agonizingly slow pace and after a little while gave up.

The hours passed in the cold darkness, and Kata again started to crawl, feeling her way along a wall to her right, which quickly curved around to the left until she felt that she was moving back in the direction from which she had come. Before long she came to a door blocking her way. She passed it by and realized, as the wall curved around again, that she was moving in circles. The only exit was the poorly constructed door, its frame bolted cheaply into the stone, with gaps between the two where she could slide her fingers. There seemed to be no door handle, and the door was fixed fast. Eventually, she lay back on the ground and waited. She was trapped, there was no way out.

More time passed. Darkness hovered around her, and again she wondered if she would die here, on the cold stone floor.

Eventually, she heard sounds and with a flash of light, the door was thrown open. Kata averted her eyes from lamplight, which seemed brilliant after the hours of darkness.

Into the room walked the same middle-aged woman who had trapped her. The woman walked with a low center of gravity, with a tense energy as if she were ready to spring. From her belt hung a dangerous-looking weighted chain. She placed a large leather bag, the kind an apothecary might carry, on the ground. Kata thought about the young apothecary who had first suggested her medicine. Where was he now?

Next to the woman, holding the lamp, was a tall blond man with very pale skin: a northerner. He stood extremely still, his head rigid on his neck, his eyes unblinking. He looked like a statue: cold and severe.

"So, a seditionist." The blond man placed the lamp on the floor. "You've made a very poor mistake. How do you enjoy House Arbor's dungeons?"

Kata looked down at the floor. She had to think: Was she really in House Arbor's dungeons? If so, she should reveal that she was an agent for House Technis. The Houses were in an uneasy truce since the wars ended five years earlier, and though still enemies of a sort, Technis would negotiate for her release, perhaps organize an exchange of prisoners. But something about the situation made her wonder: the door was so poorly made. Why could she not hear any other prisoners? Perhaps the House kept the prisoners away from each other, the way that Technis was said to do.

"So." The man kicked her on the arm. "Not talking? Oh, but you will, my little dove. We have a thousand ways to make you talk." He turned to the woman. "The bottles."

From a bag the woman took out four bottles, each filled with a differently colored liquid: one red, another blue or perhaps green, a third gray, the last clear.

The northerner picked up the gray bottle. "House Arbor's newest development —wrigglers. See how they writhe, like little spirals twisting in the water. But once you swallow them, how they move! They twist all through your body, forming little clusters, then they erupt from your skin."

Kata stared at the bottle. She had heard of wrigglers in the cafés along Via Gracchia. Arbor was well known for its designs and control of plants and animals. Perhaps she should tell them the truth—but not yet, she would wait until the final moment. She was not a woman easily frightened; she had little to live for in the first place.

The northerner uncorked it and sniffed close to the bottle's neck. "So, my little seditionist. Talk. How many of you are there?"

"An entire city."

The man laughed a steely laugh. He grabbed Kata by the arm and dragged her through the door and into the darkness. She scrabbled along, trying not to scrape her legs. He turned right, along a rough tunnel into a nearby grotto. On its floor lay a dried cadaver, its lips shriveled back over its teeth, its skin sunk into its face as if it were collapsing inward, its arms and legs like the twisted branches of a long dead tree.

"You see." The man whispered in Kata's ear. "There's a seditionist for you. That *is* the insurgency for you."

He dragged Kata and tossed her onto the corpse, which crumpled beneath her—just a bag of bones. She rolled onto the stony floor.

"How many of you are there?"

The lantern, now carried by the woman, shone from behind the northerner, gilding him with light, making him appear like some angel of death.

Now Kata burned with anger and obstinacy. She had always had it in her: a stubbornness, an endurance. "An entire city," she spat out.

"The bottle." The man took the bottle and pulled back Kata's hair so that her mouth was facing up. The woman held Kata's nose and pulled at her jaw as the bottle cracked against her already swollen lips. She struggled and tried to turn her head. She groaned. Eventually, when she took a great breath, the liquid coursed into her mouth and she gulped it down: one, two, three great gulps and then more until the bottle was pulled away from her mouth.

Kata collapsed onto the floor, spitting out the remains of the liquid from her mouth.

"Talk." The man looked down at her. "Talk and we will give you an antidote which will kill the wrigglers."

Kata broke into a derisive laugh, her tone full of ridicule and hate. She would never tell these people anything. Memories of Aemilius came to her, memories of growing up on the streets, memories of her mother's death. What did any of it matter?

Suddenly the man was next to her, and there was a knife cold against her throat. "Don't you understand? You're going to die."

Kata's felt her emptiness more desperately. Blackness filled her— annihilation. "Kill me then."

The man sat back. "Very good. You're not a House agent. You can join our group, if you wish."

Kata looked up at the man in disbelief. "The wrigglers?"

"What wrigglers?" he held the bottle to the light. Nothing wriggled inside. "You understand why we needed to test you. Josiane will let you out. Meet her at midnight tomorrow at the university. Bring what you need, and anyone you trust absolutely."

Kata sat grimly in the dirt. She had penetrated a seditionist group.

FOURTEEN

The following night, Kata waited in the alcove with Louis, a young hireling of Technis, a slavish follower of orders whose shifty eyes darted from side to side when he spoke. Louis had the air of a man prepared to do anything to rise to power. He was not cruel, like so many, but rather the reverse: It seemed that at any moment he expected to be the object of some brutishness, and so he was eager to instigate some preemptive misdeed. Right and wrong were not a part of his calculations; rather, to him the world was some morally empty labyrinth. Autec had paired the two, and one did what the officiate decided. Supplicate yourself to those above you, kick those below you, that was the rule of the Houses.

The cloisters were filled with shadows and moonlight. Far away the sound of students drunkenly laughing could be heard. Fops and dilettantes regularly stumbled around the universities at night: high on Numerian weeds and opium, searching for some transcendental or romantic vision; laughing at the strange immanence of the world at night, when things are somehow other, where everything takes on an inner life trying to break through its own form.

"She's not coming," said Louis, shifting uneasily on his feet.

"She's coming." The shadows moved as the trees in the courtyard rustled in the breeze.

"She's not," said Louis.

"She's listening to us right now," said Kata.

"Very good," said a voice from a shadow near the alcove. Josiane approached them. "Stand still," the woman said. She put hoods over their heads in the manner of the Order of the Sightless, apocalyptics who stumbled through the streets, chained together and blindfolded to symbolize their belief that the world had no sense of its future, that it stumbled blindly through history.

"You understand the need for secrecy." Josiane tethered them together and pulled them along. Through the night they walked. Kata could not tell exactly where they passed, though clearly it was through the winding routes, through the squares and up the stairs near the cliffs and on toward the peak of the mountain. She heard laughter from passersby, and the occasional gust of wind against her throat.

At a certain point they passed underground and stopped briefly. Kata heard a clicking, and a soft rushing sound, the *phht* of a wick being lit. They headed on again. The ground became rough and she lost all sense of direction. She started to sweat, and her mouth became dry. Again she was at the mercy of this radical group, who might discover her and Louis to be House agents. Like the philosopher-assassins and agents of the Houses, such seditionists were equally cold to the deaths of others. Politics was not an affair for the virtuous.

Across the rough ground they walked, the air cold. Occasionally Kata struck her shoulder against a wall, rocky and rough. They were probably beneath the city now, near the catacombs perhaps. Behind her, Louis whispered words of encouragement to himself.

She heard the sounds of people moving about, of broken sentences whispered. The smell of burning oil drifted through her hood. She drew in as much air as she could: the place smelled damp.

The hood was whipped off her head and she stood dazzled in a cavernous room that rose like some great ancient church dome. Figures moved around a small kitchen constructed in its center, surrounded by slanted tabletops with buttons and levers and plate glass indicating some long forgotten function. She barely registered her wonder at ancient technology before she focused on the present.

Josiane stood beside a tall and thin man who ran his hands through his curly hair, and eyed them curiously. On the other side of him stood a lithe woman, with a ball of red hair that looked like it was about to burst off her head. No one spoke. To Kata, there was a romance to the scene. The darkness and dinginess, the simplicity of the space, the rough-looking seditionists who worked together—all these befitted a group who spoke of a better world, a more communal world where people lived in harmony, not in competition.

Eventually the man said, "Thanks, Josiane. Take them to Kamron's room."

"Kamron is in there."

"It's time he was out of there. Tell him to prepare his things. We must be pure, above reproach. Ascetic. There can be no privileges."

"But Kamron is old," said the redheaded woman doubtfully. "It would hurt him to sleep on the floor."

"We cannot have favorites."

Josiane led Kata and Louis to a side room lit by hundreds of glittering white lights that moved gently across the walls. Again Kata wondered at the ancient technology hidden here beneath the city. She knew that much of the world of the ancients had been ruined, buried, during the cataclysm as the ground itself had broken and shifted, that beneath the world's crust lay lost wonders. While a ghostly pall hung over the blackened ruins in the communal area, these lights were some of the last working remnants of a former glorious age. Before long, she reasoned, they, too, would run down and join the rest of the skeletal remains.

An older man, his head bowed, shuffled around the room, looking for something. His body was bent and his features slightly skewed—the signs of a life of thaumaturgy. He stopped at a bookshelf, pulled a book from the others, opened it up, flicked through it absentmindedly.

"Kamron," said Josiane. "You're being moved to the common room. Collect your possessions later; leave the books, though."

The old man looked at them as if in puzzlement and said, "Josiane, after everything."

"History marches on, Kamron, you taught me that. Get out now."

The old man's face fell as some internal structure gave way, and he shuffled to the door and out into the central room. The lights changed to a slightly yellow color; perhaps they responded to change, or even emotion. Why someone would design them so was a mystery to Kata.

"Sit down." Josiane gestured to a couple of chairs. "Maximilian will be with you in a minute." She left the room.

Louis fidgeted nervously, looking around the room. Kata walked back to the shelves, which stood next to the door. She examined the books: history, philosophy, thaumaturgical tomes and grimoires, including Karlova's *Basics of Thaumaturgical Vision*. On the shelf stood copies of *Resisting the Unbearable: A Treatise in Morality* by Kamron Andrenikis, and *Kamron Andrenikis: Selected Shorter Works*. As she took in the books, the name Kamron rang in Kata's ears. Andrenikis was a master pamphleteer; he had composed rapid-fire a hundred and more denunciations of the Houses. But he had done more. He had inaugurated the illegal research of thaumaturgy and argued that control of thaumaturgy was key to the Houses' hegemony. Could that be the Kamron who had left the room, the broken old man?

As she pulled a book from the shelf, she heard voices from the central cavern. She stepped closer still to the door and listened.

"How do we know they're not working for the Houses? We're letting in too many. What does that make now, fifteen? I'm telling you, Maximilian, it will endanger us. We'll be riddled with agents." Kata recognized the voice of the redheaded woman.

"It's all right, Giselle," said the young man with curly hair. "You know that if Ejan tests you, then you are truly tested. We'll keep them here for a while. There's plenty of work for them, just like the others."

"All of them?"

"Yes. But in the meantime, look at how we're growing! I'll talk to them now."

Kata slipped the book back in the shelf and sat back in the chair. The curly-haired man, who must be Maximilian, came into the room and sat on the bed pushed up against the wall. The twine on one of his boots was unravelling, a thick wire springing clear of the leather. He examined them, his head cocked sideways with curiosity, as if they were specimens in a laboratory. The lights increased their diameter and glowed a soft red.

"I'm Maximilian." His brown eyes glittered with interest as they introduced themselves. "So, your broadsheets, *The New Tomorrow*, you wrote them yourselves?"

"Yes, the two of us," said Kata.

"You're lucky the Houses haven't taken you away. Their dungeons are filled with the likes of you."

With his shifty eyes Louis looked at Kata and then back at Maximilian. "Dungeons don't frighten us."

"They should," said Maximilian. "They have all kinds of ways of breaking someone there. They have machines designed to inflict the most horrendous injuries. They have potions to induce fear. They have molds and fungus that grow upon you. You should be afraid." The man looked at Kata. "You're apocalyptics."

"The world is coming apart," said Kata. "The Houses have kept the knowledge for themselves. It is hidden up there in the House Complexes, ready to be used. While all the time the great wastes, where Aya and Alerion battled, encroach more and more. All those chemical streams issuing forth like white poisonous mucus. All that red dust that blows like an assassin's powder, burning whatever it touches. We are at the end of an age. Only the knowledge kept in the Houses' libraries will save us. Or else we shall descend into a new dark age when people will eat their young, when nothing will hold together, when the buildings will be razed and the ties between people will dissolve, leaving us nothing but lone atoms in a sea of flux."

The man stared at her. She kicked herself. She had rehearsed the speech, and it had come out as rehearsed.

Maximilian kicked at the unraveling twine of his boot, pressing it close to the leather. "But that is very much modern thinking. The trend of day is to see things as falling apart, to think that we still live in a world of cataclysm. Yet in the long view of history, have things not been rediscovered? Surely we are on the path of development back toward the time of the ancients. Are not our populations growing? Aren't we emerging from that dark age of

which you speak? Isn't this the very basis for the growth of seditionism itself? With each step in our knowledge and our production, are we not better placed to build a better world?"

The philosopher in Kata was now alive. "You are relying on the
illusions of the ancients before the cataclysm. They were wrong.
There is no inexorable progress. Nor are the laws of history on our
side. There is no line of improvement between the knife and the
bolt-thrower, the sword and the incendiary device," she said. "The
Houses control everything. They ruin everything. They kill—"
She stopped and thought of Aemilius, of his long lashes, of his
black eyes. "They—"

"They must be destroyed," said Louis.

"Destruction?" said Maximilian. "We must be purer. We must
be the new people we hope a better world will create. We must avoid
revenge."

"Revenge is for those who have lost their way." Again Kata
thought of Aemilius. She would do the House's bidding. She would
survive. She always had.

Kata and Louis were given the task of researching the Sunken
City. They spent their time in Kamron's old room, which had now
been converted into a small library.

Ukka's *Before the Cataclysm,* considered by many to be one of
most accurate histories, explained that the Library of Caeli-Enas,
as the storage point of all the knowledge of the ancients, was protected by powerful thaumaturgy. It could resist fire, earthquake,
and flood, physical assault and internal decay. Not only was it
capable of complex methods of self-regeneration, but could develop its own innovations in self-preservation. When Kata showed
these passages to Maximilian, he had smiled. "The entire thing is
intact," he excitedly said. "Protected by thaumaturgy. Protected."

Still, mostly the Histories of the Sunken City were fragmentary. Kata wished she could have asked Aemilius; he would have
known much. It was four hundred years since it had sunk, a final,
delayed, consequence of the cataclysm four hundred years before
that. Each History told a different story, and debates were wide-

ranging. How was it that so much knowledge had been lost over the centuries?

Scattered through the books there were fragments about the Great Library of Caeli-Enas. At one point Kata came across a particularly perplexing passage. She stopped and said to Louis. "What do you make of this?"

"If you keep interrupting me, I'll never make it through these books."

Ignoring him, she read the passage. "'The Library at this point felt that it was not in its interests to allow the Gods to deposit their memories in its storage, for it felt that given the war that was occurring, no new knowledge was safe. The Gods claimed that the Library was paranoid, but the Library held firm.'" Kata turned to Louis. "The Library held firm?"

Louis shrugged. "Let's just do what we're told."

"And what are we told?"

"To research the Sunken City!" Louis hissed.

"Oh, I thought we were researching this rebel group."

Louis looked at her alarmed, "Keep quiet! Who knows if they're listening to us? They'll kill us, you know."

Kata laughed at him.

"You're mad," Louis said. "I'm not going to have you risk my life."

"Fine," she said. "Let's hope they haven't heard. Let's hope there won't be any more deaths."

Louis looked at her.

"Fine," she said, "Let's hope that *we're* not the ones to die."

Kata had slowly come to understand that though there was no formal structure to the group, there were a series of unspoken and interlocking power structures. Maximilian sat near the top of a complex set of interrelationships that crisscrossed the group. Josiane, the middle-aged philosopher-assassin who had accompanied Ejan during the interrogation, was Maximilian's constant companion, who always had a chain with a metal weight hanging ominously at her side. Kata wondered with what style Josiane fought. The chain suggested one native to Caeli-Amur, whose philosopher-assassins had developed combat with unusual weaponry: not just chains, but throwing stars, rope darts, fighting fans, and others, many that had been imported and modified. In any case, Josiane was like an attack dog circling around him, on the lookout for threats, or else scurrying off on one errand or another. Maximilian also had a little coterie to whom he taught thaumaturgical knowledge and he spent much of his time with them, or pursuing his own thaumaturgical research. He seemed obsessed with various forms of water magic and transmutation. He studied the biological differences between water-breathng and air-breathing creatures. Fish, he explained to her, his eyes alight with wonder, absorbed oxygen from the water, but Xsanthians were amphibious, able to breathe both water and air.

Meanwhile, the blond-haired man of the North, Ejan, had a group around him, which included the redheaded woman, Giselle. They seemed interested in all kinds of military and logistical research. At the markets, they sold the goods created by the group. A number of newfound seditionists had been given various jobs, including the forging of various weapons in a makeshift smithy. A young man—dark, brooding, surely only in his teens—looked after the terribly burned Omar. Only Kamron Andrenikis wandered around listlessly.

At night the groups mingled and talked, and these occasions sometimes became open discussions about the direction of the group, the number of newcomers they should accept, the strategies and tactics for fighting the Houses.

Sometimes Omar's groans permeated Kata's dreams, which were filled with frothing mouths and bulging eyes. One night she stepped lightly across to Omar. Feverishly, he turned his head from side to side. The skin on the side of his face had been blistered and now was hardened and dead, ready to flake off. What had happened to this man?

He opened his eyes. "Don't let Ejan take control. He's a killer. He's mad."

"What?"

"Panadus! By Panadus! Don't let him take control. Promise me, Max. Promise me. He'll destroy everything. He's cold."

"Hush." Kata placed her hand on his shoulder. "Sleep. Regain your strength."

Kata felt someone squatting next to her. She turned to see Maximilian looking down.

"It makes no sense, the things he says," said Max. "He speaks in riddles and fevered dreams."

"It is a sign of the times," said Kata. "Riddles and fevered dreams for an enigmatic world dreaming of its own future."

"You truly are an apocalyptic," said Maximilian, still looking at the man below. There was tenderness in his eyes that Kata had not seen before. So, thought Kata, this seditionist has a heart, after all. In that moment, she sensed Max's generosity, hidden so often by his dedication. He cared about others, the weak and the damaged. He was motivated by feelings, not just ideas. Feelings were a weakness in this world, but something about that look moved her.

Kata planned to escape at the end of her second week and report to Officiate Autec. Each night, as the others slept, she sneaked along the passageways around the hideout, taking light steps in the darkness. She found her way, her eyes trying desperately to make out the shadows in the dark. Once she was beyond the sight of the central cavern, she lit a lamp. During these expeditions, she felt like a little bubble of light, moving through a vast sea of darkness, occasionally illuminating shadowy forms—angled tables with flat glass squares, chairlike objects that were too heavy to shift—before leaving them behind in the dark.

She passed through the vast room filled with terrifying-looking machines the size of elephants. On the far side stood great black metal doors; she could find no way to open them. She returned to the central cavern and ventured to another passageway. Halfway along a man-sized hole in the wall opened out to a tunnel that looked as if it had been dug by hand. Her body tensed when she came to this, for surely it was the way she had entered. Through there—somewhere—was the way out to the city, to the light. She waited for a long time at the opening to that tunnel, tempted now that she knew the way out. Eventually, she turned back and reentered the central cavern. The following night, she decided, she would explore farther in that direction. She lay down then on her mat and tried to sleep a dreamless sleep. She woke a few hours later, exhausted, with the feeling that something was in her eyes. She rubbed them to try to clear them and looked up to see Josiane watching her like an owl in the night. But Josiane only stood up, looked away, and went about her business.

In the reading room, Kata said to Louis, "I've found the way out."

He looked at her with wild eyes. "If you are caught, we'll both be killed. It's better to wait until we gain their trust."

"And how are we to do that, sitting in here with nothing but books?"

"We do a good job. We wait." Louis nodded to himself, as if the force of his own argument impressed him.

"No. We act. We inform Officiate Autec of the whereabouts. They come in and arrest everyone. We are rewarded. It's simple." Kata pictured the villa in the hills, a vineyard she would tend during the day, or perhaps a place where she might train horses. To be left alone in such a place: that was all she wanted.

"You've seen these people. They're killers: Josiane; that blond-haired man—Ejan. There's something calculating about them."

"There's something calculating about you," said Kata.

"That's why I know."

The door opened and Maximilian entered. Kata tensed. How long had he been at the door? Had he heard them speaking? He stepped in, his eyes watchful and intelligent as ever.

"I've found the best map yet of the Sunken City," said Louis, "Look at this!"

Maximilian's eyes lit up, and he and Kata perused the ancient parchment that Louis held on the table in front of him. Inscribed on the cracked and yellowing paper was a detailed map, showing great boulevards radiating out from a central plaza. Around the area were the great buildings of the city: the Library among them.

"It's a reproduction of an earlier map," said Louis. "But the plan is fairly clear."

"Caeli-Enas," said Maximilian softly. "Caeli-Enas."

That night Kata lay awake in her bed, her little collection of personal items beside her: clothes, bottles of medicine that would last for another month, the small bag she carried with her. All she could hear was the soft breathing of the sleepers. She unwrapped the lantern from her bundle of possessions, slipped from her bed, and silently glided across the floor. She stepped lightly out of the central cavern in the darkness, lit her lamp, and quietly walked along to the tunnel opening. The walls here were carved from the rock. It could have been a mine, or the construction of some digging machine. She moved along the tunnels, counting her steps as she went. Eventually she came to a T-intersection and by instinct turned right. Along the tunnel she passed, counting each pace. Step by step, number by number. She came to another intersection, this one broader, and sloping downward in one direction. Some five hundred paces farther it became a long circular tunnel with smooth sides. A gust of wind touched her face. She walked along the tunnel and stepped out into the warm night where the stars shone white and brilliant. Beneath her the golden lights of the city were spread down to the water, like fires scattered by some god onto the ground. She smelled the sea and the soot from the factory district.

She quickly passed through the city and down to the Technis Complex, where she sat in a room waiting for Officiate Autec to be called. An intendant—one of the petty House officials responsible for handling affairs with the populace—sent a child-messenger scurrying off to fetch the officiate. An hour later, looking at once drawn and possessed with an unnatural and jittery energy, Autec entered the room and led her through the still-busy corridors to his room where he collapsed, rather than sat, into his chair.

"Seditionists are surprising people," she said.

"So are you philosopher-assassins," said the officiate, leaning forward, his eyes squinting. "What are they like, these rebels?"

"They're idealists. I thought they might be self-centered zealots, but no, they really believe in their causes. They're talented, and some of them are hardened, no doubt." Kata explained all that she had learned about the group and its personalities to Autec, who nodded, grim-faced, as she conveyed each piece of information.

When she was done, Autec opened a draw in his desk and pulled out a glass ball about the size of a small melon. He examined it in wonder. "Ancient technology. Incredible really. Press the top of its surface here and it records everything around it. How does it work?" He examined the intricate mechanism visible within the glass, a tiny machine of cogs and wheels. "You won't need to return here for a while, just hide this in a prominent position. I have a second scrying ball of my own, and the two will speak to each other. I will be able to observe the rebels myself."

Kata took the ball in her hands, examining the complex clockwork mechanism inside, as impressive as its complexity was its intricacy: its delicate workmanship, like lacework, marked it immediately as the work of ancients.

"Be discreet with it." Autec took a swig from a flask and grimaced. "Idealists are the most dangerous of people."

Kata returned to the circular entranceway, so much cooler than the air outside, still warmed by the bricks and rocks of the city. Counting her steps she came to the place where the T-intersection should have been. But it wasn't there. She'd counted her steps. She'd made the right turns. But had she made some kind of error? She retraced her steps, right back to the opening, which led out to Caeli-Amur. But she must have forgotten her memorized path, for again the T-intersection was not where it should have been. She started to panic. The light would soon be coming up, the insurgents would be rising, and her identity would be uncovered.

As Kata despairingly placed her head in her hands, she heard the sound of footsteps and listened hard. They seemed to be coming from the rock wall itself. She pressed her head up against the wall, and staggered forward. What had happened? She stepped back and tried again. Losing her balance, she fell through the wall, her lamp making a clattering sound.

From the floor of the tunnel, filled with shame, she stared up at a figure, which stared back at her.

"Giselle," said Kata involuntarily.

"Kata." Giselle stared at her wide-eyed.

"Where are you going? It's still dark."

"Where have you been?" asked Giselle.

There was silence then, but Giselle's eyes accused Kata.

Finally Kata said, "What House do you work for?"

Giselle looked at her in horror. "Marin. You?"

"Technis."

"Then we're enemies."

"We don't have to be. We're both doing the same task. We could be of assistance to each other."

Giselle examined Kata, a roguish smile on her face. "Well, there's no point on carrying the House Wars around all the time, is there? I have only half an hour. But my contact meets me nearby."

Kata nodded, watched Giselle scurry off, and sneaked back into the central cavern and tried to sleep. But her body resisted and her mind raced. Beneath her ratty blankets, in her hands she held the ball that Autec had given her. Exhausted but awake, her eyes roved around the cavern until they fixed on the six black pillars that stood to one side. Horizontal fissures ran across them; perhaps they were vents of some sort. She covered the ground almost silently, and scaled one of the pillars like a cat, ascending to the top in a split second. She pressed the smooth, cold surface of the ball. She dropped to the floor, squatted down and looked around at the sleeping seditionists, lost in their dreams of the future. She slipped across the floor and back to her bed, aware of the scrying ball hidden in the darkness, watching from above. She wondered even now if Autec was looking down upon the group of seditionists, dreaming his own dreams of violence and desolation.

FIFTEEN

Boris placed the scrying ball on his desk and swiveled his hand around its surface. A point of light shimmered inside the ball and the mechanism began to spin, little interlacing cogs whizzing around. The point of light intensified and grew into a blue sphere that quickly filled the ball. The mechanism hummed and the events in the seditionist's hideout were all of a sudden projected into the room. The images came superimposed upon the material world around Boris. He adjusted the focus by running his fingers over its surface as if he were drawing something out of it. The images shrank a little, though still they surrounded him—what a wondrous thing it was. Kata had done well, placing the device somewhere high, where it captured the vista of the base, and yet could be focused on the actions or words of an individual.

Boris watched the curly-haired Maximilian, the idealistic dreamer who thought he would create an army of liberation-thaumaturgists to bolster mass activity of the citizens against the Houses, the way a skeleton holds up a body. The glacial-featured Ejan's plans of military action against the Houses seemed more clearly achievable. Still, there was something about the wild idealism of Maximilian that unsettled Boris. Each of them contained an element of the other's personality: just as Maximilian was conspiratorial, Ejan had an element of the dreamer combined with his hardness.

With the touch of a spinning finger on the sphere, Boris focused the ball on Ejan, who was talking to Giselle near the door to their workshop. Boris had watched Ejan's followers carry all kinds of materials—metal and wood and crates and vials of chemicals—into that workshop.

"It's dangerous," Giselle said to Ejan. She looked around to make sure no one overheard them.

"The question is: which House?" said Ejan.

"House Arbor," said Giselle. "They're like a parasite on the city. At least Technis and Marin are developing new technologies. Arbor is just a decaying corpse strapped to us. And anyway, they're the weakest, the least able to strike back."

"You misunderstand," said Ejan. "The point is to create the greatest symbol. We need to make ourselves into a legend. Our actions must rouse the citizens. We must be the spark that starts the fire."

"The strongest House then," said Giselle. "We start with Technis."

Ejan nodded his head slowly. "But why stop at one House? Why not strike at them all? Then the officiates of Technis won't be the only ones to learn a lesson."

Boris spun his hand over the scrying glass. The image shrank around him, so small now that it almost disappeared inside the ball itself. The officiates of Technis won't be the only ones to learn a lesson, he thought. No, indeed they won't. A plan hatched in his mind. If the Houses united against the seditionists, they could reassert their authority over the city and quell the strikes and disturbances. Then, once this was done, they could return to struggling amongst themselves. Would the Elo-Talern, who for so long had stood aside from the Houses, allow this? A part of Boris wondered if perhaps there the Directors of Marin or Arbor were proposing precisely the same idea to the Elo-Talern. But no, he thought, Arbor was conservative, caught in the old ways, and Marin was an observer whose focus lay across the seas as much as in the city.

Boris left his room for the dry and cold corridors deep in the mountain. No matter how many times he made the journey, he could not accustom himself to it. Each time he thought he would be calmer, but each time the sight of that creature—the unnatural planes of its face, the spidery length of its limbs, the gaunt cadaverous eyes—unnerved him. Each time he found himself stammering, looking down at the floor, hoping to avoid the flashes of the decaying thing that he imagined to be the *real* Elo-Talern, the essence behind the appearance.

She was waiting for him in the throne room, lounging lethargically. In her hand, she held a smoke-filled bottle, from which she inhaled deeply and exhaled a long gray plume. The bottle filled once more with curling smoke.

Boris looked between the pillars to the fog that hovered in the darkness. He tensed his body. "The seditionists are planning a wave of assassinations. There is unrest on the streets: riots, demonstrations, strikes. I think it is time for the Houses to collaborate with each other."

Elo-Drusa stood, placed the bottle on the throne, and stepped slowly across the room. She passed behind one of the pillars and emerged on its other side, her movements jittery. She disappeared completely and then emerged several feet closer as if out of thin air. Boris's legs trembled.

"It can be a lonely life, can't it? It can be so very long." She stepped close to him, her long fingers touching him on the cheek. She produced from her gray and tattered robe some kind of measuring equipment: a long rod with two metal grips at its end. She loosened one of the grips and placed it over his head, cocking her own as she was performing internal calculations. "You have done well, Boris. We haven't had the role of Director since Hausmann was killed in the House Wars ten years ago. And it makes sense for there to be a Director now. I don't want to oversee this world of petty dramas. The position of Director, is that what you want?"

Boris looked down away from her face, which was all too close to him. As it flashed briefly into the deathly corpselike visage, like the shrunken skull of a long-nosed dog or a horse, perhaps, he felt a blast of cold air.

"Keep still!" She turned her measuring rod at a different angle, again measured his head.

Boris held his head motionless. "There is something else that I'd like."

Elo-Drusa pulled back, "Oh there is, is there?"

"You said that I could have anything I wanted." Boris steeled his voice.

In an instant one of her hands was closed around his throat, the long fingers viselike, like thin metal clamps. He reached up and grabbed a chill arm; its fingers tightened slowly.

His body tried to force out a cough, but all he could do was heave, as if he were trying to vomit something up.

She brought her face close to his and bared her lips, her teeth too long for a human skull, her forehead high and alien. Her large eyes, a purplish blue color with flecks of green and set too far apart, looked at him slightly askew, as if she focused on something slightly behind him.

She dropped him to the floor and he collapsed and scuttled across the floor a few feet like a crab.

"Well," she said, "What is it?"

"There is a Siren . . . Paxaea . . . She sings at the Opera."

"The new one."

"I," Boris started. "She." He looked up and eventually settled for, "Her."

"Ah, you search for love, is that it? Or is it simply adoration and power?" The Elo-Talern croaked a horrible laugh and leaned over him like some gigantic stick insect. "Why *her*?"

Boris scanned his thoughts but could find no answer. Eventually he ignored the question altogether. "She has the power of suggestion. I cannot—"

"We will have to silence her then. In the meantime, you may begin to work with the other Houses. What do you plan to do about the seditionists?"

"Arrest them, break them, ruin them."

"Perhaps we have something in common." She took his hand and extended his arm. She ran her fingers along his inner elbow. "Look at your veins. Beautiful." She caressed him with long skeletal fingers.

Back in Boris's office, the pneumatique whizzed through the hole in the wall and stopped above him. He opened the little door and unrolled the paper within it. There printed with black ink was a message: *Pick Paxaea up from the Opera in the evening. She'll wait for you. I think you'll find her amenable to your friendship. You may need this to achieve the silence you so obviously need.* At the bottom of the note was written the command word for Paxaea's torc—*Taritia,* the archipelago in the eastern sea where the Sirens lived —and beneath that was simply printed *Elo-Drusa.* Boris smiled sadly at the black joke: to use the Siren's home as the command word was an act of cruelty by whichever thaumaturgist had fixed the torc.

In the afternoon, Boris racked his mind for what he could do to impress the Siren. What would she want? She was a prisoner, the torc around her neck like a ball and chain. Once he had won her over, convinced her to care for him, he could release her from the torc, set her free. He imagined that future now. They would live in his house, so empty now, and fill it with life. Saidra would happily visit, and she and Paxaea would be like sisters. Boris would have a family again. A family—he rolled the word in his mouth.

Boris took a carriage along Caeli-Amur's boulevards, bypassing the chugging steam-trams. Crowds amassed on the streets in little groups: grime-streaked workers, scarlet-scarved students, street urchins slipping in between them. The cafés and salons had long been the province of philosophy, especially among the philosopher-assassins, but now the debate had spread, and it had moved beyond philosophy, to politics. Politics—it was in the air, it was catching, like some kind of plague.

The carriage came to a stop at a crowded intersection. Boris looked out to see a group of House Arbor militia dragging a man across the street, striking him with batons as a small crowd yelled abuse at them. Force had always been the Houses' way, and it had worked until now. But the crushing of the tramworkers hadn't discouraged anyone. Every day came news of riots and protests. Yesterday someone had set one of Technis's new apartment complexes alight. The day before a mob had run through the Arantine beating whomever they found. At least one Arbor servant had been stripped naked and forced to run from the jeering crowd.

As the carriage jolted again into motion and left the crossroads behind, Boris continued to reflect. It was his role to restore order by a new means. Now was the time to unite Caeli-Amur and show that they were all citizens together—as in the time of the ancients. Yes, the workers and citizens had grievances, and such grievances needed to be heard. The extremists—insurgents, seditionists—would be crushed, cut off like a dead limb. The rest, good people like Mathias and the tramworkers, would be shown that everyone had an interest in order, in peaceful development. In Boris's mind images of a glorious future arose, with him as a benevolent overseer.

When he arrived at the Opera, he noticed a small oily stain on his gray suit. He licked a finger and tried to wash it out, but it was fixed. He pulled his long coat around him to hide it.

He walked as regally as he could into the Opera's great entrance hall. High above the balls of light joyfully danced around the domed roof. One of them dropped down to hover behind him, illuminating everything around him. He looked back at it, and like a frightened bird, it skittishly rose into the air, but as he continued on, it descended again.

A few suited figures hurried across the white marbled space. Behind a long desk a man looked up, buttoned his carmine waistcoat, brushed it with his hands and rushed over to Boris.

"Officiate Autec, Officiate Autec, we've been so looking forward to seeing you." The man's hair was oiled slickly back.

Boris looked at the man silently. There was a tone of respect in the man's voice that Boris liked.

"I'm Intendant Moreau," said the man. "Let me summon Paxaea for you."

"No," said Boris. "Take me to her."

Moreau looked at him, "Yes, of course."

Boris followed the man through the winding labyrinthine passages, past the changing rooms and into an elevator. All the time the globe of light followed Boris until at the elevator he glared at the light as it drifted through the doors. Seeing Boris's annoyance, Moreau waved his arms and raised his voice. "Shoo!" The light nervously darted away back in the direction of the Entrance Hall.

"Sometimes they take a liking to people," said Moreau.

When they emerged from the elevator, they passed along a corridor and came to a door. The intendant knocked. "Paxaea. Officiate Autec is here to see you."

There was no response.

Boris's heart beat rapidly at the thought of her, at the thought of her eyes, large and emerald, at the thought of her voluptuous hips.

The intendant opened the door. "Why don't you enter, Officiate Autec?"

Boris walked into the room and was immediately struck by the deep solar hues—burgundy, vermillion and cerise—so common in the east. A sheet of deep crimson fabric with small glittering mirrors embroidered into it was suspended from the roof like a tent. Two stained glass lanterns hung in opposite corners, while a large four-poster bed complete with curtains and roof sat squarely in the middle of the room. Incense burned an exotic sweetness, and there she stood, Paxaea, her back turned to him. Surveying the city through a barred window, she wore the dress that shifted subtly around her like an animal, grouping together at her back, then spreading out and thinning again. In that moment Boris felt that he was somehow broken before the Siren, and that only she could fix him. He yearned for a closeness he had not felt since the death of his wife. He imagined himself pressing against this magnificent creature, the curves of her breasts, her thighs, soft against him. He imagined her pressing against him, the two of them whispering to each other in the soft light.

"Paxaea," he said.

She didn't respond.

"Paxaea, I've come." He waited for what seemed a vast stretch of time.

Eventually she turned and her huge eyes were a brilliant jade, beautiful and cold, like gems newly uncovered in the dark recesses of a mine. "Officiate Autec, I've been expecting you." Then, her tone dropped half an octave and reverberated deeply as she used her second voice. "How kind of you to come."

The sound unnerved him; a thousand needles pricked his skin. Again he was excitedly repelled by the disproportion of her face and body. Her too-large jaw intimated a reptile, and the smoothness of her olive skin suggested a ceramic statue. A shiver ran into his stomach—a clutch of fear and desire.

SIXTEEN

Boris led Paxaea through the passages of the Opera and into the square. He opened the carriage door for her and they sat opposite each other in plush cushioned seats. The wheels rattled over the cobblestones as the carriage headed south up along the cliffs, not far from House Arbor's plant covered palace. They passed through the city's southern gates. The houses continued on past the city's high stone walls, like froth bubbling from a bowl. It was darker out here; the gas lamps that lit the outlying areas shone weakly in the darkness. The air was warm and still.

"Where are we going?" asked Paxaea distractedly. She had a strange impassive air around her, as if she looked down on everything from a distant height. As when they had first met, she spoke only with one voice, the second a soft reverberation below it.

"It's a surprise," said Boris.

She didn't react.

"What's it like, the Taritian Archipelago?" he asked.

The features of her face were still, as if she were carved from porcelain.

"I want to know about you," said Boris. "I want to understand you."

She looked away from him, through the window and into the darkness. "*This* is all you need to know about me." She pointed to the torc around her neck.

She was newly captured. She had not yet been broken by servitude—a good thing. Boris racked his mind. How could he penetrate this defense of hers, while she was still defiant? "I hear the islands are beautiful, that there are rock pools of aquamarine water, in which orange and red fish swim with little blue octopi.

I hear that the reefs around the islands are littered with ships filled with treasures."

She smiled sadly. "They're filled with the corpses of dead sailors. The dead lay everywhere, don't they?"

He reached out and touched her hand but it was cold and lifeless. "I'm so glad we have a chance to talk."

"Isn't it something?" said Paxaea obliquely.

"I could take the torc off, you know," said Boris.

She looked at him. There was something carnivorous in her eyes; her inner eyelid twitched forward and retreated again. "But you won't. You'd be too scared of me."

"I'd like to trust you," said Boris. "I hope we can reach that stage in our friendship." The word *friend* echoed jarringly in his ears.

When they arrived at the gardens, south of Caeli-Amur, overseen by House Arbor, they passed through a great cast-iron gate imprinted with images of the god Demidae, crying alone in her boat on a great flat ocean. Like the water palaces and the Opera, the gardens were neutral zones; even during the most vicious House Wars they were safe for House agents to frequent.

In any case, Boris had armed himself with a knife, which he kept hidden beneath his suit, and employed a philosopher-assassin, called Tonio, to protect him. Now Tonio, a short, stocky man, with hair shaved close, was driving the carriage. There was something thuggish and menacing about his wrestler's gait. Tonio was an advocate of Cynicism, a philosophy descended from Ioga, who was called "The Weeping Philosopher." Ioga's most famous work, *Considerations on Pessimism,* argued through a series of dialogues that failure was the defining factor in History. The cataclysm, Ioga claimed, was the crucial pedagogic event, teaching everything one needed to know about the nature of humanity. Boris hoped that Tonio's study of failure didn't extend too much to his own career.

Shadows sat brooding beneath the garden's trees. White marble statues towered in the moonlight. The park was magnificently crafted. The trees, each placed in exactly the right position, were sculpted just so. Their branches reached over the canals and paths like the arms of gentle giants. Fountains and small waterfalls fed into the canals, while small walls crisscrossed the gardens, disappearing into the shadows. Statues of the gods and heroes towered over the park from little constructed hills, said to be ancient burial mounds. Some said the statues moved around at night, acting out in some crazed game of charades the last dreams and desires of those buried beneath.

Eventually, the carriage came to a halt in front of one of the larger canals where a finely constructed gondola stood with a small table set in it. A blue-uniformed boatman with a long oar stood in the rear of the gondola.

Dressed in black, looking all the more for it like a small gorilla, Tonio opened the door for them and they stepped over a small gangplank onto the gondola.

"Dinner," said Boris self-evidently.

The boatman rowed them off and they passed softly over the water. They passed under small bridges, which spanned the canals that traversed the park. Compared with Caeli-Amur, the park had an eerie serenity, which disturbed Boris. So used to factories and smoke, he found the brooding trees and the sweet scent of pollen to be alien. Rumors had been circulating that ghosts lurked in these parks, just as they haunted Caeli-Amur's Ancient Forum. These specters had been prophesying doom from the dark shadows of the trees or the burial mounds. Despite these stories, or perhaps because of them, the park was a favorite of the ladies of Caeli-Amur. Perhaps they desired a thrill that was otherwise so often denied them.

"Won't you say something?" Boris's voice tightened as he spoke.

"You think this impresses me?"

"I'm not trying to buy your affection. I'm trying to create an, I'm trying to, you know what I mean."

"Look at *you* and look at *me*," she said derisively.

Boris took his flask out from his suit then, unscrewed the lid, and took a swig in front of her. Hot-wine burned his lips, the way he liked it. His voice was more strident now. "You're just a scared lost thing; you're a captured thing. There's no way out for you. I'm your only hope."

She curled her beautiful lip in scorn. "That's what it always comes down to, doesn't it? It always comes down to power, or lack of it. But you can't control everything, you know. Things slip away; things refuse to be controlled."

He looked at her frostily. "You would know, if anyone did."

They sat in silence then, and Boris felt the hot-wine creep up on him. The boat floated between a knot of densely clustered burial mounds, on which a group of statues stood imperiously. Sculpted in the image of long-dead heroes, they seemed to look down upon him from a different, more powerful age. He fancied that there was movement above, but when he fixed his eyes on the statues, there was nothing.

Eventually he said, "Each of us is surrounded by shadows of our own making. And you can never escape your own shadow, can you?"

She brushed the hair from her face. Her lip was no longer curled. She spoke softly, but both voices spoke in unison, warm and powerful. "You aren't like the others. They're only interested in sating their lust," she said. "They're full of anger and desire. But you: you are sad somehow. I can see it. I can feel it."

Boris looked away, his face troubled.

"There was someone," she said.

"I would never treat you like that," he said. "I would never use you for my animal desires. What can I do?" he said.

"Nothing," she said. "Things are just the way they are."

Boris could not think of a response, though he searched for one. Eventually he settled for, "We can change things, perhaps, if you trust me."

But Paxaea simply stared at the lake onto which the boatman was now rowing them. Not long after, he turned them around and took them back to the carriage.

When they returned to the city, the beauty of the park long behind them, he walked her back to her room in the Opera. As Paxaea entered the room, she left the door swinging open. Boris stood at the door awkwardly.

She sat on the bed and looked back at him. "Close the door."

Boris closed it behind him and followed her to her bed, hidden by cushions covered with delicate lacework and with mirrors sewn into the fabric. Warm and inviting, it was the kind of bed that one yearned to sink into.

Mechanically Paxaea reached up, unbuttoned Boris's coat. He felt the urge for her then, and reached out and touched her face, the skin so smooth and soft. He pushed her down onto the bed and she didn't resist. Her eyes, large and magnificent, like those of a god, stared out disinterestedly. In some way he was afraid of them, now that he was so close. He looked down at the full lips.

He froze. "Not like this."

"What?"

"No," he said to himself. "No . . ."

Boris looked away from her and his eyes lost their focus. He looked out into the distance, into a world that no longer existed. Images of his long-dead wife, Remmie, came to him, of how they had first met, circling each other in the factory district, quick glances taken and noticed, neither of them with the courage to speak to the other, until finally one day he turned a corner on the way home from the Tram Factory and she was there, standing outside the mill, her eyes alight beneath the dirt smudged across her face.

As he thought of Remmie, he became aware of a soft sound beneath him. He looked down to see Paxaea with hands over her face. As she cried, her voice keened in two tones at once: a low hum and a high wail.

Boris turned from her and let himself out of the room quietly. As he passed along the Opera corridors he took another swig of hot-wine.

Instead of home, Boris returned to his office, where he touched the scrying ball. An image of the seditionist's hideout superimposed itself onto his room. He watched as the shapes moved around, congregated in little discussion groups. He was now filled with hatred for those subversives. They were dreamers and he would smash their dreams.

Their discussions slowly diminished to whispers in the night until they were quiet. But in the background Boris could see two of them coupling quietly; in the darkness it looked like one dark creature changing shape, struggling to transform itself. Eventually that, too, finished and Boris stared alone into the dark.

SEVENTEEN

At the evening meeting the debate raged, seditionists standing and yelling over one another. Maximilian ran his hands through his curly hair and looked on in frustration. With each day the tensions had grown until now members of the group yelled recriminations at one another. The influx of new agitators had increased these tensions, the newcomers knowing little about the history of the group or the competing philosophies.

"A major demonstration on Aya's Day!" yelled Maximilian over the ruckus, which quieted. Five weeks away, Aya's Day was a traditional day of festivities, when pranks were not only ubiquitous but encouraged among the citizens. Children fooled their parents, workers played jokes on their employers. It was a day when citizens thumbed their noses at authority. Even the Houses were fair game. But this would be a thumbing of noses of unsuspected seriousness.

"Demonstrations?" said Ejan, standing on the other side of the braziers. "We already know how those are dealt with: The House thaumaturgists strike against any public demonstration."

Maximilian seized the momentary quiet to speak. "If it is large enough, if we build enough momentum, if we have some defenses against them, then people will come out. There have been strikes already. They are yearning for common action. Of course, we must seek the Collegia's support."

A young woman called Aceline, whose short-cropped black hair and bone-white skin made her look like a child, stepped forward, "We could publicize it in the broadsheet, make posters, graffiti the walls." She was one of the leaders of the recently joined *A Call to Arms* group, a collection of seditionist-artists who had brought their printing press, replacing the old and constantly breaking machine that had been used to print up Kamron's pamphlets. Now there were daily debates about what should be written, who should control its content. Their own policy had been to create and distribute seditionist art. In their minds, this art—avant-gardist poems, symbolist posters produced by lithograph—would help people to see their place in the House system anew and reflect upon its oppressive nature. Their paper was filled with vorticist and cubist images of machinelike forms bursting through into a changed future. Aceline herself was a woman whose appearance belied her erudition. Beneath her calmly and patient words lay a deep thinker.

Ejan responded resolutely: "Joining forces with the Collegia will only compromise us. They're little better than criminal networks. Better if we could strike against the Houses physically. Build an army, a trained force, capable of fighting the Houses. Strike and then melt away before they can respond. It's time to jam their levers. To show them that we won't let their machine operate. We will become myths, legends, symbols that rouse the people." In recent weeks, Ejan had built his group into a closed unit: tight, disciplined, ruthless.

Kamron stepped forward from the darkness from where he had been observing events. He spoke for the first time since he had been deposed and the Veterans had lost their authority. "Without a way of neutralizing the Houses' thaumaturgists, we'll never achieve anything. And even if we did, what would Varenis do? The Directorate of Varenis would not allow a free Caeli-Amur. No, they would march from the north with their legions. Even worse, what if we roused the Sortileges? Who among us would face a Sortilege?"

There was silence as the seditionists weighed his words. The Sortileges—the most powerful thaumaturgists in the world, sitting up in the twelve towers of Varenis.

"Varenis will leave us alone and the Sortileges—who has even seen them?" said Maximilian. "Caeli-Amur has always been its own city-state. You are doing nothing but holding us back."

Several jeers were directed toward the old seditionist. Weariness of Kamron's timidity had turned to antagonism. No longer was he a revered figure, but rather a somewhat pathetic old man. Max was sad to see Kamron's fall, and surprised at the speed with which the group marginalized their former leader. Kamron still deserved some respect, and yet, Max, too, found the old man's arguments vexatious.

Ejan interjected. "It's time for you to liberate yourself, Kamron, from the oppressive duty of taking action. It's time for you to leave."

There were a few cheers. Others remained silent. Kamron looked on fearfully. Was the old man being banished?

"All those who think Kamron should be exiled from the group?" Ejan's voice rang out, strong and metallic.

As Maximilian saw a sea of hands raised, he refrained from raising his own. In his view, Kamron was only holding the group back. Banishing him would help the group to carry out its activities. Kamron was nothing but a ball chained to their legs. Covered once more by a blanket of guilt, Max raised his hand and pursed his lips. The vast majority had raised their hands. When Ejan called for those opposed to the banishment, even the Veterans failed to raise their hands. They had been cowed into submission. Something had broken in the seditionist group, and now it was like a wild horse, galloping on its own course. A wave of concern rose in Maximilian's chest. He would have to try to rein it in and guide it.

Maximilian called out: "Ejan can make weapons for defense. I shall search for the thaumaturgical power to defend us. And meanwhile, we plan a demonstration on Aya's Day. We arrange a meeting with the Collegia to convince them to take part. It will be our first show of strength, the first of a wave of demonstrations. It will not change the House system by itself. But what a change it would be, to stand freely in the streets and squares. What a challenge it would be. Of course there are risks. Of course we will be scared standing out in the open when for so long we've been hiding away. But we will also be exhilarated. The citizens themselves will be emboldened. But before this time, there shall be *no* preemptive strikes against the Houses. After Aya's Day, the landscape will have changed."

There was an uneasy quiet. Ejan sneered.

"All those in favor of the path I propose?" Maximilian demanded.

A sea of hands was raised again. The seditionists were not yet ready to risk Ejan's plan of violent action.

Ejan turned on his heel and stormed away. He was not the sort to take kindly to being outmaneuvered. Though Ejan possessed a discipline that Maximilian envied, Ejan was the sort to pursue his own fate, just as he had when he struck his chieftain father, riding off into the wilderness and leaving behind everyone he knew.

Later, Kamron trudged alone to the exit from the Communal Cavern, a figure warped and bent by thaumaturgy and defeat. The remaining Veterans were too attached to their place in the group; they cleaved to it like children afraid to be left alone. As for Kamron, he would not betray the group to the Houses. The old man didn't have it in him.

As Kamron reached the doorway, he stopped and looked back to where Maximilian stood, not far away. "Mark my words," he said, "this group will be ruined before your very eyes. If it's not already infiltrated by the Houses, it soon will be." He turned and shuffled away.

Maximilian watched him go. He threw off the blanket of guilt. The cause—that was the ultimate law. Individual attachments had to be sacrificed for the good of the cause. He thought of Nkando and all the Nkandos of the world. He acted *for them*. Sometimes small evils needed to be performed for a greater good. Even as he thought these things, the guilt fell onto him once more. This time he could not throw it off.

The following day, Maximilian and Kata left the hideout to visit the Xsanthians. They could swim hundreds of fathoms beneath the waters without drawing a breath. He would convince the fish-men to help him reach the Sunken City. As he and Kata stepped out into the brilliant light, he squinted and turned his head away from the glaring sun. Sometimes, in recent weeks, humid summer clouds had rolled over the city, only to move on again without unloading themselves. On the street, Max and Kata heard citizens: "This summer—when will it rain?" or "You could fry eggs in this sun!"

Max was impressed with Kata, who had studied Caeli-Enas and possessed a steely intelligence and a determination to bolster her knowledge. He wasn't sure if she dreamed of a city of pure community, as he did, but she was the kind of recruit they needed: the sort who would break barriers, the sort that would not be deterred by failure, who was emotionally unattached, and so unlikely to have conflicting loyalties. He sensed that they had much in common.

They passed through Market Square to the stairs, where the puppet-seller played out the story of Domina and Cassia, a pantomime of violence between two sisters. The story was well known to Caeli-Amur's people. Living always in harmony, the two sisters had shared everything in their lives. But when Dominia had been given an opulent gift by a suitor, she had initially concealed it, and she agonized about how to tell her sister. When Cassia discovered the gift her envy broke into violence. The puppets jiggled and struck out at each other clumsily.

"There," the puppeteer said, Cassia lashing her sister. "That's for your betrayal." Dominia struck back. "That's for your lack of trust." A group of children sat around the puppeteer laughing and clapping their hands.

As they reached the piers, great lines of Xsanthians were unloading goods from one of Marin's new class of steamer. Unlike the majority of great hulking ships, these new boats combined the sleekness of Marin's fleet of cutters, with the new steam technology. Instead of great wheels attached to the sides of the boat, these had a single powerful one at the rear.

Halfway along the pier a Xsanthian sat desolately, one of its scaled arms wrapped in a seaweed poultice. Beyond it, before the streamlined steamer, a group of blue uniformed Marin guards joked, long tridents in their hands.

Warily, Max and Kata approached the Xsanthian. "Santhor?" asked Max.

The Xsanthian looked up, "On the boat. They're having trouble with the leviathan."

As one of the Xsanthians stepped from the gangplank, he dropped one of the small caskets he was carrying. The lid broke open and a branch of a water-crystal spilled onto the pier. As it struck the wood, the crystal broke and in an instant its brilliant orange and yellow faded to a dead gray. Like bloodstone, the crystals had powerful thaumaturgical properties, but unlike bloodstone, which was inanimate, the crystals lived and grew. Once cut from their seabeds, the slightest disturbance would kill them and rob them of their powers. Max sighed as he saw the power die out in the crystal.

One of the guards stepped forward and struck the Xsanthian with a trident. "You fool! The thaumaturgists are unhappy enough without you destroying the crystals."

The Xsanthian fell to its knees and the rest of the guards took to beating it. The Xsanthian collapsed onto the pier, great webbed hands wrapped protectively around its enormous fish head.

Max and Kata took this opportunity to slip onto the ship and seconds later they descended into the hold, where what they saw stopped them in their tracks.

In a pool in the center of the hold thrashed a half-submerged creature. Its gray slippery body seemed circular, with many tentacles: some were thick and powerful and used for swimming; others were long and thin with stingers at their tips. Beneath the net that restrained it, a hundred and more disturbing plate-shaped eyes whirled and turned, each one independent, each one filled with a baleful intelligence. Max backed away a step and heard Kata beside him give out a little groan of horror. A long thin tentacle, with a leaflike cluster of horrific-looking burgundy nodules at its tip, had broken through the net. It whipped though the air and struck one of several Xsanthians scampering around the pool and attempting to subdue the creature with a second net. The Xsanthian staggered toward Max and Kata as the tentacle whipped around dangerously. Over its shoulder a red welt had risen. It looked up at Max and Kata as it fell to its knees. A gurgle came from its throat as two other Xsanthians seized their injured colleague and pulled him up onto the deck. As they passed, Max could hear the Xsanthian's ragged and struggling breath.

One of the thing's eyes fixed on Max and he was rooted to the spot. The eye pierced him with malevolent intelligence and he felt that he was looking into a dark abyss. In unison, the hundred other eyes fixed on him, and Max felt something give way in his mind. The leviathan faded out of existence and beneath the net lay a pretty Numerian girl, helpless in the grip of the nets. Max was filled with sympathy for the girl; he thought of Nkando; they must free her. Briefly he looked around for a blade to cut the net away, but stopped himself.

"Beware its illusions," said Santhor, who stood nearby, directing the other Xsanthians. "It will confuse you with its tricks."

Max shook his head and the creature emerged once more from beneath the disappearing image of the girl. Four Xsanthians threw a second net over the tentacle and, rushing around the pool, pulled it close to the creature's body. The creature collapsed into the water as the net pinned it. A second later it again thrashed powerfully against its constraint, then once more seemed to be subdued.

Santhor said, "Another exotic creature for the pools in the Marin Palace."

Maximilian said, "What use could they possible have for it?"

Santhor shrugged, "Their palace is filled with waterways, pools and canals, aquariums. All of them are filled with sea creatures. It's said that Marin throw their enemies into the water with the most dangerous beasts."

Max ran a hand through his curly hair, felt a knot, left it alone. He straightened himself and said, "Santhor, we need somehow to journey to the Sunken City. There lies the Great Library of Caeli-Enas, where we can discover thaumaturgy to unlock your torcs, which can combat the Houses. Vast stores of knowledge. Vast reservoirs of power. Secrets which will liberate us all. Could you perhaps suggest a way?"

"Swim?"

"Could you take us?"

"Even if you could breathe water, *we cannot take you*. We will

not disturb the dead who lie in that city's embrace." The Xsanthians had a strange communal culture in which the whole was more
important than any individual part. Thus when they swam together, they moved in unison, as if they were one great organism.
Sometimes Max sensed that they almost *thought* in unison.

Some said that when Marin captured the Xsanthians a decade
earlier they had used thaumaturgical nets. Once the thaumaturgists had captured a few, the rest came drifting into the nets as
passive victims, drawn by their collective bond to the others.

In an extension of this collective impulse, Xsanthians believed
that their past generations were as one with the living, that they
still lived among them, watching, participating.

A Xsanthian turned a nearby lever and the pool was lifted up
out of the floor. Through the translucent sides, Max could see
great coils of tentacles, some covered with thousands of little suck-
ers, others like long thin whips. Some of the eyes roved, others
fixed on Max.

Max's entire body tensed. He tried to focus on the Xsanthian.
"Life is for the living—all the rest is just superstition. In the city
lie all the secrets of the old world, the secrets of thaumaturgy. If
we can discover them, we can liberate ourselves. We can unlock
those collars that trap you. I promise it."

"There is more to the world than power and knowledge. There
is spirit."

"That's just fancy. We live in the here and now," Maximilian
said.

"When you start abandoning your beliefs, where will that lead
you? What will you stand for, in the end? Caeli-Enas is sacred."

Maximilian looked at the shadows moving away underneath
the docks. "Such thinking will be the ruin of us."

As he and Kata stepped back onto the deck, the Xsanthian who
had been struck by the leviathan lay unconscious and shuddering.
Two others crouched over it; another held its head helplessly.

Leaving them, Max and Kata sneaked back onto the pier as the
Marin Guards directed a great crane to lift the pool, complete with
its trapped leviathan, from the steamer. The first injured Xsanthian
continued to sit on the pier, holding the seaweed poultice to his

arm. He glanced at them as they passed and looked away miserably.

In the Market Square, the puppeteer was gone. They turned and watched the pool swinging in the air above the steamer. Elsewhere the piers were bustling with blocky steamers, great wheels running along their sides and lean, graceful cutters, distinguished not only by their smooth lines but by the intricate patterns of ropes running between mast and boom or the deck. Beyond them the sea glittered with a thousand sheets of sunlight.

"Even if we could take one of those out over Caeli-Enas, what good would it do? How does one descend to the ocean floor?" said Maximilian.

"Sea serpent?" said Kata.

"Ha! That's a myth. Kaeori never rode a sea serpent. Thaumaturgy—that is what we seek. And that is the very thing we need in order to find it." The gentle salty wind caressed Maximilian's face in little gusts. A thousand and more crests of waves danced on the sea.

"Aya flew the skies and burrowed beneath the earth, Kaeori rode a sea serpent—and why not? All things are possible." Kata touched him on the arm and he tensed. Kata withdrew her hand. An uncomfortable silence hovered between them until he said, "Let's go."

The Market Square was quieter than usual beneath the oppressive summer sun. The stalls were spaced far apart. A group of exotic animals were gathered in one corner: two chained panthers pressed themselves to the ground in fear; cages of monkeys chattered and bared their teeths at each other; a melancholy elephant stood alone. Numerian guards leaned against long spears. In the center of the square was a pile of wonderful furs from the north, their thick grays and browns incongruous in the Caeli-Amur summer. Close to the piers, a small group of black-suited thaumaturgists stood darkly around several small crates marked VARENIS. Perhaps they contained bloodstone, mined from the prison camps in the mountains. Max eyed them jealously.

Just as he and Kata were about to reach the nearby Via Attica, which ran to the south of the Opera, a foul smell drifted toward Max, caught in his nose, and seemed to fix itself there. Turning, he noticed the bone-thin Anlusian he knew as Quadi, sitting on a stool. The New-Man puffed on a cigarette from which drifted a terrible stench and examined a chessboard. His opponent was an extraordinarily large man whose body seemed so soft that it could have been a big bag of liquid with a head. Together they looked incongruous, like actors in another pantomime, the skinny man and the huge fat one. Beside the New-Man were crates filled with bottles of liquid—Anlusian hot-wine. The New-Men had been arriving in Caeli-Amur the last fifty years, first a couple of explorers, then little groups of them, and then a constant stream, usually strange exiles from their country. Some said they were building a train through the mountains toward the city.

"Do you play chess?" Max asked Kata.

"Of course."

Max had already seen this New-Man with his marvelous diving equipment in the Xsanthians' compound. Anlusians were known for their technological prowess. Here then was someone who might help him reach Caeli-Enas by technological means.

When they approached, Max saw that Quadi was not far from victory.

The huge man pushed a pawn forward with a finger. Max groaned quietly.

"What?" said the man.

"Nothing."

The New-Man glanced up at Max, amused. "We have here a player?"

Max smiled down at him. "I wouldn't be letting your elephants rampage over the board they way they have."

The fat man studied the board, shifted himself as if he was in discomfort and with a grunt knocked over his king. "I resign. It's just delaying the inevitable. Anyway, it's too hot and I've breathed enough of that malodorous smoke of yours, Quadi. May as well play in the sewers. I'm going to the baths."

Quadi took the florens that sat in the bowl by the side of the board and slipped them into a small box on his belt. The box whirred and clunked as it performed some hidden action. "Would either of you like to challenge?"

"I won't pay," said Max.

The Anlusian brushed away dust that had settled on his stacks of wine with his skeletal hand. "This dust, it's everywhere. When's it going to rain?" He turned back to Max. "So, a gentleman's game then, to pass the time."

Max sat and they set up the pieces as Kata perched herself on the side of the crate. "Don't think your elephants will have such an easy time of it."

Not ten minutes later Quadi's elephants were rampaging along the wings of the board.

"What was it you said?" The New-Man smiled weakly. His eyes were drawn, as if he hadn't slept for days.

"It's still early in the game," said Max confidently. He shifted a minotaur to the center of the board, a key strategic position. "Do you judge a painter by a half-finished picture?"

"What is your name, stranger?" Quadi asked.

Max hesitated.

The New-Man smiled again and looked at Kata squatted beside them. "You don't have to tell me. Did our friends the Xsanthians give you what you needed?"

"Who ever gets what they desire?" said Max.

They fell into silence then and concentrated on the game: the subtle shifts of position and strength, the dramatic moves, the damaging exchanges. At first Quadi had the upper hand. Later Max struck back.

"You are too aggressive, too arrogant." Quadi captured a poorly defended war tower and threatened one of Max's Tritons.

"You think you have me in a gambit now?"

"We are all caught in gambits," said Quadi.

Max examined the New-Man with his skeletal features, his gaunt tired eyes, and wondered what endgame he was relentlessly heading toward. "Do you know that beneath the sea, not far from here, lies Caeli-Amur's sister city, Caeli-Enis."

"So I have heard."

"They say it is filled with wonders: instruments of the ancients; machines and contraptions long lost."

Quadi looked up at Maximilian with interest.

"Wouldn't it be something to discover that technology? To ex plore that lost ancient world?" said Maximilian.

Quadi said nothing, but instead made an absentminded move of one of his legionnaires.

Maximilian struck with a minotaur, unhinging Quadi's defense. "Do you think it would be possible to construct a machine which would allow a man to walk beneath the water? To breathe beneath the water?"

Quadi moved an elephant along his back row, aligning it with the center to try to stabilize that part of the board, but it was no use, his lines were broken. For the New-Man the game would now be a series of moves simply averting the inevitable defeat. "Beneath the water? A breathing apparatus? Why not?"

Max felt the rush of excitement. Impulsively, he said, "Because we need someone who understands such technology, we need someone to help us construct such a suit. We need you."

Quadi moved a piece on the board without looking at it. "Check."

"What?" Maximilian looked down at the board with alarm. He cursed himself. He had become too involved in the discussion, too satisfied with luring Quadi into the seditionists. Suddenly he saw an entirely new pattern in the game he had missed, and now he knew that *he* would be the one delaying the inevitable defeat. "You . . ."

Quadi smiled, "Now, what was it you were saying about technology? I was a bit distracted."

Maximilian knocked over the piece that represented Aya and laughed furiously at himself. "You treacherous—"

Quadi looked up at him. "Wouldn't it be really something to find what lies beneath the waters? We should try, don't you think?"

Max explained to the New-Man the utter secrecy of the task and the nature of the seditionist group. The New-Man would need to submit himself to the demands of the group, if he was to help them.

"I do not care for politics," said Quadi. "But this venture excites me. I accept."

EIGHTEEN

Quadi picked up his few possessions from a boardinghouse over-flowing with refugees: Numerians lying in fevers; wastelanders with horribly changed features, their faces rearranged so that their eyes seemed to be slipping down their cheeks, extra limbs sprouting from their other limbs like cancerous trees; petty criminals or agents of the Collegia, shadowy men who crept along the corridors and refused to make eye contact. As Quadi packed a pouch of stinking weed—even unlit the smell wafted odiously—into his bag, Maximilian bit his tongue. They all had to make sacrifices, he supposed.

Together they returned to the seditionist base. Shortly before they reached the tunnel that led underground, they blindfolded Quadi. Kata leading him by the hand, Maximilian in front.

In the days that followed, Maximilian worked with Quadi in a makeshift workshop they constructed in the machine room. Quadi had brought bulky new-technology drills and clamps, sharp metal saws and mechanical nail-guns, his driving contraption with its propeller and engine. Maximilian was captivated by these machines, which steamed and heated and grumbled and rattled. To the collection he added his own looking glasses and measuring equipment, ointments to stop the helmet from rusting, carefully prepared binding spells (complete with symbols, equations, and the usual incantations) for the screws and bolts.

Together they debated the possible solutions. The problem, of course, was air. "Provide the air, and I'll provide you with the cart." Quadi sat on the floor and looked over the rows of machines in the darkness. Max could see the New-Man's curiosity at these ancient technologies.

Maximilian suggested a great, long tube that would reach all the way to the sea surface. Great bellows or perhaps a pump could push the air down to the suit-wearer. But Quadi objected that the sea floor would most likely be too deep. It would be too difficult to pump the air down all that way.

In the meantime, they prepared a suit and the cart's frame, in the hope that they would find a solution to the problem of air in due course.

So Max and Quadi and Kata spent the mornings together, cutting the suit, welding the helmet, placing carriage wheels on the air-cart. Sometimes the others, particularly Oewen and Ariana, helped. The others Max instructed to continue to study thaumaturgy and they were relieved to avoid the ubiquitous smoke of Quadi's weed.

Quadi was animated, his movements quick and precise; he seemed to gain strength from the work. During these times Maximilian came to know Quadi's sharp humor and strange vitality. He came to admire him, yet sometimes in the afternoon Quadi would be overcome with heavy eyes and a lethargy that would overwhelm him. For hours he would sit alone.

"Do you ever eat?" Maximilian asked him once.

"It takes a long time to kill a New-Man, and longer a New-Woman. Anyway, what's the point? After this I intend to get back to dying."

"But why?"

"Have you been to Ariki-Aki, so full of vitality and savagery? Have you seen the relentless self-cannibalization of that world? The endless growth? I could no longer bear it." Quadi deftly rolled one of his cigarettes, plucked the weed, which poked from the ends, lit a match.

"There are other ways to escape that."

"Not for an Ariki-Akian." Quadi took a deep drag, blew out a plume of smoke.

"What is that stuff?" Max grimaced.

Quadi grinned and his face was full of life. "Would you like to try some?"

Max grimaced. If only he could force Quadi to eat, or prepare some kind of invocation or conjuring that would keep the New-Man alive against his will. Maximilian stopped and thought: thaumaturgy to keep things alive. An image flashed in his mind: gills siphoning air from the water. Could that be the solution to the problem of oxygen?

Maximilian buried himself in the thaumaturgical tomes, reading restlessly. He found the sections of the tomes that dealt with suspended animation. The task was a combination of zoological thaumaturgy and transmutae. Death was not only a complex matter, but a fundamental one, built into the universe's deep structures. Death made sense of life. Life possible only with death. As Alyx argued, for example, in *A Study of Transformational and Evolutionary Thaumaturgy*, the consequences of suspending or allaying death were grievous, costly, and dangerous. Of course, it was more easily achieved with simple organisms than complex ones. Averting death, then, cost life. One might make a sacrifice of one creature to regenerate another. The cost of reanimating a hundred gills would be the life of a small animal: a sheep, a large dog, a goat, a child. But there was one path that avoided this trade. Maximilian could use the group's small supply of bloodstone. Not even Kamron had seen fit to use it, so valuable and dangerous was it. Indeed, Kamron had acquired the stone from a former prisoner in Varenis, who had worked in the mining camps and had, for some unknown bureaucratic reason been pardoned. But his release had come too late, and the bloodstone disease had already started to take him. He had passed the bloodstone on to Kamron and said, "Use this to free the prisoners in the mines, I beg you. You should see how the work and the disease ruin them. Help them!"

Instead, Kamron had brought the bloodstone south with him, to Caeli-Amur, and it was now in Max's hands.

Maximilian studied theorems relating to chymistry, transmutae, and zoologism until he knew their basic relationships. The difficulty would be in combining them, for they were different disciplines and relied upon different laws. This was, of course, the most difficult of thaumaturgical tasks: three different worldviews, three different disciplines, three different trances. Not for nothing did thaumaturgists focus on only one discipline. Should Maximilian fail to intertwine the equations properly, seamlessly moving from one to another, the consequences would be dire. Even one mistake in the equations, one error in their application, and the thaumaturgist might end up sacrificing himself. Maximilian weighed the options. It was a risk he was prepared to take.

Still, he needed the formula to interrelate three disciplines. For that he needed his intellectual friend Odile. She would be able to acquire it at a price from her friends among the thaumaturgical students at the university. Max wrote her a letter and passed it to a street urchin he sometimes employed for such tasks. She sent back a note: They would meet at their regular café, La Tazia, as soon as she possessed the formula.

Preparations for Aya's Day continued apace. The *Call to Arms* group, led by the childlike and bone-white Aceline, printed leaflets, undertook nightly graffiti runs, sent out agitators into the city. Maximilian directed his followers, if they did not wish to or help build the cart or continue their study of thaumaturgy alone, to join with them. The results were immediately apparent. The idea spread through the city in whispers, philosopher-assassins debated it in the cafés. Most obviously, more and more citizens joined the seditionists. Ejan's brutal tests had long been discarded and now he conducted them quickly with Aceline, whose artistic temperament allowed a quick and intuitive assessment of prospective members.

Now that the process was less rigorous, the risk of agents infiltrating the group was high. The current of fear spread through the group. The seditionists now kept an eye on one another. Rumors were whispered; trust was eroded.

Max kept Josiane close to him, and used her for many of his practical tasks. Josiane was his strong-arm and his defense, though he was not sure how far he could trust her. In the evenings, Maximilian sat close to Omar, whose strange fevers never seemed to break, but rolled over him like waves. Sometimes Maximilian would find Omar covered in sweat, mumbling his strange words, speaking in other languages. Omar's burns had begun to heal, leaving great welts on his body. A hundred little scars pinpointed where the machine's needles had pierced him. Max wished he could spend more time with his old friend, but instead a young, dark-haired, and brooding seditionist called Rikard had volunteered for the task.

Toward the end of the first week of constructing the cart, news spread that the Order of the Sightless were staging a march through the city. Maximilian and Josiane walked down to Boulevarde Karlotte, which led to the northern gate. The walls here were covered with graffiti, anti-House slogans mixed with the usual sexual jokes and crude pornographic pictures.

Lines of apocalyptics shuffled past, blinded by black hoods, chained together in a groaning chanting mass. The apocalyptics gave the appearance of a great, injured beast, heaving its way toward its final resting place. The city was filled with portents. It was said that spectral figures in the ruins of the ancient Forum had prophesized apocalyptic events, that on the hills surrounding Caeli-Amur sheep were giving birth to two-headed lambs. Flocks of birds wheeled in the sky above.

As they watched the procession, Josiane spoke determinedly. "You are a fool, pursuing this mad plan of yours. As you hide yourself away from the group, building your cart, Ejan grows in strength. Soon he will have more supporters than you. Your alliance with the *Call to Arms* group is not enough."

"Ejan and I both have the same destination, but we are just pursuing different paths."

Josiane stepped in front of him and looked up at his face. "Have you thought that perhaps the paths you tread lead in fact to different destinations? Have you thought that Ejan in fact is leading the group to a frontal assault against the Houses, and that in such a fight, the group can only come to destruction? I think you should reconsider. Abandon your plans for the Sunken City—organize your group, outmaneuver Ejan, take control."

"What hope do we have without reaching Caeli-Enas? What hope do we have to protect ourselves against the Houses in the long run? A demonstration on Aya's Day may be a success. The Houses may not even choose to attack. We may indeed have a long wave of demonstrations before winter. But after that, what happens? You think this mood will stay in the citizens forever? No, sooner or later there will be a test of strength. Sooner or later we will face the Houses on the cobblestoned streets as two armies. Then, we must have a way of combating their thaumaturgists."

"That isn't the reason you want to visit the Sunken City. No, it's purely for your own interests. You have visions of becoming a great thaumaturgist yourself, a vision with little to do with seditionism."

Josiane's words struck Max like a blow to the chest. She spoke the truth: He did have hopes to become a great thaumaturgist. But his hopes were not for his own gain. Rather, he would use his knowledge for the good of others. He hoped to serve. But even as he thought this, he knew there was more to it. He hoped to serve, but he hoped he would take a special place in seditionism. He hoped that others would hear his name, and repeat it to each other. Confusion gripped him. When he returned from the Sunken City filled with thaumaturgical knowledge, then the value of his expedition would be clear. He would be able to train an army of liberation-thaumaturgists, even as waves of demonstrations rolled through the city following Aya's Day, he would be able to face down the House thaumaturgists with their own weapons.

When Max did not respond, Josiane said, "When enough citizens oppose the Houses, then their thaumaturgical power will become impotent. What would the Houses do? Massacre the entire populace?"

"Citizens!" laughed Maximilian. "Do you know what being a citizen once meant? It meant representation at the Forum. It meant having rights. But look at the Ancient Forum now—nothing but ghostly ruins. The citizens' strength is degraded. No, we must go to Caeli-Enas." Now he was simply being obdurate.

"You trust too many of the people surrounding you. Not only Ejan, but others, too. Kata is efficient, yet there's something about her that I don't trust."

Maximilian stopped. "Kata?"

"She moves like an athlete. She moves like she's been trained. Most would not be able to recognize it." Josiane stood motionless before him.

"You're imagining it. She's trustworthy, I feel it. And you and Ejan tested her. It's the others, the newest ones, we should worry about." Maximilian felt a slight tug of fear. Was his judgment in error when it came to Kata? No, he wouldn't believe it; he pushed the thought from his mind, but it resurfaced.

Josiane looked back at the apocalyptics as they passed through the crowds of the boulevard, downward toward the docks. "What does it matter anyway? Ejan will destroy you in the end."

That evening, Maximilian found Omar lying quietly, staring at the ceiling, fully conscious. Though his face had healed considerably, it was still scarred horribly.

"Maximilian," he said. "There is a coldness in the night. Do you remember how sometimes a cold wind would whip across to the Dyrian coast from Varenis? Remember how we'd play dice there, when we were children?"

"You'd always win. The luck always fell your way."

"Even though you could calculate the odds," laughed Omar. "Can you calculate them now, with Ejan and the others? With the city?"

"I'm not sure," said Max. "Everything seems hard to judge. Everything's in motion."

"You keep your façade of confidence too fixed," said Omar.

"I know," said Max, looking down at his boot. The twine had unraveled a little more, like everything else, he thought. He pressed it against the leather with his hand, but it made little difference. Soon it would unravel completely and he would need new boots. "I know," he repeated.

"It's all right to be uncertain, you know."

"Ejan is certain," said Max.

"Look at him!" Omar spoke again softly. "Look at him."

"Sleep." Max touched Omar's shoulder. "Rest. Rest is important."

Max returned to his own bed and lay down. He realized that he, too, was exhausted. But he could not stop his mind from racing. Josiane was right about the changes within the seditionist group. Tomorrow he would meet with Aceline, convince her that

Ejan's violent strategy must be stopped. Together they would demand that Ejan abandon his plans, give up his workshop and join with the rest of the group. Faced with the two of them, Ejan would be unable to refuse. If he did, perhaps they would banish him also. Aceline's support would be crucial.

Maximilian closed his eyes, and when he opened them again he was not sure how long he had slept. It was dark, and when he looked across at his friend's mattress, Omar was gone.

"Omar?" He sat up. He caught a glimpse of a light—now yellow in the darkness, now obscured—bobbing in the direction of the machine room.

Max lit his own lamp and adjusted it. Putting on his shoes, he pursued Omar. He moved along the purple-misted corridor, into that cavernous crypt where the machines seemed filled with menace. At the far side of the room, he again saw the light. He hurried on.

When he came to the far side of the cavern, he stopped and gasped. The huge black round doors they had thought immovable had been opened. Beyond lay a corridor leading to a hexagonal room the size of the communal chamber. Shapes—perhaps thirty of them—hovered above him in the darkness. They looked like long backed chairs. Filled with wonder, Maximilian raised his lamp so that it illuminated the walls of this new room. Like many of the works of the ancients, it seemed built for giants. The very walls seemed filled with unknown technologies: circular eyelike protuberances, glossy flat spaces, levers and gears, rough surfaced ideograms of unknown meaning. As always, the ancients seemed a long-lost race, alien and incomprehensible.

There was no sign of Omar.

Maximilian continued on, crossing the room and passing through the doorway on the other side. He came to a small chamber circled by four archways. Through each archway lay even smaller chambers, the size of storerooms, in the shape of hexagonal prisms. He stepped into one and with a rushing sound—*phht*—a wall appeared where he had entered. It must have been a door, but the sheer rapidity of its motion meant he did not see it close. He felt gentle pressure on his feet—the chamber was in motion. One of the walls disappeared with another rushing sound and he stepped out into a hexagonal-shaped corridor that disappeared into the darkness. Along the walls, the floor and the roof, every ten feet or so were square black pads. He placed his hand against one, and a previously unseen doorway opened. This time he just caught its movement as the door disappeared into the wall.

Maximilian looked into a hexagonal chamber, its sides about eight feet long. Inside lay a barely visible human form on a long table, shadows cast oddly over it. He leaned in with his lamp and the light struck the figure. It was the dried-husk of a cadaver, an elongated human, or humanlike creature, its skin shrunken and brown around its bones. Into both of its arms, at the elbow joints, plunged a number of wires, each a different color, two of them translucent. Some form of tube ran from beneath the table, while another one descended into the thing's mouth. The creature did not seem to have died in pain, for the cadaver was relaxed, and that very relaxation made the image all the more horrific: not the clean white bones of those long dead, nor the fresh calmness of the newly dead, but something in between.

On the walls were more black pads.

Maximilian stepped down through the door, onto the slanted side of the cell. He put his hand down to steady himself, heard a rush of wind and stepped onto nothingness. He fell and his last image before his lamp shattered was of another cadaver beneath him, at an odd angle, as if it lay on a table not on the hexagonal room's floor, but one of its sides. He struck the body and felt the hardness of skin over bone and the two of them slipped off the table and crashed onto the floor. The cadaver tugged at the tubes plunging into it, and he grabbed on to the thing's waist as a drowning man clings to a plank in a stormy sea.

Everything here was made of odd angles: these chambers, it appeared, were stacked one on top of another in some kind of honeycomb formation. The corridor above him seemed designed so that its floor was exactly the same as its ceiling, that their relationship to the cells around them was exactly the same, so that all one needed to do was rotate them to make the floor become a ceiling, and the ceiling become a floor. Everything was perfectly symmetrical.

Max scrambled around for the lamp, touching something dry and hard, perhaps the limb of the cadaver. He found the lamp and, taking a match from the little metal compartment at the lamp's bottom, lit it through one of its broken panes.

Beside him lay the cadaver, its back bent like some acrobat frozen in mid-backflip. Some of the tubes had been torn from its arm and long thin needles hung from their ends. Maximilian scrambled up and the floor gave way and he fell into another room, this time the lamp continued to burn. In this little cell, the table was above him, and the cadaver hung from the tubes and wires like a trapeze artist. Again the floor gave way into another cell and when Maximilian struck the corner of a table, the lamp went out. He reached out for it, the floor gave way and he fell, struck something else and everything went black.

When he came to, Maximilian was lying in a long corridor, much like the one through which he'd entered, lit by a dim light. How many cells he had fallen through, he could not tell. There was no sense to this place. His lamp was gone, but green beads that ran along its roof lighted the corridor. Max pulled himself to his feet and walked to the end of the corridor, his arms aching, his ribs burning. There a door opened into an elevator, much like the one he had arrived in. He stepped into it and with the gentle lessening of pressure on his feet, he recognized it was again in motion. When the door opened he stepped out, passed into another hexagonal passageway. Again he pressed the walls, and they rapidly opened onto more hexagonal cells in which lay dried, dusty cadavers. He continued along the corridor to a crossroads. Here his corridor was intersected by another which ran in one direction at an obtuse angle, both up and away, while in the other it ran acutely downward and closer to the direction from which he had come. He marched up and to the left, occasionally touching the walls to see the emaciated bodies of the dead, lying in repose. Finally he came to another intersection, where the new corridor ran again in one direction at exactly the same obtuse angle as the first. This one was so steep that he could not climb it. With horror, Max sat down. He was lost in a labyrinth of corridors, surrounded by the dead, in a place where the angles seemed to make no sense at all. He put his head into his hands. He was lost.

He turned back. How long he wandered those corridors he could not be sure. He came to hexagonal elevators, stepped into them. Sometimes they came to black hallways without lighting and he crawled along until he was sure that they were not the way to the machine room. Tired and hungry, he rested for a while. At other times he cursed out loud, his voice echoing down the empty corridors. Time stretched out indefinitely. He pictured the seditionists far away in the Communal Cavern, going about their business, his apprentices, learning their thaumaturgical formulae, the printing press for *A Call to Arms* rattling away—and Ejan and his troops, carrying their explosives out of the cavern. He slept briefly, woke in a fright, his heart racing. He walked and traveled in more elevators, searched more corridors until at some point, scrabbling down a darkened corridor, he looked up and noticed great chairs hanging up in the dark. As he stumbled through the machine room, he heard a deep rumble from behind him. Curious he headed back from where he came—perhaps it was Omar. He stopped and again he gasped. The great circular doors were once again closed. The path to the strange labyrinth was closed. He struggled to reopen them, pressing the pads around the doors, pulling on levers that shifted and turned but seemed to have no effect. If Omar was behind the doors, he'd have to make his own way out.

Max pressed his hand against the cold metal. "Take care, friend."

He passed through the machine room, and in the far distance, the glint of a light.

When Maximilian came back into the Communal Cavern, the place was abuzz with activity. Three seditionists lay blackened and bleeding on the floor, while others tended to them.

Ejan stood overlooking the situation. "Fools!"

Maximilian walked across to them. "What happened?"

Giselle looked over from the corpses. "Some of the Xsanthians died. The docks. They were planting an incendiary on the docks."

"The Xsanthians are not our enemies," said Maximilian.

"It was an accident. We were hoping to sink a steamer. Anyway, in a war, people die," said Giselle.

From the entranceway to the cavern came the sounds of a scuffle. Josiane and another two seditionists were dragging in a guard dressed in the blue uniform of House Marin. The guard was bleeding profusely from the stomach. "He followed them to the underground entrance. Josiane stabbed him. Who knows if there were any others?"

A crowd gathered around the guard, whose face was white and drawn. He was breathing heavily.

"Were there more of you following us?" asked Josiane. When he didn't respond, she slapped him once, twice. "Did any others follow?"

The guard looked up. "Water."

"Get him water," said Maximilian. But when Giselle came with a flask, Ejan took it from her and held out of reach before the guard. "Did anyone else follow with you?"

Blood was dribbling from the man's mouth, and he gave what looked like macabre smile and his body relaxed.

Maximilian grabbed Ejan by the shirt. "You fool. You've endangered all of us. You kill our friends. You lead our enemies here. For what?"

Ejan's forearm crashed down on Maximilian's wrists, forcing him to lose his grip. Ejan's two fists punched into Max's chest. Max found himself falling. His legs, weakened by his recent ordeal, failed to hold him. He hit the ground, his back striking the stone floor followed by the crack of his head. Everything went white for a moment. Ejan looked down, his face still and cold like that of a statue. From behind, Giselle wrapped her arms around Ejan to stop further violence. Josiane appeared beside Max, her weighted chain in one hand, a bloodied dagger in the other.

Max's mind was already racing; he knew intuitively that he'd made a mistake. He looked up at the northerner.

Ejan sneered. "It's a war, Maximilian. The sooner you understand that, the better."

NINETEEN

Kata had witnessed the confrontation between Maximilian and Ejan with amazement. Many of the seditionists were afraid of Ejan, who seemed cold and fearless. Maximilian had gathered his own group around him. There were only fifteen of them. An original small group and ten or so recent adherents, all of whom hoped to develop their skills in thaumaturgy. In a meeting, Max explained that he would ally himself with Aceline to put a halt to Ejan's plans. They might even exile him. But Oewen urged against any confrontation. Max tried to push the issue and with that move, lost the confidence of his adherents. The dark-haired Rikard, who had been looking after Omar, stood up and, without a word, left to join to Ejan's group. Max backed down. He felt their weakness as much as the others did. When they finally left, Kata caught Max looking away past the machine room, toward the great doors that Omar had passed through. There was sadness in his eyes that again moved Kata. Max had weaknesses also, she knew.

In the last weeks, Maximilian had come to rely on Kata more and more. She liked his dream for a world without the Houses, even if she realized it was impossible. In other ways—in his decisiveness and drive—they were alike. But while she dreamed of an escape from the Houses, of a villa in the countryside, he thought always of the struggle against the Houses and of his ambition to reach the Library of Caeli-Enis. At times, Kata wondered if these were not contradictory goals.

Still, for the first time in her life Kata felt that there was some meaning in her work. She was no seditionist, yet the idea of a purpose greater than her own personal desires was more than seductive; it allowed those very desires of her own to fade away. The seditionists talked with passion about things that to Kata had always been only words: freedom, justice. If they were captured or killed, they felt that this was of little consequence, for their movement was larger than themselves. Each of the tasks she was assigned seemed now to be of greater import, and even if they were difficult or boring or dangerous, she carried them out with some feeling of happiness. This was not an experience that Cajiunism of apocalypticism could encapsulate. It was an experience beyond her understanding of free will and determinism. Somehow it was about existence, about the way that particular goals were connected to her sense of self. Yet, even as these feelings grew in her, she pulled herself away from them. She was an agent of the Houses. She had a task to perform.

Now allowed to come and go from the hideout as she pleased, the day after Ejan and Maximilian's confrontation, Kata, moving randomly around the city until she was sure she had not been followed, visited Boris Autec.

The officiate sat in his little office looking like a frog. He had a tinge of green to his slippery-looking skin, and though he hadn't lost his roundness, his eyes had sunk back into their sockets like the bottoms of deep wells. His hands shook as he incessantly moved papers around on his desk. He sweated in a way that couldn't be attributed to the relentless summer heat; great wet patches stained his shirts beneath the armpits.

"This Maximilian, the dreamer the seditionists call him behind his back. What do you make of him?" Autec said.

Kata felt a slight tug of guilt. "His strategy is complex, perhaps contradictory. He thinks that true power lies in the citizenry who will one day rise and that the seditionists need to obtain knowledge of thaumaturgy to fight the Houses. The first overestimates the potential of the people, and the second . . ." She trailed off.

At that moment, there was a knock and the head of a handsome young man with a long, aquiline nose popped his head around the door. "Officiate Autec, forgive me for interrupting, but the games—you wanted me to remind you."

"Thanks, Armand. Wait a moment, we'll accompany you." He turned to Kata. "You'll have to endure this entertainment with me. It's one of Technis's, uh, 'social gatherings.'"

They walked with Armand into the Palace grounds. In between buildings and through gardens, which, when observed closely seemed poorly tended: the flowers wilting, the bushes tinged with gray in the rainless summer. A stream of Technis agents and officials was heading toward the southeastern corner of the Complex, where an amphitheater stood, a smaller version of the Great Arena that sat in the Lavere district at the base of Caeli-Amur's Thousand Stairs. There battles occurred in carefully constructed environments. At times the floor was flooded with water, and gladiators fought great squids. Recently Kata had heard that Collegium Caelian had equipped its gladiators with great metal exoskeletons, powered by rumbling steam engines mounted on their backs.

The Arena, the slums, the Collegia—all these gave the Lavere its criminal tone, its base culture. For these reasons Kata avoided it. She had no desire to venture among a population where all relationships had been stripped to their basest economic interest. But now she wondered if the self-interested individuals of the Lavere were in any way different from the officials of Technis.

As they entered, a number of officiates and subofficiates approached Boris. "Congratulations on becoming an officiate, Autec! We must dine one night." "Officiate Autec, do visit my wife and me when you have the time."

"Apparently, one must be seen," Boris said to Kata.

"This way, Officiate Autec." Armand gestured gracefully toward one of the stands. There was something charming about the young man: the straight back, the way he nodded his head, the gentle smile on his face. He had the nobility that one might have expected from a House Arbor official. Grace, that's what it is, thought Kata. He does everything in the simplest way.

"Call me Boris, please." Boris turned to Kata. "Armand is the subofficiate responsible for coordination and administration of the Palace building. He's an adjutant to the officiates."

Their seats, as befitted an officiate, were close to the sandy arena floor. Beneath the grounds surface, Kata could see the faint outlines of structures. Like the Great Arena in the Lavere, tunnels presumably ran beneath it, and the floor itself might open up to reveal rising elevators on which stood gladiators or exotic beasts.

"So how does this Maximilian plan to discover thaumaturgical knowledge?" Boris asked.

Kata hesitated. What was it, that she should feel some kind of loyalty to the seditionists? Yet there it was, a heaviness inside her, as real and substantial as any of her feelings. She thought about the air-cart, and settled for, "He wants to visit the Sunken City. He has us searching through old books."

"As if he could reach the Sunken City! Dreamers, fools."

"Ejan, though, is the most dangerous," she said. "His workshop is filled with secret activities. Only a day ago, some of his followers carried chemicals into the hideout. The other seditionists are intimidated by the northerner. And until now he has been responsible for most of the group's income. He holds the levers of power."

"As I thought. I want you to move the scrying ball to Ejan's workshop." Autec licked his lips and looked around the crowd, as if he were expecting spies or enemies to be hidden among it. "Do you think we should strike now, crush them?"

Kata hesitated once more. "We should wait. They are no threat yet. We have time."

At the side of the amphitheater, a gate opened to their left. Hesitantly, a group of eight gladiators trepidatiously entered the arena floor. Armed only with long spears, they walked forward, stopped a little, looked up at the audience, which yelled and cheered. House Technis was ready for blood.

"Who are they?" Boris asked Armand.

"Some of the captured tramworkers who refuse to submit," said Armand. "Officiate Matisse instructed the master torturer to bring them up. He thought you would be especially pleased."

Boris grimaced and looked toward a thin middle-aged man sitting nearby who waved and grinned malevolently. His bottom row of teeth was broken and blackened.

Another gate opened on the opposite side of the amphitheater. Lumbering through the opening came a great elephant, its back painted in extravagant reds and greens. The crowd gasped. Brought with other wild animals from Numeria, elephants were sometimes used in the Arena games, but only rarely were they killed nowadays. They were too expensive and too magnificent.

With the back of one hand, Boris wiped the sweat that beaded on his forehead. "It's really quite beautiful isn't it?"

Armand touched Boris on his arm. "Officiate Autec, you're not the only one to recognize Matisse's . . ." He hesitated and finally settled on, "joke."

"Kill it! Kill it!" yelled the crowd.

Five of the spearmen surrounded the elephant, their spears ready. Kata could sense the fear emanating from them. These were no gladiators, only workers from the factory district. The three remaining retreated to the amphitheater wall where one worker seemed to have wet himself.

The elephant stood still and blinked dumbly, unaware of the danger it was in. Kata found herself watching the delicate elephant eyelashes interlacing as the eye closed. There was something soft and gentle about those lashes, and the uncomprehending eyes they protected.

One of the gladiators ran at full pace and plunged the spear into the side of the elephant, which roared, leaped onto its back feet, threw its trunk in the air, let out a powerful trumpet, and turned on the man. Its giant feet came down on the sandy ground and dust billowed around it. The spear was torn from the man's grasp and jutted from the elephant like the pin from a cushion. The gladiator turned, but had barely taken a step when the trunk lashed at him. He flew into the amphitheater wall and the huge feet trampled over him. No longer still, the elephant was now a picture of power and motion. Its trunk swayed; its feet moved from side to side; its head swiveled.

The other spearmen charged. Spears plunged again into the elephant. Again, it roared and turned, trampling another man. Again, and yet again the men charged and again the elephant struck at the gladiators, crushed them beneath its gigantic weight. Finally, the elephant stood alone and still with spears jutting from its belly. Blood ran down its giant legs and dropped onto the dusty amphitheater floor in black pools. Around it lay the bloody corpses of the gladiators, legs and arms askew at odd angles. The crowd bayed like dogs, an ancient tradition from the Veiled Years, when all knowledge and meaning had been hidden from the world, after the cataclysm. Officiate Autec took a swig from a flask, moved to replace it in his jacket, but instead took another swig.

For a while the elephant stood motionless, the three remaining gladiators pressed against the wall. The one who had wet himself had dropped his spear and was shaking.

Autec looked away from the carnage toward Kata, his face strained. "We have enough to deal with on the streets. They're strange creatures, these seditionists, aren't they? Dreamers. But then, we all have dreams, don't we? We all have things we want and cannot achieve, no matter how hard we try."

"What do you mean?" asked Kata.

"Have you never wanted something out of reach?" Autec focused in on her with a kind of desperate curiosity.

Kata thought of Aemilius, and then the image of Maximilian flashed into her mind. "No matter where you go, there is always something you cannot have."

"That's the difference between us and the seditionists," said Autec. "We accept that and make do. They strive for the impossible. There is no realism in their views. There is no realism in absolute love. And yet, what we would do if we could have it!"

"Love! Has that anything to do with it?" asked Kata irritably.

"Exactly!" said Autec. "Nothing! And yet . . ."

"Everyone you love must leave in the end," said Kata. "Or you must leave them. There is no other alternative, no matter how wonderful the journey."

"You're a good woman," said Autec urgently, caught in some daytime reverie. "You will do well. I will make sure you have a good life if you serve the House well. Your star shall be bound to mine. We will rise or fall together. And I say we will rise, higher than any other, to shine in the vast darkness of the night!"

The crowd now screamed at the gladiators. The denouement to the fight was turning out to be an anticlimax. The elephant dropped to its knees; its body heaved, and a dimness had come over its eyes. The remaining two men charged toward it and plunged their spears in again and again. First the elephant groaned, then it emitted a keening sound, and finally it collapsed in on itself, its trunk making a couple of attempts to lift before resting still.

"What a sad end," said Autec. "What a grubby little spectacle. One day, we'll stop these gladiatorial events. One day the world will be at peace."

After she left Technis, Kata was in despair. The elephant's death, the gladiators' deaths, her complicity in it all. She walked back through the city with its evening crowds, with the graffiti on the walls: FOG IS BLOWN AWAY BY A NEW WIND, TOMORROW A NEW SUN DAWNS. And where did she stand with the seditionists? Why hadn't she told Boris about the cart that Maximilian was building? Yes, Ejan was the real danger, but she had protected Maximilian. She had downplayed the group as a whole.

She looked around at the city that surrounded her like a besieging army.

Louis had joined Ejan's group, and Kata now saw him only occasionally, which suited her. His presence had always unnerved her: his shifty eyes, forever moving from side to side, the way he turned away and looked at the ground when he spoke. She had always been the dominant one, for Louis seemed by nature conservative, perhaps even frightened. This time Kata resolved that Louis would move the scrying ball. She had scaled the pillar the first time and now it was only fair that he should perform the task.

The following morning, she sidled up to Louis in the little circle around the pot of the morning's potato and sardine broth. Each of them waited as an old woman called Lara, said to have been with the group for decades, scooped the breakfast into the waiting bowls. Kata wondered at the backwardness of the group: that it should fall to a woman to make the food, that with the exception of Aceline, the leaders—Maximilian, Ejan, Kamron before his exile—were men. The same divisions occurred in the Houses also. For the philosopher-assassins such prejudices did not exist. For them a woman was just as deadly as a man, and just as wise. Indeed, there was one whole school of philosopher-assassins—the matriachists—who believed that women should rise to positions of power because they felt more deeply than men and so were more likely not to be led astray by Olympian abstractions, by the tyranny of pure rationality. They would be bound closer to the real world of people. The matriarchists were not all women.

When their bowls were full, she sat next to Louis, away from the others. "Officiate Autec wants you to move the scrying ball to Ejan's workshop."

Louis swallowed a mouthful of broth. "You know when I was a child, we ate this every week. I come from a fishing village to the south, where sardines and anchovies are in everything. It's funny the way certain things bring back memories, isn't it? Just the sound of the water on rocks, or the taste of salty fish. The days I spent on my father's fishing boat, dredging up the nets. And then returning home to this."

"They sound like good days," said Kata.

"They were terrible. I dreamed always of escape to Caeli Amur."

Kata laughed. "Some dream of escape *from* Caeli-Amur."

They ate the broth quietly beside each other until they were finished. Kata said, "So you will move the ball?"

Louis shrugged. "I'll try. But you know that you are better suited to it. I am just an agent. I am not . . . a philosopher. It is wrong of you to endanger me, when you could shift it without the slightest worry."

Kata softened her voice and looked deeply into his eyes, which for once were transfixed. "Come, we're in this together, you and I. We should share our tasks."

Against all her instincts, Kata reached over and took his rough hand in hers. A lascivious look crossed Louis's face. He was not a man, Kata realized, with a great knowledge of women. He did not have the confidence or decisiveness to be attractive. Kata had always know that men found her lithe body and her dark flowing hair appealing, though she could never imagine why. She knew now that she was using this appeal, and though she herself did not have an intimate knowledge of men, that she was blurring a line between herself and Louis, intimating something that repulsed her. And yet, some part of her liked this newfound, strange power over him.

His voice came out softly. "I'll try."

Kata smiled sweetly at him and let go of his hand. She let her eyes linger on him as she stood up. As she walked away, her bowl in hand, she felt dirty. She ignored the feeling: she would do what she had to. A villa awaited her, and with it, escape from this petty world of intrigue and betrayal and cruelty.

Kata spent the morning with Maximilian and Quadi, Oewen and Ariana, planning the air-cart with Quadi. The whole venture had started to take hold of Kata's imagination: the sheer daring of it, to build an underwater apparatus and descend to Caeli-Enas, that ancient metropolis of legends. The fragmentary knowledge she had gained had made her all the more curious. What would they find? Shadowy figures of broken statues, like the ghosts of the past? Great palaces on the Arrian Hill to the east of Caeli-Enis's center?

She hoped she would be the person to accompany Maximilian on the mission. She fulfilled all the criteria. She was athletic, healthy, trusted. But she stopped herself: she should not think like this, for there would be no venture to the Sunken City. The House would intervene before any such thing happened. The House would crush this little group.

In the afternoon, she ventured into the Quaedian with Maximilian and Quadi. There they bought screws and washers, springs and metal bars.

As they neared the university, they found two groups of students facing off against each other, each a sprawling mass of two or three hundred, alternately surging forward, backing away. The group farther along the street was dressed in more sharply cut suits, with cleaner colors, while the other was slightly more ragtag in its dress, green pants mismatched against blue coats, their shoes scuffed. The near group loosed a volley of stones that suddenly stopped midair and dropped into the street halfway between the groups.

"Apprentice thaumaturgists," said Maximilian, looking at the well-dressed group.

The apprentices opened their ranks and a heavy, muscular student walked through from the rear. He held against his hip what looked like a large bolt-thrower: a box-shaped chamber, from which jutted a long barrel. Hushed silence hung over the street before the apprentices broke into sinister laughter. The second ragtag group close to Maximilian and Kata turned and scattered. The air burst with a huge explosion. Whatever the mechanism was, it was no bolt-thrower.

Students dashed past Kata like a herd of deer. She dodged between them as they ran, their faces twitching and fearful, hats falling to the cobblestoned street. One of them collapsed in front of her, screaming. He looked over his shoulder, rolled onto his back and started clawing senselessly at his face, as if some unseen enemy were attacking him. Another screamed nearby and began tearing at the skin on his legs.

Knocked from his feet by one of the students, Maximilian sprawled on the ground beside her. He got to his knees but was knocked down again. She grabbed him and with a surge of strength lifted him across to the wall. Standing between him and the rushing crowd, she looked for Quadi, but the New-Man was gone.

When the rushing mob had dispersed, the street was littered with students clawing at their faces and arms and screaming hideously. Kata stood, Maximilian sprawled on the ground behind her.

Sneering apprentices stepped through the bodies, laughing at those on the ground, kicking them absentmindedly. One of them came toward Kata and Maximilian, who dragged himself to his feet.

A tall apprentice with a scar that ran along one side of his imperious face examined them. The square, muscular one fell in beside him and pointed the thaumaturgical machine at Maximilian.

Kata stared at the student. "We're not involved in this dispute."

"Likely story. Make them scream," said the tall one.

There was silence as the heavy apprentice looked coldly on them, still pointing the barrel of the contraption.

Kata dropped to the ground and in an instant rolled to her left, her two knives already in her hands. A fraction of a moment later, she stood next to the tall apprentice. Her daggers pressed into his chest. "We're not a part of this."

There was silence as the apprentices sized up the situation.

"Leave them alone." A third apprentice ran his hands through his sandy hair.

The group began moving on, and after another moment of

silence, the tall one, with knives still against his chest, nodded. The heavy apprentice walked away and the tall one backed out and followed him.

Kata brushed the dust from Maximilian's clothes, aware that she had betrayed herself. She was unable to look him in the eye. "Are you all right?"

He looked at her and didn't respond. "Who are you?"

"I'm a seditionist."

"There's only one seditionist I know who can do things like that. Josiane." There was a challenge in his voice.

Kata tensed and her thoughts seemed to freeze. No explanations rose to her mind, and she became terribly aware how much rested on this moment. Her body was awash with conflicting emotions. She didn't know where her loyalties lay: with Maximilian, with House Technis, with only herself. Her mind kicked into gear. "It's true: I was once a philosopher-assassin. But I didn't think I should advertise the fact."

Still she could not look at him, but she knew he was sizing her up. She could almost hear the thoughts rattling through his mind. She prepared herself to flee in disgrace. Waves of fear and guilt flooded through her. She kept her face impassive, unemotional. She hid inside herself.

"I revealed myself for you." She looked up into his brown eyes.

His eyes softened a little, with a touch of confusion, as if he felt something that surprised him. He reached out and touched her face with the back of his hand. "We should get back."

TWENTY

On the way back to the hideout, Kata could still feel Max's touch on her face, a tingling warm spot. Quadi had fled with the crowd of students. Kata and Max found him in the Communal Cavern entertaining a group of seditionists with stories of Tir-Aki. "In Tir-Aki there are machines that do everything for you. They tie the laces of your boots, they pluck your eyebrow hairs, they even carry you everywhere you want to go."

"Really?" asked Oewen.

Quadi glanced at Maximilian mischievously and continued apace. "And there are places where it is illegal to wear clothes, and other places where you must not run or walk but instead must dance, no matter what else you're doing."

He rolled a cigarette and looked surprised as the audience, a moment before enraptured, took to their feet and scampered away.

"Everyone believes there are House spies among us, and it will not be long before one of the Houses raids us," said Max. Again his eyes seemed to be sizing her up. He was testing her, after she had revealed that she was a philosopher-assassin. Kata was conscious of the ball still sitting up on the pillar in the center of the room, Officiate Autec's third eye bearing down on them. Always she felt its presence.

The storm of guilt and anxiety rushed into her again. Why did she want him to think so well of her? Why did she want him to approve of her? "How would the House know where we are? Only the trustworthy can come and go as they please."

Maximilian nodded. "And all our work on the ca—"

"Anyway," interrupted Kata, eager to keep him from discussing his plans for the cart. She must keep him safe from Autec's spying eyes. "Perhaps we should prepare for such a raid? We have no real escape plan, only Ejan's guards, no real method of defense."

"Ejan would have us stay and fight to the death. And who can say that he is wrong?"

Kata reached over and touched Maximilian on the arm. She needed reassurance. She needed— No, she wouldn't admit it. But she had seen the effect she'd had on Louis and she knew with this touch she was trying to marshal the same forces in her favor. Maximilian didn't tense this time, but let it rest there. "Some of us must escape. Some of us must continue on if the group is arrested. The most important of us."

Maximilian looked at her, puzzled. "But each of us is important. Each one of us as important as the other."

"You know that's not true," said Kata. "You know that your survival is critical to our success. You are a thaumaturgist, but you are also a dreamer. The world needs dreamers, as things are falling apart. Not just for the overthrow of the Houses, but think of the world after that. What can be done for the wastelanders and the wasteland itself? How will the influence of the New-Men affect Caeli-Amur? Who thinks of these things, even here? Not Ejan. Perhaps Aceline. Few of the others."

"Do any of us really know what role we will play in this history?" Maximilian spoke reflectively, as if his inner life were now being bared to her. He looked over the other figures, each playing his little role. "But then perhaps you're right. I am often surprised by the narrow-mindedness of people, even seditionists. It's as if they can't see beyond their own petty horizons. They're caught in their own little worlds."

"You must be prepared to save yourself," she said.

"And we must try to save the cart from—"

"We must," said Kata, interrupting him again, "save all our important possessions."

He placed his hand on top of hers. The two of them rested on his arm. "You are a good seditionist."

She felt a swell of pride within her, and as he walked away, again she felt a stab of fear. With great effort, she cut off the feelings within her: she had no room for them, no room for him. A second later the feelings returned. In her mind she did the calculations. The group was doomed, but perhaps she could save *him*. But how?

On the pillar the scrying ball looked on, recording everything. The way to protect Maximilian would be for Louis to move it.

But Louis did not move it. In the following days she worked on the cart with Quadi and Maximilian and each time she wandered down the long straight corridors and emerged into the central cavern, the ball was sitting at the top of the pillar, where she had placed it, like an eagle watching its prey on the fields below. Each day she became increasingly angry with Louis, who nodded his head and smiled greasily at her from across the communal area, or from the doorway of Ejan's workshop, as if he had forgotten entirely about moving the scrying ball. Finally, as she watched the seditionists move obliviously around the cavern, she snapped.

In a fury, Kata walked toward Ejan's workshop. She stopped at the door, taken aback as she looked over the room filled with cobbled-together weapons, bubbling chemicals in great vats, and various ceramic receptacles and canvas packages. The place smelled bitter and acidic. Black boxes stood along one side of the room, with crude levers on the top. Dressed in thick gray or blue work clothes like factory workers, several seditionists wandered about moving liquids or powders from bowl to bowl. Ejan *did* seem the most dangerous of the group, and this seemed the place where *things* were happening.

"Have you come to spy for Maximilian?" asked Ejan from the far side of the room. His face was smudged with a brown substance, which only highlighted his severe beauty.

Louis looked over at her from a table. Before him were laid many wires of different colors: reds, yellow, copper. His darting eyes lit up at the sight of her.

"Because we don't take well to spies here," said Ejan, brushing his hands against his tunic. "What's the penalty, do you think, Louis?"

Louis shrugged, looked down shyly, continued connecting wires together.

Ejan smiled a brilliant smile. "But of course Maximilian wouldn't stoop to spying, would he? He's too pure for that, and a good thing, too."

"Maximilian wants me to assess the state of things in the city. Perhaps I could borrow Louis for a while. It's been long since we talked, isn't it, Louis? Would I be able to take him out to the city, Ejan? He is my former comrade, after all. We became apocalyptics together."

Louis turned to Ejan, who gave a rapid nod.

Gliders hung above the city as they emerged into the bright light. The heat of summer was on them, and there were occasional wafts of city smells: refuse and fish, smoke from factories and fires.

"Come. I'll show you something." Louis headed northward through the narrow streets. She could feel the heightened focus he kept on her, his awareness of her every step.

"It's about time you moved that scrying ball, don't you think?" said Kata. "I'm not going to ask you again."

"Of course," said Louis. "But I've not had a chance. You know how difficult it is. I'll do it as soon as I can. But you understand I must be careful. And people are paranoid. I've seen them looking at each other, with these squinty eyes. I've seen them looking at *you.*"

"Who?"

Louis looked over his shoulder along the narrow street, as if someone might be following them. "Josiane, for one."

They came to a large burned-out factory in the Factory Quarter. Dirty children sifted through the ash and ruins. In the center of the building stood the shell of a blackened steam tram.

Louis nodded. "Ruined."

"Not—"

"Yes," said Louis. "But a long time ago. This was one of the first attacks. We struck at House Technis and look what we've achieved. The tramworkers were spurred into action. There was a strike. It may have been crushed, but in retaliation someone set fire to the factory. We've shown the House that things can't just go on as usual."

"This is madness," said Kata.

Louis grasped her hands. "No, Kata. Don't you see, this is the most effective of the seditionist methods. It's a war between us and the Houses. It must be fought with weapons."

"There could have been deaths."

"In a war, there are no neutrals. Everyone is complicit is some way. If they stand aside from the cruelties of the Houses, then they de facto support them. If they oppose the Houses, then they must fight them with everything they have. They cannot still participate in this charade."

"Just whose side are you on now, Louis?"

Louis looked over the brick factories that ran down the hill. Smoke billowed from chimneys, then back at her with impassioned eyes. "Kata, you said that we were in this together, you and I. Well, come and join Ejan and we can be together—truly together. You and I."

Kata fought the urge to recoil. "Are you suggesting we shift allegiances, we abandon the House for the seditionists?"

Louis stepped in to her, so that his leering face was close to hers. "If we side with Ejan, we align ourselves with the strongest of the seditionist factions. If the seditionists are victorious, we'll be well positioned. If the Houses win, well, we've already been on the side of the Houses. Either way, you and I are victorious. You. And. I."

Kata struggled to contain her revulsion, but she could not. She felt her distaste for this man fix on her face. Her lip curled and she spoke coldly, pushing his hands away. "Move the scrying ball."

Confusion settled on Louis's face, then sudden bitterness. He became aware of her rejection. His eyes narrowed. "You bitch."

Kata kept her voice calm. "I have taken all the risks so far. Now it is your turn."

Louis brushed a hand across his face and spat out. "You were the one the officiate gave the order to. I don't see why I should have to do it—whore."

Kata grabbed him by the back of the neck and he tensed. "I think you've forgotten who I am, what I can do."

Louis tensed and up looked at her; now there was fear in his eyes. He knew that she was no everyday agent but a philosopher-assassin. She had killed; she could kill again.

His eyes darting once more from side to side, his voice rose to a higher register. "Fine. I'll move it. Fine."

Kata pushed him away and Louis fled up along the street, through the sooty air. Squatting in a nearby alleyway was the urchin Henri. A dirty blond boy squatted next to him while a third leaned alone against the wall. She glared at them and they, too, scuttled away.

Kata returned to the hideout, her anger bubbling within her like a brew. Her hands shook, and her teeth were clenched. But shortly afterwards, the anger was replaced with the cold grip of anxiety. She had let her dislike of Louis get the better of her. Threatening him had been a mistake. It was possible that he would betray her somehow, and that way gain more respect in the group. Suddenly she was aware of her dangerous position. She should not underestimate these seditionists. She had grown too lax and comfortable in recent days. All day and all night, anxiety gripped her like a clamp.

The next day Louis did not move the scrying ball and Kata realized that she would have to. After all, she needed to protect Maximilian. It was a fine line between Technis and the seditionists that she was treading, but some part of her knew that she wanted to take the risk.

As she stared at her feet late in the evening, she considered when would be the best time to move the scrying ball: late at night, when the seditionists were asleep.

Aware of a figure beside her, she looked up, from her feet at Maximilian. Her heart skipped: Had she been discovered? Had Louis betrayed her? She sprang up, prepared to strike out, run.

"I wanted to say, thank you," he said. "You've been a great help to me. You're busily making yourself indispensable to me."

Kata looked at him, that lanky man with his curly hair, who could have been a librarian or scholar, but who chose to be a seditionist and fight the Houses. She could look at him all day, with those curls. He was softer on the inside than he presented himself. She had seen the way he looked at the urchins in the street, the broken and elderly, even the skinny stray dogs that darted through the Factory Quarter. He felt compelled to defend the lost and alone. She could see now the man he might become. Now she wanted to reach out and hold him. But by the time she took a step forward he had already turned and began walking away. He stopped, turned back to her, and said, "Was there something?"

She stepped forward and grasped his hand as he looked at her blankly. With a gentle step she leaned in, her heart pounding, her lips opening a little as she craned her neck up, up toward his face.

As she moved to kiss him, he blinked rapidly and took a step back. "Anyway, I must get back. . . ." He shook her hand from his arm.

Ashamed, Kata looked down at her feet. As he walked away, she felt tears in her eyes. He's rejected you in the way you rejected Louis, she thought bitterly. He's never been interested and never will be. You're nothing, she said to herself. Nothing.

TWENTY-ONE

Six House Technis officiates sat in a large carriage, two sets of three facing each other.

Boris sat next to the door facing forward, looking out at the streets of Caeli-Amur and thinking about the Siren, Paxaea. The last time he saw her, a week and a half earlier, he had left her crying on her bed. How she had manipulated his emotions; how she had appeared pathetic before him. Yet in that prostration he had seen *something* and he had taken pity on her. Everything had turned out wrong: he wanted her to *like* him; he wanted her to *want* him. But when he had visited her the following day, she had been as cold as when he had first met her, and had turned away his affections as one would those of a lowly attendant. Furious, he had concentrated on his work—the Elo-Talern had given him license to unite the Houses against the rising insurgency—but each day his thoughts of Paxaea had become more intense.

From the carriage he stared out into the darkness at the warm lights in the apartments, at citizens moving around with their families, each in their own little comfortable world. Then they had passed onto Via Gracchia whose late-night cafés and bars were brimming with clientele. The area's famous cats sat on the eaves of the buildings, were silhouetted in the windows, or scuttled along the alleyways.

Sitting opposite Boris, the skinny Officiate Matisse waved his insectlike arms in small circular motions without any apparent reason. "You'd better be right about this, Autec. Imagine if this is an Arbor trap and we're all massacred. You'll go down in history as the one who presided over the death of the entire House Technis leadership." Matisse grinned nervously.

Boris glanced unimpressed at the man and remembered the deaths of the tramworker-gladiators in Technis's amphitheater, deaths that Matisse had organized. He reached into his waistcoat, took a swig from his flask. "I don't think anyone will miss you too much, Matisse."

The others laughed uneasily. Like Boris, they understood just how fragile the balance was in Caeli-Amur. The strikes, the meetings and discussion groups, the broadsheets, the subversive plays performed in little theaters in the Quaedian, the new philosophies springing up. If these continued, the populace would take even greater liberties. Two days earlier, Boris had sat at the House Technis executive meeting with the other officiates and argued that it was time for the Houses to unite, to strike together against the restless subversives in the population. The others had agreed. They were hard and efficient men, but none had seen days like this. They had insisted that the suggestion for a forum of the Houses come from the executive itself. They were trying to keep Boris in his place.

Boris held one secret to himself: Only he knew about the growing seditionist group hidden away in some cavern somewhere, planning their demonstrations and their actions against the Houses. The impulsive action of the population was one thing, but a group like that was another. Tonight Autec would unite the Houses into a single steel machine. It would be the scene of his greatest triumph.

The carriage entered the grounds of House Arbor's Palace, great manicured lawns ending in sharply cut hedges, and beyond that meticulously designed gardens with trees and statues perfectly placed. Beds of flowers were shadows in the dark, but he could imagine their splendid colors. Walkways cut through the garden, sometimes rose up into the air in gentle curves and there met aqueducts, which fed the ponds and fountains. It was said that one could travel along those high waterways in gondolas, looking down on the perfect gardens from above. In the distance, far off in the darkness were what appeared to be thick, junglelike woods. Out there roamed man-sized blood-orchids and other deadly flora. Even now, Boris could hear the crying tear-flowers, a wail that at times seemed like a warbling song. He felt the sudden urge to find those flowers in the darkness, to lie down at their base, to let their nectar drip on him, and to fall into a strange floral-reverie as the flowers and he became one. He took a swig of hot-wine to calm the urge and waited for the surge of energy through his body. The surges came less and less nowadays, and he drank more and more of the wine to compensate. Soon he would need to visit the New-Man—what was his name?—at the markets for more.

They circled a huge circular statue depicting the gods at war: Aya, the rebel god throwing lighting bolts as the others chased him. A short while later the carriage halted. The door was thrown open and Boris stepped down in front of House Arbor's grand palace; how unlike the Technis Complex it was. Rather than the constantly growing mass of contradictory styled of its competitor, the Arbor Palace was classical in its construction. Built hundreds of years earlier, it was a single unchanged chateau. Towers on one end spiraled into the night. Arches suspended the opposite wing over a placid lake. The palace's stately balconies were made of delicate curlicues of wrought iron and windows were set high in its walls, through which Boris could glimpse candlelit rooms. House Arbor, the most ancient of the Houses, still did things in the old ways.

A row of carriages already stood quietly in front of the palace, joined now by the four from Technis—two carrying twelve officiates, and two others containing an entourage of guards, including several undercover philosopher-assassins. Boris's bodyguard, Tonio, a bundle of muscle and repressed energy, was one of them.

A suited intendant stood on the steps. He bore the air of ceremony that so often hung around Arbor. "Ah, dear friends, welcome."

Thirty years had passed since anyone from House Technis had officially entered the House Arbor Palace. Now they followed the intendant through long halls lit by candled chandeliers, the flames flickering above them, little lights of hope. Along the walls, shadows moved. Boris glanced at them, but as soon as he fixed his eyes on them, they were gone. Perhaps it's the hot-wine, he thought to himself. But immediately afterwards he wondered, what if it wasn't?

Halfway along the corridor, tendrils of vines climbed along the walls: at first spidery little things, like great splayed hands, but then thicker, with candle-flowers branching from them, replacing the lamps that had hung on the walls. Finally, the entire corridor had become a wild organic mass, hundreds of candle-flowers gleaming white in the greenery. The vines even grew along the now uneven floor and were worn flat by the passing of many feet.

The corridor opened into a great semicircular theater. Boris could not tell whether it was a part of the palace's internal structure, or a transformed courtyard, for the faraway walls were all composed of the same thick wiry vines, candle-flowers glowing brilliantly around them. The air was redolent with the sweet smells of the flowers' perfumes. Furnace trees stood like pillars throughout, their bulbs emitting the softest warmth, an ingenious method of heating, for as the air in the room became colder, the bulbs would emit more heat to compensate. To survive, the trees needed sun, yet the roof was shrouded in darkness. Perhaps some secret method was used to overcome this. Seats were carved intricately from the aboveground roots of trees and vines that intertwined just so around each other; interlaced as they were, it was unclear to which particular flora the seats belonged. All in all, the theater was a brilliantly, carefully tended, construction—a forum of great imagination that could house close to two hundred people.

The right-hand third of the theater was occupied by thirty or so green-suited men—Arbor's officiates. In the center of the semicircle sat twenty officiates dressed in the traditional aqua suits of House Marin. The left side was vacant for House Technis. At the table at the front of the forum sat three Arbor Directors, and two from Marin.

Boris walked toward the table, but Matisse clasped his arm. "We are all equals. We have no Director. We sit in the theater seats."

Boris clenched his teeth. First the death of the tramworkers in the Arena, now this. I'll get you, Matisse, he thought. There will come a time when the scales will be once again tilted in my favor.

Ancient Director Lefebvre of House Arbor, a shock of gray hair above his still dark eyebrows, his face stern but his eyes fierce, stood from the table and raised his arm. "Technis have called this gathering. But I don't see any reason why we should cooperate. The waves of strikes can be crushed, as they have been. The dungeons are currently carrying out their reeducation of these subversives. None of us is directly threatened."

Boris raised his hand, but Lefebvre chose an officiate from Arbor to speak first. Bitter at the decline of his House, the officiate claimed that Technis had upset the balance of things. Their relentless growth, their rejection of the old traditions of stability, principle, and responsibility toward the society as a whole, had caused these troubles.

Immediately, a hundred arms were raised. Officiates stood up and called out to Lefebvre. As Boris himself was only an officiate, he too took to his feet and raised his arm, but to no avail. First one, then another officiate was called to speak before him. Like the others, Boris sat again, his arm raised, stood up as another officiate was chosen, then sat once more. The debate raged around him. Marin argued that Arbor had always monopolized wealth and power. Both Arbor and Marin claimed that during the wars, Technis had broken the House laws by assassinating officiates at their houses or the forbidden places: the Opera, the steam baths, the parks. No wonder order had broken down in the city. Technis responded that Arbor and Marin had refused to change with the times, and that *that* was the underlying cause of discontent. Each argued that the other was responsible for the situation.

From Technis, Matisse was called to speak. "You are fools. You are sitting in your own houses while the gardens around them burn! We have all seen the rise of dissatisfaction with the Houses—"

"Upstarts. You don't even have a Director!" yelled a hoarse voice from the gallery.

A Marin officiate leaped to his feet. "Technis manipulations. How they speak with honeyed tongues even as they undermine the whole order themselves. This gathering is nothing but a waste of time!"

Boris sat uncomfortably in his seat. The meeting was turning into a farce. In desperation he looked at the other Technis officiates. No help was to be found. He had suggested this meeting. He would have to be the one who took control.

Pushing through the officials who blocked his way, Boris strode onto the floor at the front of the forum, his face red with anger. These fools would get them all killed.

Behind the table, Director Lefebvre stood in anger at Boris's audacity.

"Sit down!" yelled Boris, but the red-faced Lefebvre, eyes like serpents, stood motionless. Next to Lefebvre the other Directors eyed Boris with wide-eyed surprise.

"Only Directors can—," said Lefebvre.

Ignoring him, Boris took the ball from his bag and placed it on the table. Rare though they were, the officiates knew the scrying ball's function. As they quieted, Boris said, "Watch."

Three-dimensional images of the seditionists' hideout sprang to life in the forum around them. There was a great gasp from the officiates, not only at the size of of the seditionist group as they industriously went about their business, but also at the dark visions of the ancient technology that surrounded them: the panels, levers and wheels barely visible on the shadowy walls, the six black pillars of unknown function.

Boris manipulated the image he had recorded earlier so that it focused on Ejan and Louis, who stood close to the door to Ejan's workshop.

Ejan held a bolt-thrower in his hands and turned it over, as if examining it. "It's all very well for Maximilian to have his plans, but we need everyone to be part of the army. And an army needs discipline. There's no room for formlessness in an army. So we shall have to impose this from above. When Maximilian is gone searching for his precious knowledge, but before Aya's Day, before the great demonstration—that will be the moment we strike against the Houses in open warfare."

"Maximilian's followers?"

Ejan nodded with menace, as if to say, yes, we shall have to deal with them. "Anyway, you have the list?"

Louis rolled out a scroll. "Most of the Directors' and the officiates' mansions: Matisse, Strazny, Thorel, Dosois, Autec, Lefebvre. There are some that we haven't yet located, but we will soon. And the subofficiates. When do we strike?"

"As soon as we can. In the days before the demonstration, we shall behead the Houses and liquidate the officiates and their families. The whole system will collapse and a new order will reign."

There was silence in the theater after Boris halted the image.

Director Lefebvre said, "Our houses? Our *families*?" Behind those words, Boris sensed a changed attitude. Lefebvre saw the world now at a different angle.

Boris spoke: "They are organized and experienced. They are building an army of seditionists. Until after Aya's Day, I suggest we maintain more than a truce. I suggest we cooperate. We will crush these subversives. We ruin them, we tear their lives asunder, we break this demonstration, and we show the people just who rules this city."

At first there were a few nods and then a few claps around the room, until the clapping grew and grew, reverberating around Boris like the sound of victory itself.

Flushed with his success, Boris came to the Opera and strode through the labyrinthine tunnels. He would share his triumph with Paxaea and she would feel its colossal significance. She would see him as the architect of this new world, and see a place for herself within it. Boris could sense the inevitability of their union, and the idea of a family filled him with savage joy.

Boris threw open Paxaea's door and was already speaking as he walked inside. "I have united the Houses! For the first time in history, they will be working together. An agreement never before seen! Those fools knew nothing. If it were not for me, they would barely be hanging on to their precious system. Me! Once a tramworker!"

Paxaea stood by her window, her back toward him. "Do you know that if you lean close to the window, you can catch just the smallest glance of the sea?"

Boris stopped. "Don't you realize?" he said. "Don't you comprehend what this means for us?"

"Far away lies my island."

"Forget that," snapped Boris. "I'll get you a room where you can see the ocean. Once I'm Director, I'll get you an entire palace."

She leaned forward, craning her head, pushing her face against the bars.

Boris continued, regardless. "They thought I was a no one. I brought them together, and I unified them. I showed them the real state of affairs. In a sense I'm a prophet, an oracle."

"Have you visited the Augurers?" asked Paxaea.

"No," he said. "It is a long climb through the mountains, and they speak in riddles. They are nothing but obscurantists."

"But they can show you your future," said Paxaea. "Can't they?"

"So they say."

"Everything they showed me would be as if seen through a barred window."

Boris strode over to her, grabbed her by the arms and turned her around. "Enough of such talk. You wallow too much in your misery."

She spoke some words, which he could not quite comprehend. An irresistible urge overtook him, as if his limbs were driven by a part of himself that he could not control, and yet it seemed like the obvious thing to do: He walked from the room. As he walked, the motion made sense to him, but once he was outside the room, he struggled against himself, took control. He pulled out his flask, took another swig of wine, and stormed back into the room.

"Don't use your voice!"

Again she was looking out the window, and she did not turn around.

As he walked to her, he noticed the hundred little muscles on her back, revealed by her low-cut dress. They were finely cut, as if chiseled from rock. He touched her neck and ran his hand softly along the top of her shoulder, onto her dress, and down to her upper arm. He leaned in to her raven black hair and smelled its exotic spices—ginger and clove perfume. "Have faith in me," he said. "I'll take you out of this night and into the day. I'll take you away, wherever you want to go."

She turned to him. "You're my only hope. Take off the torc. Set me free."

Boris felt close to her. She was confessing her true feeling to him, and of course it made sense for her to be emotionally cold.

She was, after all, under his control. But sometimes, like now, she opened up to him and he felt he could trust her.

He touched the torc that was fastened around her neck. He ran his finger along the top of the winding metal, where it touched her skin. He could set her free, and perhaps she would stay with him of her own volition. He grasped the thing between his fingers.

"Let me go to Taritia," she said. "Let me go back home."

"But you would want to stay here with me, wouldn't you?"

She looked up at him, and he was lost in her huge eyes, the lights from the room's lamps reflected in their glistening whites.

"Say it," he said. "Say you'd want to stay with me."

"I'd want to stay with you," she said, one of her voices trilling softly. "We could go together, to Taritia, and then we could return here."

He knew it! He knew that ultimately she wanted him; ultimately she saw something in him. She had said it herself: You are not like the others.

He leaned in and his lips met hers, so soft and large. He pushed her against the wall. Musk and clove-scent aroused him and he felt her body—her breasts, her thighs— voluptuous against him. He pushed her toward the bed, but she slipped aside. "I have to perform tonight. I must get ready."

He nodded, "I'll return tomorrow. Then we'll have more time . . . for each other."

She nodded and looked away, no doubt shy. He liked the way she would turn her head away to hide her feelings. Timidity wasn't something that he had previously associated with her, but he saw it now. Their bond was strengthening.

As he left the Opera, a crowd milled in the Market Square, waiting for the night's late performance. Boris was pleased with himself. Everything was coming together; everything was turning out as he had hoped. He took another swig from his flask and licked his lips, which felt bloated, like those of a deep-sea fish. He wiped them with the back of his hand and noticed a white sheen. He wiped them again, licked his lips and then realized that his mouth was producing a strange froth. He swigged the bottle of hot-wine, but the froth came again. He spat it out onto the cobble-stones and concentrated on stopping his salivation. Finally it abated. He took a final swig from his flask and stepped into his waiting carriage. Tonio flicked the reins and the horses hooves clopped against the stones, a rapid drumbeat accompanying the rattle of the wheels.

He examined his final bottle of hot-wine, with its complex Anlusian wax stamp depicting a machine composed of cogs and wheels and pistons. In the back of his mind, something stirred, but he couldn't bring it to the fore. It had to do with the New-Man, but what was it? What was his name again? He grimaced as he tried to recall the man's name, then put the thought aside. He had things to do. In the morning, he would demand the Directorship from the Elo-Talern.

Boris had come to know the long journey through the empty Technis corridors, deep down into the mountain, into the heart of things. His bursts of laughter echoed eerily down the passage-ways and back. He kicked at the dust-laden floors; little puffs of dust motes billowed up.

"I see you! I see you!" he yelled madly at the shadows around him. He laughed at them, as they flickered around him, shifting and moving like animals in the night. "You don't scare me. You're nothing."

He walked into the emptied hall and called out, "I'm here. Come see me." He laughed again and ran his hand across one of the pillars to his right. It felt smooth to the touch, made of pol-ished stone, marble perhaps.

A voice echoed into the room. "Boris, pass through the double doors, and I will guide you."

Boris moved to the double doors behind the throne. He hesi-tated. What lay behind the doors? The empire of the Elo-Talern—but what was it like? Visions sprang into his mind: a wondrous space of light and calm, but were then quickly replaced by other, darker images of shadows in blackness.

He pulled on the double doors and they creaked toward him. A long corridor led away.

"This way," the voice rustled from somewhere farther along the corridor.

Boris continued on. Some opened out into vast ancient eating rooms, filled with chaises longues and tables, or ballrooms decorated with statues arranged just so, or gaming rooms with carefully arranged chess sets and dice tables. The rooms followed one after another, a vast complex. Rotting rugs and cushions lay strewn about the place, collecting dust and mold. Beside them lay strewn empty amphorae. Thick rugs hung from the walls, their once glorious colors—reds and golds and sky blues—now barely discernible beneath the gray dust. Yet others rooms were filled with empty pools, their mosaic tiles cracked. Indoor fountains, their water long gone, stood close to broken statues. In its time, the place would have been lush and magnificent. People would have lounged and played, paddled in the baths, drunk from fountains and amphorae. Here they would once have held all-night parties. Now the place was just the shattered remnants of an ancient pleasure palace, emptied by vast stretches of time. There was something sad about its abandonment, which intimated the passing of all things. No longer was it a place of pleasure or laughter. The main passageway continued on into the gloom.

"Now, left," the disembodied voice of the Elo-Talern called.

Boris turned at an intersection. The corridor led into a large room filled with a series of baths, some larger than others, all connected by small channels filled with fetid black water. Unknown shapes floated in the pools. Were they the rotten corpses of birds or other small animals? The room reeked of death.

Something moved in one of the nearby pools. The water churned as something floated to the surface: a cadaverous face, like a horse's withered skull pushing from beneath a burial ground.

The Elo-Talern stood, the water coursing down her naked torso, her breasts, withered things over a far-too-long rib cage. "It's good for my joints, the water. Won't you come in?"

Boris looked at the rank water, the floating bits of matter on the surface. He looked up toward the ceiling. "I have unified the Houses to crush this insurgency. I have put the pieces together. I think I am ready to be made Director."

The Elo-Talern flickered into its cadaverous form and then was gone, just like that, from the pool. One moment she had been there, and then—flick-absent from the space. He blinked, silent. A couple of seconds later she appeared several feet closer to him. The water in the pool displaced around her, churning. Again, she was gone. Boris took an involuntary step back. For a long time, nothing stirred.

The cadaverous face burst into the air next to his, horselike and horrible, its teeth large, its eyes gigantic, its voice whispering in his ear. "Oh, I know, Officiate Autec."

She moved slowly behind him; water dripped onto the tiled floor. He remained as still as a statue. Her head craned in, close to the left hand side of his face and her spidery and huge hand rested on the opposite shoulder. He felt water on his skin.

"Boris, you have talent, you have . . . the necessary merciless-ness for greater things."

"I'm not merciless," he said. "I'm not cruel."

"Oh, but you are, Boris. You are, and it's magnificent! I see beyond this weak flesh that you are clothed in. I see your pitiless gaze on the things around you. You are like an ancient King, gaz-ing imperiously over your subjects. Yes, Boris, I see into that hid-den part of you."

"I only do what is necessary," said Boris. "I do what I must to keep the peace. I reward the Houses, a system that has rewarded me. I work for a better Caeli-Amur, a fairer one."

She laughed, the sound like the rustling of paper in the dis-tance. "I will make you Director. You can now move to the Direc-tor's offices. But, Boris, crush these seditionists and we shall find an even *greater* role for you."

"What greater role could there be?"

She leaned in even closer, her dry lips now brushing the side of his ears. "Boris, are you afraid of death?"

Boris was stunned into silence.

Her head brushed slowly against the side of his. "Imagine if you didn't have to die. Imagine if you could live forever. The elixir of life—what would you trade for that? What would you be prepared to do for that? You could live with your precious Siren for centuries, rather than waste away and die in those brief decades that your decaying body will offer you. Imagine that."

Boris remained quiet, but his mind was rushing. He had heard of the Ascended in old wives' tales: those who transcended death. To live without the fear of dying, that emerging blackness coming for them all—that would be truly something—something he could share with Paxaea, who would herself live for hundreds of years or perhaps longer. They could live together beyond the vale of death.

As Boris stood in reverie, the Elo-Talern's horselike head nestled wet against his cheek.

TWENTY-TWO

When Boris arrived back at his office, Subofficiate Armand stood motionless before him, radiating calm, his hands clasped behind his back, his eyes piercing and projecting a sense of control. He seemed the very opposite of Boris: Where the tramworker was stout and common, Armand was thin and aristocratic. "The Elo Talern have instructed me to show you to your new offices and suite. As subofficiate coordinating the Palace, it's been my task to prepare for a new Director, as much as I could."

Armand led Boris up through the Complex toward the uppermost levels and there threw open great double-doors leading to a vast office dominated by a wide dark-wood desk. On the floor a great mosaic pictured Alerion's triumphant march into Caeli-Amur after the battles in the wastelands. The reds and blues of the mosaic's tiles were wondrous and alive.

In the corner of the room, close to the desk, stood a machine the size of a person. It was oval, like a black egg perched on a stand. On its surface, silver ideograms formed complex interweaving patterns. Between its egg-shaped body and its base, it was held up by a metal pole, around which were pistons, a group of thin tubes, small hand-wheels to adjust aspects of the machine, it seemed to Boris.

Along its sides were fixed small metal bolts, but they were unlike those from a normal bolt-thrower. A transparent window in its midsection revealed a thousand little black specks, tiny mite-sized mechanical creatures.

"It's a memory-catcher. Here's the trigger for it." Armand showed Boris a button underneath the desk. "Have your enemy approach the desk, then pull the trigger. As easy as that. The bolt is loosed, the memory drained, leaving the victim mindless. The memory can then be imbibed later." He gestured to the machine behind him. "You see the bolts attached to the side? They're the vessels for the victim's remembrances."

Boris was transfixed by the splendor of the room, but he couldn't stop thinking of Paxaea. He should concentrate on the office, on his work, on quelling the disturbances that threatened House rule, but the image that rose in his mind again and again was of great emerald eyes and raven black hair. She had suggested they travel to Taritia together, and he imagined her showing him the little rock-pooled coves, the steep sheer cliffs and ridges on the islands, the wondrous views of the archipelago as the hundred and more little islands scattered across the warm seas.

Boris opened the doors that led to his personal rooms, which were warmly decorated in frescoes of red and orange depicting Caeli-Amur under the rein of Alerion, after he had thrown Aya from the city. A huge bed stood along one wall. At the opposite end of the room sat couches and chaises longues around a little semi-circle, close to a fireplace. Through an open door at the other side of the room Boris could see the base of some great machine, a tangle of pipes and tubes. He walked to the door and examined the huge round object. "A sphere!" he said. A staircase led around the sphere to its open top. He climbed the stairs and looked in at the pale water. "Incredible: just like the water palaces." Boris thought again of Paxaea. Tonight they would lie together, he had decided. He would take her to one of the water palaces and then . . . He shook off the alluring vision.

Armand stood tall and straight. "It has been ten years since the House has had a Director. He lived for the House and he died for the House. I hope you'll not be a disappointment."

Boris stared at the young man. "Whom do you think you're talking to?"

"That's better." The side of Armand's lips twitched slightly.

"But I'm going. I have things to do."

"Before you do, one last thing." He led him to the corner of the office, where a great ball sat on top of a pillar, from which jutted a lever. "It's a scrying ball: to communicate with the Director-ate of Varenis. They are expecting your contact."

"What do we owe them?"

Armand examined him calmly. "Nothing; everything. Varenis has left us a free city-state. What is that worth? It's simply a matter of courtesy." He waited as he thought and added: "Remember, failed Directors never come to a happy end. I look forward to making your Directorship as brutal as necessary and successful as can be."

Armand turned to leave, but Boris halted him. "Armand, I re-member well your kind words at the amphitheater. Congratula-tions, you are now an officiate, if that is what you wish."

Armand smiled coolly and nodded his head. "A fine first deci-sion, Director." He turned and left, inscrutable and aloof as ever.

Boris stood before the pillar. He wanted desperately to leave. The thought of Paxaea engulfed his mind like a drug. Instead he looked with dread at the lever. Varenis was ruled by the Sorti-leges, but was run by the Directorate, a great bureaucracy that held all the levers of power. Unlike Caeli-Amur, theirs was one unified power under the watchful eye of a single Director. Boris wondered how it worked. Like most workers, he had never ven-tured to other cities. He had never even seen the Dyrian coast. But his concept of Varenis set his imagination alight. Into Boris's mind sprang visions of a new Caeli-Amur: a Forum to replace the ruined ancient one. It would be composed of the Houses, with voting rights, and for the citizens, a tribune with speaking rights. Perhaps Varenis would help? Boris pressed his lips together. He rubbed his hands against the side of his suit. Fear gripped him. He continued to examine the lever.

Boris reached forward and gripped it, hesitated for a moment as fear rushed down into his stomach, then shifted it down.

A pinpoint of light began in the center of the ball. Quickly it spread out to fill the entire thing. Finally it radiated into the whole room.

The sister ball seemed to be in a room atop a circular tower of some sort. For in front of him, Boris could see a balcony with a railing. Nearby stood the circular walls of other towers that dwarfed even this one. Beyond these lay a vast plaza surrounded by gigantic forty- or fifty-story buildings. His mind leaped: Varenis's Plaza of the Sun in which stood the twelve towers, one for each of the Sortileges, as every Caeli-Amur schoolchild knew.

The image of a man walked into Boris's office, though his body was leagues away in Varenis. "Ah, my counterpart for House Technis. Welcome. Your man Armand has sent us word of your rise to power."

Boris said, "I'm Boris Autec."

"The Sortileges greet you. . . ." The man had no need to introduce himself: when a man ascended to the position, he gave up his name and became only known as the Director. Instead, he hesitated for a minute and looked to his right, at something out of Boris's vision. An odd light shone from that direction, as if someone were holding an lamp with a warped lens that distorted the image. Boris squinted, but could not make anything out in that misshapen part of the projection.

The man's voice trembled. A twitch appeared beneath one eye. "The Sortileges ask how you . . . how you intend to enforce order in Caeli-Amur."

"The Elo-Talern and—"

"The Elo-Talern are nothing but withered degenerates!" The man burst out unexpectedly. He seemed angry with someone other than Boris, perhaps himself. He glanced briefly again to his right, toward the shifting and contorting light. Something was standing out of view: *someone was watching the conversation.* "Forget the Elo-Talern. They have retreated from this world. Why they have suddenly taken interest in the Houses after so many years is a mystery. Perhaps you think they rule Caeli-Amur the way the Sortileges rule Varenis, but that would be an error. Those days are long gone."

Boris blinked rapidly. Rudé had mentioned that the Elo-Talern had only recently reemerged to turn their attention to matters in Caeli-Amur. Boris suddenly wondered why. Boris pushed the thought from his mind and said, "No doubt the Sortileges are great indeed. It is a great comfort that we can rely on their support."

The Varenis Director's legs began to tremble. "It would be unacceptable to Varenis for there to be some kind of . . . lawlessness, some tyranny of liberty, in Caeli-Amur. We rely on all our neighboring regions to remain stable. How else might peaceful rule continue? The Directorate would be unhappy if it needed to intervene. Many of our legions are engaged with the wild tribes of the northeast. The ones stationed in Varenis have already spent years campaigning. They deserve some rest. In any case, keep us informed."

Boris nodded and pursed his lips as the Director leaned forward and the image shrank rapidly back into a point of light within the ball.

Boris blinked again. Words rattled in his mind: "The Elo-Talern are nothing but withered degenerates."

Replaying the scene, Boris rushed from his new rooms to the courtyard, where Tonio waited with his carriage. From there Boris rode back to the Opera. As he waited in the carriage for Paxaea, the world was a writhing sea of shadows. He could make them out more clearly now. They seemed to be on a different plane, so that they appeared to walk up invisible stairs or inclines, or else dip beneath the ground. He gulped the last of his hot-wine from his final bottle. Tomorrow he would acquire some more at the market.

When Paxaea stepped into the carriage, he pulled her close to him so she almost toppled onto him. She tensed: she was perhaps nervous, now that things were progressing well between them. Doubtless she didn't want to ruin her chance for happiness, her chance to return to her Taritia. She sat down awkwardly next to him.

"I am Director of House Technis. I have been given the finest offices overlooking the city; all the officiates will report to me; we are on the road to our triumph."

"That is good news," she said tersely.

"There is more. The Elo-Talern have offered me the elixir of life. It seems incredible, a child's tale, but it's true. Do you know what that means? It means that perhaps I could live forever, beside you."

She looked at her delicately sculpted maroon boots, a fine

combination of Taritian style with Caeli-Amur workmanship. She did not, however, reply.

The carriage carried them north, along the low-lying area overlooked by the Northern Headland on which perched House Marin's palace and many of the mansions belonging to the Marin officials. They passed over the canals that crisscrossed the area, the carriage climbing over bridges, some miniature, others wide and long. Through the windows, boatmen could be seen pushing their gondolas along the canals, which stank of refuse in the warm summer air.

The carriage stopped at a colossal building, almost as large as the Opera, and cut in the manner of the ancients, giant pillars running along the front of it. Boris stepped from the carriage and held out his hand for Paxaea.

Up the stairs they climbed, and into the Water Palace of Taium, the largest of the baths in the pleasure district of Caeli-Amur. Led by an intendant, they traversed the long halls, seeing the many steam baths to their right and left, some surrounded by gardens, others like rock pools, one below the next, connected by waterfalls.

Eventually he led them to a door. He touched the wall and the door dilated open, revealing a spherical room with a round door on either side. "Undress, and place your clothes into these slots in the wall. When you are ready, tell the chamber and it will begin."

Boris began to disrobe, but Paxaea stood still.

"What is this place?"

"The baths of the ancients. Disrobe," said Boris.

She reached for her shoulder. With a subtle rub of thumb and forefinger, her dress dropped to the ground. Boris stood there, mesmerized by that hourglass figure, the heavy breasts and the wide hips, the rounded belly. She looked like a painting, with her black hair swept back severely, and her emerald eyes challenging him, fierce and proud.

He placed her still-moving dress together with his clothes in the slot, which then closed.

"There is no water," she said.

"We are ready," Boris said to the room.

The circular door closed behind them, sealing them inside. A soft gurgling sound issued from the walls. From a thousand little openings around the base of the walls, water poured into the room. The water was warm as it touched their feet. A few moments later it had risen to their ankles, and then their knees. There was a faint perfumed scent to it; it was infused with vanilla and another more robust aroma. When the water reached their waists, Boris dropped down and kicked his legs. He floated toward Paxaea, who remained still. He took her by the arms and held himself horizontal. The water was now above Paxaea's breasts, then her neck.

She kicked off the floor and slowly treaded water.

Together they floated toward the ceiling, the both of them kicking their legs as the roof neared.

"When will it stop?"

"What?" asked Boris mischievously.

"The water. When will it stop rising?" Her two voices spoke with a desperate unity.

Boris laughed again and waited until the water carried them higher. Paxaea put her hands to the roof in a panic, tilting her head as it came near. Boris enjoyed the fear and surprise in her eyes. It was like playing a wonderful prank. He dropped his head beneath the water and was seized by panic himself. No matter how much his mind told him to breathe in the water, his lungs would not do it. The water had now filled the whole chamber, and he looked over at Paxaea's desperate eyes. His lungs still refused him, and he found himself straining. Everything slowly faded to white, and his lungs burned, as if they were aflame. He sucked in a big mouthful and, his body heaving, his lungs filled up with water. He convulsed a couple of times, though there was no pain. Again he looked across at Paxaea, whose black hair wafted around ethereally. She grimaced and opened her mouth and then she, too, breathed the superoxygenated water.

He took her by the hand and they dived down into the center of the chamber and to the circular passage that had opened up on the side of the sphere. Along the circular tunnel they swam, into the labyrinth of the water palace.

They passed through a succession of rooms and passages,

which were slowly filling with kaleidoscopic lights cutting at angles. Before long, they seemed to drift through an aqua sea, at times forests of seaweed wavered around them, schools of exotic fish, of brilliant yellows and oranges moving in unison. They entered caves, dark and craggy, and in those murky depths watched giant lobsters retreat beneath little rocky outcrops. The caves opened out to a vast open seabed, where giant crabs scuttled along the floor.

The world shifted and they were flying like birds, high above Caeli-Amur. Beneath them the city gleamed white in the summer sun like a miniature version of itself, and across the water Caeli-Enas still sat upon the water, beautiful and white, like a gleaming jewel on the sea. They kicked their legs in its direction and flew across the high winds. From above, Boris could see white-robed figures gently walking through the tree-lined promenades. The buildings of the ancients below were cut so cleanly and smoothly, not at all like the newer, crumbling versions in Caeli-Amur, which were piled upon each other. The magnificence of that city, there in the light!

But already Paxaea was kicking ahead of Boris, southeast, toward the Taritian Archipelago. He kicked his legs and followed her. They passed above cutters sailing through the water below. They passed over reefs breaking through the surface of the water like bones breaking through skin, perched on them the ruins of ships, like the decaying bones of beached whales. Finally, in the distance a hundred and more little islands came into view: rocky little things with craggy peaks. Waterfalls fell from their yellow cliffs into the surrounding shoals and reefs. Deadly water currents coursed through narrow channels as the islands spun and shifted around one another in their wondrous geological dance. Boris looked at Paxaea, and a gurgling sound came from her throat.

The world shifted and they were swimming out among the stars, as if their bodies were ships passing through the blackest night. A terrible cry pierced that space. Paxaea had opened her voice and it came through the water and Boris covered his ears with his hands. Still he heard that voice, resonating in his body, vibrating his cells. A blinding pain seized his head like a clamp.

He kicked out and gurgled; he could barely breathe. He was being swept away on a dark sea, about to lose consciousness. He struggled to remember the word. What was it?

"Taritia," he spoke into the water and the scream was cut off suddenly. The pain disappeared and Paxaea struggled and kicked as she held the torc, which closed around her throat. Boris spoke again and released the torc.

He swam then to Paxaea, who held her hands to her eyes. He held her and they floated through an asteroid belt, a million drifted by, a thousand rocky ships. Little sounds escaped from her throat as her tears were lost in the water around them.

As they took the carriage back toward the Opera, Boris stared down the narrow alleyways and the lamp-lined canals, romantic in the night. Paxaea sat next to him, silent. She was like the water herself, one moment stormy and gray, the next moment a flat surface, hiding hidden depths, sunken cities that he couldn't venture to. He looked across at her dress, which molded itself to her, accentuating the curve of her belly, the strong thighs. Energy radiated from his chest and his groin. He needed her; he needed to be beside her, within her. He wanted to leap upon her and take her that very moment, but instead he looked away. Inside him, the hot-wine still burned, stoking a fire of murky emotions.

He followed her along the corridors of the Opera. When they reached her room, she said, "I'm tired. I think I might sleep now." She started to close the door, but he placed his hand against it.

"I want to talk to you, don't you understand?" He looked at her dress, so flimsy around her body.

Paxaea stared at him coldly. "I'm tire—"

"But don't you want me to stay?" Confusion reigned in Boris's mind. She had said that they would travel together. She had given him indications that they would be together. Yes, he understood that she was a prisoner, but he had sought to build a bond between them beyond that of master and servant. He had been true and honest to her, offered her the world. And yet, as he thought these things, hidden far away in the corner of his mind was a soft voice that said that these were nothing but delusions. In his mind he silenced that voice. He needed her now. He could not wait any longer.

She looked at him angrily. "Want you to stay? I never wanted you to stay. I never wanted to see you in the first place. I never wanted you and your bloated body and your petty ambitions and your grubby past." With both voices, she said something more, something incomprehensible to him, and he took his hands from the door as she closed it.

Anger welled in him. He grasped the door and tore at it, the hot-wine coursing through his veins, his muscles, his nerves. There was a terrible cracking as the door broke from its frame. He threw it open and it hung like an old and battered coat. Paxaea was already halfway across the room.

He pointed at her. "Don't use your voice."

Again she spoke and he turned and walked out through the door. He forced himself to stop, turned, placed his hands over his ears. "Don't use your voice!"

She turned away from him. "You don't scare me. You may be Director now, but we both know you're nothing but a deluded tramworker."

He slammed the shattered door back into its cracked frame where it lodged. He turned again and strode across the room. Paxaea opened her mouth to speak, but he spoke first. "Taritia." Her eyes filled with fear. She raised her hands to her throat as the torc tightened. He grabbed her by the hair and dragged her across the room and threw her onto the bed, scrabbling and crawling. Again he spoke the word and the torc tightened further. A little gurgle escaped her lips and the emerald eyes were filled with alarm. Those eyes—the same ones he had seen at the water palace—excited him. He pushed himself down onto her and the warmth of her body close to his aroused him further. He reached down and undid his pants. As he forced up her dress which he felt shift around his arm, Paxaea's hands still held the torc. He looked down to see her high and wide ribs, too high to be a human's. As if to protect her, her nictating membranes closed over her eyes. Beneath the milky white eyelids, her pupils were just visible. All around Boris the shadows moved, like animals fighting in the dark.

Boris strode down the corridors; they shifted around him as if they were made of some ethereal substance, like gray sheets blowing in the wind.

He returned to the great bed in the Director's chambers, but he could not sleep. Part of him wanted to return to the Opera, to see Paxaea, to apologize to her, to make love to her properly, to take her again and feel that exquisite pleasure. A flash of her eyes came to his mind, and he was again excited, and then immediately repelled by himself. He lay on his bed and the world around him seemed composed of shadowy shapes. The very walls of his apartment seemed insubstantial wavering things. Shadow walls from the shadow world wavered where no walls should have been. Stairs climbed up to rooms in that second plane's existence, where things scuttled in the blackness. Then a great black shadow seemed to emerge, darker than the darkness, and loom before him. It had a familiar shape, a tramworker's shape. It shifted toward him, and he backed himself up against the wall behind the bed.

"Get away, get away," he whispered.

But the shadow remained in front of him and Boris thought he saw eyes there in the darkness, staring evilly at him.

"Mathias, is that you? Mathias?"

The eyes bored into him, and they were red now, like blots of blood in the darkness.

Boris closed his eyes. "Go away," he whispered.

He held his eyes closed for the rest of the night, in the darkness, alone. Slowly the strength of the hot-wine drained from him. Dawn broke and when he finally opened his eyes, the shadow was gone, disappeared with the shadow world around it.

Determined to acquire more hot-wine, Boris ventured to the markets. But the New-Man Quadi was not there. Boris needed the wine's strength and power. But search as he might, the New-Man was gone. A horrible thought crossed his mind as he rushed back to his office. He scoured the images captured by the scrying ball, and he saw the New-Man, walking among the subversives—that was what he had tried to remember, days ago, that vague notion nibbling at the edge of his thoughts.

Knowing he would be drained for a while, he took the ball with him to his old apartment, where he collapsed on the bed. As he surveyed the images, he heard the seditionist Maximilian discussing a plan to build some kind of air-cart. Boris rubbed his temples with powerful fingers. The hot-wine, the time spent with Paxaea, his plans to unify the Houses—they had taken his focus from the seditionists. Rather than have a subofficiate monitor the seditionists, he had chosen to perform the task himself, and keep the knowledge to himself. Now he was about to pay a price. He tried to raise himself from the bed, but his limbs were leaden and lifeless. Around him everything started to lose its color, as if it were painted in a shade of gray. He was filled with a terrible anxiety. The image of Paxaea on her bed rose in his mind like a floating corpse, and each time he tried to push it away, it rolled up again. He pressed his palms hard against his eyes, but that was no help. Things were falling apart.

TWENTY-THREE

After House Marin's guard followed Ejan's group to the hideout, Maximilian began to feel the pressure of events. Aya's Day was three weeks away. Finally, a meeting had been secured with the Collegia, who were essential to the plan, for they united the small traders, craftsmen, shopkeepers. If the seditionists could ally themselves with the Collegia, then the masses of the Lavere and the slums might march with them. The meeting was set for the coming Jolisday, five days hence.

Meanwhile, the members of the *Call to Arms* group were out in the streets with their broadsheets and graffiti. During the days, Ejan's group piled head-sized canvas-covered incendiary devices, tightly wrapped and tied with rope, along a wall already lined with swords and long-knives. He had seen Josiane walk from the workshop with Ejan, who talked fervently. She shook her head at whatever he said but he took her arm and led her back into his workshop.

Meanwhile, building the air-cart was proceeding apace. Maximilian knew that he should leave the journey to Caeli-Enas until after Aya's Day. He should ally his own followers with *A Call to Arms*. Together they still outnumbered Ejan's group, but not for long.

But the pull of the Great Library of Caeli-Enis was too strong. Yes, it was a risk, but one worth taking. He would discover the Library's secrets, and return a few days later, well before Aya's Day. He would return with all the knowledge necessary for a great thaumaturgist. He needed Odile to provide the equations for the weaving of chymistry, zoological thaumaturgy, and transmutae. Then, under Quadi's direction, they could finish the cart. So he was pleased that his street urchin had delivered news from Odile: They were to meet in two days at the café La Tazia.

When Max arrived in the machine room, neither Kata nor Quadi were at work in the workshop area. He frowned, marched forward, stopped. Kata looked up from where she was squatting. Quadi lay beneath her, unconscious.

"He collapsed," she said. "He just collapsed."

They carried Quadi back to the central cavern and laid him on a bed. When he awoke they gave him water. Maximilian paced beside Quadi, up and down. Emotions ran through him, one after another: frustration, disappointment, anger. Omar's disappearance had disturbed Maximilian. At nights he lay awake wondering where Omar was, and what was the function of this strange underground world they inhabited. Now Quadi was possessed by this strange death wish. The New-Man had been gaunt when he had joined them. Now he was positively cadaverous. This self-starving was common among New-Men in Caeli-Amur, but to Max it was alien and inscrutable. It grieved him to see the New-Man's bony features.

When Quadi had regained consciousness, Maximilian gathered his circle in the machine room and explained that they would abandon the plan to build a second air-cart. He would travel to the Sunken City alone with the first.

"You cannot go alone." Kata's voice seemed to tremble a little.

Maximilian had figured her to be a hardened member of the group, but more and more she seemed soft to him, as if she were unveiling weakness underneath. He liked it, and yet they needed weapons made of steel, not of tin. A few days earlier, he fancied that she had moved to kiss him. He felt confused by the event. First, he had been surprised and turned away. Yet later he had thought about what it would have been like, to kiss her, to touch that athletic waist. Something stirred within him, not just an interest—a desire. She was lovely, precisely because she was imperfect, had weaknesses as well as strengths. He sensed that she was lost and he thought of Nkando. He brushed his hand through his hair, found the knot that had been there for sometime, pulled away at it angrily. There was no room for such things in his life. He had dedicated himself to seditionism.

"There is no time to build a second air-cart. I am the most qualified to recognize the tomes in the Great Library. I have memorized the code. And you." Maximilian looked at Quadi; again he thought of Omar. "You shall start eating. We need your strength."

"Have I failed you yet?" asked Quadi.

"I cannot have you fail at the last hurdle."

Quadi broke into one of his distinctive grins. "Oh, the last hurdle is a while away. Until then I'll be fine."

Kata said, "I think we should work tirelessly to keep these plans secret. There may well be House agents among us now."

Maximilian nodded: that was better; that was why he valued Kata.

Two days later, the cart stood in the workshop, an image from a fevered imagination. Round carriage wheels held its weight. Delicate slats ran vertically along the inside of the cart, like a boat's sails, able to shift in the wind, to which the fish gills would be attached. From these slats thin tubes ran into a central oxygen chamber, just as from from this chamber larger tubes ran forward to the suit. Attached to the cart's sides were compartments and pouches. Now it was time to perform the thaumaturgy and animate the fish gills.

Maximilian, Quadi, and Kata left the hideout and ventured into the city. They would meet Odile at La Tazia. It was two months since he'd seen her at the printworkers strike. How things had changed since then. Kamron had been deposed, the seditionist group had grown, the streets were alive now with anti-House sentiment.

As the little group passed along Via Gracchia, tension seemed to hang over the cafés and bars. Even the cats seemed on edge, pacing up and down on the cafés' roofs. A nasty-looking one-eyed black cat scurried along the street as they approached La Tazia. It stopped and looked back at them ominously, then darted along an alleyway and was gone.

In La Tazia, two small groups of philosopher-assassins were drinking coffee and stretching out languorously. As Max and the others found seats in the corner, they surveyed the scene. On one balcony outside, a couple held each other's hands lovingly and seemed in the midst of profoundly intimate talk. Five thaumaturgists sat on the other balcony where they argued animatedly, gesticulating as they spoke. This was a strange sight, for thaumaturgists rarely ventured to the cafés; even more infrequently did they argue in public. Inside, a fat philosopher-assassin sat alone at the bar, a huge bowless bolt-thrower hung from his waist.

One group of philosopher-assassins baited the other. "You gratificationists wouldn't understand. The Aya's Day demonstration will rearrange things in this city, you mark my words. But you gratificationists, you're incapable of thinking of the future. Wouldn't you say, Fat Nik?"

The fat man at the bar turned his head, looked silently, and turned back to his coffee.

The café's owner, Pehzi, walked from behind the bar to Maximilian's group. "I've some new mince pies if you'd like to try some."

Maximilian screwed his face up. "Mince pies?"

Pehzi cackled until the cackle became a wheeze and then a burbling cough.

"Some cheese, please," said Kata.

"What's so funny?" said Quadi. He rolled a cigarette with one hand, almost like a magic trick. Max was horrified to realize he'd grown accustomed to the smell.

Pehzi wandered off without answering.

On the other side of the room, one of the gratificationists spoke loudly. There was a charge to his words that grabbed Maximilian's attention. "Perhaps the Aya's Day demonstration will turn out to be a hitherto unseen moment of pleasure. Perhaps it will be extremely *gratifying*. Perhaps you're wrong to assume that we wouldn't understand. And if you're wrong about that, what else might you be wrong about? Perhaps your entire theoretical foundation? Perhaps thought is not the most pure form of experience. Perhaps feeling is."

Maximilian wondered if some factions of the philosopher-assassins might serve also as allies. He pushed the thought from his mind. They were mercenaries, nothing more.

A few minutes later Pehzi brought to the table a platter of cheese with thinly sliced bread and a wicked-looking hooked knife. Kata sliced a piece of cheese with one hand, grasped a piece of bread with the other. She held it out to Quadi.

"You should eat," said Maximilian.

"No."

"You should," said Kata. "We don't want you dying before we're finished."

"I said no."

They sat in silence for a minute.

"What happened to you in Anlusia? What is this strange self-destructive disease that you New-Men are so prey to?"

"I'm sorry." Quadi stood up, lit another cigarette, and walked toward the exit of the café. As he passed, both groups of philosopher-assassins sniffed the air and grimaced. They looked appalled.

Kata ate some more cheese and bread while Maximilian sat somberly.

At that point, Odile slipped into the seat beside Kata. Side by side they looked quite unalike: Odile, slim with her short-cropped blond hair and lighthearted demeanor; Kata, with shoulder-length flowing hair and brooding visage.

"Here it is, the interweaving formula." Odile passed a small notebook to him. She then looked around, sniffed the air. "What's that smell?"

Max shook his head to say, "Don't ask."

Odile continued: "You're going to combine the disciplines, aren't you?"

Max smiled at her. "How are things at the university?"

"You know students, always up in arms about something."

Max pushed the remains of the cheese toward Odile. "The whole city is up in arms. Soon we'll be able to help them direct it."

Odile picked at the cheese. "Oh, that's exactly what the city needs. Another group directing it."

"You've always been enamored of the impulsive moods of the population. You think there's something pure in them," said Max.

"You think there's something pure to your own dreams." Odile pushed the cheese away again.

The two stared aggressively at each other, then burst into laughter.

"It's good to see you, Odile." Max grasped his friend's hand. "This is Kata."

Odile slipped from the seat. "We shouldn't be seen together. The city's not safe anymore. There are spies everywhere. Don't combine the disciplines, Max. Two, perhaps. But three—surely not even you are that mad. I still want to hear about your wild dreams, you know."

With that, Odile walked away through the café and a gratificationist called to her. "Hey, would you like Aya's Day to be one of great pleasure?"

Odile looked back, smiled. "As long as it doesn't involve you."

Shortly afterwards, Max and Kata left the philosopher-assassins to their debates. Fat Nik looked up from his coffee at them as they passed him. They walked along one of the winding side alleys that led down to the cliffs. The view across the sea was spectacular. At the base of the cliffs before them, to the south of the Quaedian, the necropolis lay sprawled before them, filled with a thousand and more tombs and headstones. In its center lay the Mausoleum of the Gods.

"Soon Quadi will be down there," Max spoke bitterly.

"You need to understand philosophy," said Kata. "To understand his position."

"I *don't* understand."

"What do we know about the New-Men? They are intensely driven, they must build and create and grow. You have heard the stories of their great city, growing like a cancer. Remember, they are *not* men, they are *New-Men*. They are filled with restless energy. They can never rest, but are condemned always to *do*. Their minds are different."

He turned from her and placed his hands on the rail. The sea was deep blue. White breakers crashed along the Southern Headland. In the south of the city, the Arena could be seen at the base of the Thousand Stairs, and close to it the ruins of the Ancient

Forum, crumbling buildings, pillars standing alone amongst the rubble, the great arch of Iniria, somehow still intact. Even on days like this, when the sky was blue and clear, there seemed to be a fog that sat over the Forum. During the nights, the citizens avoided it, for the ghosts of the ancients were said to haunt the place, grieving for their lost world.

"Come here," Kata said. From behind, she wrapped her arms around Max and rested her chin on his shoulder. Her voice was so soft, he could barely hear it; its half-broken tone something he had never heard before. "The world is a beautiful, generous place, isn't it? And this city, how hard it would be to leave." Her warmth radiated through to him, and he yearned to hold her arms to him, to relax into her. To his surprise, he felt the first stirrings of arousal. He turned and faced her dark lustrous eyes, her dark hair. Caught in her intensity, he pulled her close and his lips touched hers. Desire coursed through him like lava churning within a mountain. Entwined, they staggered against the wall of a building, his hands pulling her dress up over her thighs. The sky was blue above then, the sun hot on his face. Somehow, his belt was already unbuckled and his pants dropping down to his knees. He was drawn into her blazing intensity, sucked like a planet into a sun. He moved in her, his hand placed against the cool stone of the wall, her breath in his ear, the touch of wind on the back of his thighs.

"Maximilian," she said. "Maximilian."

When they were done, he leaned against her, filled with guilt and shame. He closed his eyes as she ran her hands through his hair on the back of his head. He tried to think of ways to extricate himself, finally settled on, "That can't happen again. You understand that, don't you?"

Kata's voice was strained in his ear. "Of course not."

"We have much work to do. Let's return," he said.

"To the little hole that we hide in?" she said bitterly.

"Yes."

The guilt did not abate when they returned to the seditionist base, nor did his confusion, for that sudden moment of intimacy had awakened worlds he had cut off from himself long ago. He yearned now for Kata, for her combination of decisiveness and vulnerability, for her touch. He saw in her not only the movement of a philosopher-assassin, deadly in a crisis, but also a kindness beneath. He could see her as a true leader of the seditionists, if only she believed in herself and her destiny. Together they might make a formidable couple, and yet, there was no time for such attachments—thus he had always believed.

Quadi was nowhere to be seen and he did not return that day. Max worried about the New-Man, for it was Quadi's task to attach the gills. But the New-Man was not a seditionist. He did not hold the cause to be the highest value, the greatest goal. To Quadi, the expedition was simply an adventure.

That night Maximilian avoided Kata, though it hurt him. She, too, would need time, he realized, to dissociate from him. Instead, he plunged into his work. He studied the formulae to transform the bloodstone energy into the gills of the fish. The equations were complex and subtle: as if moving smoothly from one language to an entirely different one. Later, as he slept, Maximilian dreamed of the Sunken City, before it had collapsed into the ocean. White caparisoned horses drew carriages down its wide boulevards. Everything was marble and glittering. But the people stared at him, as if he was an impostor, a foreigner. They knew he was there to steal their riches, to take what wasn't his.

"You will never escape." A man wearing bloodred robes stared at him evilly. "The city will keep you here. You will never make it home."

He awoke on his mattress, exhausted. His eyes felt as if sand had been rubbed into them. He blinked rapidly.

Shortly afterwards, Quadi straggled into the hideout. He spent the day lying on his back, staring at the ceiling. Max was filled with guilt. He always strained to hold seditionism as the highest cause, to which all others were submitted, but did that not make him uncaring? Did he not use those around him? He thought of Kata holding him the day before, on the cliffs. Now he looked at Quadi, who had become his friend.

"Quadi." Max knelt beside the New-Man.

The New-Man's eyes wandered aimlessly.

"Have some water, at least."

Quadi sipped, most of the water dribbling over his cheeks and onto the floor.

"I'm sorry that I pressed you yesterday."

"No matter," said Quadi. "I can't expect you to understand."

Despite his misgivings, Maximilian found himself saying, "We lost time yesterday."

"I'm sorry. It won't happen again."

"Quadi. Why do you do this to yourself?"

Quadi reached up and place his hand on Maximilian's shoulder. "You're a friend. You're a good friend."

But I'm not, thought Maximilian to himself. To create a world where people around me are treated with humanity, I treat those around me in precisely the opposite manner. But he had cast his die. There was nothing to do but to see what number he had rolled.

"Tomorrow we complete the cart," said Maximilian. Or I lose control of the formulae and I die, he thought.

TWENTY-FOUR

With the entirety of his little group around him, Maximilian prepared himself. Kata and Quadi stood ready to detach the gills from the fish. It was essential that the gills were freshly cut, that they still retain the resonances of life before Max infused them with the uncanny power of the bloodstone.

In one hand, Maximilian held the vial of bloodstone, heavier than lead. The large fish swam in the barrels beside him. He closed his eyes, remembered the incantations, the gesticulations, the complex algebra. He was struck by doubt. The risks of the thaumaturgy were extreme; it was possible that he might never reemerge from the trance at all, but be trapped within while he died rapidly. It was possible that the bloodstone might infect him with its disease, or infuse him with weird transformations. He steeled himself.

Maximilian began his incantations. He opened up his perception to zoologism, the life structures beneath the phenomenal. In this deep structure of things, he felt the numinous vitality of the fish as they swam in their barrel, ghosts within their scaled bodies. He focused his trance on the quick words between Kata and Josiane, the brief struggle of the fish as they were put to the knife, their vitality shaking and shifting within their bodies, struggling against its form, yearning now for release from their dying husks.

Holding that perception to one side, Maximilian invoked the chymical equation to trap the weird power of the bloodstone and threw the red crystals into the air. There they hovered, a cloud of red dust, as he held them, suspended. He felt his own energy seeping out of him. The bloodstone cloud gave a shudder and radiated heat, burned him as he held it suspended the air, adding his own strength to the unnatural power.

Maximilian invoked the formula he had acquired from Odile. He held the bloodstone in one part of his mind and shifted trances to transmutae, which he would need to move the bloodstone's energy into the gills. He lost a sense of the bloodstone and panicked. Thaumaturgical energy flooded toward him, threatening to warp him. Desperately he held it at bay, but then lost his grip on the transmutae, which he had to begin all over again. Again, he invoked the laws of biological zoologism, and saw a different set of structures. He began the invocation to bind the bloodstone's powers to the gills. His strength was weakening now, and he felt his body shake. It was too much for him, controlling these complexities. He fell to his knees. Somewhere nearby he heard a call, realized it was from his own throat. He knew, then that he would have to give up his defenses, allow the thaumaturgical forces to flow back into him, warp and poison him. That was the only way to complete the task. He prepared himself, let go of his defenses, aware as he controlled the last part of the equations, as the bloodstone's powers coursed into the the gills, that injurious forces were also entering his body. He was being changed.

When the suit and cart were finished, Maximilian vomited repeatedly. He shivered and sweated as if he had been poisoned. That night he lay wrapped in blankets and he felt like there was a hot wet towel inside his chest. He drifted in and out of sleep and dreamed that a serpent was asleep inside him, though he knew soon it would awake and force itself out of his mouth.

In the morning, the fever had broken, but Max felt exhausted, and somehow *altered*. There was, as yet, no external sign of the thaumaturgy's malign influences on him. But he could feel something growing within him. Was it something physical or psychological?

Maximilian shuffled down the corridor to the workshop, where the suit lay on the table, the great spherical bronze helmet at its head, the densely woven Anlusian fabric, thick and silvery. Beside the suit stood the cart, with its hose jutting out the front and its wheels large so it could be dragged along the ocean floor. Maximilian leaned against the cart and smiled weakly at Quadi, who had accompanied him. Kata stood glancing between the two of them. The task was finished.

Maximilian's entire group ventured to the café La Tazia to celebrate. The lovers Oewen and Ariana hid themselves away on a balcony. Gilli and Philippe sat along the bar next to the great fat philosopher-assassin who seemed a permanent fixture in the place. Clemence and Usula joined Maximilian, Quadi, and Kata, who had been circumspect about their encounter in the alleyway, around a table.

"He doesn't look well," said Quadi, looking at Pehzi.

"He looks just like you."

Quadi broke suddenly into a grin. "Perhaps it's time to smoke."

In unison the entire group—Max, Kata, Clemence, and Usula—leaned forward and said, "No!"

Quadi looked nonplussed, then shrugged his shoulders and left his pouch of weed alone.

When the coffee arrived with accompanying Numarian sweet-melon, noted for its red sugary pips, Maximilian made a toast. "To the underwater suit."

They took their coffee in one gulp and Maximilian looked over to Quadi: "A piece of fruit for celebration?"

"You know," said Quadi, "I think I will. Today is a good day." He took a piece of fruit and popped it into his mouth. It seemed that in his own way he had found meaning, or at least a reason to live.

Though still weakened by his use of thaumaturgy, Maximilian insisted on accompanying Aceline and Ejan to the great complex of Collegium Calian in the quarter known as the Lavere. They traveled with Josiane; Rikard, who had become Ejan's young dark-haired lieutenant; and the thickset Thom, a garrulous and passionate painter and muralist from *A Call to Arms*. Each of them was aware that all three important leaders of the seditionist group were venturing into a foreign neighborhood and needed protection. When Max told Kata that she would not be coming, her face was a study of control, betraying no emotions. He was relieved. He felt that even the slightest outburst of feeling from her would weaken his own defenses. Then he might fall once more into her arms as he fantasized. Perhaps one day, he allowed himself to imagine. But not now.

Past Market Square, toward the Southern Headland, lay Caeli-Amur's slums. Here lived the dispossessed and the dissolute. The streets narrowed. Many of the houses were built of rotten wood; stagnant pools of water and sewerage fouled the streets. Dirty children sat in piles of rubbish and fought with rats. Whores called out to them from dark alleyways, promising quick release in the darkness. Toothless old men sat in the corners, grasping their worthless possessions as if someone might steal them.

They passed through the slums silently. To speak seemed to trivialize the brutal poverty that surrounded them. Still, Maximilian burned with the injustice of it all. While up in the Arantine, Caeli-Amur's most wealthy lived in opulent mansions, here the poorest lived without hope.

Past the slums, the streets of the Lavere brightened a little. Here streetlamps were lit, and the whores called from their balconies or doorways, inviting them to play word and number games, to solve riddles and puzzles. "If you can separate these wooden balls, you can have a free visit." One held out a contraption. In its center, two wooden balls hung together on a piece of string that passed through holes in two wooden slats. The whores of the Lavere knew how to entice the mind as well as the body.

"Where are you, my un-true love?" called others, echoing each other along the streets.

In the center of the Lavere, Collegium Caelian's great complex dwarfed those around it. The building was built entirely of metal: great iron and steel walls rising coldly above them. Representing all small traders involved with metal—merchants, smiths, mechanics—Caelian had grown to become the most powerful of the three Collegia. Their guards were said to rove with impunity through Caelian's territory in the Lavere.

Two of Caelian's guards let them through the gates where they were met by two tall Numerian intendants, dressed in black uniforms. A long silver entrance hall, its roof catching the light of bright lamps and giving off shimmering waves of light, gave way to a courtyard, which was filled with the sounds of hammering and sawing, the booming of machines at work. Caelian had workshops of its own within its walls and the red glow of embers was visible through the courtyard's open doors. The silhouettes of workmen could be seen moving about in these workshops.

The Numerians led them across the courtyard, where they entered the great hall of Collegium Caelian, a warren of metal and stone, resembling the insides of a vast machine. One might have thought that the hall would have been a great monotone of gray but the iron and steel was subtly worked so that the metals caught the light and shimmered with waves of purples and white. Elsewhere delicate engravings pictured traders and adventurers traveling the world, plying their wares in markets of Numeria, Varenis, the ivy halls of the north, and the Ruined Cities in the south.

Around a shining silver table, in the Caelian meeting room high in the hall, sat three Collegia officials.

A heavy man with a sagging face like a bloodhound gestured for the seditionists to sit. "Welcome to Collegium Calian. I am the Director, Guillam Dumas." He introduced the other two men as Director Suuri and Director Parsyn, of Collegium Litia and Avaricum respectively.

Parsyn turned to the Numerians. "Bring us refreshments, slaves."

Maximilian knew already that the Collegia were known to enslave Numerians and others from beyond the sea. But the sight of the slaves aroused his anger. He saw Nkando in them. And yet, he knew the Collegia's support was essential. Even with their support, a demonstration against the Houses was dangerous. Without it, the seditionists would be smashed.

"How do you live each day, knowing that you own living men and women?" he said.

"Anything that can be bought or sold freely," said the Collegium man. "That's the nature of commerce. Everything has a price."

Aceline spoke first. "You understand that we, of course, do not support such human bondage. We hope Caeli-Amur will return to a situation where all are real citizens, as in the time of the ancients."

"But surely there are other rights. The right of a man to buy whatever he can, with his own good earnings?"

Maximilian bit his tongue. To break ranks would mean there would be no point in belonging to the group at all. Decisions must be made together, and once made, were binding on all. That was the point of the meetings in the Communal Cavern. Across the table he watched as Thom's dark eyebrows quivered with rage. The artist was prone to passionate outbursts and, apparently to stop one of these, he clamped his own hand against his mouth.

Ejan leaned forward. "None of this is relevant to the question at hand. A call has been made for a show of anti-House sentiment on Aya's Day, two weeks hence. We ask that the Collegia and their members join us."

Surri of Collegium Litia, whose members were composed of independent fisherman and boatbuilders, leaned forward. "Our members are freemen. Consider the Collegia more a flexible web of individuals than a closed body. Still, we have our own watchmen—"

"Death squads, you mean," said Max. "Isn't it true that what loyalty you claim is won by coercion?"

Dumas shifted behind the table and ran his tongue along the inside of one jowl. "We can call on our members, if need be. But, if we do, then there must be a cost. We know that you seditionists have wild theories about the kind of Caeli-Amur you would see, should the Houses be overthrown. But any city after the Houses must allow for freedom of commerce: Anything a man can sell, we must allow. There must be no constraint on a man's ability to buy or sell."

"Or a woman's," said Aceline.

"Or a woman's," agreed Dumas.

"Slavery, for example," said Max.

"Perhaps," said Dumas, rubbing his jowls with one hand. "But more likely there are things which we have not yet realized might profit a man. At this point, the Houses only allow us a small autonomy, here hidden away among the slums in the Lavere. They allow us to unite the small traders and craftsmen. But much of the large-scale trading they control, Marin across the seas, Technis to Varenis, Arbor the South. We want to be able to import or construct anything we like, however much we like, to hire as many people as we like, whoever they are. Agree to that, and we will march on Aya's Day, and at every manifestation of dissent after that."

Maximilian thought instantly of the consequences: everything under the control of the Houses would now be free to exploit. Was that a better world? Certainly, it was not the one he had in mind, in which all things would be put to the use of the people.

Aceline looked first at Ejan, who nodded, and then at Max, who stared blank-faced. "Agreed," she said. "In two weeks, we will have the first of our demonstrations."

At this moment, the Numerian slaves entered with wine, fruit, and spiced flat-breads from a bakery somewhere on the Thousand Stairs nearby.

"Let us celebrate!" said Dumas.

As soon as they left Collegium Caelian's complex, Max could hold his tongue no longer. "They are our enemies. Slavery is worse than the House system. This will be a regression."

"We use whatever we can to overthrow the Houses," said Ejan.

"Yes," said Aceline. "One step at a time. First the immediate enemy, with whoever supports us against them. Then a second step, against the second enemy, shedding those who no longer walk beside us."

Maximilian admired Aceline's strategic thought, but he thought Ejan to be purely a pragmatist. Here they were united against him. He argued that this would lead the path to a new system of cruelty, in which the rich would be served by a legion of slaves. Each time he mounted the argument, the other two replied as they already had. It was a question of strategy. They would defeat the greatest enemy first. Who knew, perhaps the Collegia themselves would come to change their minds.

Thom finally burst out, "They are filth. Rotten like fruit on the ground—the skin looks fresh but if you eat the fruit, you'll make yourself sick. That's what we are doing. Mark my words!" He then burst into melodramatic tears, which took even Max aback. Aceline smiled at Max in embarrassment.

"He's right," said Max.

Once they were back at the hideout, they finally stopped arguing. There, Maximilian stood alone and watched the seditionists as they walked around the cavern. They seemed beautiful to him, all these people with one transcendental mission; all these people whose lives were greater than their individual interests and desires.

As he stood there, Quadi walked over to him. As he nibbled on some spiced bread, he said, "Tell me, Maximilian, why do you record all these activities?"

"What do you mean?"

"The recording device—why do you have it up there?"

Maximilian looked up to see a round object placed on the top of one of the pillars in the room. "A recording device," he said softly.

TWENTY-FIVE

The scrying ball had remained on the top of the pillar watching everything, like a symbol for Kata's bad conscience. Each time she considered moving it to Ejan's workshop, she stopped herself. Now more than three hundred seditionists were crushed into the place, sleeping side by side, picking through the piles of belongings, calling to one another across the cavern. There was always someone up at night, moving about: workaholics and insomniacs. Hidden somewhere deep inside her swirled a feeling of dread. Every now and then awareness of the pillar rose up to the front of her mind—she did not want to be caught; she did not want Maximilian to know who she was—and as quickly as she could, she pushed it down. But the longer the ball stayed there, the more dangerous it was for Maximilian. She was bound to him, after their moment in the alleyway by the cliffs. When Maximilian had said it would not happen again, she had been filled with terrible bitterness. But then she had considered things. Of course, they were seditionists. Though others formed attachments, she knew Maximilian's dedication. She had then begun to hope. Once the seditionist group was broken, then she might hide him away from the Houses. Then, perhaps, they could be together. Louis would not move the scrying ball, so she would have to do it.

As she tidied her possessions around her mattress, Louis squatted beside her. His eyes moved about as if he were about to be attacked. "I think they know."

"Don't be stupid," said Kata.

"I've seen Maximilian meet with Ejan and I swear he looked up at the ball. Josiane's been prowling like a dog on a scent."

"You're imagining things," said Kata. But underneath, she

knew what he said was true. The group was filled with suspicions now. Only days before, Aceline's passionate lieutenant, Thom—his thick black beard giving him a slightly mad look—had clashed with the brooding Rikard, whom he accused of spying on *A Call to Arms*. Kata had no doubt about Rikard's fidelity to seditionism, but as Thom shook Rikard, she had known that it would not be long before such fractures turned to violence.

"Leave the scrying ball. Think only of our survival," Louis pleaded.

In the afternoon, Kata excused herself as the final preparations for Maximilian's journey to Caeli-Enas were being completed. She felt cooped up in the hideout.

Padding along the tunnels that led back to the exit, she passed groups of seditionists carrying bags. She nodded to them. As she headed on, she felt one stop behind her.

Turning, she said, "Giselle."

"Follow me."

Giselle led her back toward the hideout. Their lanterns threw shadows onto the rocky walls. Some seemed to move and shift into the shapes of animals or great distorted faces, looming large and then fading away again. Rather than passing through the hidden passageway, they continued on deeper into the mountain. Giselle passed several more forks in the tunnel and turned right into a dark opening. The only thing that Kata could hear was the soft sound of water trickling over rocks.

They moved along the side of a cavern, where vast murals were painted on the wall in orange and black: a group of elephant-headed humanoids walked down a long pathway in the hills, their trunks brilliantly made into bas-reliefs by the ripples and ridges of the rock. Whether part of that same picture or another one Kata could not tell, sleek machines hovered in a blue sky.

"Who painted these?" whispered Kata, quieted by the spiritual feel of the paintings. "I've never heard of such elephant-men. Is it possible they date back to before the ancients? A species before minotaurs and Sirens?"

Giselle shrugged and sat on a ledge close to a large underground lake, the water dead still, only the trickling sound of water coming from far away in the dark. "Only yesterday I saw a mino-taur in the city."

"You did?" The words leaped from her throat. "Where?"

"He was climbing the Thousand Steps. Sometimes I wonder if those creatures brought all this on. All this trouble."

"What did he look like?"

"Tall, with the strangest head—something like a bull," joked Giselle.

Kata elbowed Giselle in the ribs and narrowed her eyes. But her mind rushed with thoughts and images. A flood of excitement and fear filled her.

"So." Giselle changed the subject. "Does Technis plan to strike?"

Kata hesitated. Officially Marin was still Technis's enemy; it was not long since the protracted wars between the Houses were open and vicious. "At some point, but not yet. Marin?"

"Not until later," said Giselle. "Marin has made the decision that as long as the greatest hatred is focused against Technis, they will allow the sedition. Perhaps Marin will finally rise to domi-nance." Giselle picked a small stone and threw it into the water. There was a loud plop as it disappeared beneath the surface. "Now, are you going to lie to me all the time?"

Kata looked at Giselle coldly. "What makes you think I'm lying?"

Giselle pursed her lips. "Because you're a liar."

Kata began to protest and stopped herself. What could she say? She *was* a liar. But who wasn't, she wondered? Who didn't keep little secrets or large ones? You had to keep secrets to survive; she'd learned that on the street.

"It's of no concern," said Giselle. "I just want to know *when* Technis plans to strike. I want to make sure I'm safe."

"I'll let you know," said Kata.

Giselle took Kata's face in her hands. "I'm relying on you."

Everyone is, thought Kata. And they have all made a terrible mistake.

Kata waited until late at night when the slumbering bodies of the seditionists were enshrouded by darkness, only a few lamps hang-ing from the distant gloomy walls. Finally, the room was filled with only the soft stirrings of the sleeping. Here someone rolled over; there another mumbled words from a dream.

Kata padded softly to Louis's mattress, which lay by one of the benches fixed in the center of the room. With a firm finger, she poked him. "Get up. If anyone awakes, I want you to distract them, or alert me."

"How?" He whispered as he pulled himself quietly to his feet, pulled on his pants and his shoes.

"You'll think of a way. Break something. Start screaming."

Kata stepped quickly and lightly through the sleeping bodies, like a cat in the night. Without hesitating, she scaled the black pillar, placing her hands in the little vents that ran horizontally along it. In seconds she had reached the top, some fifteen feet above the ground. She took the ball in her hand, placed it beneath her arm, looked down to prepare her descent.

A bright light illuminated her, a white ray in the darkness. Kata froze.

"Well, well," said a voice.

Sleepers stirred at the beaming light and the sound of Josiane's voice. Kata dropped to the ground. Still the light shone on her. She could sense Louis slipping back into the background, leaving her alone.

Seditionists stood around the room while Kata remained fixed to the spot, her mind racing. They probably didn't know what the ball was—at least not yet. That would buy her time to think of a reason. Perhaps she could claim that she just noticed it up there. But then why did she not retrieve it during the day?

Other lamps were now being lit and seditionists were stirring or pressing in closer to her, eyes wide with anger and fear.

"She climbed that pillar and fetched the ball." Josiane spoke to no one in particular. She kept her lamp, shining a single beam through one open shutters, fixed on Kata.

"What is it?" said Kata, her mind scrambled to deflect attention.

Maximilian stood beside Ejan. His face was ashen. "It's a recording device."

"What are you doing with a recording device?" asked Ejan.

Kata looked around the room. "I saw a figure in the dark approach the pillar and I thought they were about to scale it. It was then that I saw the ball sitting there. Curious, I scaled the pillar to see what it was."

Ejan's beautiful face was impassive as ever. "Oh, and who was this 'figure'?"

Kata surveyed the crowd gathered around her. She looked from eye to accusing eye. It sounded like an excuse. It *was* an excuse. There would be no escape in that direction. Her eyes settled on Maximilian, whose eyes were round in disbelief. To see him was like a blow to her stomach. She felt as if she would collapse there, among the crowd, under the weight of all the things she had lost. But that would only hasten her death—for death was what awaited her. It was a war, as Ejan had said many times. She looked into the ball: Could the officiate see what was happening? Would he send rescue?

"So," said Ejan. "Who was this figure?"

Kata looked around at the crowd again. Desperation filled her as she saw the faces of the seditionists, of people she had come to care for in these recent weeks. Shame welled within her like nausea. She was bereft of principle, bereft of anything that mattered in this life. Yet some part of her wanted these seditionists to accept her as one of their own. Especially Maximilian, whose worried eyes lingered on her. Her eyes roved the crowd, knowing that there was no way out. This was the end for her. She had not even experienced one day in the villa she had dreamed of. But dreaming: that was all that it had ever been, her entire life.

Ejan smiled malevolently. "Kata, this figure, this person you accuse. They don't exist, do they? No, you're trying to avoid the truth of matters, for you know that this is the end of you."

Kata's eyes roved the crowd and finally settled on one face, staring from the back of the crowd guiltily. "It was him! I saw Louis approach and once he had done something with this ball, I examined it. It was him!"

Louis yelped and looked on with horror. "No! No, it's not true. I'm not an agent. It's her: she's an agent for House Technis. She placed the ball herself." As he was panicking, words flooded from his mouth, one falling over the other like a stampeding crowd. "I have nothing to do with that ball."

"It was him." Kata spoke with confidence. She saw a way out of this disaster, if she held her nerve. And holding her nerve was something she was practiced at.

Silence reigned in the seditionist hideout. The weight of the moment seemed to hang in the air like a pall, connecting them all in a silent shroud of emotion and power. Everyone looked to be lost in thought: Maximilian, his face troubled; Ejan, calm and cool; Josaine, shifting from foot to foot like an animal. Collette and Oewen and Aceline and Thom. Each of them seemed to be assessing the truth of Kata's words. Could they trust her? Was Louis the agent, as she claimed? Each of them appeared to be rejecting the notion. Maximilian dropped his head and, still shaking it, looked at the ground. Ejan smiled coldly at her, Josaine took a step forward as if she were preparing to fight. And Kata realized that there would be no escape. They saw through her desperate gambit. They saw her as the liar she was. She prepared for the bitter last moments.

"It's true." Through the crowd walked Giselle. "I, too, saw a figure in the dark approach the pillar. It was him. It was Louis."

Louis stood pale and trembling, seditionists stepping away from him so that he stood alone in the dark.

Maximilian looked up, nodding suddenly and stepped forward. "I, too, will vouch for her. I trust her. She is one of us. But *him*, I cannot vouch for."

Ejan nodded. "To tell the truth, I have had suspicions about him myself."

Kata did not feel the relief she had hoped. Instead, she felt dread at coming events. She looked at Louis's guilt-stricken and terrified face. I'm sorry, she thought to herself, at what the seditionists are about to do to you.

TWENTY-SIX

Louis was strangely passive as Thom and Josiane tied him to a chair in the center of the cavern. Once strapped down, he alternated between shivering silently and then bursting out with words that tumbled over each other. "I'll do anything. It was wrong of me. I'll become an agent for you. I'll spy on the Houses. Yes, that's what I'll do." Some internal wall had broken within him, and he no longer protested his innocence. He was not hard, like Kata.

Around him, the entire group stood silently. No one could be exactly sure what would occur now, for Louis was the first agent to be discovered in the group. What would be the punishment for such a crime?

"She's a part of it, too." Louis looked across at Kata.

At that moment, she felt the tingling of her illness. Oh no, she thought, for she could not move. Not now. Always the fits came at points of emotional pressure, she knew. She looked over to her possessions, where her medicine flask lay.

Maximilian stepped forward and struck him on the side of the face. "Stop trying to divert attention. Stop trying to blame others."

Louis laughed madly, as if a terrible joke were being played on him. His teeth were covered in red: he looked like an old man with rotten teeth. His eyes darted to and fro, as if there were some means of escape hidden in the crowd or the darkness.

"How long has the ball been up there?" asked Ejan.

Louis's face was suddenly filled with hate. "The Houses will get you. They'll crush you and your pathetic little group. They'll get you and break you. It won't be long before you're tied in a chair speaking to the officiates or thrust into one of the terror-spheres." He started to laugh manically.

"How long?" said Maximilian.

"Oh, they'll hurt you, they'll make you cry," mumbled Louis.

Giselle took out a long and sharp stiletto. At the sight of it, Louis laughed again madly, stopped just as suddenly, and looked down at the floor. "She's in on it, too. Kata's in on it."

Giselle struck him again on the face. "Stop lying." She turned to the others. "His testimony will be filled with things to mislead us. Untruths mixed with truths. Only long hours of pain will un-ravel his story."

Ejan nodded and they all stood around in silence.

Louis looked at the floor as if something there might help him. "I beg you. I'll tell you everything. There's a second ball in the Technis Complex. They can see you as if through a window, perhaps even now. It's been there for three weeks. Technis knows all your plans now."

Kata was now filled with horror. For her, the best thing would be for Louis to be killed. She could not afford to have him speak, for soon enough the truth would be uncovered and she, too, would find herself strapped into a chair. Yet she could hardly bear to have more blood on her hands. During the House Wars, she had killed agents of Arbor and Marin. They had been part of a cruel system; there had been no moral transgression in killing them, for there was no question of right and wrong; at that time the world for her had been a war of all against all. But now things had become murky. She had sensed that somewhere in the mess of it all there was a right and wrong. As she thought these things, the tingling in her body became a slight trembling. The fit was a slow one, but she knew that meant it would be all the more powerful for that.

Finally Maximilian spoke. "We cannot use the methods of the Houses. We are not the same as the Houses. To act like them would be to become them."

"Yes." Louis's voice brightened and he looked up. "You are not. You are seditionists. You live by a higher morality, a higher sense of purpose."

Ejan crossed his arms and stood with legs slightly apart in a powerful stance. "The higher purpose is the struggle against the Houses. When they are gone, we will have room for your niceties. But we don't choose the field on which we fight."

Maximilian paced around the chair. Louis swiveled his head, trying to follow him.

"You know the wisdom of his words, Maximilian," said Aceline. "The time for a better way will be after the defeat of the Houses."

Maximilian glanced at Kata as he considered things. His face twitched, he pursed his lips and ran his hands through his curly hair. She could see the struggle occurring within him, between the words of Ejan and Aceline and his dream that seditionists should somehow act better.

Kata's hands felt moist. One of her legs was shaking, threatening to give way. With immense effort she steadied herself. She was starting to see everything through a mist of white. She concentrated. She knew she should agree with Ejan, before Louis had a chance to betray her. She shook herself. Louis must die. She stepped forward and, against all her interests, tried to save Louis's life. "Ejan's words have wisdom. But if we resort to these methods, it means we have already lost the war. It means we are too weak to fight by our own means. It means they have lured us onto their ground, a sign that we should not engage in the battle at all and Kamron was right, we should have waited."

Ejan's eyes rolled back in disappointment. He then stared at Maximilian frostily. "I'll do it."

"No!" cried Louis.

Some internal resistance seemed to give way in Maximilian. His face stopped twitching; he straightened his stance and spoke. "Death. Louis must die. All House agents must know that just as we risk death opposing the Houses, so they risk death upholding them."

"Then you carry it out," Ejan said to Maximilian. He took the stiletto and placed it in Maximilian's hand. "Does anyone challenge this verdict?" he asked of the group quickly. A few responded with, "No," and "Death it is," and "It's a war." Others remained silent, watchful, fearful.

Kata watched Maximilian, the stiletto in hand. He stared at Louis, who looked down at his feet, a crumpled and disheveled wreck of a man.

"Maximilian," said Ejan.

Still Maximilian did not move.

"Maximilian!" said Ejan.

Maximilian looked up at Ejan. His confidence seemed to be flagging with the pressure of the task. Kata realized now that he had never killed a man. Indeed, she knew that he was probably incapable of it. Yet to fail now would mean that he did not have the courage of his convictions. The group waited, silent in the tension of the moment.

A small whine came from Louis: "Please."

"Fine," said Ejan definitely. He took three long strides across to Maximilian, took the stiletto from his hand. Louis's face convulsed with fear as Ejan strode purposefully in front of the chair. Looking out into the darkness over Louis's shoulder, Ejan pulled his arm back. The stiletto glinted softly in the darkness. Ejan plunged it into the agent's chest: one, two, three times. Louis grimaced but did not scream or cry. Instead, he let out a series of growls, like a dog in the dark, one after each strike of the stiletto. His body shook violently, like a broken engine, lurching and jumping. The chair creaked and shuddered and shifted over the ground. Again and again Ejan plunged in the stiletto and again and again Louis growled, but the rough sounds became softer and softer until they were almost sighs. All the while the crowd looked on in horror. Finally Louis's head slumped to the side, his eyes staring at the ground. It was done.

Ejan strode across to Kata and aggressively took the scrying ball from her hands. He placed it before the body of Louis. "You see," he said to the ball. "That is what awaits you and your Houses."

Ejan then took the ball in his hands and threw it onto the stone floor. The sound of glass shattering echoed through the cavern. On the ground lay the remnants of the intricate contraption, fragile pieces of metal crushed against each other like the broken wings of a butterfly.

Kata dashed to her mattress and took long swigs of her medicine, the preparation as pungent as ever. Her body trembled all over and she was struck by a cruel headache. She lost track of events as the migraine took her over, but the medicine halted the fit. Later, as she regained a sense of things, the images kept replaying in her mind. She felt herself tremble again as a second fit came on. She drank quickly from her flask again. Perhaps she was building up a tolerance to the medicine. Several times recently she had felt oncoming fits and had to drink twice the amount of preparation to halt them. After some moments, the trembling again ceased. She finally drifted into a weary reverie that was plagued by terrible dreams. In these, it was Louis who walked around Kata, and she who was tied to a chair. In his hand Louis held a stiletto. He leaned in toward her. "She's in on it, too," he said. Then he leaned back and smiled. His teeth were red with blood, and there was madness in his eyes. "She's in on it, too."

TWENTY-SEVEN

Boris lay on his bed without the strength to move. The bedclothes were sweat-soaked and fetid, as if they had not been washed in months. In the first hours of his withdrawal from the hot-wine, he had vomited on the floors of his apartment what little liquids he had in his stomach, and after that, in great uncontrollable heaves, as if his body was fighting for its life, yellow bile, until it seemed impossible that he could vomit anything else. Some hours later, the lethargy had settled in, draining his limbs of strength, so that all he could do was lie on the bed. Unable to reach the toilet, he had relieved himself so that he wallowed in a great dampness of sweat and other excretions.

A bottle of water, some bread, and the scrying ball rested on the bed next to him. Throughout this torment, he had seen many of the seditionists' activities that he had not previously noticed. Maximilian had constructed an air-cart for breathing beneath the water—with the help of the New-Man, Quadi—the very man who was responsible for Boris's predicament. Ejan had stockpiled all manner of incendiaries and hand-weapons. The group around *A Call to Arms* busily ventured into the city, stirring up trouble and anti-House feeling. It seemed that they even had the Collegia on their side, a development that surprised Boris. Aya's Day now loomed as a decisive moment, when the seditionists and the Houses would face each other in open war.

When things were worst with Boris, these developments meant nothing to him. He was in too much pain. The yearning for hot-wine had now become something deeper within him. The whole world had been emptied of meaning, had lost its color and was painted in shades of gray. But several days into his ordeal things gradually regained a terrible import. His own actions flashed through his mind. He was filled with rising panic and despair: images of Mathias, dying in front of the Tram Factory, visions of Paxaea lying on the bed before him. Again and again these visions occurred in his mind, no matter how he tried to pushed them away. What had become of him? Disgusted with himself, he thought of escape, somewhere, perhaps to Varenis, perhaps across the sea. Maybe he and Paxaea could leave for Taritia after all, and live there, away from everything. But then, the Elo-Talern had offered him the elixir of eternal life. Immortality. How could he leave such a promise, when it might mean that he and Paxaea could live together forever?

Days later, as he lay in the darkness, he watched as Ejan, with the coldness of an assassin, stabbed Louis as he sat tied in a chair. Motionless on his bed, Boris looked on as the agent had growled and shaken the chair in rapid side-to-side movements as if he were having a fit. Ejan had then stared through the glass into Boris's eyes. "You see. That is what awaits you and your Houses."

Boris stirred, and a flicker of anger emerged beneath the depression that overwhelmed him. He had allowed the seditionists to grow and plan while he obsessed about Paxaea. If he acted quickly, he could still crush them. Kata would need to lead the House guards to the seditionist hideout, hidden somewhere beneath the city. She would need to do it soon, yet Boris did not know when he would see her next. The acrid taste of defeat hovered over him. Already he could imagine the other officiates moving against him, jostling for position of Director now that he, an ignorant tramworker, had failed.

The following day, when Boris was able to crawl to the water pump and drink a little, there was a knocking on his door. A voice called out, "Director Autec? Director Autec?"

Boris tried to get to his feet, but collapsed on his weakened legs like a baby.

"Direcor Autec?"

There was the rattling of metal in the lock and Boris felt despair at his incapacitation. When the door opened, the final days of his Directorate would begin. News of his enfeeblement would spread among the officiates. Boris could see Matisse grinning malevolently and clenching his insectlike hands with glee.

The door swung open and Tonio stepped through the door, a bunch of thin keys in one hand. He scrunched up his face at the smell and stepped inside. Craning his neck around the doorway was Officiate Armand. The two of them stared at Boris, who turned his face away in full knowledge of his ruin.

Armand turned to Tonio, "The physician, quickly."

"No!" called out Boris.

At this, Armand held Tonio back and instead closed the door. "Director, you are unwell?"

Boris could see his own vulnerability and desperation registered in Armand's eyes. Armand surveyed the scene: the bottles of hot-wine lined the walls, lay strewn on the floor. Armand pressed his lips together and touched his chin. "All right, Tonio, we must keep this completely secret."

They carried Boris to the washroom and cleaned him. They stripped the sheets from his bed and replaced them. All the while Armand was talking, telling the others ways in which to cover for Boris's absence. Boris admired Armand's calm at he outlined the story they would tell. Boris, Armand explained to the other two, had been to the Dyrian coast, rallying support for the Houses among the villa owners, fish and oyster farms. They would claim that Boris had negotiated for the Dyrians to send their watchmen to the city, if necessary. Armand drafted instructions for the other officiates, which Boris signed. They were to make lists of all the factories that were still functioning, the level of support for the Houses, assessments of the morale of the guards and the thaumaturgists. Tonio, Armand decided, would stay with Boris and help him recover.

After they left Boris resting in the bed, he examined the scrying ball once more. But it it revealed nothing.

Tonio attended to him later that evening and offered him a simple potato soup. To Boris it tasted sweet, something he had yearned for. "To think that life can be made so much more bearable by something so simple."

Tonio stood calmly, his hands behind his back. "Some say that our lives have become filled with too much sophistication, too much pleasure, too much of everything. Our mistake has been to think we need more and more. But really, we need only the basics, the simplest of things. Potato soup."

"Some say? You mean that's what you Cynics argue," said Boris, smiling weakly.

"This is the ground where we meet with the Cajian philosophers. They, too, suggest that the world has lost its way with its constant obsession with becoming smarter, better, more complex."

Afterwards, Boris wondered if perhaps he too was mistaken in his goal of changing things for the better. But what other choice did they have? The Cajiun philosophers simply emptied their lives of material objects, lived alone with nothing, hermits in the city. That was possible for a philosopher-assassin, but not anyone else.

The following day, Boris felt the world coming together once more, and to his surprise, there were no more shadows. But the horror of events and his place within them still overwhelmed him, and the flashes of the past came just as frequently. Although Armand had saved his Directorship, Boris's priority was clear: He would escape with Paxaea. There was no future for him in Caeli-Amur. He felt guilty for Armand, who had surprised him with his efficiency and grace and would be betrayed by this decision. He mourned his loss of the elixir of life, promised by the Elo-Talern. But perhaps she had only been seducing him with an idea. For if she had access to it, why had no one else drunk that draft? Perhaps it was only a myth, invented to manipulate him.

Tonio fetched his carriage and Boris rode along the boulevards, their walls covered with graffiti and posters calling for insurrection against the Houses. With each moment, as he approached the Opera, the feeling of dread grew in him. Surely Paxaea would understand; surely she would see that he had not been himself. He had been overtaken by anger, by hot-wine. The feeling of dread did not pass; rather, it intensified.

When he arrived, the usual intendant rushed from behind the desk area, "Director Autec, Director Autec," he said. "Do let me know if there's anything I can help you with."

"Get away." Boris pushed the intendant in the chest, took a few steps past him. He turned back. "Paxaea?"

"In rehearsal," said the intendant.

Boris climbed the stairs up to the grand gallery where he looked on from one of the theater seats in the the vast empty expanse above. A group of six was rehearsing a tragedy, in which an upper-class girl's family forbid her to marry a poor small-town fisherman. In a desire to enrich himself, the fisherman heads out into the terrible storms beneath which the priceless gem-fish swam in schools like great rivers of multicolored treasure, a current of red and sapphire and emerald. Each day the girl waits, singing out into the storm until one day a body washes up onto the beach, still grasping his net with his clawed hand. Wrapped inside the net is a glorious gem-fish. He has returned rich after all, but dead.

When Paxaea sang to the wind, one of her notes rose to unnatural plaintive heights, the second trembled low, a rhythmic gutteral sob. The exquisite pain of these melodies washed over Boris and he found himself crying. Filled with longing, he grasped the armrests to stop himself from throwing himself from the balcony and onto the stage. This desire, he knew, he shared with all those fishermen who had been drawn onto the deadly rocks and shoals of Taritia. There the lucky ones would drown or be dashed against the rocks. The unlucky ones would wash up on the shore, to be come captives of the Sirens.

"Just a little softer, a little less, Paxaea," said the Opera director from offstage.

Boris slipped from the seats and made his way to her room. The door had been repaired, and he entered the room, sat on her bed, and waited. His heart thumped madly and emotions coursed through him with an intensity he had forgotten possible. What had the hot-wine done to him? Emotions had raged within him, but there had been a distance between his mind and everything else, as if he had seen the world through the haze of the industrial quarter. Now he felt a terrible maelstrom of guilt and fear and self-loathing.

The door opened and Paxaea stepped in. Her face quivered, as if it might suddenly crumble. She composed herself. "Director Autec."

He looked at the ground, "Look, I'm sorry."

"I wondered where you have been," said Paxaea.

"I've been getting well. The wine—it was making me into something I did not care for."

"Ah." Paxaea walked to her window and craned her neck.

Boris walked behind her, and stood close. They were silent. He touched her lightly on the shoulder. She started—her entire body convulsing—and then she was still.

"Can you forgive me?" asked Boris. "I want you to forgive me."

"There's nothing to forgive, Director Autec," said Paxaea.

He took her hand and turned her around. He held her for a long time, though her arms hung loosely at her sides.

He pulled her to the bed and held her there against him, his desire growing in him. He held it at bay, but it welled up in him irresistibly. He kissed her. She still had a strange passivity; she was away somewhere, in a world far from this one. Perhaps it was just her spirit, her nature, to be detached. She must have developed that nature as a defense against the world and its demands. He kissed her again, and his desire grew greater for this magnificent creature before him. He put his hand on her thigh and pulled up her dress. She trembled again, perhaps in anticipation. Slowly he unbuckled himself and pushed himself closer to her.

"Paxaea," he said.

She trembled but did not move.

"I saw your rehearsal."

She closed her eyes—her nictating membrane followed momentarily afterwards by her main eyelids—as if she hadn't heard.

"You never sing like that to me," said Boris, moving slowly.

"I did not know you would like it." Great tears squeezed themselves through her long black eyelashes. A second later a strange trilling sound came from her throat, accompanied every now and then by clicking, as if she were a lizard out on the rocky foothills to the north.

When they were done, he walked to her window and looked

out. It was true, if a person craned his neck, he could see a little patch of the sea, blue with little crests of white.

"I came to take you away," he said. "Let's escape this nightmare city. Let's go. Let's go to Taritia after all. Let's get away."

She didn't respond.

"Paxaea. Let's escape."

Eventually her answer came, soft and passionless. "It's not escape if you bring the horror you're escaping from with you. You can have me. You always could. But I will not defile my homeland with you."

He turned and looked at her, lying there on the bed, her eyes open now and staring still into some faraway place in her mind. "I'm offering you freedom. I'm saying let's escape this place, this death-filled place."

"You *belong* here." Her words were short and sharp and spoken with disdain.

"Let's escape," he said again without conviction. He comprehended her words, her contempt.

"No."

"I'll kill you," Boris whispered. He walked to the bed and looked down at her.

She looked up at him. "Or *I'll* kill *you*."

He grabbed her by the hair, pulled it backwards. He yanked back her head. "But don't think you'll ever escape my grasp. Don't think you'll ever be free. You're mine now, to do with what I will. And you'll like it, damn it! You'll grow to love it."

He stormed from the room, his teeth clenched, his nostrils flaring. Despair filled him. All his dreams of escape were delusions, Paxaea nothing but a deceitful creature who had allowed him to love her. Something broke within him, changed irrevocably. He felt it give way deep within and knew it could never be repaired. He headed to the Technis Complex. He had a city to rule.

TWENTY-EIGHT
❦

As Boris strode through the Technis corridors, Tonio slightly to one side behind him with bolt-thrower in one hand, subofficiates, intendants, thaumaturgists, and all stood aside. Filled with rage—at Paxaea, at the seditionists, at himself, at life itself—Boris moved with an newly discovered force.

He entered the Director's offices, his voice booming at a group of secretaries. "Summon the officiates. I want those reports on the state of the House guards, the House thaumaturgists, the state of the factories. I want them now!" He looked out over his new grand balcony down at the city twinkling below him. "I want to know everything that occurs in Caeli-Amur."

He placed his scrying ball on the dark-wood desk and surveyed the room. In the corner of the room, close to the desk, stood the memory-catcher, bolts clipped in to its sides. Tonio stood to one side of the room, next to the scrying ball whose twin lay in Varenis.

Boris sat behind the desk and read through each officiate's records, which Armand had left for him. There were twelve officiates and he skimmed through their histories. Mostly they had come from the House families, having been raised by their fathers to inherit their positions. There were the usual privileges and luxuries: the best lycées, time learning the Classics at the university beside the elites of Arbor and Marin, drifting and misspent youths, then a sudden turn to serious affairs, marriage, fingers to the grindstone. Then the usual combination of political machinations: here a betrayal, there an unexpected death, here a rapid rise, there a terrible descent. Amid all this two histories stood out: Armand's grandfather had been an Arbor official, many years earlier. But Arbor had expelled him and the family had fallen on hard times.

Armand's grandfather had died a broken man; his parents had struggled. But Armand had known where the future lay: He joined Technis. The other file that stood out was Boris's own. As a tramworker, he would never be one of the inner circle. He would need to reaffirm his authority, and these men understood only one thing: naked power.

The officiates entered Boris's office, something suspicious and animalistic in their eyes—all except Armand, who stood calmly.

"Director Autec," said the sluggish Fournier, his angry eyes drooping. "You have been indisposed for some days."

"You think I should spend all my time with you?" Boris's voice rose slightly.

"Of course not, Director, but events move quickly." Fournier blinked slowly. He was from one of Technis's oldest families, who had been responsible for the forging of new agricultural equipment, which seemed appropriate to Boris. The man himself seemed about as interesting as a plow.

"Events? I make them," said Boris.

Officiate Matisse, who stood behind the others, smirked and clasped his long fingers. "Let's hope they don't unmake you in return."

"I think you forget whom you are talking to." Boris stood up from his seat behind his desk.

Matisse smiled again knowingly. "We all know that you are the Elo-Talern's favorite. That there was no good reason to promote you—you—above anyone else. All these years they avoided interfering in House affairs, and when they do, they favor . . ." As he let his words peter out, Matisse looked Boris up and down with contempt.

Boris smiled grimly and said in a soft voice, "Matisse, would you come a little closer, perhaps."

Matisse took a few steps toward Boris.

"A little closer yet, Matisse. I have something to say to you in private."

Matisse took another step forward.

"Just a few more steps. Just up to the desk here please, Matisse."

Matisse took one more step and Boris struck the trigger beneath his desk. There was the sound of air rushing—*phhht*—and then something struck Matisse, who took a step back and looked down at the little bolt that protruded from his stomach.

Matisse looked up again as if he couldn't believe what Boris had done. He laughed. "The bolt is too small, Autec. It's like a child's weapon." Matisse reached for the bolt. But before he touched it, its sides burst apart, like the rapid blooming of a flower, and a thousand and more little black antlike specks rushed onto Matisse, who looked in horror. He tried to brush them off, but they climbed and crawled, a swarm of tiny mites. He laughed again, this time in fear, as the things seemed to multiply and climb higher up his chest, and higher still to his neck. Laughing hysterically now, he brushed feverishly at the swarm coursing up his neck like a wave. He struck at them and as he opened his mouth to scream in fear, the mites coursed into his mouth like water. Farther up they moved, and plunged into his nostrils, his ears. They rushed over his eyes, and he gurgled, twisting and shaking like a madman in some strange dance. The scream became horrible: not so much of fear as of pain, and the things entered him, a black seething mask disappearing into his face. He fell to his knees, crying piteously, the sound of someone so lost in his own experience that the world dropped away to nothingness. He gurgled again and his entire body trembled. He collapsed onto the floor, still convulsing and shuddering, and finally was still. The swarm of black things emerged from his mouth and nose and descended back into the bolt as quickly as they had emerged. The bolt's sides closed back around the mites.

Boris looked at the others. "Now, let me have your reports."

When they were done, Boris turned to Armand. "Bring the Siren Paxaea to me."

Boris turned away and looked coldly from his window over the city over which he now had so much control. Even if it resisted, he would bend it to his will. Kata, where are you? He wondered. It all rests on you. As he looked out over the twinkling lights, he straightened his back and stood rigidly, his head held high as was befitting the House Technis Director. It would not be long now, until Paxaea arrived.

TWENTY-NINE

Maximilian strapped himself to the top of the air-cart, which the boatman winched over the water from a lobster boat. Farther out, a cutter headed across the seas, toward Numeria. A steamer headed north, smoke billowing from its chimneys, its great wheels crashing against the waves. Dotting the horizon were many fishing boats of a similar size to theirs. If any of them were equipped with telescopes, they would have no trouble making out the air-cart hovering above the water.

Max grasped the metal chain as the whole thing lurched from side to side. Through the glass faceplate, the rest of his group stood gazing intently at him. His breath was loud in his ears, amplified by the heavy helmet. Before he had climbed onto the cart, Kata had stood before him, her face a jumble of emotions. She had tried to say something, but it had caught in her throat and instead she stood forward and hugged him a little too long. He had been moved by the softness and warmth of her, pressed against him.

When they had tested the suit the day before, in the underground lake near the hideout, it had sprung a leak where the helmet joined the rest of the suit. His boots filled with cold water unnervingly quickly. By the time he dragged the cart from the lake, his entire lower body was submerged. They had made repairs and the second time, the cart and suit had seemed to work well, but Max was keenly aware of the danger he was heading into.

Now water splashed around the cart as it crashed into the sea, rose again as the lobster boat rocked on its side, then plunged down once more. This time the water rushed over the top of the cart, where Maximilian sat strapped, holding grimly on to the chain. He could feel the coolness of the water through the thick mesh suit. A few seconds later it rushed up over his legs, up to his waist and finally over his shoulders. He looked out at the figures on the boat and they were momentarily obscured, visible once more briefly as his head bobbed up over a wave, and then gone.

Currents moved against him, but he held tight as he descended. He looked down and took a deep breath. The water was rushing over the gills of his cart, providing him with oxygen. Far below, like some hallucinatory dream, the decaying city was a ghostly memory of its former self: there in the center, stately buildings of white marble, gleaming and somehow intact; farther out, broken spires pointed to the surface, surrounded by thousands of crumbling buildings; elsewhere, the city was entirely buried beneath silt and coral or had fallen into vast open chasms. Cobblestoned streets sprouted swaying seaweed forests. Beams of light broke the water at an angle, weakening as they descended, casting dark and surreal shadows. Here and there schools of blue and gray fish swam. Maximilian did his best to forget about sharks and sea serpents.

As he descended, Maximilian's breath, loud in his ears, measured the time like a clock. Through the faceplate, everything seemed as if viewed from a tunnel. The lack of peripheral awareness disturbed him. He kept turning his head, expecting that something might be lurking just a little out of view, watching him. His heart beat with fear and exhilaration.

Beneath him the city became clearer, though the green water was thick with motes of submarine matter. Miniature carriages lay collapsed on the streets, skeletal horses lying half-buried gently before them, harnesses still strapped to their bones. Far into the distance was a spectral port, complete with decomposing ships moored to the piers. Along the larger boulevards, odd-shaped street-vehicles pushed up against one another like a row of ants heading to honey: old, lost technology. Perched on a hill at the center of the city, not far away, the circular dome of the Library beckoned him. Like the Opera in Caeli-Amur, the Library was constructed classically. It was one of the best preserved of the buildings and he thought of Ukka's claims in *Before the Cataclysm*:

The Library was thaumaturgically protected from fire, earthquake and flood, external assault and internal decay. In front of it lay a grand circular plaza, surrounded by walkways. Boulevards spread like a spider's web from the plaza while surrounding the Library were buildings built of white marble and equally preserved, yet others were towers of strange metals and stones side by side with crumbling mansions.

Halfway to the ocean floor, the cart jerked to a stop. Quadi had explained that he would need to adjust to the pressure beneath the ocean. Even now his suit was clamped around him like embracing arms. He waited, like a little balloon in the sky above Caeli-Enas.

Sometime later, the cart jerked once more and began descending. Max was at the same level as the Library's great dome. Again he examined the city below. Caeli-Enas had been a planned city, with its Library at its center. But the city had torn and broken as it sank, so that some sections now lay on top of others. Its thoroughfares and walkways now lay scrambled. Yet more seemed to have descended into chasms in the ocean floor. It was now a city of cliffs and abysses.

Finally, Max came close to the ground. He could see clearly into the ruins of buildings, where the decayed remains of their interiors lay rotting, covered with silt and sludge. Underwater weeds and vines overran others. Schools of golden fish darted through broken walls while large gray ones hovered watchfully in the water above.

The wheels of the air-cart struck the cobblestoned streets of the Sunken City, which stood before him, shadowy and magnificent. Around him billowed a cloud of sediment, obscuring his vision. He climbed off the air cart and unhitched the chain. He stood on a narrow street, the walls of roofless buildings running down to a main boulevard—one of the radial arteries that led to the library.

It took effort to walk down the street—its cobblestones jutting up at odd angles as the sandy floor had shifted beneath them over the years—and he set off slowly, dragging the air-cart behind him. Each step took effort, the cart heavy in the water, its wheels striking the uneven cobblestones. The only thing he could hear was the sound of his own breath.

The water was cold. As he walked, he occasionally looked upward, toward the fractured light playing on the ocean surface far above. Foot-sized crabs scrabbled along the walls beside him, while little black fish darted around his legs. Small streets led off to either side, crumbling buildings visible in all directions.

Breathing heavily he reached the boulevard, looked right, toward the ruined carriages and horses. There he saw, splayed out on the floor of the Sunken City, his first human skeleton. Its bones had collapsed on themselves. Its jaw lay open as if it was caught in one last desperate scream. The remains of leather clothes hung over it, decaying in the water. To the left of him, towering above a seaweed forest, stood the Library, its monolithic structure hulking in the semidarkness. He looked back at the skeleton. Though its ligaments and tendons had been nibbled away long ago by fish, still its bony hands looked tense and expectant.

He headed up a gentle incline toward the forest, thick and dark and rising from what might have been a park or a city square.

As he neared the forest, the forty-foot-long seaweed tendrils blew over, as if pushed by an enormous current of water. He froze. A rush of water hit him with physical force and he staggered to his left. He glimpsed something immense from the corner of his eye, but when he turned, it was gone. A gigantic cloud of silt billowed up into the sky. He turned the other way: only ruined houses, their windows gaping like empty eyes. He drew his knife from the scabbard attached to the side of the cart. It seemed pathetic in his hand.

Maximilian stood still, his heart pounding, his breath now fast. He would have to move, for the cart's gills needed the water to move through them in order to draw oxygen. He took a step forward just as the house-sized head of a sea serpent passed directly overhead, followed by its gigantic dark-gray body, its white underbelly. He collapsed to the ocean floor, breathless, as the colossal beast passed over him. The rush of water stirred the sand around him, and he was pulled to his right. He let out a little groan as the serpent's tail flicked, sending it on its way. He lay there, momentarily paralyzed by fear. He could make himself and the cart invisible, but it would drain his strength, sicken him, and he could not afford that yet.

Gritting his teeth, he forced himself to his feet and trudged on toward the seaweed, until he reached the first small stalks at the forest's edge. Inside, the forest was dark and shadowy. His breath was ragged in his ears; his heart thumped like a drum; his nerves tightened to breaking point.

Bracing himself, Max walked on. The seaweed was surprisingly soft and supple. The cart passed through it, only occasionally catching on a stalk, which he would sever quickly with his knife. Before long he was deep in the darkness, the stalks close around him. With vision in front of him now obscured, he expected at any moment the giant head of the sea serpent to burst through the seaweed, its jaws open, its great mouth revealing its yellow teeth, each one tall as a man.

He emerged breathless from the willowy seaweed.

Above him towered the Library, vast and white in the water, like the dream of some sleeping god. The sheer size of it made him take a breath.

Max crossed a wide boulevard flanked by the palatial buildings built of crumbling marble. Interspersed with these were older towers, cut in unusual styles using acute angles so that they seemed to be leaning and warping before his very eyes, the buildings' silvery-black onyx darkness at home in the watery gloom. These were unlike any structures he had seen. They lacked the external classicism of the ancient architecture. Instead they resembled the interiors of the ancient buildings in Caeli-Amur. Their angles were unhinging, seeming to have no logic to them, even though they were composed of geometric shapes, and finely cut angles. They were at once mesmerizing and disturbing.

The boulevard opened into the wide plaza; he had now reached the top of the gentle hill he had been climbing. Opposite him stood the Library, colossal and imposing. Around the plaza, walkways rose gently, supported by white marble pillars. Like the petals of some beautiful flower, they intertwined with one another. Here the ancients must have taken their afternoon promenades. Max yearned to see the city in its full glory, back before it sank beneath the sea. It must have been wondrous and strange.

Max glanced behind him. The seaweed forest, murky though, swayed in the distance below. Deep inside it, some of the weeds jerked unnaturally, as if something large moved among them; then they were still. He watched a moment, but there was no more movement. As he walked across the plaza, he felt he was a miniscule figure amid these majestic ruins. The immensity of it all pressed upon him: these deserted streets that no one had walked for over four hundred years. He felt like an outsider, disturbing a city of the dead. He glanced behind. The plaza was empty, but floating through the water slightly over its crest was a small cloud of sediment. Something had moved down there.

THIRTY

Maximilian hurried on through the great underwater plaza and came to the long flights of stairs, each step over a foot in height, which led up to the Library. He climbed the Library stairs as quickly as he could, the cart thumping behind him—*clunk, clunk, clunk*—and his heart pounding with fear and exertion. He passed through one row of pillars, wide enough to be towers themselves, and then after another flight of stairs, yet more pillars. The gigantic doors of the library were already open. He looked down toward the square and from the corner of his eye caught a glimpse of rapid movement beneath a walkway curving around the plaza. The thing was smaller than the sea serpent, and moved in a quick pulse, before slowing and then pulsing again, like a carriage-sized jellyfish. The thing seemed disturbingly familiar.

Max turned and increased his speed to a great foyer, vast and wide. The interior reminded him of the Opera in Caeli-Amur. Patterns shimmered on the walls, outlining geometric shapes constructed from strange angles. Red globes of light danced near the ceiling, rising and falling, even in the water. He could not shake the feeling that the Library was built for beings altogether larger than humans. Two giant doors stood, one on either side of him. Across the foyer, another wide flight of stairs led up toward the center of the library. When he was about halfway across the foyer, a terrible sense of vulnerability came over him, and he headed straight toward one of the pillars that stood to the side of the stairs. He stepped behind the pillar, which glowed with a silver scrawl that spiraled around the marble surface, and chanted his illusionism incantation. He placed his knife on the air-cart, drew the ideograms in the air, and shimmered out of sight.

The thing came floating through the water like a monstrous balloon. Max closed his eyes to avoid dropping to his knees in fear. His breath was loud in his ears and the image of the creature was seared onto the back of his eyelids. His heart skipped a beat, started up again rapidly. His stomach lurched. Would his small incantation be enough to hide him? Perhaps with those hundreds of eyes packed close together the leviathan could see other spectrums. There would be no way out for him, should the creature notice him. When he opened his eyes, he became aware of the current of water the beast displaced as its hundreds of tentacles kicked it across the hall. It hovered now near him, at the base of the stairs. He imagined it was thinking. It was close to him, some of its eyes moving slowly and independently, others fixed beadily. One of the eyes, as large as a small plate and filled with an alien intelligence, roved over him. But then the eye moved on and the creature drifted up the stairs. Max remained rooted to the spot with fear. The thing drifted quickly across the foyer and out of the library.

Max felt ill. The sickness seemed more profound than before he had animated the gills for the cart, as if he had been poisoned and any added touch of toxin caused his body to react. He swallowed back bile as nausea hit him. Lethargy flooded his limbs.

Max waited for a few minutes, clasped his knife tightly in his hand and walked with heavy legs toward the stairs as quietly as he could.

He felt a disturbance in the water behind him. Turning, he was astonished to see another figure dragging an air-cart toward him. He looked closely. It was Kata! She smiled at him from behind her faceplate and he was filled with a rush of joy. He would not be alone down here. She moved quickly through the water toward him. The question rushed into his mind: How had they completed the air-cart in so short a time? It was impossible. Max looked at the image coming toward him: beneath the image of Kata, he fancied he could pick out a hundred glistening eyes.

Max turned and ran. His legs burned as they moved slowly through the viscous water and up the stairs: *clunk, clunk, clunk.* He moved far too slowly and could feel the thing coming at him, rushing through the water with its alien eyes fixed on his back and its tentacles and stingers ready to grasp him in a deadly embrace.

Clunk, clunk, clunk. Above him was a kind of film over the water, but he could make no sense of it, only that the area above him was lit more brightly. Up more stairs he climbed, and he thought he could feel a rush of displaced water as the thing propelled itself toward him. The film was close to him now and instinctively as he ran he reached up and his arm passed through it. With three more steps—*clunk, clunk, clunk*—he burst through the film, which turned out to be the surface of the water. Max found himself in a pocket of air. Here then was one of the Library's defenses. He slowed down now, heaving for breath as he dragged the air-cart from the water and moved up a couple more steps to safety.

Max was standing in a great domed reading room. Above him, by some clever arrangement in the Library roof, the windows still let in light and perhaps even magnified it. Hovering in the center of the room were the strange chairlike platforms he had noticed in the control room back at the seditionist hideout. Shelved around the walls were books—books of every type! Large and leather bound, thin pamphlets, red-and-black spined books, short squat ones. He laughed to himself. The greatest library in the world, and he was the only one with access to it.

Max laughed again. In that instant, he was pulled with fantastic force off his feet. He struck the ground and slid across the marble floor. Behind him the cart was being dragged toward the water by long, thin tentacles. He scrambled for something to clutch on the floor, but the marble was smooth. The cart crashed into the water and submerged. Max's feet hit the water, then his body, and finally he was clumping down the stairs fully submerged.

Fear clenched his heart in a fist. He reached for his knife but in his desperation missed it altogether. Again he tried, and this time—his hand shaking —drew his knife from its scabbard and slashed out at a tentacle, which pulled away. Something whipped his arm, and he felt his suit tear. He caught a glimpse of a long appendage with a flat leaflike end covered in burgundy nodules whisking away.

Water rushed into his suit and a warm pain grew on his arm. He gasped and cried out. The pain increased in intensity, as if someone were placing burning coal against him. But at the same time the water rushed up beneath his suit and into his helmet. He hacked into another tentacle that grasped the cart, but knew it was no use—the tentacles were too many. Desperation flooded him. He could barely think. His actions were impulsive and desperate. Again and again he lashed out at the tentacles. With each strike of his knife a tentacle retreated, only to be replaced immediately by another. Each moment he was dragged farther down the stairs. Frantically he reached out, unclipped the chain that connected him and the cart, and severed the air-tube. The cart rushed away across the submerged foyer. He turned, breathed in water, and coughed it out again. The burning pain now consumed his entire left arm and shoulder. He could no longer move his arm. He stumbled up the stairs, his lungs yearning for air. One foot clipped the stairs and he fell. Climbing to his feet, he looked up at the surface of the water shimmering with light. He took another step. His lungs filled with a fire and his entire body screamed, "Breathe!" He held his breath a moment more and clambered desperately forward. Finally, involuntarily, he took another breath of water and his body convulsed. He coughed violently, burst through the water's surface, scrambled across the marble floor coughing up water and bile into his helmet.

His body spasming, Max released the first lever that held his helmet clamped tight against his suit. He reached over to the other side of the helmet with his good arm, released the second. The helmet fell to the floor with a clatter.

On his hands and knees, he scrambled across the floor to the middle of the reading room, far from the water's edge, heaving for breath. As he lay there, the hot-coal burning had now covered his arm and shoulder and he found breathing more difficult. Breathe, he told himself, but his arm and shoulder would not move, and his breaths were slowing. He tried to draw air into his lungs, but it was no use, his breaths slowed themselves down. The entire left side of his body now surged with pain. His left leg would not move. And then his right side. He tried to scream, but all that would emerge was a little gurgle. As the paralysis overcame his body, his lungs were slowly starved of oxygen and his vision shimmered before him with a whole new form of light, until the whiteness eventually enveloped him.

THIRTY-ONE

Once Maximilian was gone, Kata found herself at a loss. Things had changed so rapidly, within the seditionist group and within her mind. She was a jumble of thoughts and feelings and hardly knew where she stood. That morning, as she had watched the air-cart descend to the bottom of the ocean, her heart had been gripped with worry. Now he was gone and the delicate equilibrium in the seditionist group would disintegrate. Maximilian was to return in four days, but by then, she feared, the group would have been transformed into Ejan's army.

Her plan had been simple: She had hoped to save Max, and Quadi, perhaps warn others before House Technis struck. She knew that House Technis could not strike until she betrayed the base's location to Autec. Then Technis would descend on the base with guards, perhaps even thaumaturgists and Furies summoned from the Other Side. The decision lay in her hands. And yet, unthinkably, she had come to love these seditionists. Was the overthrow of the Houses not a just aim?

Kata could not resolve these conflicts within her. Rather she sat passively in the communal room with Quadi and watched the seditionists prepare for Aya's Day, a week and a half away.

"Busy as bees," said Quadi. "Just like Tir-Aki."

"Eleven days until the demonstration, and then we will see if all of this means anything." Kata looked on grimly.

Rikard, his brooding expression fixed on his face, his eyes squinting suspiciously at them, sat himself next to them. He was always heading here and there, speaking for Ejan, passing on messages. It had seemed not so long ago that he had been aligned with Maximilian.

"There will be a meeting tonight," said Rikard.

"So Ejan wants to assert his authority," said Kata.

Rikard did not answer immediately. "Maximilian has abandoned the group for his own selfish aims. He's only ever thought about his own place. He wants to be a great leader."

"And Ejan doesn't?" Kata spat back. But Rikard's words rocked her, for there was truth to them.

"You know that Ejan is without personal ambition." Rikard stood again, looked back at them briefly, moved on.

"Ejan builds them in his own mold," said Quadi. Rikard had the look of many of the seditionists these days. They were less idealistic than the first members of the group. Where once the seditionists were dreamers, living in abstractions—Kamron and Maximilian—these were simpler and harder folk, workers from the factories or former urchins from the street. Their visions were not of grand future worlds where everyone was free, but immediate and practical: The desire to defeat the Houses drove them. They scared her, for they were her people, and she understood them better.

"What will Aceline say tonight?" Kata said.

"She will be silent," said Quadi. "Like the others, she will not fight Ejan in the open. She hopes that once Aya's Day has come, the sheer momentum of demonstrations will make Ejan's militarism obsolete."

"If she will not fight him, then we must," said Kata.

Quadi put his hand on Kata's arm. "No. We wait for four days and pick up Maximilian. Then we'll have the upper hand."

"By then it will be too late. If this group is to remain a positive force, then we must act now," said Kata. As he spoke, she wondered: she sounded like a seditionist herself.

That evening the central hall swelled with the members of the group. The room was hazy with lamp smoke. Ejan took the floor with Josiane hovering closely beside him.

Ejan paced, his voice steely, his face radiant in the soft light, his white-blond hair brilliant. "Today Maximilian descended beneath the waters to the Sunken City. He risks his life for the cause. With him in mind, we must do the same. The battle lines have been drawn between the enemy and us. On the one side, the seditionist movement, on the other, the Houses. In the middle, the great apathetic mass, who by their inaction support the Houses. Why do they not stand up and fight? Why do they blindly allow the Houses to control, to dominate, to destroy, to kill and torture? Refusal to act—that is tacit support of those in power!"

Kata was horrified by Ejan's invocation of Max's name, his claim to Max's allegiances. Ejan was prepared to claim that they were on the same path, no doubt to win over Max's supporters.

Ejan continued to pace, feeling the audience, pleading with them, arguing with them. He seemed to draw energy from them, and they from him, as if together with him they formed one giant organism. Never had he looked so certain of himself. There was a magnificence to him, no doubt, as if he came into his own on a larger stage.

Ejan's speech was clear in its logic: The group must provoke a clash with the Houses on Aya's Day. In the heat of battle, everyone in the city would be forced to choose sides. He stopped and waited in the deadly silence, before he added, "We must all prepare together now. We must prepare for the confrontation. Tomorrow we shall begin to arm and train you. In a fortnight we will be an army that even the strongest of the Houses will tremble before! When Max returns a liberation-thaumaturgist, then no force in the city will be able to resist us."

As Ejan swept off the stage, Kata watched as mesmerized as the rest of them. Across the floor, Aceline watched with concern. Quadi was right, she would not risk a confrontation with Ejan. Kata knew she would have to act, if she was to save the group from this destructive path.

Josiane stepped forward, and said, "The meeting is over."

Kata leaped to her feet and stepped forward. As she spoke, she felt a tingle of energy rush over her skin. "It's not over! It would be wrong for us to concentrate solely on military concerns, or to spark a confrontation. We're still only a few hundred, in the face of all three Houses. We must grow, we must increase our influence, Aya's Day might only be a show of strength, not the final measurement of it."

The tingle rushed through her and Kata watched the faces of the seditionists. They looked at her with closed mouths and un- blinking eyes. They did not disagree with her, but they would not cross Ejan. His influence was more than a matter of persuasion now; he was a man who had acquired power, and that power was itself argument.

Kata formulated her argument anew. "In any case, Maximilian would never—" She stopped speaking. The tingling turned into a trembling within her. Her legs shook as she felt the waves of a fit rise within her. This one came on with a rapidity for which she was unprepared. Oh no, she thought, not now. She grasped for her flask, tried to unscrew the lid, but it fell to the ground as she shook. The sedtionists looked at her blankly, unsure of what was occurring. No, she thought, as she fell to the ground, her entire body shuddering. She could feel her limbs clattering against the ground. The roof of the cavern faded into white slowly above her. She fought against the fit, struggled to stand, failed.

Quadi's blurred outline appeared above her. "Kata!"

Kata lost all sense of the world and was pulled away into the black sea on a dark tide.

When she regained consciousness, the meeting was over. Her tongue was swollen, for she had bitten it during the fit. Her head pounded and she was filled with bitterness. She had failed to make Maximilian's arguments, to defend him in his absence. Quadi gave her some broth and they sat in silence, realizing that things were coming apart. Eventually, Kata fell asleep and by the morn- ing, she was well enough to move around the cavern.

Not long after, Ejan approached her. "Are you feeling better?"

"Oh, it's just a temporary ailment, nothing serious." She would not show weakness.

Ejan nodded. "I don't think we should be opposed to each other. You've proved yourself a good seditionist."

"Maximilian will return soon," Kata said simply.

Ejan pursed his lips. "I need you until he returns. I need you in one of the attack squads. We strike soon against the Houses. I know how good you are under pressure."

"I won't do it."

Ejan leaned close and to Kata's shock, dropped to his knees in supplication. He looked up at her. "I know many people think me cold and calculating. My father taught me to be this way. For when you live in the ice-halls, surrounded by mountains and snow, you are forced to calculate chances of survival at every moment. As a child, he would take me out onto the glaciers and leave me to find my own way back. Do you know what that is like, at ten years of age, with the snow cold enough that it is like powder? When snow giants roam through those mountain passes? I assumed it was because my father didn't love me, but then I saw that it was his *way* of loving me. He taught me, you see, that the end justify the means."

"But not all means lead to the same end," said Kata.

"I need you, not just for your skills, but as a symbol. If you accept, then the group will be unified. The group agreed last night, voted to accept my plan, and the rest of Maximilian's group have agreed. This is what Max would have wanted: a united group. I know you understand the reasons for it. Without unity, why be in a group at all? To say no would be to say that you aren't really a part of the group. What would that mean?"

"It wasn't a true decision. I could not make my arguments against you."

Ejan pleaded, "But you know that even had you made them, you would not have gained the majority. I know you won't force us to exile you, as we exiled Kamron. I know you won't fail us, will you?"

Kata knew the truth of his words. Even had she put her arguments to the group, she would not have been able to sway the other seditionists. Ejan was now undisputed leader of the seditionists. To oppose him would be to lose her place, to be cast out. Or worse, face imprisonment at Ejan's hands. Yes, he implored her on his knees, but she knew the consequences should she say no.

Kata looked away into space. "No. I won't fail you."

————

Not long after her conversation with Ejan, Kata slipped away from the base and walked the streets of Caeli-Amur at a loss. She felt detached, like a boat that had broken away from its anchor and floated adrift on the sea. She had slowly been seduced by these seditionists, but now that Maximilian was gone, she realized how fragile the entire enterprise was. Questions buzzed in her head. Would Aya's Day be the beginning of the wave of actions that the seditionists hoped? Would the code that Omar had provided allow Maximilian to drink the knowledge of the Library of Caeli-Amur, as the Histories would have it? If he returned, would he be able to shift the strategy of the seditionists away from the confrontation which Ejan proposed? Ejan's coming attacks on the House, his wave of assassinations, would surely provoke a violent response. Meanwhile, Autec would be waiting for her at Technis, waiting to discover the location of the hideout. If she did not return, soon he would send in another agent. Perhaps he already had. Would she return to Technis? Or would she once and for all throw her lot in with the seditionists? The moment of no turning back was approaching fast.

As she walked along the boulevards, she was amazed to see the graffiti across the walls calling for the manifestation on Aya's Day. The entire city seemed to be caught in the grip of an ominous tension. She could see it on the faces, hear it in the voices of those who scurried around the streets attempting to avoid the stifling heat and burning sun. In the endless summer, the atmosphere seemed overheated, overcharged. Buildings shimmered in the air, perspectives warped, painted walls became sheets of brilliant white.

To escape the unpleasant mood, Kata passed along the white cliffs, up along the narrow staircases to the Artists' Square, where it was always peaceful.

Kata approached a small huddled figure sitting on one of the benches that overlooked the city beneath. The sun was baking and the day was bright, but many years earlier the artists had constructed great sail-like covers that could be extended to cover the square in shade. They flapped now in the light breeze.

"Kamron. Escaping the heat up here?" She sat beside the old

man who had been banished from the seditionists in what seemed to be an entire age ago.

He looked up at her and smiled a gentle smile. "Look at the city. Magnificent isn't it? Terrible and beautiful. Look at all the people moving about their lives, all the activity. Things move on, don't they? They pass you by."

"We can always choose to participate, though. To throw ourselves into the maelstrom."

Kamron again smiled softly. "That's a youthful thought. Sometimes the maelstrom won't have you. Sometimes it rushes away and you can't catch up with it. Maximilian will learn that, you know."

Kata shifted on the seat. "I know Maximilian treated you badly, but he did what he thought was right."

"Some of the gravest injustices have been done by those who thought they were doing right. No matter, I bear him no ill will. My exile was hardly one of those injustices. We must each learn to accept our place the world. Dreams and realities rarely align. Some years ago, I ventured to Varenis. In the center of that vast city stand twelve towers. You should see them. Like mountainous pinnacles they are, soaring above the world. Each tower belongs to one Sortilege, the greatest of thaumaturgists. To live in Varenis is to feel that their eyes are always on you, looking down from those black and glittering towers. It's as if their very dark power radiates from the stones like cold from ice. During those days, one of them had died and another was elevated to take his place. It happens rarely, for they have the knowledge to extend their lifespan. The dark festival was extraordinary. For the first time in fifty years the population was allowed three days of freedom to do as they wished, free of the tendrils of the Directorate. Well, I remember that feast. It was as if all bonds had been released from the most animalistic of impulses among the population. Drugs drove people into heightened states of arousal. They coupled in the dark corners of the parks, vendettas came to their final bloody end on the city's high walkways. All of it was looked upon by the Sortileges up in their towers. I imagined them up there, laughing. I had never seen them, for their ceremony was held in secret and they abandon their names when they are elevated. I fear that one day soon they will come down upon a free Caeli-Amur with their full darkness, as they have to so many other cities of the world."

"Perhaps they will, but what alternative do we have? If you do not fight, what are you? You're not moving: you must be dead." Kata looked around the square. Sitting and playing chess on the far side was a tall and young minotaur, laughing occasionally as he played. Kata was knocked off balance by the sight.

Kamron kaughed. "Spoken like a true woman of action."

Kata placed her hand on Kamron's forearm. "You should be assured of your place in history. You should not grieve, but be content."

Kamron's old eyes filled momentarily with tears. He blinked them away. "One does the best one can."

Kata left him then, just as the minotaur was standing after the end of the game. She walked quickly across to the creature. "Dexion."

Dexion took several great steps toward her and she was afraid. He towered above her, the compressed energy in his body radiating. She stopped, waited for him to crush her. And then she found herself high in the air as he laughed, "Kata!" He then held her to him, crushing her in a bear hug, still laughing, and finally placed her down.

She looked up into his inky black eyes. "I thought you'd left."

"The island of Aya awaits." He placed a hand on each of her shoulders. "But now I stay in Caeli-Amur, bejeweled city."

"You don't miss the others?"

"Yes. But now is my time to see the world. You know how it is: to stand alone, to travel where no one knows you."

The words cut at her like a razor. To stand alone: the very thing she had tried to avoid; the very thing she could not avoid.

"And you," he said. "I thought you had perhaps left with Aemilius. He spoke of it, you know."

She looked down at the ground. No longer could she look him in the eyes. "He spoke of it?"

"Yes. He hoped to take you across the sea to Aya, and from there he said he would build a boat on which you would both sail the seas, to Numeria perhaps, I don't know."

Kata buried her face in her hands, as if in the hope that if she shut out the light, the world would disappear also.

"I'm sorry he left you here." Dexion spoke quietly. "But I am surprised. The way he spoke of you . . ." His voice became lighter. "Anyway, we still have Caeli-Amur!" He laughed.

Kata took her hands from her face. There was a joyfulness to the minotaur that she couldn't resist. "It's good to see you, Dexion. It is good to see you well."

He did a jig on the spot, to show how excited he was. It was ludicrous, given his size, and he stopped suddenly, looked around to see if anyone had seen.

Kata could not stop herself laughing.

THIRTY-TWO

In the quiet of the night, Kata walked into the machine room and moved among the great sleeping conglomerations of pipes and plates. The lamp hung from her hand, swaying and casting great looming shadows. She felt at peace there, among the lost machines, like hibernating creatures, waiting for spring to come so that they could awake.

She passed along line after line of machines until she reached the middle of the cavernous room. She heard something move in the darkness. She froze and listened: the sound of feet padding somewhere behind her.

Kata turned the knob on her lamp and in a second the light guttered, leaving her in the dark. She placed it on the floor, drew her stilettos from their scabbards and slipped across the floor, silent as a cat.

The footsteps stopped, but the sound was enough for her to locate them: they came from behind a nearby machine.

She moved silently circling around a silent figure that stood in the dark. With rapid movements she crept behind the figure, so that she could hear his breath. "So Ejan had you follow me."

The figure flinched slightly and faced her. "No, I chose to follow you myself. There are those that say you are untrustworthy." Rikard spoke matter-of-factly. His honesty appealed to Kata, and frightened her.

The young man looked around the room. Somehow he looked in his element. There was something brooding and dark about him, something both troubled and romantic in his dark eyes. "What is this place? What are these machines?"

Kata looked at crouching machines. "They're the dead dreams

of the past. When a dream has nowhere to live, it comes here and collapses in on itself, becoming one of these creatures."

Rikard's face was impassive. "Your thoughts are feverish."

"No. It is the world that is in a fever."

"Well, we need calm heads. House Arbor is having a feast in one of the parks to the south of the city. It is a perfect chance for us to strike. They will be far from the Arbor palace. They will be unprotected."

"What's the occasion?"

"Director Lefebvre's birthday."

"When?"

"Tomorrow." He tilted his head, challenging her.

"Who are you, Rikard?" she asked.

"My father was a tramworker, well respected, at the head of their strike. After Technis crushed it, my father was little more than a blackened ruin. The tramworkers were buried in a mass grave on the other side of the mountain, out of sight of Caeli-Amur. There was not even space for him in the necropolis here. He had a friend in Technis, a certain Officiate Autec, who betrayed him. He had once been a tramworker, but now is nothing but a House apparatchik. As we threw lime over the bodies, my mother weeping with the other widows, I vowed to avenge my father. I vowed to kill this Autec."

Kata yearned to explain to Rikard that she knew the monstrous Autec. "Yes, the Houses have much blood on their hands."

"Now, Kata, who are you?"

"Just a seditionist."

"You love Maximilian, don't you?"

Kata breathed deeply. "Yes, I do." There, she had said it. The truth.

"He won't return, you know."

"I know," she said.

The following day, the cart rattled along the cobblestoned roads just south of the city, whose walls stood ominously nearby. Here the sun beat down on little shantytowns, which sat on the dry and dusty slopes. Smoke rose miserably from hovels. Kata held a shirt over her head to protect her from the sun. Beside her, Rikard wore a wide-brimmed black hat. The summer burned on, with no sign of abating. The stink of refuse rose from piles of waste around them.

Josiane, in charge of Kata's group, sat at the rear, spinning her weighted chain expertly.

"You change allegiances easily," said Kata.

"Yet you're on this mission also." Josiane waved the chain in front of her face, to scare away the flies that had descended on them the moment they'd entered the area.

"Sometimes I wonder if there's anything you stand for at all."

Josiane stopped spinning the chain. Her sudden smile was shocking to Kata, who was so used to seeing the seditionists serious and grim. Josiane's entire face changed; her cheeks rose, her eyes shone; she looked younger. "Think of life as a game. I was a child once, you know. Children play games to learn the skills that they will use as adults. What games do they play? War. Hide-and-seek. Dice and other games of chance. That is exactly what all of life is like. It's fun and exciting. People maneuver around each other, allegiances shift, but there's always one goal. And behind it all, I do what I think is right and necessary. And what is it you stand for?"

Kata looked away as Josiane's words reverberated within her. What did she stand for? A hand closed on Kata's and she looked up to see Josiane quietly withdraw her own hand, lean back against the rear of the cart and look out over the landscape.

The cart descended from the slopes of the mountain. Bushes and copses of trees punctuated the landscape. Before long, they passed through an ancient iron gate into the water-parks, which were so cleverly irrigated that they were lush and green, even in the relentless summer.

Josiane directed them to an embankment, which overlooked the small, delicate bridge, its sides built with wooden planks and iron lacework. It was a beautiful thing. Beneath it, Josiane placed barrels filled with explosives.

Kata could hear the sounds of the preparation for the party not far away. Lefebvre's carriages would carry the revelers from the city and along the path through the park to this very bridge. When they arrived, the bridge would explode, killing those in the first carriage. The survivors would be slain by the seditionists waiting in the groves of trees or hidden behind hedges or embankments.

To Kata's right, not far away, lay Rikard. Kata gripped a short-sword in her hand. Rikard had an old bolt-thrower and a short-sword in a scabbard.

She looked behind her. Towering on a nearby embankment stood a statue of Iria, goddess-lover of Aya. Before the gods went to war, Iria and Aya had walked the pleasure gardens of the world together. But the war had driven them apart, and after Aya's defeat she had retreated to a fabled Tower—now long lost—there to renounce her immortality and grow old and die. Who knew how much truth there was to these myths. Still, the statue looked out at the world in stern sorrow, tall and magnificent and frightening.

Kata looked back at the path, but there were no signs of the carriage. She looked back at the statue of Iria. Had the statue moved? It looked as if it had shifted slightly: its head cocked a little more, its arms moved just slightly across its body, its weight a little more on one marble foot. Kata pressed her eyelids together, hard, and opened them again: no, she was only imagining it.

"Here they come," said Rikard.

Kata looked down from the embankment toward the path. Four carriages pulled by magnificent white horses emerged from the copse of trees to their right. The horses pranced joyfully along the path, their legs rising high like those of dancers, their heads shaking, their powerful musculature rippling with their movement. They seemed so beautiful to Kata, obliviously galloping toward the bridge. She could barely look. They were now halfway toward the bridge and she could see silhouettes through the windows of the four carriages. She closed her eyes, concentrated on her breathing. But she could not keep them closed. When she opened them, the carriages were three quarters of the way from the copse to the bridge.

Kata looked back up to Iria, who now seemed to be looking at the bridge with imperious curiosity, like a parent watching children, uncertain of their actions. Kata looked back at the carriages, the first only seconds away from the bridge. Everything seemed to slow down: one of its horses tossed its head, its long mane rippling like a wave crashing on the shore; Kata blinked, her eyelids dropping languorously, rising again like a curtain at the theater. The carriages seemed to be standing still, even as the horses pranced, as if the ground was moving beneath them, rather than they over it. The bridge seemed no closer, and then they took a leap forward, and they rushed toward the bridge. The lead horses had just placed its hooves onto the planks when Kata heard the terrible explosion. Somehow things seemed all mixed up: the sound of the blast first, then the splintering of the planks as debris and shards of bridge burst upward, and finally a great ball of flame. The horses were thrown back like children's toys, the carriage behind them tossed into the air by the force. The second set of horses ran headlong into the falling carriage as the second crashed into them from behind. The third set of horses veered leftward at an acute angle, and the third carriage lurched onto its side while the final horses came to a halt safely.

The seditionists were already rushing from their hiding places toward the carriages, intent on pressing their advantage.

Kata staggered after them, vaguely aware of Rikard moving to her right.

There was a pall of smoke now over the scene, affording only glimpses of the action within: the figure of a horse, standing motionless, a scattered carriage wheel, figures milling around. Everything seemed silent, even though Kata was aware of screams and yells. A man burst from the pall, red blood splattered across his green arbor uniform, blackened with soot. He raised a ceremonial sword, took two steps before a bolt struck him in the middle of the chest. He dropped to his knees, leaned back, and collapsed to the ground, his hand scrabbling ineffectually against the bolt.

Rikard stopped to reload his bolt-thrower.

Kata ran into the smoke, and gagged on the acrid fumes hanging bitterly in the air. A horse writhed on the ground, still harnessed to a carriage. Its beautiful white head was blackened with soot, splattered crimson in places, almost black in others. Where its forelegs had once been, now there were only stumps, which it wiggled ineffectually as it tried to stand. Great flaps of skin hung from the bones. She turned away to see a man with throwing knives: a philosopher-assassin. The man loosed one: it spun fast through the air and stuck a seditionist in the throat. The seditionist put her hand up to the protruding handle and started shaking her head like a dog with a stick.

Kata dived to the ground, rolled once, came to her feet, but dropped down again and rolled once more as a knife whizzed past her ear. She rolled a third time, came to her feet directly beside the philosopher-assassin and, her two knives in hand, plunged them into his sides. He struck her in the neck with both hands: sharp hard chops. She collapsed to the ground and everything went white.

A man's face stared at hers, its eyes blank as they looked beyond her into the realm of death itself. She dragged herself up. The smoke was dissipating. She staggered to her feet and pulled her knives from the dead man's ribs.

Before she took a step forward, a figure staggered from the smoke. Kata dropped to one knee, ready to strike but stopped. It was only a servant girl, not even out of her teens. In her desperation, the girl lurched clumsily over to Kata, unaware even of the seditionist's presence. She staggered directly into Kata, who found herself holding the young woman up. The girl looked at Kata blankly, in shock.

Kata turned, and together they staggered from the smoke and the violence, back toward the embankment. The girl could barely stay on her feet; every now and then her legs gave way. They made it up the embankment, where Kata laid the girl down.

The girl's face had freckles scattered over it like confetti. "Don't let me die."

"You're not going to die, you fool." Kata looked at the girl's face; she saw herself in another life. If she had managed to acquire a job in one of the Houses, this girl might have been her. "You're out now, and I'll make sure you're all right."

"I've a man. I've a true love," said the girl. "He's waiting for me in the city."

"He'll be there when you get back. I, too, have a love. He's away at the moment." Kata leaned back, looked out over the bloody scene. Seditionists were picking over the corpses, finishing off those still alive.

Rikard dragged a body by a leg. The body's shock of white hair was practically the only thing not covered in scorch-marks and soot. Rikard called out, "Lefebvre is dead!"

Kata turned and looked back at the girl, who now appeared pale, a sheen on her skin making her look sicker than before. Kata looked down. The girl's left arm was missing. "Oh, no." She grasped the girl by the shoulder, to keep her awake. She looked down helplessly as the girl's face turned ever whiter, draining of energy, of life. The girl opened her mouth, closed it, opened it again like a fish.

Kata looked around, as if she might see help arriving. When she looked down again, the girl had stopped breathing and now stared coldly over her shoulder up at the statue. Kata turned and looked up at the figure of Iria, who still looked over the scene imperiously, as if she had always known exactly what was going to happen.

From below others had taken up the cry, "Lefebvre is dead!"

THIRTY-THREE

News of Lefebvre's death sent shock waves through the Houses. Officiates hurried around the Technis corridors with a look of terror on their faces. Intendants whispered to each other in the corners. Recriminations were sent from House to House. House Arbor saw it as an attack from House Technis, and Boris was seen as responsible, despite the fact that he had sent out a wave of guards to round up anyone talking sedition in the streets. The new Arbor Director Thorel released a public statement, which Boris now received from his trusted agent Armand. Armand was somehow above the grubby politicking of the others, no doubt due to his background. Arbor had always done things with a grace that Technis lacked. They made much of their traditions, their ancient families, their principles. Principles, damn it—did no one have them anymore?

Standing before Boris's desk, Armand read it to him in an ice-cold voice, the words pressed together tightly. "The seditionists' brutal attack, in a designated haven, was clearly kept secret by House Technis, who had the technical means, as Director Boris Autec had demonstrated, to know of all seditionist activities. Retribution will be swift and righteous. House Arbor names Autec of Technis responsible. Justice will prevail."

From behind his desk, Boris scrunched up his face in distaste. "Fools."

Armand looked up at him. "And Director Autec. A strike has broken out at the docks. The Xsanthians."

"House Marin will crush that in a flash."

"They haven't." Armand held Boris's eye. "There are rumors

that Marin's thaumaturgists are no longer following orders. And Director Bourg of Marin requests an audience. He's in the waiting room."

Boris placed both hands on his desk as if he were holding it down. Here was a chance to take the ascendancy over the other Houses. Arbor was in decline, decimated by the assault against their leaders. Marin crippled by the strike at the docks. Having united them, now Technis could rise to a hegemonic position. But Boris hesitated. The Marin thaumaturgists would not act. What was the meaning of this?

Armand continued. "Director. It is nine days until Aya's Day. Perhaps we should consider that the citizens might come out in their thousands. Perhaps—"

Boris cut in: "Armand, I am former factory worker. Believe me, the citizens are not capable of such a show of force. They're disparate and defeated. Yes, we have witnessed strikes, but most citizens look on like spectators. If anyone understands this, it's me. No—we must focus on crushing the seditionists. Send Bourg in."

Director Bourg, a willowy man with large hands, entered. His pockmarked face—a sign he had suffered from chickenpox as a child—was gray like the skin of a drum. He crossed the room like a man condemned to die, Armand striding calmly behind him.

Boris smiled broadly. "Director Bourg. So nice to see you." A lithe female bodyguard followed Bourg; everyone had them nowadays, just as in the days of the House Wars.

Boris led Bourg and Armand to the seats that formed the semicircle around the fireplace. Sitting down with ease, Boris smiled again at the grim-looking man. "I trust this is the first time you've entered the Technis Complex. It's most impressive, is it not?"

"Director Autec"—Bourg's eyes were deeply lined—"you are going to die."

Throwing his head back, Boris laughed loudly. "Bourg. Bourg. Why so morbid?"

"Arbor blames you for the death of Lefebvre. It was a clever ruse, to convince the other Houses that you would ally with them, and then allow the seditionists to murder Lefebvre. I must admit, it took me by surprise. You possess a cunning which is admirable."

"Arbor are nothing but a decaying old House. Arbor is the past, Bourg."

"Exactly my point, Autec. Exactly my point. But House Marin and Technis must keep our alliance—for we are the future."

Boris held Bourg's eye, the tension slowly building between them until the Marin Director looked down and away. "Is House Marin really the future?"

Bourg looked back up, his voice rose. "With these seditionist attacks, this protest on Aya's Day, it is essential that we bond together, no? Wasn't that your entire point?"

"Well, is Marin's House in order?" Boris was enjoying the conversation. He leaned back and stretched out on his chair.

"What do you mean?" Bourg's pudgy face was the color of canvas. The collar of his shirt seemed to clasp at his throat, for he continually reached up to loosen it. House Marin's officials' had a reputation for langorousness to which Bourg did not conform. Marin officials were said to spend most of their time floating like jellyfish in their palace's steaming baths and water-spheres.

"Technis is in a position of strength. How does Marin stand?" Boris smiled slightly.

"Marin is, all things speaking . . . Well, we have our troubles, as do all the Houses."

"Oh, but some have greater troubles than others." Boris's voice was soft and pleasant.

"What could you mean, Director Autec?"

Boris leaned forward and yelled directly into the man's face. "You know damn well what I mean!"

Bourg started, his head jerked back as if he'd been punched.

"The Xsanthians' strike is the least of your troubles, Bourg. It's your thaumaturgists. Have you no control?"

"They want things to change."

"Everyone wants things to change! Damn them! What do the Elo-Talern say about this? Do you speak to them?"

"As usual, they seem to take little interest."

The thought stopped Boris. The Elo-Talern seemed to take little interest in Marin, and yet they took interest in Technis. Why? Beneath these cryptic clues, he tried to discern some pattern. The Elo-Talern recently emerged from a long hibernation to take notice of—what? What had changed?

Boris pushed the thoughts away. "Well, what would you have us do?"

"Help us with the Xsanthians. The thaumaturgists use them as bargaining chips. Their torcs tighten if the Xsanthians venture too far way, but otherwise they are useless. Now the Xsanthians refuse to work. Instead they swim in the harbor and bask on the piers."

"Bloody Tritons." Boris spoke to no one in particular, using the derogatory term for the Xsanthians. "Alas, our own thaumaturgists are busy at the moment."

Bourg's face turned turned even grayer. "Please."

"Sorry, what did you say?" Boris pretended not to be able to hear the man speak.

Bourg looked at him with baleful eyes. "I beg you."

"You beg me?" Boris looked around the room as if there were more important things elsewhere in the room. His eyes fixed on the scrying ball twinned with Varenis. "Get on your knees and ask me again, and I'll see what I can do."

"What?"

Boris looked straight at Bourg. They waited there a minute before Bourg shifted from his chair, dropping down to on knee before Boris, then the other. "Director Autec, please."

"We will intercede. But you are indebted to me now, Bourg. Expect me to call on this favor one day."

Bourg stood again. "Director Autec, thank you. And I feel it is my duty to warn you. Director Autec—there will be an attempt on your life before long. Arbor will not forgive you. After all, you have the scrying ball and could have warned them before Lefebvre's assassination."

Boris tried to hold his face calmly, but a tiny twitch came over it.

Bourg looked at him curiously. "You have the scrying ball, don't you?"

"Of course." Boris's voice was tight.

Bourg's face shifted subtly, this time with curiosity. "Of course." He looked at Boris. "Of course," he said softly.

With Armand behind him, Boris stormed along the Technis corridors. Armand was still silent. Yes, Boris liked the man, but his silence was unnerving. He had almost *too much* principle, almost *too much* respect for station, too much respect for *proper process*.

The thaumaturgists worked in the east wing, past the private apartments where House agents sometimes lived. As Boris approached, great double doors sensed his approach. Intricate ideograms inscribed on them glowed a soft green, and the doors slid open of their own accord.

The room was vast, lit dimly by glittering squares along the roof. Small movable walls divided the room into hundreds of smaller enclosures, where suited thaumaturgists sat at desks sealed off from each other, working on formulae, copying manuscripts, working on equations, researching the various disciplines. Gas lamps hanging from tall thin stands threw cones of light over each desk, heightening the sense that each thaumaturgist worked alone. Just like a factory, Boris thought, a factory of knowledge.

Boris and Armand walked toward a large central platform, held up by a huge piston. As Boris approached, the piston let out a great hiss and the platform lowered slowly to the ground. Boris stepped onto it, Armand a step behind him and to his right. Behind a desk sat a huge gray-suited man with olive skin, a close-cropped white beard, and a great bald head, curved and smooth like the dome of the Opera House.

"Director Autec." The man remained perfectly still as he raised his eyes from his ordered desk: piles of paper in trays before him, a tome to one side, geometric shapes and diagrams inscribed on its open pages. He appeared unchanged by the use of thaumaturgy, which unnerved Boris, for that meant his mutation might be internal and invisible, perhaps in personality or intellect. Only his dead-white irises were extraordinary; Boris had heard that such unsettling eyes occurred naturally far south in the Teeming Cities.

"Prefect Alfadi," said Boris. "You've heard about the Marin thaumaturgists?"

"Marin has always been the most liberal of the houses. They run their affairs as if they were one great collection of equals." Alfadi sat motionless, like a statue. Was it perhaps because Alfadi was from the Teeming Cities, or was he simply self-possessed, centered, at peace, like the mystagogues—the great Magi of old—were said to be? "Have no fear. Look around. Our thaumaturgists have only one priority: loyalty to Technis."

Boris looked at the scores of men at their desks around him, writing, and muttering to themselves, like little cogs in a great wheel. "Good, because I need them to help put down the Xsanthians' dock strike."

Alfadi leaned back. "If you are suggesting the Furies, I would advise against it. You do not understand the effort it takes to invoke them from the Other Side. The demands are terrible." Alfadi looked around at the thaumaturgists at work. "There are always consequences."

"What other way is there? Our guards are not equipped to fight Xsanthians, especially not when the creatures take to the water."

Alfadi's pupils widened noticeably within his icy irises. "What could you offer us, to help offset your demands?"

Boris shifted on his feet in anger. He held it at bay, for he did not want to upset Alfadi and the thaumaturgists. And yet, a House must function with respect for authority. An army must have a chain of command. "Loyalty is loyalty. It's not something that can be bought."

Alfadi blinked rapidly. "If I may be so bold: I would hesitate to demand of our thaumaturgists too much. There will come a day when the well will be dry."

Now Boris felt like begging, but as Director, he could show no weakness. In any case, did he not have the support of the Elo-Talern? With such weight behind him, he could force them. But then again, he had not heard from Elo-Drusa recently. "I will not ask for an invocation of the Furies for a long time. Also, we will find a way to reward you all. What if I was to offer you lost knowledge from the Library beneath the Sunken City?"

Alfadi's eyes narrowed greedily. "What knowledge?"

"Lost knowledge of the ancients," Boris continued. In the rear of his mind, he knew that this promise would most likely not be fulfilled. The seditionist Maximilian would have died beneath the sea. But once they were quelled, why not force the Xsanthians to swim there and return with whatever secrets survived? "I will tell you more as things progress. But I expect the Furies to be invoked this afternoon."

Alfadi continued to look at Boris in silence. There was a hiss and the platform began once more to rise as the prefect turned back to his work. "It will be done."

Boris took a few steps before Alfadi called out to him. "Remember your promises."

Boris stormed out, Armand following him silently. As they marched along the corridor, Boris stopped and turned. "What?"

Armand looked Boris in the eye, calm as ever. "Nothing, Director. Nothing at all."

That afternoon, Boris and Armand stood on a balcony overlooking the great courtyard at the rear of the House Technis Palace. Lines of suited thaumaturgists stood below. Before them were the Furies, roiled and warped, black stains in the air. Fragments of limbs and bodies—wiry, taloned arms; rib cages; yellowed fangs—emerged from the other side and then fell back into darkness. Around them, the air itself took on new dark and unnatural qualities; it shimmered with alien energies. Again Boris felt horror and fear at the sight of these creatures. He yearned to turn away from them and run to safety, far from the hideous sight. But he forced himself to watch on coldly.

Boris realized that the Furies must have some connection to the Elo-Talern. The Furies come from the land of darkness, beyond the wall of death. However the Elo-Talern did not seem to live wholly in this plane, nor in the Other Side, but were lodged somewhere between life and death, shifting from one to the other. To be lodged between life and death—what did that mean?

"Events have a terrible logic to them, don't they?" Boris said to Armand. "When I became officiate, I never considered I would have to order such things. I would have railed against it. Yet, I've tried everything else I could."

Armand raised his nose to the air as if he could smell the Furies.

"That's why we must rely on tradition, principles, honor. When my grandfather was exiled from Arbor, his heart was broken. Principles were what stopped him from collapsing into nothing. He cleaved to tradition like a shipwrecked man to flotsam. They held him afloat. My father worked for the Collegia in the Lavere, at the base of the Thousand Stairs. It was hard work, some of it criminal, in the eyes of the Houses. But he was no ordinary criminal. No, he, too, held to the traditions: loyalty, honor, civilization, education. When Technis came searching for agents, they recruited from the Lavere, not from the factories. That is the difference between you and I and the rest of them. We have our own traditions. You are a factory worker at heart, and I am one who believes in the noble right of the Houses to rule. Only the Houses can control the rabble out there—the uncivilized mob. We must protect the people from themselves. Events brought us here, and who are we to question their logic?"

A great grinding sound came from the courtyard's rear gate, which slowly rolled open. The Furies strained at unseen bonds. The gray-suited thaumaturgists appeared like dog handlers leaving for a hunt. As soon as the gate was fully open, the whole monstrous conglomeration passed through the gate and out into the city, to descend upon the Xsanthians in a storm of horror. Behind them, a squad of Technis guards followed to put the half-dead to the sword and to clean up the mess.

"Fetch Tonio for me," said Boris. "He and I will follow the detachment to the docks."

Armand looked at him sternly. "Remember Bourg's warnings. Arbor may be decaying, but they are still one of Caeli-Amur's ancient Houses."

THIRTY-FOUR

When the carriage arrived at the docks, Tonio leaped like a monkey from the top of it and landed on the ground with a soft padding sound. He looked around protectively as Boris stepped out.

Already the Furies had been and gone. Along the docks a few corpses of Xsanthians lay like great beached fish rotting in the sun. But most of the conflict would have happened beneath the waters. Boris imagined the Furies, plunging into the sea and pursuing the fleeing Xsanthians like black-stained currents. He remembered the tramworkers' strike, which seemed so long ago. History itself seemed to have sped up, and a few months seemed like whole lifetimes. He still felt the grief, though. It clutched at his heart and made him yearn for hot-wine again. The corpses of the Xsanthians made him think of Mathias, lying blackened before the factory, the fishlike things emerging from him. Boris felt like crying.

He walked along one of the piers, where some remaining Xsanthians, their heads hung low, unloaded caskets from a cutter. Elsewhere sails fluttered in the breeze and the wind whined past masts and ropes. Order had been restored.

Across the Market Square, citizens watched from afar. Boris could practically feel their despair. This should dent their enthusiasm for the Aya's Day demonstration, thought Boris. Let them run through the city, spreading word about who was the real power in the city.

Content, Boris returned to his carriage. Tonio leaped to the platform attached to the rear of the carriage as Boris opened the door. But Boris didn't feel like being alone. He wanted company, someone to take his mind off the horror of things. As he placed his foot on the step, Boris looked up at Tonio. "Why not ride in here with me?"

Tonio raised his eyebrows. "Are you sure?"

"Come and talk."

Tonio shrugged and leaped down again.

As the carriage rattled over the cobblestones, Boris said, "Technis's thaumaturgists resisted this action today. They suggested that loyalty needed to be bought. What do you think, philosopher?"

The Cynic's eyes lit up with excitement. "These days it is hard to tell who is bought, and who is a true ally. What is certain is that he who fails the least will triumph. These are the questions the great Ioga would have us ask: What mistakes have your opponents made? What mistakes have you made?"

Boris laughed involuntarily. He could barely think about them, piling one on the other like corpses in a mass grave. Eventually he joked halfheartedly, "Mistakes? I've never made a mistake in my life. What mistake could I have made with the thaumaturgists? To punish them, that would be the mistake. But I bought them off with promises. After all, I need them to deal with all—" Boris waved his toward the window, "—this."

The carriage climbed up Via Persine, through the mobs looking on like carrion-dogs from the drylands to the south. To Boris, the people looked increasingly gaunt and pinched-faced. There was a meanness to them that frightened him. This was the mob that Armand feared also, the base masses living without belief or principle, without a sense of honor or order, without education. They rutted in rooming houses in front of their children, whom they left to run wild in the factory district or the slums of the Lavere. Family, that was what had always driven Boris. He thought now of Saidra. How he missed her. Why had he not visited her in the Opera while he was with Paxaea? But he knew the answer, for she would be full of contempt and disgust for him. The thought filled him with even more misery.

The carriage drew to a halt and Boris looked out the window to where a cart blocked their way. "Move that cart!" he yelled. But strangely there seemed to be nobody in charge of it. Instead it sat motionless on the street. A gray-haired woman looked at him through a window and retreated into the shadows. From a side alley, a man looked suspiciously from a doorway, then hurried away.

Boris frowned. Something was wrong; he could sense it. A feeling of panic rose within him. He looked farther up and down the streets, where people backed away as they, too, perceived something awry.

Tonio reached rapidly for the door just as his side of the carriage exploded inward. There were no flames, but a thousand and more shards of wood and metal showered the two men. Tonio held his face in his hands and screamed terribly. Blood poured through his fingers and dribbled down his arms. When he took his hands from his face, it was nothing but a bloody mess, the skin and flesh gone, a red bony structure revealed below. He fell toward Boris, who pushed the body of the philosopher-assassin away. The body fell backwards through the gaping hole that had been the side of the carriage.

Boris threw open the door to his right. Hitting the ground, he staggered away from the carriage. The crowd had backed still farther away. A washerwoman dropped her basket; a maid raised one hand to her face; a young man clenched his jaw. The carriage driver scrambled away over the horses, one of which had tried to leap the cart unsuccessfully.

Still moving, Boris looked back. A great fat man burst through the carriage after him, a huge bolt-thrower in his hand. Boris turned and ran. He heard a smaller explosion and to his right a heavy woman with a scarf on her head was thrown backwards, her chest a gaping ragged circle of blood.

Boris stopped and turned, knowing that he had no hope against this fat philosopher-assassin. Around him the crowd fled and Boris was left alone, standing on the wide boulevard.

The gargantuan assassin, his weight shifting as he walked forward, held a heavy bolt-thrower against his hip, its barrel composed of a hundred little holes. It was one of the new incendiary-throwers, imported by the New-Men from Tir-Aki, or Ari-Aki. Boris laughed grimly to himself. Technology, progress—they seemed to destroy everything.

"I am Fat Nik. You know why I'm here." The killer strode toward him.

"Arbor sent you to kill me."

"You understand it's nothing personal. Is there anything you'd like me to do before I take your life? Words I should pass to anyone?"

Boris thought of Paxaea. He thought of Mathias. He thought of Saidra. He looked around him at the emptied street. The people were gone and with them, the life of the city. In its place stood a ghost town, the memories of long-gone people whispering around the gray stones. There was no escape. There would be no way that he could run. The killer would cut him down before he had moved two paces. The place was a desolate place to die.

"There is nothing I have to say." Boris looked Nik in the eye. "There is no one who will care that I am gone. There is nothing I can say that can redeem me."

Nik looked at Boris and shifted on his heavy legs, his body moving around him as his equilibrium shifted. "I've ridden the trains in Varenis. I've sailed the seas past Taritia. I've killed many men in this life. Never has one of those men had nothing to say, no one to beg forgiveness from, no one to tell that they love them. You are unique."

Boris nodded.

"Boris Autec. I've killed many men in my life. On behalf of House Arbor and Director Lefebvre, I'm here now to kill you."

Boris closed his eyes but opened them again. Better to face his fate.

Fat Nik pulled the trigger and the bolt-thrower exploded in his hand, as if the assassin had been holding a bomb. The malfunction caused the entire mechanism to blow apart, and Nik's forearm with it. A look of terrible pain shuddered across his face, he fell to his knees, and he glanced down at the bloodied stump of his arm. In desperation, Nik tore his shirt from his back with his left hand and wrapped it as quickly as possible around his stump.

But already Boris was beside him. Boris pressed his knife to the throat of the philosopher-assassin. "Is there anything you'd like to say, before you die? Any words for anyone?"

Nik looked up at Boris, his face gray and slippery with pain and shock. "You can't do this. I'm not meant to die yet."

Boris cocked his head and smiled. "So your last words are for me?"

Nik nodded sadly and looked at the ground. "I have a sister, she works at Café Legras, on Via Gracchia. Send her word that I am sorry about Father's disappearance. Beg her forgiveness. She'll understand. Now, just do it quickly. Don't make a mess of it."

All Boris's problems rose in his mind: the strikes, the pressures from the other officiates, the thaumaturgists, the other houses. He was filled with a blinding anger, and he would take it out on this fat assassin.

Nik started to tremble just a fraction and Boris was immediately shaken from his rage. Looking at the assassin, he saw himself only minutes ago reflecting back on his life. And how had Boris's life turned out? He never meant things to turn like this. He wanted to make things better in the city. He wanted to find someone to share this with. He wanted a family again.

He took the knife from the man's throat. "Go."

Nik looked up in surprise. He staggered to his feet, his face still blank with shock. "You really are unique."

The philosopher-assassin turned and ran past the carriage and into a side alleyway, there disappearing like an alley cat down a drain, leaving Boris standing alone and alive on the boulevard.

After the assassination attempt, Boris stood in front of the carriage, where Tonio's body lay, his face just a bloody pulp. Your mistake, thought Boris, was to accept my invitation to sit with me in the carriage. He calmed the skittish horses with soothing words and gentle patting of their necks. Alone, he pushed the cart from the crossroads, mounted the carriage, and drove it back to the Technis Complex alone, for the driver had long since fled.

When Boris returned to his office, the city was shrouded in the shadow of the mountain. Darkness was falling and Boris had thought much about mortality. How he feared death. What would have happened if Fat Nik's bolt-thrower hadn't failed? Even now,

Boris would be living in the dark lands. The thought sent cold needles through his body. He thought of the Elo-Talern's elixir of life. Was it true? Would he be able to avoid that terrible moment when his soul struggled to free itself from the cage of his body? When his heart rattled and then was still?

Armand had brought Boris a bowl of spicy lamb stew, though he was barely hungry. "The Xsanthian leaders are in the dungeons. You can interrogate them whenever you wish."

Boris put his hand to his forehead, as if struck by a headache. "Leave me alone."

As he sat at his desk, the image of Tonio's ruined face—blood over bone— returned again and again in his mind, so that he could barely think of anything else. He tried to conjure other thoughts, other memories—but all he could think of were bad ones. He needed something to take him away from his nightmarish past.

Looking across the room, Boris eyed the man-sized, egg-shaped memory-catcher in the corner of the room. He walked across to it, examined its intricate machinery: the carefully carved bolts, the silver ideograms decorating its shell, the pistons and pipes and little wheels that surrounded the pole that held it erect.

Clipped alongside the other bolts was the one that he had fired into Matisse. Boris unclipped it, held it in his hand. Long and black with a silver head, through a transparent window swarmed the thousand mites that had swarmed on Matisse, stolen his memories and his mind.

Boris placed the bolt into a hole in the side of the machine and a mechanism clasped it. There was a whir, a click, the sound of rushing liquid. Beneath the bolt a panel slid open, revealing a glass of black liquid. Without thinking, Boris took the glass and drank the strange and metallic brew. He sighed as he finished drinking.

Boris walked into the great bedroom and lay on the bed, images of Tonio still flashing in his mind. The horror of the day was overwhelming, he felt it in his body: a tightness that started in his calves and shuddered up along his back. Horror—there had been so much of it in his life, and he wondered if perhaps he had always been destined for it, or perhaps if he invoked it the way thaumaturgists could invoke unworldly powers. When he was a child, his father had been a smith who spent his days hammering molten metal into the form of hinges and vises. One day his father had spilled the molten metal onto his foot, which had melted like wax. His father hadn't cried or screamed, but held out against the pain with a barely controlled white face. Something had changed in the family that day, and his mother stopped talking to his father. Instead they lived their lives in rooms at the far end of a long corridor along which servants moved.

No, wait, his parents had not been estranged. That was not his memory, thought Boris. No, it was Matisse's. Boris became aware then of the slow creep of Matisse's memories—an entire new lifetime, slowly entering his consciousness. He is a child, playing in the parks to the south of the city. Those are happy days, of running and laughter—the days of the rich whose childhood is a time of happiness, so different from his own. He savors those memories, as one would rare fruit. He recalls his youth—no, not his, Matisse's youth—moving among House Technis circles: balls, summer parties in the parks, trips north to Varenis. There is always something strained about those rituals in the House. Where Arbor and Marin could rightly claim centuries of tradition, the Technis officiates and Directors, the entire privileged stratum, participate in these events with a slight air of desperation. The memories come to Boris with the rush of blazing reality, the colors intense, the smells vivid, the feelings coursing through his body as if he is experiencing for the first time.

As a youth, he finds it all vaguely pathetic, and he gossips with the other youngsters—Karel and Tashna and Vikri and Efram—about their parents' pretensions. At other times they play teenage games in the bushes of the parks. They take off each others' clothes. One day he finds himself alone with Tashna, her long hair black and curled, her mouth slightly downturned, freckles scattered almost absentmindedly over her face. Without thought he puts both hands on her shoulders and she drops to her knees. He unbuckles his pants and, drunk with his own daring, presses himself against her face. She takes him in her mouth, warm and wet and almost immediately he is shuddering and crying out and it is over. Boris feels that memory with all the lust of the teenage boy.

He found that he could shuffle through Matisse's memories as if through the sheaves of a manuscript. He jumped through them, searching out all the moments of pleasure and power, and found joy in discovering Matisse's dirty little secrets: the moment he betrayed his childhood friend to rise to officiate; the petty affairs he had, surreptitiously cheating on his wife.

Boris ingested these memories as one would a wine, getting drunker and drunker as one by one he lives them—Matisse's whole life there for Boris's perusal, until he finds himself standing before the new Director Boris Autec. Autec is a round man who has somehow weaseled his way up from the factories into the position. Somehow the Elo-Talern have favored this grubby little man who speaks with a rough and undignified accent, whose clothes hang stylelessly around his body. He cannot understand how this man has become Director. It makes no sense at all. He knows that the Elo-Talern have been through a time of weakness where they have retreated from the world. His father suggested to him once that the Elo-Talern would never return to being a power in the city. Perhaps now they have now restored their strength and it will take some time longer for them to make sensible judgments. In any case, he hates Autec and will destroy him. He has already turned the other officiates against the former worker, who has disappeared for the last few days. Together they stand with him before the new director's desk, and he plans to force Autec's hand.

"Director Autec," says Fournier, standing slightly in front of Matisse. "You have been indisposed for some days."

"You think I should spend all my time with you?" Autec looks tired, as if he's been weakened by some trial.

"Of course not, Director, but events move quickly," Fournier continues, along the lines that Matisse has encouraged him.

"Events? I make them," said Boris.

"Let's hope they don't unmake you then," he says, provocatively smiling. The Director has only recently been promoted. He must feel at a little insecure. Show the other officiates, Matisse thinks—that's the way. It is time to test Autec, see if he weakens.

"I think you forget who you are talking to." Autec stands and his voice is cold.

Matisse smiles again at Autec provocatively. Show him no fear, no respect, undermine him with every chance.

"What?"

"We all know that you are the Elo-Talern's favorite. That there was no good reason to promote you—you—above anyone else. All these years they avoided interfering in House affairs, and when they do, they favor . . ." He goes on the attack now, looking Autec up and down with as much scorn as he can muster.

Autec smiled grimly. His voice is softer now, as if he is being cowed. "Matisse, would you come a little closer, perhaps."

He takes a few steps but not enough to let Autec speak to him without the others here.

"A little closer yet, Matisse. I have something to say to you that I would prefer that the others did not hear."

He takes another step forward, teasingly, making Autec ask again. He enjoys this little power game. With each request, Autec loses face.

"Just a few more steps. Just up to the desk here, please, Matisse."

Matisse takes one more step and something strikes him in the chest. What? He looks down to see a little bolt protruding from his stomach. He laughs. "The bolt is too small, Autec. It's like a child's weapon." Matisse reaches for the bolt. But before he touches it, its sides burst apart, like the rapid blooming of a flower, and a thousand and more little black antlike specks rushed over the bolt. Fear grips him. Technology of the ancients—no, it can't be. But it is. The specks crawl up toward his face. He tries to brush them off, but they have a powerful grip and do not fall to the floor. He laughs again, though he becomes aware of it only when it becomes hysterical. The swarm of black things is now on his face and he is filled with dread. The specks are now pushing into his mouth. No! His nose. His eyes. His ears. Desperation grasps him even as pain overwhelms his consciousness, as if someone were driving a spike up into his head, and he starts to forget as thoughts start to disappear from his mind. First feeling in his arms and legs, then a thought here, a memory there, blanking out like candles guttering in the darkness. Then great swaths of his mind: gone, leaving only vast vistas of blackness. He is lost.

Boris, lying on the bed, is racked by the final deathly memory that he savors more than any of the others. The disappearing of a soul, the feeling of slipping into eternity, the terrible darkness—death is truly something to experience.

As he drifted in and out of consciousness, a dreamlike sleep, Matisse's memories having exhausted him, Boris was aware of a presence. Above him stands a tall and terrible cadaverous figure.

"Elo-Drusa."

She reached down and her immense, many-knuckled fingers covered his brow. "Boris. Boris."

Boris was scared, but he could not move. It was if his mind had disconnected from his body and now he lay prostrate and paralyzed. She was above him, distorted in his vision. He could not tell if it was simply his fever, the warping of his memories, but her hand appeared grossly large, her head tiny and far away.

"Boris." She leaned over him, her face looming large and close, the side of her horselike face close to his so that her cheek brushed against his.

He groaned softly.

"Boris—so full of life. You will save me, reawaken the passions of the world into me. Rejuvenate—yes, rejuvenate. We'll achieve great things together. Great things." She took his manhood in her hand and squeezed softly.

THIRTY-FIVE

Images flashed into Maximilian's mind: sheets of white light, a curved roof far above, with great metal supports, chairlike things hovering in the air. His stomach contracted involuntarily. Instinctively, he rolled over onto his side, heaving. He lay there for some time, until he realized that he was alive, on the floor of the Great Library of Caeli-Enas.

After a while Maximilian pushed himself up with his hands. He couldn't be sure how long he had been unconscious and paralyzed. He could remember his heart slowing down, his body on the edge of blissful rest. He stood uncertainly and looked around at the vast reading room. Stale, humid air hovered around him. From the ceiling, a little glowing sphere descended and hovered behind him as he walked, illuminating his path with warm golden light.

Maximilian wandered unsteadily through that room, enchanted by its age, mesmerized by the thousands of books that still lined its walls. Everywhere his eyes wandered, he found lost gems of history. He saw the huge red spine of *A Chymicall Treatise of Arnuldus of Novilla*. He noticed *The Secret Book of Artephias,* and side by side in different editions the *Alchemical Catechism of Barone Tschuldi,* and quite close the *Epistle on the Mineral Fire.*

With hands trembling, he took down from the walls a metal-covered copy of Sumi's *Necromancy and Agency* and placed it on one of the reading tables that ran out like spokes from the middle of the room. He opened the front cover. In spidery writing the title was written on the front page. Carefully, he reached down to turn the page. With just the gentlest of touches, the edge of the paper crumbled. He drew his hand back in alarm. With even greater sensitivity, he tried turning the page. Again the edge of the page crumbled, like water retreating from flame. And this time the pages beneath crumbled a little also. He touched the top edge of the parchment and again the paper decomposed beneath his fingers. In frustration, he turned the book on its side and opened both covers, hoping the sheets would fall open. Instead the entire insides gave way, sloughing into a mound of crumbled papery stuff, leaving him grasping the covers.

Ioto's *Histories* also disintegrated beneath his touch. He grasped Eribal's *Structure,* and the covers themselves decayed in his hand.

He laughed, the manic sound echoing back at him from the roof and the vast spaces of the empty hall. Stumbling in disbelief across the room, the reality of Maximilian's situation finally struck him. He had reached the Great Library. Wondrous books surrounded him, but they were ruined by age. He would need to study formulae to preserve them, and yet he had no access to those formulae. And he had no way of escape. His cart was gone, dragged beneath the waters by a creature that waited for him in the murky depths. With it had gone his food and water. He would die beneath the waters and his bones would join all the others in Caeli-Enas. But no: there were still the legends of knowledge that could be drunk like an elixir. There was still the code.

He staggered from the empty reading room and through the massive archway that led farther into the library. Through long corridors and into drafty halls he passed, entering rooms with chairs that hung like balloons in the air. He wandered past offices separated by shimmering glass walls, ideograms descending their surfaces like snowflakes. In these deeper sections, the architecture took on the sleek lines and unusual angles of ancient architecture, obsessed as they were with geometric shapes, sometimes symmetrical, at other times seemingly without any logic.

As he walked, his perceptions slowly changed. Ill from his traumatic arrival and the creature's poison, he passed, thirsty and hungry, through the labyrinthine corridors. Things seemed to Maximilian as if in a dream. Images of the library rose before him and disappeared just as quickly: snatches of corridors, and rooms, walls that flickered with brilliant imagery of unknown worlds, cities that had existed only in myth: the ancient tower of Payrris, the archipelago of Tarynesia, the broken land of Chinar. He came to grand stairs lit by a red glow. As he descended, he heard frightened whispers from figures that moved inside the walls. He could see them, shadows like those that lived in the great ice-halls of the north, where Ejan was born. The shadows twittered to each other nervously and darted along beside him, disappearing in the angles where the walls joined, some obviously rushing away in hidden directions, others emerging trepidatiously. One shadow crouched down and giggled near him, then ran back to join the others.

Six archways surrounded him. As he stepped into one, he dropped into a shaft. An unseen force picked up so that he descended at a controlled speed. He hovered for a moment and then popped out into another corridor, this one lit by purple and green balls of light. Staggering along the corridor, he lost his sense of the proportions of things. Perhaps this was the result of a combination of the strange light and the effect of the poison.

The air around him was now heavier and reverberated with a deep sound, like that caused by a faraway engine. There was a soft whisper as if air were escaping from a valve. It felt more significant than those that came from the figures moving in the walls. The whisper increased, beginning softly and increasing in volume. At first, he thought there were many voices, but then as they became louder, he realized it was one voice; the words were repeated so quickly that they were superimposed upon each other, each time increasing in volume, like an echo slowly building.

Maximilian stopped and cocked his head. But he couldn't make out the words. He walked on. The whispers continued, and though now he could make out the words, he still couldn't understand them. They were in a foreign language. The voices said, *"Panadus, eperantus, el minio el tritian. Espa?"*

Along kaleidoscopic corridors he passed, colors of blue and red and green shifted in patterns that distorted his senses and ruined his perception. Again he was buffeted by a force that lifted him off his feet, across rooms, up shafts that opened in the roof, along corridors, and down, down, always down into the depths of the earth, as if he were plunging deeper into the soul of things.

Along the walls ran gleaming ideograms and numbers, or geo-metric shapes that seem to break the laws of physics, as if the angles of their sides were impossible, as if they existed suspended in a four-dimensional space. At times these forms peeled away from the walls and moved through the air itself, before sinking back onto the plane of the wall.

The whispering continued, and the repeated words, once echoing each other, were now more clearly superimposed. The voice seemed to be cycling through languages, and Maximilian recognized words from the ancients among them. Until finally it spoke and he understood.

The voice said, *The world spins and the wind wears down the buildings of creatures. Things fall apart.*

"Are you speaking to me?" asked Maximilian.

Elentra? said the voice. *Disparus?*

Maximilian looked at the hexagonal room in which he found himself. Its walls and roof were formed by moving plates. Some of these plates broke away from the others, shifted and spun. On their surfaces ran the words spoken by the voice—Elentra? Disparus?— in many-sized scripts: some written in huge letters that moved slowly across the walls, others infinitesimal, fast-moving versions of the word, catching up, superimposing themselves, overtaking the larger ones. Max looked down to see that he also stood on a drifting plate with words drifting across it.

He said, "I am Maximilian."

No, said the voice. *That is your name. Who are you?*

"I am a seditionist," said Maximilian. "I come in search of knowledge. Who are you?"

Knowledge is not to be used to gain power over others, said the voice.

"But it has, and only knowledge will set it right," said Maximilian. "Knowledge and action together."

The voice said, *You would use knowledge to control things, to warp them to your will. But the universes react back upon you, and warp you in turn.*

"But what use is knowledge if it is not to be used? Should we not put it to our ends, to defend us?"

I am here not for you, but for knowledge. I am here to defend it, the voice said.

"Can you help me with what I seek?"

The fall of the ancients was a great one, said the voice. *And you and your generations are their children.*

Maximilian said, "We all stand on the shoulders of our fore-bears."

But some of them fell, said the voice. *And their children had no shoulders to stand on.*

"Who are you?" asked Maximilian.

I am the defender. I am the Library.

Maximilian paused. His mind raced. He struggled to think of the words he wanted to say. Eventually, his body tense and his heart racing, he said, "Can you help me? I need to learn the secrets of the ancients. I need to drink them like an elixir. I have the code."

And what knowledge do you seek?

Again Max paused. Knowledge that might unhinge the dominion of the Houses, his own image of himself as a great thau-maturgist of liberation—these hopes rested on this moment. Yet he was aware that he stood before an entity that predated the House system, that predated the cataclysm itself, that transcended his desires and viewed history with a wider perspective. But he himself was not such an entity; he was a seditionist. So he spoke: "That of the mystagogues. That of the greatest Magi."

And what is this code you speak of?

Maximilian began to recite the numbers. Zero, one, zero, one, zero . . . On and on he spoke the numbers.

There was silence. When the Library spoke, there seemed to be the hint of laughter in its voice. *Continue on if you dare. Perhaps you will come to adulthood or perhaps you will be ruined. The choice is yours.*

Maximilian waited. When the Library did not speak again, he moved through the labyrinthine passages. The deeper Maximil-ian descended, the stranger were the arrangements of colors. Light crisscrossed the spaces at unusual angles, as if he were walk-ing not on floors but on ceilings.

Lost beyond hope, Maximilian found himself bathed in colors, as if he was again beneath a great ocean and lights hovered around him in the water, cut through it at angles. He waded through this timeless space and came upon a huge glittering pillar, composed only of horizontal bars of light that rose above him like a tower. He staggered on and came to another such tower. Stepping close, he reached out and placed his hand into the luminous structure. His hand disappeared as trays of white light emerged from the pillar's side. A deep sonic hum resonated inside his body, as if his internal organs were shivering. The white light became blinding, a sheet of brilliance. He closed his eyes, but the light pierced his eyelids. He dropped to his knees, cried out, a pain like needles drilling into his head. He placed his hands to his ears, to try to block out the sound, but it was no use. He screamed—a long high-pitched thing that was lost in the sea of sound that enveloped him. Deep thumping sounds vibrated in his chest and he could not tell if it was simply his heart rattling around like a wild animal throwing itself senselessly against the bars of a cage. He collapsed onto the ground.

Overwhelmed by light and sound and pain, Maximilian frothed at the mouth. His chest thrust up from the ground as if he were having a fit. Now, surrounding him was a bright band with some kind of complex mathematical structure. The band oscillated and coalesced and descended upon him. Maximilian screamed, and felt something splicing into him, interweaving with his body and mind. He cried out again, as some new information of the universe, which was floating in the white ether only a moment before, merged with him. It vibrated against him, and for a while his body struggled back. Some part of Max's mind tried to process these events. This, he thought, must be the elixir that he is drinking. But that was only a metaphor. Rather, he was somehow fusing with the Library, opening himself up to its world and knowledge, and now he was scared.

There was the cry of a word. "No!" But it made no difference. Maximilian rose to his knees and hands. His chest heaved. And as he lay twisting and turning in the whiteness, he realized that he, too, was only a band of information waving in the brilliance. And the two bands—his and the Library's—struggle and fight and threaten at any moment to tear each other apart. Everything around is lost in a sheet of brilliant white—until now he is the light. He is the sound. It has pierced him, and merged with him and now he is the sound and the light. And they are him. He has dissolved into the whiteness around him and is now connected with the entire universe of the Library. Everything he is dissolves into the Library and as he disappears, he screams a final scream as everything fades into the whiteness and is no more.

THIRTY-SIX

Max stood in a clearing in a thick forest. High above, the great canopy shut out all but a soft light. Around him grew furnace trees, larger than those that line the streets of the Arantine. Their bulbs glowed like hanging lamps. Farther away stood gigantic tree trunks, as large as apartment blocks, their roots spreading out from their base like huge curved tentacles. Hanging from high above were thick emerald vines. The scent of rotten vegetation wafted among the sickly perfume of the furnace trees.

An insect the size of Max's head buzzed over his shoulder; he backed away. It settled its long spindly legs on one of the bulbs and touched its proboscis to the bulb. When it tried to pull away, it found that it could not. It pulled at one leg, but the others sank farther. It tried another, and the same thing occurred. The more it struggled, the more profoundly it was trapped. As it tried to twist and turn, it was finally absorbed, its delicate lacework wings the last to go. When Max examined the furnace tree, he noticed the silhouettes of giant insects and bugs inside; he assumed they were being slowly digested.

"They're quite amazing, aren't they?" said a voice.

A man squatted on the other side of the clearing, watching Max. His powerful arms rested comfortably on his knees. He had the look of an athlete, at ease, but capable of bursting into action at any moment.

"I've never seen such a place," said Max.

"Numerian jungles are something to behold, aren't they?"

"Am I in Numeria?" asked Max.

"After a fashion." The man stood, looked at his feet, ruffled his blond hair, and walked across to Max.

Max looked up at the man, who stood many inches taller. "There is something about you."

The man turned and ran to a group of little blue flowers. As he passed them, they lit up like candle-flowers in the night. "You could spend epochs here."

Max examined the man further: the powerful physique, the happy disposition. A thought tried to rise from deep in his mind but sank back. It needed more time to grow, and Max had other things to think about. "How did I get here?"

"Would you like to see the waterfall? It's really something. Come on." The man ran from the clearing and Max followed as quickly as he could. At times the path climbed giant tree roots that rose from the forest floor like bridges. To the left of the path lay a swamp over which hovered dog-sized dragonflies. Several plants rose from the water and snapped up the insects in mawlike fronds, dragging them, still struggling, back into the water.

"Come on!" called the man over the sound of a great roaring, like a wildfire burning across the hills near Caeli-Amur.

When Max emerged from the forest, he stopped in terror. He stood on the edge of a gigantic cliff, higher than he could have imagined. From this height, the canopy below looked like growths of moss. Nearby, a vast river plunged over a waterfall; misty vapor obscured its bottom. Beyond the waterfall, the cliffs continued, an enormous wall curling through the forest into the distance. Every aspect of this jungle-world was alien to Max. The very air was thicker than that of Caeli-Amur, the light softer, the greens deeper.

"I'm not really in Numeria, am I?" said Max.

The man put his powerful arm around Max's shoulder. "Once that jungle below was all water, all sea. Look at how beautiful it is. You could almost stay here forever. Almost."

"I need to get back," said Max. But where to? He wondered. He knew he had left Caeli-Amur on a mission, but for where, for what?

"I'm bored here. I need life."

Max's mind was working now. He looked at the vast wonderland. He thought back to his final memories before arriving at this place. They came to him now: the air-cart, the descent beneath the sea. "If I didn't know better, I'd say that you're almost . . . godlike."

The man said nothing but continued to look out over the forest.

"I asked the Library for the knowledge of the greatest of the Magi. Is that you?"

The man laughed. "Some would say so, but I wouldn't."

"Will you teach me? Teach me the secrets of the mystagogues. Teach me to use all the disciplines of thaumaturgy as you can."

The man stepped back from Max and looked into his eyes. "Why do you need to know these things? Will power make you happier? We thought it made us happier, and for a while perhaps we were right. The strength to move mountains, to drain seas, to create a playground. But did it make us happier in the end? Alerion and I had once been the best of friends, you know. But light does not exist without darkness. There is no method of thaumaturgy in the world of life without engaging the Other Side. That is your first lesson and the secret to moving from discipline to discipline."

Max tried to make sense of this. Yes, the warping of the thaumaturgists when they use the art—the Other Side seeping through into this. That made sense. He could see it now: Kamron's body, the illness, the House thaumaturgists in all their distorted forms. But how was this the secret to unification, to mastering all the diciplines?

"Tell me more," said Max.

The man still did not answer.

Maximilian tried to speak, to bring the man's name to his lips. He was surprised that he knew the name, that he'd known it for some time. The truth of it set of cascades of thoughts in his mind, thoughts of gods and legends and history. Finally, he forced it out "Aya." He started again. "Aya, I beg you. Tell me the truth of it all."

Aya turned back to Max. "And you, you must help me. This was my favorite playground once, so I created it to keep me entertained while I lived here, in the Library's great memory. But it's not real. None of this is real. Can you see how if you examine things closely, you can almost see their flaws—it's fake. After a while it disturbs you. You start to feel like everything is constructed to deceive you, that this world is just one big lie. Sometimes you try to catch the Library out: you turn quickly, you peer at the most minute detail. Then you lose sense of what you're seeing. You must help me to escape this place."

"How?"

"There is only one way."

Max looked at Aya in confusion.

"Let me join you," said Aya.

"How?" A terrible feeling crept over Max.

"You won't have all of me, only fragments—that's how it works. Information is lost in the transfer: memories, knowledge. You will still be you, but you will be parts of me also. Free me. I was born to be free."

"No," said Max. This pact would destroy him. What are people, if not their memories? To take on someone else's, to let them integrate into you, that would be a kind of death. The idea terrified him. He would never be Maximilian again.

Aya looked sadly at Max. "Well, at least I won't be so lonely if you stay." He looks around. "Come on, I want to show you something."

Through the jungle they walked. Max could never quite become used to the strangeness of it. Just when he thought he had grown accustomed to its cycles of life and death, of predator and prey—the way the jungle itself seemed one vast interconnection of creatures devouring plants, of plants devouring animals—he would be startled by a new image. A fern that opened out to reveal an open mouth at its base; a deadly looking lizard with razor-sharp teeth swallowed suddenly by a bed of red spongy moss.

"Be careful of these." Aya pointed toward beautiful flowers the size of a human. Their white petals shivered, as if they sensed the proximity of others. A clear nectar dropped from their velveteen centers where several stamens moved like worms reaching into the air. With a lurch, one of them tore its roots from the ground and shuffled toward them. The others were free of the ground and heading toward them also.

"Blood-orchids," said Aya, who broke into a run. Max followed rapidly.

Aya led Max into a dark valley where it became cool. The sound of a river drifted through the trees, then disappeared a little later. Here in the coolness, the trees became thinner and taller, covered with gray lichens and slate-colored molds. Flowers grew rare and the undergrowth more sparse.

Buried beneath the jungle were stone ruins. Here a crumbling wall was covered by lichen so that he almost mistook it for the roots of a tree. There a stone slab was overgrown by a seething bluish moss. Over a little rise, a gnarled and winding tree grew over a stone structure that might have been a one-room house; the tree's roots clamped over the building like a great hand. Then, in the middle of a clearing stood a pyramid the size of an apartment block. Small trees clung to its sides, their roots splaying out, searching for cracks in the stone. A walkway circled the pyramid about halfway up its structure; carved into the stone wall was a great bas-relief of humanoid figures and unknown histories.

Breaking off green chunks of mold as they walked, Aya and Max climbed the stairs that ran up the pyramid, and stood before the bas-relief. The humanoid creatures seemed to be waving ele-phantlike trunks at each other. "This stood before we arrived. It was built by some of the original inhabitants."

"Before you arrived in Numeria?"

Aya smiled and crossed his arms. "No. Before we arrived on this world."

Confused, Max examined the bas-relief. It told a story of deadly fraternal conflicts, of exile and banishment, of war. "What happened to them?"

Before Aya could answer, Max noticed a young boy squatting on the top of the pyramid, squinting at them. In one hand he twirled a leafy branch and absentmindedly ran his other hand over his bald head. Max took a step back from the bas-relief.

"Well, what do you think?" Aya asked the boy. "What happened to these elephant people?"

The boy plucked a burgundy berry from the branch and threw it at Aya. With a wave of his hand, Aya stopped the berry midair and propelled it back at the boy, who ducked as it flew over his head.

"You know their history, Library. Won't you tell us?"

Without answering, the boy scampered down the pyramid's face, leaped onto the walkway, threw another berry, which Aya stopped once again in midair, but this time let fall to the ground.

The boy scampered down the rest of the pyramid and ran off into the jungle.

"I don't know why it torments me. For its own pleasure, I suppose." Aya spoke pensively.

"You stopped those berries without incantations, without material elements. You stopped them, just like that. Is that a function of this world, or some kind of thaumaturgy?"

"Let me show you something." Aya stepped directly into the bas-relief and disappeared.

Max put out his hand to the stone, which was rough and impermeable. From the rock an arm grabbed his wrist and pulled him forward. A strange feeling rushed through Max's arm as it passed into the wall. It felt as if the stone was passing through him, like water through burlap. As his face was about to touch one of the elephant figures, he pulled back. Then Aya gave a tug and again the stone passed through him, as he passed through it.

Max found himself in a large chamber. In its center sat a great statue of one of the humanoids, its trunk curling up around its own neck, then down onto its own lap. The creature's eyes were sad, as if they looked out into the vast vistas of space and time, and there found only emptiness.

In a corner of the chamber the Library-boy played with stone figurines that had trunks sprouting from their faces. Whether it was a second boy, or the first who had returned secretly, Max could not tell.

Aya stepped across the floor of the chamber toward the statue. "I fear that somehow we wiped them out, when we arrived to build our beautiful world."

"What do you mean arrived? You were the gods."

Aya stared at Max and burst into laughter. "Gods! Is that what you call us?" Aya repeated to himself in the voice of a man whose worldview had just been fundamentally rearranged. "Gods!" He laughed again.

Max felt a rush of anxiety. If they weren't gods, what were they? "You pulled me through the stone. You rearranged matter as if you were stirring soup."

Aya shrugged. "Thaumaturgy." He looked back at the great statue. "There's a cost. There's always a cost. But you forget, this is not the world. We live inside the mind of the Library. We live in its fevered imaginings, however close that is to the world outside." Aya reached forward and touched the statue's trunk: "What happened to you, my beautiful alien species?"

The boy stopped playing and scampered up to Max. His great eyes looked up like pools of darkness from the round face. "Will you play with me?"

The little figurines hovered in the air behind him like a stone constellation. As they swept in the air around him, he looked up laughing and chased them. Aya laughed also, as he made the figurines fly through the air. The Library jumped up and down, trying to touch the feet of the little elephant-men. Together the Library and Aya laughed some more. Then, as quickly as things started, the boy lost interest and walked back to the corner of the chamber, where he drew pictures in the sandy floor.

"Who were they?" Aya asked the boy. "Please tell me."

The Library-boy looked up at Aya, his face serious. His voice came out deep and unnatural, an adult voice. "They're the presentiment of your failures. History is long, Aya. Even I am dying. Me, the Library, dying now. You know that. Soon my energy will run out and all will be lost: all the vast knowledge, all the Histories. Water will gush into me and ruin the books, darken my lights, destroy my memories. The history of things is vast, the sun dies, the stars blink out." The boy's face suddenly shifted. "Want to play hide-and-seek?"

"We already are," said Aya.

They left the child in the chamber and passed back though the jungle as twilight shifted. Shadows played across the foliage. Max followed Aya back to the cliffs, where they looked out over the darkening landscape.

"History is long," said Aya. "The Library will die and me along with it. Unless you save me. For that, I offer you my knowledge. I offer you the secrets of the mystagogues. The truths of the Magi. If not, we will die together. But me—am I not the last man of a dying race? The end of the firstborn on this world? The last man is also the final instance of a whole species."

Max looked out at the vastness of the forest that stretched out to the horizon. He feared letting Aya's memories become a part of him. Yet if he refused, he, too, would face his own death, along with Aya's and the Library's. He thought of the seditionist movement, of everything he had dedicated his life to. The cause is greater than any one individual, he had always argued. Had he not made that claim, when they deposed Kamron? Did he not believe it? And yet himself, his mind, his memories—how he also valued himself. He thought of the dreams he had for his own place in history. How he had wanted others to say his name with respect. Not for the sake of it, but because of the things he had done, the sacrifices he had made. What would it mean to say he returned to Caeli-Amur a great thaumaturgist, if he was not himself? He wrestled with this dilemma as night fell around him. He was filled with a nameless anxiety.

Aya led him to a nearby cave in the cliffs, where they cooked spiced meat on skewers and a red paste made with a small bean.

"How long until the Library dies?" Max said.

Aya shrugged and pulled one of the pieces of meat from his skewer. "It does not regenerate. Its energy fades bit by bit. Who knows? Any time the sky might black out, the waters cease to flow."

Max did not sleep that night, but sat at the cave's mouth and watched bats circling over the jungle below. Strange caws echoed from the canopy: monkeys or birds, he could not tell. Slowly the eastern sky lightened and high clouds were streaked with gold and red. Behind them stars continued to gleam silver, before the sun burst over the horizon and extinguished them from the sky.

Aya squatted beside him, looked out over the jungle. "There is a lost city down there: a city of the elephant-men, long gone. There you can see their histories inscribed in greater detail in towering bas-reliefs in vast dismal halls. They had their own myths, their own gods, their own terrible heroes. One cannot examine them without feeling one's insignificance in the vistas of the time. We are but specks in the seas of infinity."

Maximilian, paused, and finally he said, "Let's both escape, Aya. Let's both return to the material world. Yes."

Aya looked across at one of the vast waterfalls. "You won't be the same."

"Will either of us?" Max asked.

Part III

TRANSFORMATIONS

When the other Gods caught Aya, they dragged him from the jungles where he was hidden. The earth had been torn asunder; much blood had been shed. Aya was thrown into a small dark cell on an island from which there was no escape. The joy leached from his body until he was nothing but a naked and shivering creature. It is said that in that cell, Aya cried for the first time.

Iria, despairing, retreated to her Tower. There, it is said, she renounced godhood and all action. She allowed herself only to meditate on things and events. There she embraced her pain.

Alerion and Panadus fought over Aya's punishment. Panadus—tall and imposing—stood calm as Alerion raged and fumed.

"He has upset the balance! This was meant to be a world of joy! He must be ended!" said Alerion.

Aya was carried from his cell and thrown before the other Gods. Cold, naked, he dragged himself to his feet.

"Beg forgiveness," said Panadus. "Beg forgiveness and you will be saved!"

Alerion circled in the background like a carrion bird. He watched the scene from the corner of his eye.

"Beg forgiveness!" said Panadus.

Aya looked at the other Gods. A twinkle came into his eye. A twitch danced on his lips. He fell to the ground and waved his legs in the air, like a turtle on his back.

To the rear, one of the Gods laughed. Smiles came onto the faces of the others.

Aya hummed a jaunty tune to himself as if he was happy. "Doo-do-doo-do-doo."

THIRTY-SEVEN

At the appointed time, Kata and the others ventured to the docks to meet the lobster fisherman who would help them pick up Max. When they arrived, they stood and stared in horror. Corpses of Xsanthians lay scattered around, already stinking like great fish. Others, heads hung in defeat, were unloading cargo from the ships. Guards from both House Marin and House Technis looked on, leaning against pikes and chatting to each other. Standing at the end of one of the piers, a small group of black-suited thaumaturgists spoke quietly.

Kata walked along the pier until she came to a Xsanthian carrying a great bag. She leaned in and said, "I'm looking for Santhor."

The Xsanthian walked on.

She grabbed the creature by its scaly arm. "Santhor, where is he?"

The Xsanthian stopped. "Taken. Taken away." He shook off her arm and continued on his defeated march toward a line of carts, where cargo was being deposited.

When Kata returned to the group, they had already climbed aboard the fisherman's lobster boat. She followed them, filled with despair as they made their way out to the buoy that had been set, marking the point where Maximilian had been dropped. They lowered the winch and waited. Rikard accompanied them; now he and Josiane openly monitored Maximilian's group. Kata much preferred having the quiet brooding young man to the former philosopher-assassin beside her. There was sincerity behind his tough exterior that Josiane, despite her words back on the cart, lacked. As she thought this, Kata wondered if she was being too hard on Josiane.

After the assassination of Director Lefebvre, Ejan's people

were filled with a crazed confidence. This would be the beginning of a program of attacks, where one by one officiates would be killed and the upper echelons of the Houses thrown into a state of confusion and disorganization. And then, on Aya's Day, the people would come forth and show who the real power in the city was. But Kata was filled with dread at the thought of the young woman who had died in her arms. The death of innocents: that was the cost of politics.

But other seditionists stared off into the distance as if reliving some past horror. For the first time, some slipped away never to return; the group was shrinking slightly. Aceline's group had fallen into quietude, watching with the passivity of a threatened animal, afraid to run from a predator. The exception was Thom, who, running his hands through his wild black hair, proclaimed loudly that Ejan's program would lead to ruin. For some reason, Ejan's group left Thom alone, though at one point Josiane stood threateningly in front of him. Thom, filled with bluster, stuck his chest out, hands behind his back and said somewhat cryptically, "Indeed?"

After the attack, House guards had struck at anyone who spoke out against them; citizens disappeared into their dungeons. The spate of strikes had been crushed, most brutally the Xsanthian strike. The city itself had fallen into a deathly silence. Now citizens hurried through the streets with downcast eyes. Even the university was quiet.

As Kata stood looking into the deep waters, hoping that Max would return, Rikard stood serenely next to her. Below, Caeli-Enis was obscured by murky currents.

"Why don't you ever smile?" she asked him.

"Why don't you?"

"Nobody smiles in the seditionist group—have you noticed? It's a group of people trying to create a new world without pleasure, without smiles."

"We cannot be representations of the new world. We are only here to usher it in."

"Can't you see that the attack on Lefebvre had the opposite effect? Rather than rouse the citizens, it resigned them to their own passivity. Anyway, how can we usher something in when we do not embody it?"

The afternoon passed slowly, as the fishing boat bobbed up and down on the waters. As the afternoon light deepened, Caeli-Amur appeared like some dream-city shimmering across the water. To Kata it seemed as if she was looking back into the past, and Caeli-Amur lived still in the glorious prime of the ancients. There was no smoke in the air, no restless destruction and rebuilding; the white cliffs gleamed like marble, ancients dressed in togas promenaded along the waterfront. And then as night fell, the city slowly lit up with thousands of twinkling lights.

"We'd better get going," said the fisherman. "Looks like he's not coming."

Kata looked down at the bobbing buoy. "We'll come tomorrow."

They came the following morning to the buoy and waited. The long day passed without incident. Kata spent it watching cutters sailing out to sea, their great sails filled with wind, or else streamers churning through the water with their great wheels. When the afternoon light faded again, the fisherman said, "Looks like that's the day."

"Tomorrow," said Kata.

Maximilian did not return the following day either and at the end of the day they fisherman said, "Listen, he's not coming back. You know that he was never going to come back."

"He'll be back tomorrow," said Kata.

At the end of the fourth day, the fisherman said, "He may come back. But I won't. I'm just wasting your florens out here, and my time."

Kata looked at the bobbing waters, at the buoy, and despair as deep as the ocean rushed into her—first Aemilius dead, now Maximilian. She pictured Maximilian: his brown curly hair, the certainty of his own mission. In her heart, she felt he would not return. She felt like crying. She thought of their brief moment in the alleyway. That was all that she had of him. Everybody dies in the end, she thought. Everyone dies alone.

That evening, Kata took to her mattress as soon as she returned to the base, and she lay there alone as others walked around and Ejan's lieutenants yelled out, "Hurry up with the vises!" "Quick with the powder!" "This isn't a game!" It was five days until Aya's Day, and the end of open opposition to the Houses, the sudden quiet on the streets, had influenced many of the seditionists now. No matter Ejan's assaults: two more officiates had been killed, Technis's Fourier in his own home, clubbed to death by Josiane's weighted chain in front of his own family; and Marin's Dosois, drowned in one of the water palaces as other officiates ran naked down the steam-filled corridors for safety. Two of Ejan's group did not return from the second assassination. Thierry was slain by Dosois's bodyguard: the Cajiun philospher-assassin turned and spun and flipped across to the seditionist before driving a stiletto through Thierry's eye. The others fled, but the middle-aged Mudge, excited by her sudden elevation from washerwoman to killer, moved too slowly. The philosopher-assassin had buried his stiletto into Mudge's back before Josiane brought her weighted chain down on his head. The effect of these assassinations was unknown, for the citizenry of Caeli-Amur remained quieted.

Kata was caught in her own sea of despair. At one point Rikard passed close by, turned, and squatted close to her. "Go away," she told him.

A little later Ejan approached. "Are you all right?" he asked, lowering himself down to his knees.

"Yes," she said.

"So he's gone. Poor Maximilian." Ejan placed a hand on hers, where it rested uncomfortably.

"It was a stupid errand, a mad notion."

"We need you now. Will you help us?"

"You don't need me. Anyway, your notions are just as mad. You really think you can take on the might of the Houses with this puny force? They will come down upon you like the gods themselves and they'll throw you into the sky, just as Aya did the moon."

"*Us,*" said Ejan. "Surely you mean they will come down upon *us.*"

"I mean *you*," said Kata. "I'm not part of your group. Not anymore."

"We'll have to hold you here, you know. Until after Aya's Day."

"I'm not yours to control."

Ejan leaned close to her, his impassive face frightening. "Oh, but you don't understand—you are."

Later, Quadi, who had spent these last days examining the machines, squatted next to her.

"I'm going back to Tir-Aki," said Quadi. "I'm going home."

"I thought you hated the place."

"I never said I hated the place," said Quadi. "I said I could not bear it any longer. But now I have ended my exile and my fasting. I'm going back, to change it, in my own way. Why don't you come?"

"I have work to do here," said Kata.

"What work do you have to do? Look around. It's Ejan's group now. Anyway, Aya's Day is likely to be a failure. The citizens have become quiet, passive. Aceline argued the other day that they're waiting, preparing themselves for a demonstration. She has contacts out in the city, who say it's true. But I think it's unlikely."

Kata looked away and blinked rapidly.

Quadi shrugged. "It's never been of interest to me anyway. But you know that Maximilian is not going to return. You can't rely on him."

"I wasn't thinking of him," said Kata.

"Then who?"

"You should go as soon as possible. It's not safe here anymore." The thoughts of what Kata was about to do shook her deeply. She had come to believe in this group, or in what it stood for. But things had gone awry. Like a guttered candle, she was surrounded now by darkness. She could still look after herself. It's what she'd always done. She would return to the real powers in the city. She would return to Boris Autec and House Technis, that power that had always controlled her.

In the morning, Quadi and Kata slipped out of the base together, past Ejan's sleeping guards. Dawn was breaking over the fog-shrouded city, the sun a burning red ball over the sea. They walked toward the cable car and the Arantine, coming finally to Via Gracchia, where they stopped. Together they looked across the thoroughfare, down an alleyway, and over the cliffs in silence. Around them, the city was beginning to stir. Pedestrians were appearing on the via, stopping into the opening cafés for their early-morning shots, quickly stroking a cat or two before hurrying on.

Quadi said, "I'll miss this city. But now I must return home. It's been waiting for me."

They embraced briefly. Quadi took a few steps, turned around. "Oh, would you like this?" He held out his pouch of weed and grinned.

Kata laughed. She could smell its fetid odor, even though it was unlit. "Go!"

Quadi strode away through the early morning. Kata watched him as he walked past the cafés. Several cats danced out behind him, then dashed away again. At first she could see him clearly, despite the other pedestrians, out in the early morning, who cut across his path. He looked much smaller than she remembered—a true New-Man—in an alien city. Slowly he became a little blot of gray moving among passersby, until finally he was lost in the growing multitude.

Kata walked through the waking city toward the Technis Complex. Farther on and to her right lay the factory district, which she could clearly see as she walked along Via Gracchia, the smoke from the factories merged with the now-dissipating fog. Her apartment lay there, waiting for her: a place where she would be alone again.

She turned left and cut through the streets of a well-to-do area. Elderly couples drank coffee at tables in the front of their little white-painted houses. Children were already playing. Odd, thought Kata. For some, life moves on, as if nothing had changed.

When she came to a T-intersection, Kata stopped briefly as fear gripped her chest: she was being followed. She turned right again, this time away from the Technis Complex, across Via Gracchia and toward the cliffs. She could not risk looking behind her, but she had a good idea of the identity of her shadow. She feared a confrontation, hoped it would not come to blows.

Kata came to the edge of the cliffs, found one of the narrow pathways—half stairs, half goat-trails—that descended. To her right the precipice was sheer. The slightest false step would result in a fall to the death far below. But death did not seem the worst fate for her now.

At times the path opened out almost to the width of a cart-track, but then narrowed again so that she had to place her hands against the rock wall to her left, for there was room only for the width of one foot on the path. When the trail turned around a rocky outcrop, she stopped, leaned against the rock wall, and drew her knives. Not long afterwards she sensed a presence on the far side of the outcrop, though she could not see her pursuer. The sun had risen over the ocean and blazed against the white cliffs. Already it was hot and promised to become hotter still. The sky was a cloudless and brilliant blue. To Kata, everything was sharp and clear and alive, as if this were the morning of the world.

Kata waited. The pursuer did not emerge. She continued to wait. Still the pursuer hesitated.

"How long do you plan to wait on your side?" Kata leaned against the cliff beside her, touched her face to the cool rock. Far beneath them lay the city. Miniature figures moved along its streets, steam-trams chugged along its boulevards. Kata yearned to be among them, far from this cliff with its promises of death.

"It seems we are at an impasse," said Josiane.

"It seems *you* are at an impasse. Not I."

"Oh, but you are," said Josiane. "Where have you to go? To your masters at whatever House you work for? No, we're going to return to Ejan, and there you will meet justice."

"There is no justice," said Kata. "Not in this world."

"It grieves me, but I knew you never cared for the cause. There was always something calculated about you. You never cared for anyone but yourself."

The words struck Kata like a physical blow. Her legs trembled. "That's not true." She had loved the seditionist group. She had loved Maximilian. She hated the entire House structure.

"You can't fool me."

Kata turned and scampered along the track like a mountain goat. There were tears in her eyes and the path blurred before her, yet on she ran, up and down the little rises and falls, over the rocks that occasionally jutted from the white earth.

She came to a steep rise, where the path rose up a series of natural rocky steps. At the top she stopped, aware that Josiane must be closing on her. Instead of running, she turned. The blinding sun hovered over the water, turning the sea into a molten white. She squinted as she looked back.

Josiane had reached the bottom of the incline. In one hand her length of chain hung menacingly. In the other she held a short-sword, longer than either of Kata's daggers. She stepped forward lightly, like the athlete she was. "Running away as usual."

"Let's not do this." Kata did not have the strength for another killing.

"I have principles worth dying for. What do you have?" Josiane took few steps up the incline. With a rapid movement, she dashed up the track, swinging the chain quickly.

Kata leaped backward, but too slowly. The chain wrapped itself around her left leg. With a tug, Josiane pulled Kata's leg toward her. Kata fell backwards, hit the ground, and was dragged down the steps. She sat up, and threw one knife instinctively. It flew through the air but Josiane released her chain and ducked beneath the flying dagger. She leaped toward the supine Kata, who, in an instant, raised both feet and connected with Josiane's chest. Josiane was thrown backwards, even as her short-sword plunged toward Kata. The tip cut into Kata's stomach, a sharp shallow incision. As the older philosopher-assassin flew backwards, Kata sprang to her feet. Dust billowed around her. The sun flared with light and heat.

Josiane hit the ground and scrambled up, but the edge of the path crumbled over the precipice beneath her right foot. In an instant, her right leg gave way, and she collapsed to the ground, trying to avoid toppling over the cliff. But it was no good: her weight was unbalanced and she slid, dropping her sword and scrabbling with her hands for something to hold on to. One hand clasped a dry, dusty vine, long dead. It pulled away from the dirt for about a foot and then, with Josiane swinging well over the side of the cliff, held.

Kata untangled the chain from her leg and rushed down the incline. Several feet below the cliff's edge, Josiane held on to the vine, her dusty face grim with determination.

Kata dropped to her haunches and hung the chain over the edge. "Grab on."

But Josiane was too far out of reach. She dangled, her body spinning freely.

"You'll have to climb up the vine," said Kata.

One of Josiane's hands reached up and she clasped higher up the vine. She pulled herself up, reached again, took hold of the vine once more—now only a couple of hand-spans from the dangling chain—and pulled.

The entire vine's root system gave way and in a split-second the dried-out plant ripped from the earth. Josiane plunged toward the ground without uttering a sound. In an instant, she was halfway down the cliff-face. She twisted and turned in the air, crashed against the cliff-wall, spun like a top, arms and legs akimbo.

Kata closed her eyes. When she opened them, Josiane was gone from sight, somewhere at the base of the cliff, among the vegetation down there, or perhaps the roofs of the Artists' Quarter. Kata stood and looked away from the sea, a sheet of brilliance under the cruel sun.

Armand guided Kata into Director Boris Autec's grand room, which made her pause. Autec was right: He had risen in the darkness of the night. But she had not risen with him.

Though Autec was absent, standing on the huge balcony was a woman with the lushest raven black hair tumbling down her back that Kata had ever seen. Kata approached the woman, noticing the wonderfully defined muscles on the woman's back, the hourglass figure. Kata stepped onto the balcony and leaned against the railing next to the woman. Kata was taken aback by the Siren's alien beauty: her enormous emerald eyes, the unnatural fullness of her lips, the proportions all wrong, as if some child had drawn her. There was something repulsive about the Siren's strangeness. Anxiety and fear rushed into Kata; she felt as if she were standing before a carnivorous beast. A torc inlaid with two crimson gems hung around the creature's neck. Like the Xsanthians, she was a prisoner.

The Siren said, "The madness that this age has brought upon us."

Kata looked out over the city. She didn't want to look at the creature. "Indeed."

"One day I'll escape this city."

Kata turned and looked at the Siren. "I wanted a villa near the coast, a little place away from all unhappy events. Perhaps I would raise horses or grow grapes."

Now the Siren turned to Kata. Their eyes met. Buried beneath that alienness, Kata saw a oneness with herself.

"And I back to Taritia," the creature said.

For some reason, Kata leaned forward and embraced the Siren, and they stood there, arms around each other, strangers somehow united. It was so long since Kata had held someone like that—a pure comfort in the maelstrom. When Kata stood back, she found that she could not speak. She lowered her eyes in a shame she couldn't make sense of.

The doors opened and Director Autec entered the room. "Kata!" he cried. "Finally! Come."

He sat behind his desk, shuffled some papers on the desk ineffectually. "In front." He gestured to the space in front of his desk.

Kata walked around the desk and stood before him.

"Come a bit closer."

She stepped forward.

Autec leaned over the desk. "Now, tell me. What news? Where is this seditionist base?"

"I can draw you a map and give instructions. There's a passageway hidden by thaumaturgy, but it is not hard to find," said Kata.

Autec smiled. "Truly excellent. I have to admit, I was worried you'd disappeared. After that incident with the scrying ball. And with Aya's Day only four days away, I wondered . . ." Autec laughed. "Now we shall grind them like a bug beneath our shoe. First the seditionists, then whatever stragglers protest on Aya's Day. My agents assure me it will be only the few troublemakers. And Armand has visited the Collegia to ensure they're on our side. Now:

you shall return, so as not to arouse suspicion. But expect a raiding party this night, or before dawn tomorrow."

Kata nodded. "And my reward?"

"Armand," Autec called out. "Organize a villa for Kata will you? In the hills to the south, I think." To Kata he said, "Yes, it's nice there. Quiet. Away from the main roads to the city."

On the balcony, the Siren stood looking at the horizon.

THIRTY-EIGHT

Kata returned to the seditionist base as the sun was descending. She passed the barricades, which had been built close to the exit to the city. There two guards sat, playing dice. They jumped to their feet at her approach, but recognized her and returned to their game. In her pocket were a ring of keys and a small map that showed directions to her villa. Armand had handed to them as she left. The villa was standing empty. It had belonged, he said, to Officiate Matisse, who no longer needed it.

As she entered the hideout, Giselle eyed her watchfully from the doorway to Ejan's laboratory. Kata stared back, her face carrying all the heaviness of betrayal. Giselle needed no more encouragement; she nodded once in understanding and wandered toward the corner of the room where her mattress lay. She squatted, slipped several small objects into her pocket, bantered with a few seditionists, and wandered toward the entryway to the hideout. She, at least, would escape.

Numb to everything, Kata lay down on her mattress in the middle of the seditionist base. She did not rouse herself as the night passed. In a half daze, she lay wretched in her treachery. She wished now that she could take it back, even with Ejan's group in control. Did she have no principles? Did she not stand for anything? Was it as Josiane had said? She waited for the first cry of despair, the sound of battle.

Sometime in the middle of the night she heard a call from the cavern's entrance. So it had begun. There was more excited talking, the tense exchanges that signaled an event, but not the arrival of the House guards she expected. She raised her head. From near the entranceway a small group had gathered.

"Ejan," someone called.

At the entranceway two seditionists were holding up a hooded figure.

Kata stepped to her feet and moved toward the little group as others roused around her. The hooded figure had now been laid on the ground. Others circled around. Kata brushed through them. Lying on the ground, the man's face was obscured by his hood. Shadows were cast over his face. A foreboding crept over Kata, the feeling that she had overlooked something fundamental.

Ejan stepped forward and pulled back the hood.

They all stared in silence until Kata threw herself to the ground next to the figure, taking his head in her arms. "Maximilian."

Maximilian looked out into empty space. His cloathes were soaked, his face white. He seemed to be in some kind of fever. *"Panadus!"* he said. *"Panadus, eperantus, el minio el tritian."*

Kata looked up intensely. "Water. Someone get some water." She looked back at Maximilian. "Max, Max." But the man didn't seem to hear. Kata looked up again, as if for some kind of help. Someone passed a flask of water, but the water just dribbled from Max's mouth. Hope flooded into Kata: she would have to get Maximilian out of the base, but he was alive! She could spirit him away to the villa, but how? She needed to act quickly.

At that moment a cry went up from the guards at the cavern entranceway. This time it was the call of despair. "We're discovered! We have been found!"

Ejan called out, "Evacuate!"

Mayhem broke out in the seditionist camp. Seditionists scrambled for their possessions. Others ran toward the entrance, boltthrowers and swords in their hands, their faces set with the promise of grim death.

Kata held Maximilian in her arms. "Maximilian," she said, but he did not respond. Instead his eyes were glassy, focused inward.

The seditionists poured toward the entrance. Had they halted the House guards at the exit to the city, or closer to the hideout? The farther away the battle raged, the more likely the seditionists were to escape.

Kata tried to get Maximilian to his feet, but his weight hung

like a corpse, heavy and inert. She lifted him up desperately and
he hung limp in her arms. Someone jostled Kata from behind.
She lost her balance, staggered, lost her grip on Max, who slumped
back to the ground. Urgently, she clasped him again, pulled him to
his feet. With a great heave, she threw him over her shoulders and
made for the entranceway. Each moment was vital. Seditionists ran
ahead; cries and calls echoed from the stone walls. Already the
bulk of the group were ahead of her. They had been expecting such
an attack. Someone knocked her and she fell to her knees. Max
slipped into her arms as more seditionists ran past her. Again she
heaved Max onto her shoulders, staggered to her feet.

Finally, Kata reached the opening to the tunnel. A bloodied
woman came staggering back in the direction of the cavern, her
hand pressed against her face. "We're cut off," the woman cried.
"Some made it out and back into the mountain. But we're cut off."

Kata carried Max back to the central cavern, the clash of arms
reverberating behind. Screams echoed around the underground
chambers. Maximilian became too heavy and she rested, with her
arm around his waist, his weight propped against her hip.

"Walk!" She took a step forward and to her relief he shuffled
beside her. They staggered toward the machine room. Perhaps she
could open the great doors that led to the strange labyrinth with
the cells of the dead. If so, they might escape.

Around them, seditionists ran desperately. Kata looked over
her shoulder where Technis guards had burst through the passageway. Some fired bolt-throwers; several retreating seditionists
fell. Others charged in with short-swords. A number of seditionists fell to their knees and surrendered.

"Walk," said Kata.

And then a Technis guard was standing before them, steely
eyed, sword in hand.

Kata laid Maximilian on the ground in despair. She sat next to
him and watched as the gray-suited guards efficiently rounded up
the final seditionists. Occasionally they gave a seditionist a kick.
"Hurry up!"

When Director Autec arrived, he strutted around the hideout
like a savage-eyed peacock. Kata sensed a desperate darkness in

him. He pressed his hands together, released them, pressed them together once more. His head twitched this way and that, as if he were looking for someone on which to wreak a terrible revenge.

Autec came to Kata, eyes malevolently roving over Maximilian. "Ah, you've caught the thaumaturgist. Excellent work, Kata. Excellent work."

After the raid, Kata took her clothes and slunk out into the dull dawn. Humid clouds had rolled over Caeli-Amur in the night, threatening rain at last. She passed along Via Gracchia. Late-night revelers and insomniacs sat hunched in corners. A tall man eyed her suspiciously and turned back to his book.

She passed through the Arantine, where stately mansions could be seen, the boulevards lines with furnace trees, cold now as it was summer. When she reached the gate, she purchased a horse from the stables, using the florens she had saved from her deceit and betrayals and rode out through the dawn.

An hour past the shantytowns, the rock road cut southwestward. To her left lay the water-parks, to her right the hills climbed higher and higher into the great mountain range that ran from north to south. There, high up in their eyries lived the Augurers, waiting for those brave enough to experience their foresight.

Soon she rode along the wide, flat valleys between the rolling hills. The weather here was wetter than in Caeli-Amur, and even in this dry summer, there was a touch of green to the vineyards that wrapped many of the slopes. Elsewhere lay fields of candle-flowers and rows of furnace trees. Like the water-parks and water palaces, Opera and other public areas, the villas that dotted the area were safe areas. Some might be owned by officiates from Marin or Technis, but most belonged to Arbor. In one lush little valley, Kata saw an entire meadow of fire-roses, bursting into flame periodically in their strange reproductive cycle. In another, beds of shifting orange mosses—imported from Numeria perhaps, or developed by Arbor's thaumaturgists—grew in carefully designed paddies. A third harbored white snow-orchids, siblings of the blood-orchids, which moved together as if in a strange circular dance. Greenhouses were dotted around the place, filled, she knew, with all kinds of carnivorous shubs, narcotic flowers, sentient plants. The villas themselves sat often at the crest of ridges, or high on the surrounding hills, near to little copses of trees.

The clouds rolled ominously above her, a great gray roiling mass that now looked as if it might burst in a great storm. Yet it held off as she turned along a side road, which led her up past a crossroads and through empty paddocks. Here was her villa where she might raise horses, or—as Armand had said to her—any number of wild beasts: bears, great cats, boar, giant lizards, or crocodiles. There was a demand for all of them.

She passed through the atrium, through barren side rooms, into an internal garden complete with benches, a pool, a pergola covered with candle-flowers. In typical fashion, Technis had stripped the place bare. There was not even a chair to sit on, and so she found herself sitting alone back in the atrium.

Never had Kata felt more alone or more despairing. This place, her villa, seemed nothing but an empty tomb. Whom would she entertain here? Who would visit? Officiates from neighboring villas? Despite the wondrous flora that surrounded her, the place seemed empty of life, for she had no one to share it with. Indeed, why did she deserve the villa at all? What had she done to deserve luxury? She had not made the world a better place. Rather, she had made it worse. She knew this and it seared her soul.

Still she sat, alone as the looming clouds rolled above her. The sky brightened and though the sun was hidden, still the oppressive heat bore down on her. Night fell, and the following day was just as bad. She wandered the villa, alone and empty. As the light dimmed, she mounted her horse and rode back to the city.

She sold the horse at a loss back to the stable by the southern gate and walked through the hot wind that blew through the night, whipping around walls and rushing down streets, forcing people inside. By the time she arrived at the Factory Quarter, it was late. The moon had risen and fallen and the wind had dropped off. Even it didn't have the strength to go on. Desolate, she stumbled along her alleyway, barely taking anything in. She tripped on something, fell forward, regained her balance, looked back.

Little Henri had scrambled to his feet. "Kata," he mumbled, his voice sleepy.

Kata walked on.

Henri grabbed her arm, "Kata!"

She shook him off. "Leave me alone. I don't want any of your fudge. I don't want anything."

She slammed shut the door of her apartment and sat alone on the stairs. How long was it since she had stayed here? In her mind she still heard the cries of the seditionists as they fell before the House assault. She could still see the faces of the dead as they lay on the cavern floor. She could still see Maximilian being dragged away by guards as she looked on, helpless. Helpless—that's what she had always been, really; at the beck and call of forces around her: just a reed blowing whichever way the wind took her. She staggered to her upper room, collapsed on the bed, and lay there, staring at the ceiling. She thought of Aya's Day, only two days away, and wondered what would occur. So long had the demonstration been planned: the first show of strength between seditionists and Houses, forces she was intimately entwined with. But she knew the result: The Houses would reassert their power, the Collegia were not coming, the House thaumaturgists would loose the Furies, and like the Xsanthians on the docks, citizens would die. There was no hope to be held there.

With sudden intent she stood and rifled through her cupboards for rope. Finding none, she took one of her sheets from the bed and using her stiletto cut a long strip. One would not do, so she cut another, and taking both moved quickly to her staircase. She tied the ends around the banister, and let them drop down to the lower floor. She descended the stairs halfway, reached out, and took hold of the strips and made a noose. Then, standing halfway up the stairs, she placed the noose over her head and tightened it around her neck. She climbed over the banister and stood there momentarily. Her face felt heavy, as if the flesh of her face was dragging down away from her bones.

She stepped off the stairs and fell. The noose clamped around her neck sharply. She felt her throat close under the pressure.

Instinctively, she reached up to grasp the straps, but stopped herself. She fought the urge to swing back to the staircase. She wanted everything to end, the endless struggle that got her nowhere. Her chest heaved, her lungs trying to let in a gasp of air. Instead all she heard was a desperate croak. Her neck was being crushed, the muscles and tendons, the trachea tearing under the force. The pain engulfed her body. Again her chest heaved, and heaved, and this time not even a croak. Her body now started to shudder, tears poured from her eyes, mucus from her nose. Everything whitened, as if things were fading away. Her body now jerked violently, refusing to accept its own end. The whiteness increased with her body's jerking and shaking, until all she could see was a ghostly brilliance blanking out all forms and shapes. Death was not far away now. She slowly fell into the bleached world.

THIRTY-NINE

Boris stood beside the Technis master torturer, Delanus Tyle. Tyle had the officious air of a specialist, eager to regale anyone with his knowledge. Even now he was discussing the peculiar characteristics of skin. It could be burned, it could be stretched, it could be cut like parchment and pulled back like the sheet from a bloody bed. Tyle wanted to write a treatise on torture, he explained. This would be part of his legacy.

The elevator rattled as it descended deep beneath the Technis Complex. They passed level after level. Boris had studied the maps of the tunnels beneath the city that were stored in the Director's desk. The maps were incomplete: spidery tunnels winding into each other, some trailing off and leaving great blank spaces, a subterranean world of cave and catacombs. One of the tunnels wound beneath the city all the way to open out on the other side of the mountain. The entrance to the Elo-Talern's domain was marked, but the realm beyond was left blank. There had always been rumors of a city built by the ancients hidden beneath the mountain. Perhaps it was there.

The elevator lurched to a halt; the guard took hold of the gate and pulled it open. Two other guards sat together playing dice near the elevator. Seeing Boris, they immediately stood up, chastened.

"This way, Director." Tyle led the way along the corridor. To each side, large cells were filled with shadowy figures, some with their arms painfully chained to the walls above their heads, others in shackles around their ankles. Yet more wandered around the cells free, or held on to the bars.

"There's been a mistake, sir, please." A bony young man barely out of his teens held on to the bars of a cell.

"There's been such an influx—we're positively overflowing." Tyle waved his hand toward the cells without looking.

They came to a darkened intersection. Tyle walked left, and as he passed along the passageway, orbs of light turned themselves on above. "The corridors are kept in darkness in the section for solitary confinement. As we take each prisoner along the corridors, the orbs turn themselves on, and turn themselves off when we leave. It ensures that the prisoner is able to feel their aloneness more keenly. All powered by bloodstone, of course."

They turned down another corridor. Running along each wall was a series of closed doors.

"We keep the important political prisoners in Section B Twelve." Tyle looked back at Boris and smiled warmly. He had the look of a man proudly showing off his new house with all its luxuries.

Eventually, Tyle stopped at the front of one of the doors. "The Xsanthian leader Santhor is in here. I think he's ready to break, but to be honest, I don't think he actually has anything to hide. Would you like to see him?" Tyle pressed a pad by the side of the door and a panel slowly became translucent. "We stole these panels and the glass from the ancient parts of the Palace. Thought they might be more useful down here."

Boris found himself looking through a small head-high window as the cell inside slowly lit up. Inside a large Xsanthian leaned against the wall, his head thrown back, his huge mouth open like that of a dead fish. A salty substance seemed encrusted on his scales.

Tyle pressed the pad again and the panel window faded again to black. "The seditionists are farther on."

They took another turn and Tyle stopped at another door. The window lit up and revealed a hooded man huddled in the corner. "This is the one you want, I believe." Tyle opened the door.

Boris stepped awkwardly into the cell. His mind raced, filled with anger and sadness, and with other emotions he could barely place. This one was the dreamer. But the northerner Ejan had escaped with many of his followers. They had fought bitterly, forcing their way through the tunnels, leaving dead guards behind them. Boris had again underestimated their resilience. The guards had lost them in the catacombs deeper underground. Boris wished it had been Ejan who Kata had captured. Somehow he felt like blaming the dreamer Maximilian for it.

"Maximilian," Boris said.

The figure remained motionless.

"Now, Maximilian, we can let you out of here if only you cooperate. It's not hard. Just a little information. Just as easy as that."

Still the figure did not move.

Boris squatted down next to the seditionist and with one finger lifted the hood. The man's face was deathly pale, his eyes wide. He looked haunted and distant, his eyes making tiny movements to and fro, as if he could see into a far-off world.

"Now, Maximilian, where are Ejan and the rest of the seditionists? Where would they hide? The catacombs?"

The seditionist's eyes seemed fixed on a point slightly to the right of Boris. Finally, he spoke: "When I was young, most of the world was covered with ocean. We sucked it from the surface to reveal these continents, upon which we built that world that we desired. It's a wonderful thing, to build the world you imagined."

Boris looked back at Tyle, who stood in the doorway. Tyle shrugged.

Boris turned back to the seditionist. "Come, Maximilian, help me. And help me to help you."

Maximilian's head fell back against the wall and tilted upwards, his eyes staring into space above. "But it's a terrible thing to have such power. One must constantly improve and grow. But we became complacent. We reveled in our luxuries, we wallowed in our past successes."

"I'll return." Boris stood up. "And we can have a proper discussion. Gather your wits, man."

Boris walked to the door, where he turned and looked back at the figure of Maximilian, a huddled little pale creature against the cold, stone walls. He wondered briefly if the seditionist had lost his mind, but he knew that seditionists were trained to avoid interrogations. Even if the man was psychologically shattered, they could extract the truth from him with pain.

"Perhaps we should soften him up before you come to see him again?" Tyle said.

"Perhaps you should."

"I'll get the apprentices straight onto it. We might start him off with one of the terror-spheres. You know, they are the most amazing devices. I plan to devote an entire chapter to their uses in my treatise."

FORTY

As Boris ascended in the elevator, he considered his position. With the crushing of the Xsanthians' strike, he had won over House Marin. House Arbor still blamed him for Lefebvre's death but had retreated into quiet.

For a long time now, even before the raid on the seditionists' hideout, the city had been in a state of eerie quiet. Boris could be considered the most powerful man in the city. Aya's Day was only two days away. It would only be a trickle of oppositionists, a petty congregation of troublemakers. Still, he would smash them, too, loosing the Furies upon them. Sometimes people needed to be taught a lesson. Then, free to act without all these pressures upon him, he would change things for the good of all. Better conditions for the workers, a more unified system for the Houses, a Forum—he could barely wait to start his program of reform.

Drunk on the visions of his own success, Boris strode to the Elo-Talern's hall in triumph, his head held back, his chest out. The Elo-Talern waited for him by the great doors behind the throne. "Boris." She made a face that could have been a smile. "Boris, you have conquered the city. You are victorious. It is time."

"Time?" Boris frowned.

"Time for the elixir—your treatment against death. Come."

Boris hesitated. The promised elixir: so it was true, he might cheat death; he could avoid that terrible moment when his heart stopped. Without the fear of aging and death, he would rule Technis like a god. His program of reform could last a century or more. Perhaps later he would be able to share the elixir with Saidra, and they could be a family again. Over the years, Paxaea would come to love him. Yet still he hesitated, for he was afraid of the unknown.

"Come," said Elo-Drusa.

Boris nodded to himself and followed her. The doors opened and they passed into the pleasure palace where they continued past intersections and doorways, farther than Boris had been before, toward the Undercity of the Elo-Talern. Boris was filled with anxiety. Did he want this? Like everything in his life, events seemed to carry him along like a broken branch in a flooded river, twisting and turning, being submerged, breaking once more through the sturface.

"Wait." He stopped.

Elo-Drusa was gone. She appeared behind him, her hands settled on his shoulders. "Eternal life. Never to die. You'll be an angel."

Boris wanted to turn back. He was gripped by fear, seized with a terrible foreboding. Why him? How had he ended up in this position? None of it made sense. "Yes," he said, and walked on.

They came then to a vast circular door, larger than any Boris had ever seen. Hundreds of silver ideograms descended its face like snowflakes falling in winter. The Elo-Talern spoke a strange guttural word and the great door rolled back into a space in the wall.

Now fear clasped Boris in its vise and he could barely move. Before he knew it, the Elo-Talern pulled him by the hand and they entered the Undercity, the most secret province of the Elo-Talern.

Boris entered a vast hexagonally shaped hall as if in some strange trance. Passivity overtook his mind and his limbs; everything seemed whiter than before, as if viewed through a mist. Emerging before him came the nightmare vision of the Undercity. Somehow the architecture of the hall was wrong, so that he could not make out which walls were closer and which farther away. It was as if some painter had played with impossible perspectives, the angles of a triangle added up to more than 180 degrees. As Boris tried to make them out, he was seized with a deep sense of disturbance. Staircases climbed the sides of the walls and joined walkways that crisscrossed the room like crazed spiderwebs. All around the room a hundred and more cadaverous Elo-Talern danced with each other to a strange electronic waltz. Others lay upon chaises longues amid the scattered remnants of rich food and drink: thick syrups of extraordinary luminescent reds and yellows half spilled from their bowls onto the floor; rotten peaches and pears, like deflated balls sunk into plates; tankards knocked onto the floor, their liquids forming little shiny puddles. Yet more Elo-Talern lay on piles of pillows, their legs and arms draped over each other, long tubes seemed to be attached to the inside of their elbows. Pockets of lichen and mold—luminous greens, bright oranges, wild purples—were scattered across all surfaces: here an entire corner of the hall was submerged in a deep forest of crimson; there an abandoned feast floated beneath a lime green lichen sea. Decay and dilapidation permeated the entire scene, filling Boris with dread.

Nearby stood a pillar on which sat a hexagonal-shaped prism, the size of a child's head. From where he stood, Boris could see smoke swirling within the prism, and the thing didn't exactly shine, but rather seemed to resonate with power. This was not the unnatural sheen of thaumaturgy, but something else, something somehow cleaner.

But Boris had no time to contemplate the thing, for Elo-Drusa took his arm in her great spidery hand and led him through the carnivalesque scene. Many of the Elo-Talern were naked, and Boris could see the males' shriveled members, drooping and withered trunks attached to their bodies as an afterthought. No matter which direction he looked, the scene unfolded like some kind of mad burlesque. On the ceiling another entire party was occurring, as if it were controlled by some negative gravity, a mirrored and distorted image of the one through which he moved. Yet another party lounged on one of the walls. Pathways climbed from floor to wall to ceiling, twisting in the air to reorient themselves into the appropriate position of "up" for each location. Tower-sized pillars of mold and lichen grew everywhere.

She dragged him across the room, through a tunnel that twisted and turned upon itself like a corkscrew, so that the tilted floor became the wall, and yet he still walked impossibly on. Twisting like a spiral, the tunnel plunged down so that, by rights, he should have fallen forward as if down a shaft. The laws of physics did not apply here.

They came to a great hexagonal room where robed Elo-Talern stood in lines and chanted in an unknown ritual. One hovered down to meet them on a platform that hung in the air.

"You have brought the one of which you spoke." The robed one seemed to be male, and was the tallest that Boris had yet seen, as if beneath the red robes he stood on great stilts.

"This is he."

"I am Kalas, high priest of the ascent. Welcome, child." For a moment he was gone completely. He flashed back into reality, a cadaverous creature. "I will train you once you have ascended. Take him through."

She led him along another passageway, which branched off from the room until they came to another hexagonal chamber, this one much smaller. She pressed a pad on the wall and it opened. In the center of yet another smaller hexagonal chamber sat some kind of reclining couch.

"Lie down."

He lay upon the couch, which was unnervingly comfortable.

"Your arm. Roll up your sleeves."

Boris did as he was told, even as terrible premonitions came to him, one after the other. The Elo-Talern pushed his arm against an armrest and strapped it down.

"You won't leave me, will you?" said Boris.

She held in her hand a long tube, attached to its end a long needle. "The elixir is made from the horns and the eyes of the minotaurs killed during the Festival of the Sun. Life comes from death, and eternal life from a magical creature. Your predecessor Rudé provided this for us; the thaumaturgists concocted the liquid."

Boris felt a deep, sharp pain in the fold of his elbow. He was too afraid to look, but he knew that the needle had now pierced a vein.

"Rest. I'll return."

"No!" Boris cried. But she turned and left him in the cell. Warmth began at the crease of his elbow, spread down his arm and through the rest of his body. He could hear his heart beating like a deep drum rumbling in his ears: *boom-boom, boom-boom, boom-boom.*

He licked his dry lips, but was distracted by the pain, which crept all the way up his arm like a shadow of the warmth. He tried to sit up, but his arms were pinned, and a strap pressed against his chest. He laughed maniacally and the sound echoed weirdly in his ears, as if it came from far away, down an empty corridor. The ceiling above him shifted and warped as he watched it. One of the walls appeared to descend toward him, and then pulled away as another section spun oddly down, the angles twisting and warping. He glimpsed a flash of a dark world, superimposed upon the one he knew. It was as if another chamber, slightly askew, had somehow been placed over the one in which he lay. Shadow doorways led away to tilted corridors; a black staircase that led up through the ceiling of the hexagonal chamber and to another level. He blinked and the other world was gone. Boris lost a sense of his body . . . and then a sense of himself. He simply *was*.

The Elo-Talern appeared above him, leaning over like the cadaver of some horrible horse. "My Boris."

Boris could barely remember the journey back to his office. At some point he staggered along the dusty corridors alone. He returned to his office and collapsed on his couch. When he regained consciousness, it seemed like a long nightmare, but when he looked at his arm he noticed the dark bruise and a round swelling. From the place where the needle had pierced, his veins were an irradiant unnatural blue, creeping out from his elbow like a spider's web.

In the evening, after Boris returned to the Director's office and rested for several hours, Armand showed in House Arbor's Director Thorel, who had taken over from Lefebvre. Like Armand, Thorel had the long aquiline nose that distinguished the Arbor officiates. Years of inbreeding, thought Boris, whose own stubby little nose was the opposite of Thorel's.

"You're the undisputed power in Caeli-Amur." Thorel grinned uneasily.

Boris nodded. After his treatment, everything possessed the quality of a dream: he saw through a haze, the walls and ceilings loomed down at him, sounds echoed around in his head.

"Both Arbor and Marin are indebted to you, and personally,

I'm happy that Lefebvre is gone. I think both Houses, for the time being at least, will defer to your judgment until these disturbances have passed."

Boris gathered himself. "We shall strike together against the demonstration on Aya's Day, and crush the seditionists." The floor shifted beneath Boris. He grabbed on to the arm of his chair. "A moment, please." He ran into his private room, grabbed the washbasin, and vomited into it.

As he rested, hands clamped to the edges of the washbasin, he was seized by a cramp in his arm. He groaned and looked at his elbow. The arm seemed to be elongating, as if it were being stretched on the rack. For a minute he thought the elbow would dislocate. He groaned again, but the pain now rose up to his shoulder and dissipated into the rest of his body.

"Are you ill, Director Autec?" Thorel stood by the entranceway to the room.

"It's nothing."

"We would hate to see you ill." There seemed to be a tinge of pleasure in Thorel's voice.

Boris blinked rapidly, hoping it would clear his sight. "I hear you have a long list of organic torture devices."

"We do indeed."

"Perhaps you might allow us the use of some of them? We have a number of prisoners in our dungeons whom we would like to interview."

"I shall organize it. I recommend the truth mold—if information is what you are after. Though I understand that sometimes there are other aims to torture."

The room seemed to flicker and again Boris saw the shadow world superimposed upon the one he knew, with all its spectral tunnels and ghostly stairs leading into darker ones.

"The truth." Boris looked down at the floor and his own feet. His knees ached for some reason. "The truth will be enough for the moment. Send the mold across."

FORTY-ONE

Two apprentices grasped Maximilian roughly and chained his arms. "Don't bother struggling. It won't do any good."

They led him from the cell along a corridor. Above, orbs of light flickered on as they approached and off as they passed by. To either side there were silent cell doors. Maximilian imagined their occupants, trapped in the dark: seditionists, criminals, opponents of the House, spies. Ahead the corridor was shrouded in darkness, like everything in his life. This is what it had come to: the dungeons of House Technis.

When they had built things in his youth, they had agreed that the surface should remain a place of nature, and that beneath the ground would be a place of wondrous construction. They planned underground cities dotting the edges of the oceans, so that they might play in at the water's edge. Somewhere along the line things went awry. Was it the nature of power? Did it turn people against each other? Is that why beneath the ground had now turned not into a place of wonder, but one of horror? Everything had slipped so quickly off track. Maximilian shook his head: but no, this was not his memory. He had no knowledge of these things, and yet it persisted: he could see the cities they had designed. At some point they'd changed their minds and built aboveground, too.

Max was jostled and he came out of his memories. The apprentices led him into a dark cavern, where five great metal spheres stood in a row. As they climbed the stairs, another two apprentices pulled a woman from the top of one of the spheres. The woman came out whimpering, the look on her face like that of a hurt dog. She coughed and spluttered, vomited liquid, and collapsed onto the walkway.

"Come on, up you go."

The woman started to cry a high, hideous childlike wail that suited her appearance: she was Aceline.

The apprentices led Maximilian up the stairs to the walkway.

"Aceline," he called, but she did not seem to hear.

The two apprentices picked her up and dragged her along the walkway. "Why are we always given this task?" one complained to the other.

One of Max's apprentices turned a large spoked wheel at the top of one of the spheres. There was a clunk and the man pulled open a round doorway. The second apprentice pushed Maximilian toward the opening. He held his ground, then his legs, still weakened by his long journey back from Caeli-Enas, gave way and he dropped to his knees. He recalled that submarine voyage in dreamlike fragments: regaining consciousness, nestled within one of the pillars of light, a terrible headache like needles behind his eyes; staggering up to the ground floor of the Library barely knowing who he was; the long journey beneath the water, the necessary invocations floating up to his conscious mind in an entirely new thaumaturgical language; the staggering up the beach, through the night in Caeli-Amur, all the way to the seditionist hideout. Capture. Now this.

"Don't struggle." The second apprentice clasped Maximilian's legs and dragged him to the opening. The first pushed him from behind. Fully clothed, he fell into the sphere. Cold water embraced him. When he kicked his legs, he found that the hatch had been closed over the opening to the sphere. He reached up, increasingly desperate. He thrashed around, banged his head against the roof, his lungs burning for oxygen. Finally, he breathed in the liquid around him. But by then things had begun to change. Shapes emerged in the sphere, ghostlike wisps like roiling fog. Behind them, forms emerged slowly: a landscape gray and cold. The wispy shapes solidified into a tall and terrible figure, chasing him, calling after him in a horrid inhuman wail.

"Aya, Aya!" it screamed, for it meant to destroy him.

Across the landscape he ran, through ghostly woods at twilight. He looked back in fear at the tall, spectral figure, cloaked so that its face was obscured, and the black nothingness beneath the hood was all the more terrifying for that.

Maximilian ran, and the sense of horror and doom filled him, for no matter how fast he ran, down paths and over fallen trees, fog now descending in the quietening light, the figure came behind him. He could hear its breath, hissing darkly. There was no hope. He tripped on a log, fell to the ground, scrambled to his feet, ran again. He whimpered.

Again he tripped and fell, his hands striking the dark earth. He rolled onto his back. The figure stood above him: a thaumaturgist, but he could not tell if it belonged to a House, for it looked like a mage of old, and stood above him like a god. Unlike the magi, a terrible light seemed to emanate from it, and the light was somehow *dark* also, as if it were gleaming an unnatural chemical darkness. It was a Sortilege—one of the twelve from Varenis. Maximilian knew he had no way of fighting the figure. He was bested before the trial had begun. The figure before him was not only more powerful than he, but was also the embodiment of faceless evil.

The figure drew an ideogram in the air, and Maximilian felt a coldness run through him and settle in his bones. He tried to get to his feet, but his arms would not move, his legs refused to obey. He was paralyzed. The Sortilege took out a sharp knife, as long as his forearm, with a serrated blade. Slowly, as if measuring something, it pressed the blade against Maximilian's stomach, just below the belly button. The knife slipped through the skin and into the vital organs, as if Max's stomach were nothing but water. Pulling upward, the figure cut a deep wound. Blood and yellow stuff rushed from inside, and there was a terrible smell of something rotten and organic. Reaching into the stomach, the Sortilege disemboweled Maximilian, who looked on with horror as his white entrails came out. First, his stomach, then his lungs, so that no longer could he breathe, and finally, his black heart, beating still. Maximilian tried to scream, but could not, for his jaws were clamped shut by the cold.

Drawing his robes aside, the Sortilege took the beating heart and placed it into a wound in his own chest. As he looked down at Maximilian, the figure threw back his hood. Maximilian looked up into face of a dead man. The features were rotten and blackened, as if the body had floated beneath the grimy water of a lake. Its skin was broken and splotchy and its eyes looked like they were losing their structure: they bulged like little sacs of liquid. The curly hair was thin and patchy. The lips had begun to disintegrate, as if nibbled by tiny fish. He looked up into the face, and it was familiar: it was his own.

Maximilian was dumped into his cell. One of the apprentices said, "If you want my advice, just tell the master torturer everything you know at the beginning. It might help."

"Then again, it might not," said the second apprentice matter-of-factly.

Max lay there, staring out into the world. He thought of Ejan and the seditionist group. All that work destroyed. He thought of his expedition to Caeli-Enas, beneath the sea. He thought of the times when he had laughed as he had skipped over the skies in their skimmers, with Demidae and the others, when the world was young. He grasped his head between his hands and pressed hard. There were voices in his head, voices that raged like a storm. *By Panadus, by Marinta! You shall not catch me. You shall not take my life and make it as you want it to be.* He tried to stop the voices, which made so little sense, and yet made so much sense. I am a fragment, he thought. I am two broken halves of an unhealed whole. He could feel the smashed pieces of another entity gathering strength within the dark recesses of his mind, a lurking shadow growing. Every now and then, fragments of another mind rose up and forced themselves into him. Now, he thought, I do not know who I am. I am Maximilian, I am. I am. I am. I am.

Maximilian started to cry, for now the pain in his head had spread to his body. He didn't want to return to the terror-sphere. He didn't want to be chased again by that blackened dead thing, that creature that he knew waited for him, with its disemboweling knife. The creature he could never escape, could never defeat. His body now was racked with pain, as if poison was coursing through his body, until finally he felt that he was just agonizing white light. His body was no more.

The second self grew together in his mind, solidified. *Stop struggling,* a voice said in his head.

—I should never have agreed to let you in—said Max.

It is too late now for us both, Aya said. *But perhaps there is a way out for us, somewhere in this world. In the meantime, stop struggling. You're always trying to control things.*

Aya was right. He had reached the breaking point. All the years of struggle, of trying to get somewhere, of trying to control things, of living not now but in the future and the past, of living not in the present moment, but in the wheels and cogs churning in his head. He thought of all the time that he looked at the world as if through lenses, his mind ticking away, filtering, resisting, controlling. He thought of all the time that he wasted in the dark cave of his consciousness.

He could feel Aya gathering his strength in the deep passageways of his mind, growing, reintegrating. Their identities dissolved at the edges. The barriers of their minds were permeable, bits breaking off and absorbing into the other. Just as Max caught fragments of memory, pieces of knowledge from Aya, so he felt pieces of himself drift into the other. Periodically, each identity would surge and Max would lose a sense of who he was, at other times they would draw away from each other and for a while he had clarity.

—The secret of unification, what is it?—asked Max.

Aya did not speak, but allowed a piece of his knowledge to drift toward Max. It rushed into him, like water into a sponge. Thaumaturgy, he saw, was written in a language derived from the structures of their world, the world of life.

But there was another world of anti-matter, a second world, the Other Side, the world of darkness and death, where the Furies lived. That, too, was a part of the universe, and there was dark magic also, thaumaturgy that operated in that world. To use it, one had to learn and understand *its* laws.

Still, unification had a third source. For each thaumaturgical language—that of the world of life and that of the Other Side— was a broken descendant derived from a primary language, a pure language, the language of the Art, austere and elegant. It was mathematics to present-day thaumaturgy's physics, the primary foundation. It did not operate according to the disciplines like il-lusionism or chymistry, but according to its own subcategories of quantity, structure, space, and change. He could understand, then, how these four categories were internal properties of every-thing else.

—Tell me the language. Give me the knowledge—said Max.

No, said Aya.

—But that was the agreement. I would allow you to live in my body, if you shared the pure language of the Magi with me.

That was then, said Aya. *This is now.*

Aya's identity surged toward Max. The two of them crashed into each other, each suffused with the other's mind. Max again lost a sense of who he was and was lost in feverish reverie.

FORTY-TWO

The door to Maximilian's cell opened, and in walked a stub-nosed man whose unusually long arms and neck gave him the appearance of a spider. Along the side of his neck, veins the color of a bright blue climbed like a little luminous lattice.

Unexpectedly the man sat on the floor next to Maximilian. "So here we are, the two of us."

Maximilian looked at his hands as if for the first time. "Did you know that during the war, armies leaped across the wastelands like a sea of fleas. I remember looking down from the mountains thinking, 'We have no chance.'"

The man looked at Maximilian. "Which war?"

Maximilian continued to look out into space beyond the stone wall. "We cried and cried as they died, falling onto the battle ground like ash." He could see the scene before him now: the thunderous roars of the weapons, the rush of the combat suits, the snarls of machines and projectiles burning through the shimmering haze.

"Do you know who I am?"

"You're here to capture me and take me back to Alerion and Demidae. They plan to parade me along the Boulevard of Marshals in Varenis—the rebel defeated."

The man looked at him. "You're raving like a madman."

Maximilian turned to the man, whose face looked somehow gaunt, despite its pudginess, as if its cheekbones were a little too high for the face. "You're changing."

"Where would the rest of the seditionists have run to?"

"What does it matter? Farther underground. Out into the city. Even if you destroy them, another rank will rise from the ground, like the dead themselves."

The man pressed his hands to his face. "I don't have the heart for it. I don't have the heart for all this death and torture. I'm just a tramworker. I'm out of my depth."

Maximilian looked out back into space. "We didn't think we'd do battle there, on that desert plain, and yet what could we do? We couldn't run anymore. There comes a time when you cannot run, when you have to stand and fight and hide no more. There comes a time when you cannot just let things stand as they are. Battle must be engaged; the conflict must be resolved."

The man said quickly and loudly: "I'm the Director now! A tramworker, the Director of Technis!"

"What does it matter?" asked Maximilian.

"What does it matter? It means I've escaped from the slums. I have influence, power. I have wealth, if I want it. I demand respect!"

"And love? Do you have love?" Max thought of Iria. She had been so beautiful, dancing with him when the world was young. She had built her Tower on the rocky outcrop in the wild mountains, overlooking the Valley of Icons, built by Mountain Giants. Iria and Aya: they had loved. But he was not Aya. He was Maximilian.

The man looked away, back at the door through which he'd entered. "Who among us has that?"

Max spoke softly. "Some do, out there. The little people, living their lives away from great events. They have time for everyday cares. For love."

"We don't have to torture you, you know. I'll make sure you're not tortured."

Maximilian stared back out at the battlefield in his mind. "There's nothing we could do in the end, but flee. We fled like children into the mountains, across the sea. But at least we could always say that we tried. We could say that Aya and his followers tried, and that there was nothing else that could be done. That at least they fought for the world, even if they could not save it."

"You're mad, you realize that. Is there any reason left in you?"

But Maximilian was back in his memories. He could see the dead on the battlefield now, green and blue chemicals leaking like blood from their ruined suits. The wasteland: that's what they called it now, that place of desolation to the north.

The man stood up. "I'll try not to let them torture you. But it's their job, you understand. The master torturer has studied the art for forty years."

Maximilian looked up as the man stopped at the door. "You're changing. You're becoming something else."

"I'll try." The man looked disappointed as he left the cell.

Less than half an hour later he returned with the master torturer and the same two apprentices who had led Max to the terror-sphere.

Maximilian sat up from the cold stone floor. The apprentices helped him to his feet. They led him, without a word, past the others and down the corridor in the direction of the terror-spheres. They turned right at an intersection, and entered a room with a reclining seat at its center. Already Maximilian could see the various pins and screws and clamps attached to the thing. He sat into it without a struggle, his feet slipping into great metal boots. He was strapped in, and a helmet closed over his head.

"Should we begin our work?" One of the apprentices spoke matter-of-factly.

The master torturer looked at the Director.

In the light of the room, the spidery veins on the side of the man's neck lit up like little streams of blue lava. There was a slight sheen to the man's skin. "Just give him the mold and let us get on with it."

The master torturer took a vial from his bag and, taking the stopper out, placed it at Maximilian's lips. Looking down, Max could see something brown and green start to move in the vial. Something furry pushed against his mouth. He pressed his lips tight as the thing tried to push between them, then moved like a small crawling animal, up, up, to his nose. His chest constricted with anxiety and he clenched his fists. He blew through his nose, but it made no difference, the carpetlike creature plunged into both nostrils and his eyes flooded with tears. Up into his sinuses the thing pushed, deep into his head. He cried out then, in desperation, while the whole room remained silent.

— Aya, help! — he called.

A memory—from where? He riffled through his mind. He

remembered now. He was a child, sitting at the top of a great tower, the world far below. A bearded instructor said to the children, Rest, notice the state you are in, let go of all thoughts and really notice the things around you: the floor, the air, your fellow students. Speak the first words of pure speech and notice how as you do this, things seem to light up with new life, with a new sense of immanence. Beneath this, you see the Other Side, the dark world, superimposed on this one. It, too, burns with dark intensity. The two now, in balance. Life and death, matter and anti-matter.

Maximilian spoke the words, he let go of himself, he noticed the air around him, the chair beneath him, the figures in the room. He noticed the thing inside him, slowly pushing up into his brain. The world lit up around him, the universe of light and dark, one on the other. Yes, now he could see things in their essence, not just their appearance. He understood now the ancients' obsession with mathematical forms, with the purity of numbers and angles, with all those hexagonal prisms.

Here, said Aya. Drifting toward him came the primary equations, formulae he—Aya—had learned in those years of training. He did not need to speak them aloud, Max realized. He pictured them in his mind, pure equations that dissolved into blackness. He brought them to mind, then forgot them. *Thaumaturgy should be a forgetting.* He could see inside everything, their molecules and atoms, and farther still, into the deep structure of the universe. He saw how things were connected to each other by a million minute threads of energy, how each thing supported the other in the motion of matter. The primary language, he knew, spoke the deep structure of the universe.

In this space, looking into the skeletal reality before him, Maximilian realized that with these equations he could reach out—like that, just so—and change a piece of matter in its quantity and structure, or its space or pace of change. Like the creature, yes, with the correctly arranged words, like that, he could stop it moving, and slowly push it away, slowly push it back out of his sinuses, out though his nose, and—yes, like that—push it back into the bottle and hold it there.

"What happened?" said one of figures.

Maximilian opened his eyes. Everything before him shimmered as if it were new and alive—as if he were seeing it for the first time. Light and movement: the very walls were filled with energy. Dark and movement: another world beneath this one.

"Use the vises."

Maximilian watched one of the apprentices approach the chair. The young man took hold of a large handle and twisted. The vise clamped to his forearm tightened. At first it was firm, then tight, and then, with a third twist, pain shot up his arm. He watched curiously as one collection of matter impressed itself upon another. He watched the structure of the vise deform the structure of his arm—atoms and molecules being rearranged by the force.

Again, far in the background of his mind the formulae and equations hovered. He reached into the deep structure of things and rearranged the pieces of matter. The vice broke open. He shook his arm. Stood up, the chair bursting asunder beneath him, the helmet falling to the floor.

One of the apprentices cried out. The other cowered. The master torturer backed away, his mouth open in shock. Only the Director stood still and straight.

Maximilian walked past them. He tore the door off its hinges and walked through the tunnels, the orbs lighting up above him. Each time he came to a door he broke open its locks, sending particles of metal tumbling to the ground. Behind him the doors swung open, the way all doors should be, allowing people to enter and leave at will.

Deep in his mind, Aya spoke: *There is a price for this, you realize. No longer will the universe of the Other Side flood into you, warp you. But you will be driven away from the world of life itself. You will care less and less for its everyday concerns. Love, happiness—these are things you will lose. But don't worry about that. Worry that you are now in my debt.*

FORTY-THREE

Kata felt a deep throbbing pain in head. Her throat felt rough and she struggled to swallow. She reached up, touched a pillow. She was on her bed, somehow. She opened her eyes, sat up. Downstairs she could hear someone moving around in her kitchen. She tried to call out, but her voice came out as a whisper. She touched her throat; the skin was raw. Again she tried to swallow, this time successfully though painfully.

She sat up in her bed, and looked around her room. She was fully clothed, but everything seemed in order. Recent events came back to her: her betrayal of the seditionists, the trip to the empty villa, the return home to die.

Kata walked slowly down the stairs into her parlor. She poked her head around the corner of the doorway to the kitchen where little Henri held a pot in one hand. He turned it around, examined it curiously, as if he'd never seen one before. Noticing Kata, he turned and grinned.

Kata groaned: the damned street urchin. "This is death, isn't it? I've been sent to some hell, with you to torture me."

Henri grinned again and put the pot on the bench. "You were really heavy, you know. I had to drag you up those stairs."

Kata looked at her bruised legs. "Looks like you did a fine job of it."

Henri squatted down onto his heels, the natural resting position of street urchins, who were unused to chairs. He watched her quietly.

"Are you hungry?"

He nodded.

Kata examined the boy. About ten years old, and his face was dirt-streaked; his hair slicked back and chopped roughly around his neck. A quiet intelligence glittered in his eyes, which she knew were untrustworthy.

"You saved me," she said.

The boy nodded and waited. She could tell he had no expectations. He was ready for cruelty as much as kindness.

"I suppose I'm going to have to buy some of your fudge now," she said.

He looked up with great round eyes; somewhere in them and on his face was a hint of humor. "Best Yensa fudge."

Together they made some potato soup from what was left of her supplies. The potatoes had begun to sprout and were a little green, but she showed him how to peel them. They dashed in a little gree, a pungent Caeli-Amurian sauce made from fish entrails. Later, she made Henri wash in the communal bathroom. He wailed and groaned as she poured cold water over him with the bucket. Then, as the sun went down over the baking city, she made him a bed in the parlor from old blankets.

Something had broken in Kata. No longer did she feel the horror of her actions. No longer was she filled with anger or grief. In some way, she had died the night before and been reborn. Her sins had been cleansed. She had been given a second chance. She had no immediate thoughts about her future but was content to see each day as it came. And tomorrow was Aya's Day. What would happen? she wondered. Outside, thick, heavy clouds hung threateningly over the city. From her balcony she looked out over the city, which seemed caught in some moment of decision. Small birds darted around, people walked through nearby streets, faces strained with tension. A hot wind blew from the south and the ocean was choppy and gray. She left the feeling of apprehension behind as she closed the doors onto the balcony and returned to the parlor below.

"You can stay here for a while," she said to Henri. She thought about banning the Yensa fudge, but this was a street urchin; he would likely be gone in the morning.

She retired to her bed: not a soft cushioned bed, yet large and comfortable and full of support. She threw a light sheet over herself, though the heat was stifling. Still, she had no trouble falling into a deep and dreamless sleep.

Rested in the morning, she awoke and found Henri sprawled on his own bed, legs splayed, half-covered with his own sheets in the humid morning. Beside him lay his little pouch of Yensa fudge, a dirty spoon, some coins, a model of a legionnaire from Varenis, its shield intact but the sword broken.

She served them more potato soup for breakfast. As they sat at the table, watching each other curiously, Kata heard the sound of people outside, yelling and laughing. A little while later, she heard the booming of drums. Together they sounded like a great sea, roaring and crashing. Kata and Henri walked upstairs, opened the doors to her balcony and stepped out. The streets below were filled with people, all marching down to the square between the Opera and the docks in the center of the city. Above them black clouds churned. Some seemed to be sweeping in from the sea, others rumbling in from the north. Far over the ocean, flashes of lightning could be seen, and thunder joined the rumbling of the drums.

She returned to her parlor, and listened to the sounds as they washed around her, permeated her. Her depression had completely lifted. She had passed through a personal nadir from which there was no farther distance to fall and now was climbing back up. Indeed, she didn't know quite *what* she felt. The future seemed now a blank canvas, on which she might paint her own possibilities. It was a strange sensation, one she could never recall having had before. Curiosity gripped her. She desired to see what had become of the seditionist movement. Some aspect of it called to her. Was she a seditionist, she wondered? With no other loyalties, no other cares? The very thought excited her.

"I'm going out," she said. "You stay here, if you want."

Henri nodded and followed when she stepped from the apartment.

"Stay here!" she turned to him.

He ran off down the street and toward Via Persine. She followed, shaking her head.

Old and young they came, filing down toward the square. From the industrial sections of the city the rough factory workers trudged down in their blue uniforms and their heavy boots, covered in dust and dirt and soot. Older people walked down holding hands, while others debated loudly in small groups various aspects of seditionist theory. Now and then they glanced up at the ominous clouds, which seemed to reflect the tension that hung over the crowd. Among the marchers, urchins ran and played and Kata made sure to keep an eye on her pockets. Henri disappeared into the crowd, following whatever impulse led him. But she was amazed that she should see so many people on the streets. She didn't believe it to be possible, and yet here they were. She walked with them, knowing—as everyone there felt—that the confrontation with the Houses was yet to come.

"Where are the House guards? Where are the thaumaturgists?" she asked.

An old woman whose hair was tied back with a scarf shrugged uncomfortably. "Seems there is no need for them here."

Kata wondered at this. Perhaps the Houses were planning to leave the demonstration alone, let things blow over. But that had never been the House way. She imagined Autec up in the Technis Complex, imperiously ordering the guards to mobilize, the thaumaturgists to invoke the Furies, standing on his balcony and watching the smudges of blackness descending toward the demonstration. Yet the sheer scale of the crowd surprised her. Perhaps it surprised the Houses also. Most likely they were waiting until the marchers reached the Market Square. There the citizens would be trapped, caught between the docks and the Opera. She imagined the massacre that would ensue: the Furies tearing onto the crowd with unearthly speed, like rabid dogs into a dying corpse. She imagined Autec, cold and heartless, engorged with his hate.

When she came to the square, she simply stopped and stared. The entire place was a morass of color, a thousand dots of red and blue and green and gray—amid the dim rumble of chatter. There were no guards in sight.

Orators stood high on the corners of the Opera balcony, leaning out over the crowd, arguing for various forms of sedition. The ideas they propounded were crude amalgams of different theories. One argued for the complete destruction of the Houses and everything they stood for, to be replaced by no structure at all; another for a kind of reconstruction of the Houses from the bottom up, with elected tribunes to replace the Directors.

Kata passed through the crowd, caught up in its little currents and eddies. A group of washerwomen hung effigies of officiates from crudely made scaffolds. Three blue-uniformed workers glanced at her lecherously and elbowed each other, grinning; an old man leaned against his walking stick, his face like wrinkled parchment.

She found herself chanting bloodthirsty chants with the others, drums beating a stony rhythm: "Death to the Houses, Death to the officiates, Death to the Directors, Death to the thaumaturgists." She listened to the speakers as if in some kind of strange reverie and felt at once insignificant, and somehow part of something bigger. The crowd seemed to rumble like a single giant animal, shifting to and fro like a sprawling beast stirring from a long sleep. It had no soul, it had no consciousness—it had only an awakening energy, a ravenous hunger. It needed to find its prey.

As Kata moved among the masses of people, just as she lost a sense of herself, she lost a sense of time. She found herself lost in the never-ending moment, where her past and her future seemed inconsequential, a part of something other. All that mattered was the feeling that she had now of being something larger than herself, something broader, a part of a greater universe.

She found herself shifting one way across the square, and back again. The words of the speakers accumulated in her consciousness, until she was drunk with visions of a new world. This mattered to her, she realized. Hope for the future mattered. Above her the clouds darkened, trapping in the heat and humidity. The lighting had crept closer and the thunder rumbled more loudly over the crowd.

At one point she looked up to see Ejan clinging to a statue. His steely voice rang out over the crowd like a clarion call. With one arm holding on to the belt of the ancient hero Caladus, Ejan, all blond hair and pale skin, looked even more like a Northman. He gazed over the crowd, his head turning this way and that. He leaned out, looking as if he wanted to touch the beast, to draw energy from it.

Ejan's words came in little bursts; after each one he drew a little breath, as if to take stock, to absorb the crowd's own desires. Kata examined the crowd. What does it want? It wants to grow, to cry out in unison, to march upon the Houses and force them to surrender. Ejan voiced these desires. Let us sweep up to the Houses, surround them, he cried. The crowd roared. By sheer force of numbers, we will make them capitulate, he said. Then we will tear their very palaces to the ground and start anew. A surge. Kata shifted on her feet as the crowd moved like the ocean.

As Kata was carried along by the crowd, she heard someone say, "Where are the Collegia?"

Tension rushed into her, for she knew they would not come. She remembered Autec's words: "Armand has visited the Collegia to ensure they're on our side." Among the crowd there were worried faces and skittish eyes.

"Where are the Collegia?" some asked again.

FORTY-FOUR
❧◈❧

Ejan leaped down from the statue and joined his little army, standing near, cobbled together bolt-throwers and jagged knives in hand. Many of his supporters had escaped the seditinist hideout.

Ejan and this group marched to Via Persine, for they were headed for House Technis. Others, Kata learned, would march on Marin and Arbor, but she followed Ejan and the others. She wanted to face Technis, to stare the machine in the face. Ejan's group forced themselves to the front of the crowd, which followed them, pouring into Via Persine like water into a channel, rushing up against the shopfronts that lined the street. Most of the shops were closed up, their protective grates bolted down down like jaws in a death rictus. Other shopkeepers were busily closing up.

Lightning flashed in the sky above, and the boulevard lit up before Kata. A mighty clap of thunder exploded above. But no rain fell. Perhaps this would be one of the rainless electrical storms that sometimes rolled over Caeli-Amur.

But she knew that others around her read it as a portent. Behind her, she heard whisperings: The Collegia had not come. A storm had arisen instead. The sky was empty; the city's birds had hidden themselves away. The Collegia had left the crowd to face the Houses alone. Kata had already known that this would be the case. Despite the size of the demonstration, she knew in her heart that they would not be able to stand the force of the Houses. With the support of the Collegia they might have stood a chance, even against the Furies, for she knew that the thaumaturgists could not summon the creatures and keep them on this plane indefinitely. But she did not care. For her the demonstration itself was a little utopia. She felt free for the very first time in her life, filled with a frightened jubilation she could never have predicted. She was committed now. Now that she had been stripped of all hope and reborn from death, she knew that she was finally a seditionist at heart.

Kata pushed forward until she was close to the head of the procession. Drums beat incessantly, setting a marching kind of rhythm. To their right lay the factory district. Workers from the glass factories set down their tools and joined them. Tramps edged along the side of the crowd, as if afraid to join in, until they were finally sure that they would not be struck down. Then their voices were among the loudest and angriest. "Death to the Houses! Death to the guards! Death to the Directors! Death to the officiates!"

The crowd jolted to a halt. A hundred yards away, high up the boulevard, stood the House Technis guards. The crowd fell silent. The two forces stood facing each other. Time slowed down. The crowd faced the guards. Eyes locked with their opponents', searching for weakness, searching for resolution. Behind them, Kata could sense the mass of the crowd, poorly prepared for battle. But at the head stood Ejan and his group. This was the moment they had waited for. The tension hovered above them all, trapped in by the clouds above.

In her heart, Kata knew that the crowd could not stand up to the might of the Houses. She expected at any moment for the guards to separate, and for the thaumaturgists to come, led by the black Furies. Then the crowd would flee for its life, screaming with fear and despair.

The tension suddenly broke. Kata became aware of a movement in the sky. A storm of stones hovered momentarily in the air, launched by hundreds of arms behind her, and then came down upon the guards, who held their arms over their heads to defend themselves. Cries echoed around the streets: the pain of the guards, the anger of the demonstrators, the shock of those who had never seen anything like it.

The guards fired their bolt-throwers. With a whir of bolts through the air, black and threatening things speeding toward them. Demonstrators went down. More cries and screams. Demonstrators scattered like a flight of birds under threat.

Kata pushed herself through running figures toward a shop-front. Already others had broken into the nearby shops. As she pressed herself against the wall, others poured through the nearby door. Moments later the guards were confronted with a hail of roof tiles as demonstrators surged onto nearby roofs.

Ejan's seditionists at the head of the march fired their own bolt-throwers.

The heat of the day was greatest now, and events seemed to occur in a radiant pulsing glare. Like a great pressure cooker, the clouds overhead seemed to trap the heat and focus it back onto the city. The very sky writhed above them, in conflict with itself. Lightning slashed across it and deafening thunder boomed, so that the clash of arms and the cries of the opponents were overwhelmed.

Sweat ran along Kata's brow, dust swirled in the air, even as blood ran in the street. The fighting became vicious. People screamed, lay on the ground. The crowd rushed forward over the injured. Kata found herself farther up Via Persine. Several glass-makers held a guard between them. A woman repeatedly bludgeoned the guard on the head with a wooden beam. One of the guard's eyes fell from its socket.

Up Via Persine, the line of guards fell back. Elated and savage, the crowd swept forward. All the while Kata wondered: Where are the thaumaturgists? She knew they would come, and this momentary conflagration would be doused by blackness.

Occasionally there were breaks in the fighting, as both sides regrouped, waited. The injured were carried away from the action: men and women, their skin torn or pierced, bones splintered or broken. Neither side took prisoners, and Kata was surprised by the efficiency with which injured guards were dispatched. The citizens were tougher than she had thought.

Water was in short supply. Kata shared from a flask that was passed around. She was relieved when the water touched her parched throat, but the flask was all too soon emptied. Around her, elderly sheltered in the side streets. Many had collapsed under the shock of events. Kata wiped sweat from her dirty brow. The stormy air had an eerie quality to it. Things seemed magnified, their outlines sharp and clear.

"Will the storm pass without breaking the heat?" asked a young man near Kata.

She looked up at the sky. The clouds rushed overhead, seething and roiling. "Until now the clouds have threatened rain, then passed over as if they have made a joke. But now—"

"The Collegia did not come," said the young man. "We can't defeat the guards. There are too many of them. Others are fighting Marin on the Northern Headland and in Arbor in the Arantine. If the House thaumaturgists are loosed on us, what then?"

Kata placed her hand on the man's shoulder. "We'll face them while we can."

Again the crowd launched themselves at the guards, like a snake striking. Bolts on each side were loosed. Kata had both knives in her hands. She rushed forward, expecting at any moment to be struck by a missile. The clash of arms rang. A guard slashed at her with his sword, but she rolled away, threw a knife, and he went down. Then she was over him. Her knife sank into his chest. He gurgled, the light slipped from his eyes. She wondered at the man's life, his family. She pushed the thought from her mind.

Through the lines of the guards came apprentice thaumaturgists, students from the university. Perhaps fifty of them, carrying the thick-barreled thaumaturgical weapons that Kata had seen them use in the Quaedian against seditionist students weeks before. So this is it, she thought. This is the end of it. She called out, trying to warn the seditionists, but her voice was lost in the din.

The apprentices fired the great weapons and seditionists went down, clawing at their faces and screaming. Again the weapons boomed and again another row of seditionists collapsed. Their wails hideous and high, their minds in a far-off land of pain and terror. Nearby a seditionist tore at her cheeks, leaving ragged bloody marks.

The seditionist forces broke and fled. Kata followed them as they stampeded along Via Persine. Men and women were trampled underfoot in the great rout. An old man cowered in a doorway, his arm around a wounded young woman. Others fled down the side alleyways, driven by blind fear and desperation.

Kata was filled with the bitterness of defeat. She knew that there could be no rallying of the seditionist forces. They were not soldiers but citizens, better suited to baking bread, building houses, constructing trams, washing clothes, and all the other assorted acts of everyday people. Only the arrival of the Collegia could save them now, and she knew the Collegia would not come.

The great rout carried her back to Market Square, where there was no escape. The seditionists were hemmed in, trapped in a bottleneck. Kata pressed herself into a doorway at the end of Via Persine. In the square below her, the great panicked floods trampled over one another. Across the road, Ejan and the remnants of his army, rallying in a side street, prepared for one last defensive maneuver. Kata looked up to see the apprentice thaumaturgists marching cruelly forward. Behind them, the House guards stabbed at stray or wounded seditionists. Cries of agony sounded the approach of death. So the Houses had not even needed to mobilize the thaumaturgists in the end, after all. They had been able to rely on their apprentices.

As she watched them approach, Kata was filled with grief. She had escaped death only two days ago. She was happy enough to embrace it now. In her hands, she held her two knives, which had served her so well.

Gritting her teeth as the stomping feet approached, Kata closed her eyes and with a leap and a dive, rolled out to face the approaching enemy. She stood alone in the center of Via Persine, the cobblestones beneath her feet, the gray clouds overhead, the heat bearing down on the entire city. She stared grimly at the approaching forces: the student apprentices with their thaumaturgical weapons, the gray-suited guards behind them. Behind them, lighting seemed to strike the mountain itself, lighting the city with unearthly beauty.

At that moment, as the world was illuminated by ghostly light, the entire right-hand side column of the students and the guards collapsed, as if struck by some unseen force. The others halted, turned to their right. From windows and alleyways came spinning knives and piercing bolts. A second later lithe figures rolled and tumbled and charged, striking with exotic weapons: weighted chains, lassoes and lariats, spinning knives and impaling bolts. Kata tried to comprehend these images. Who were these deadly, athletic figures rolling and tumbling, cutting a swath into the House forces? Then she understood: Only one caste in Caeli-Amur would fight with such deadly intent.

"Philosopher-assassins! The philosopher-assassins have come!" she turned. Tears were in her eyes now and she could barely see when she turned back. She remembered now that debate they had been having in the café La Tazia. One of them had said, "The Aya's Day demonstration will rearrange things in this city, you mark my words." She recalled now the charge that his words had held. The philosopher-assassins were forever at the beck and call of the Houses, forever used and discarded. Were they not just like her, in the end?

From the alleyway, Ejan and his seditionists charged, and a cascade of citizens flooded past her to join the battle. At this, the House forces were seized with panic. Many tried to flee, but the deadly weapons of the philosopher-assassins caught them. Others fell to their knees, but the seditionists gave them no mercy. Precious few escaped back, falling upon the rear ranks with dismay.

With this, the sky opened up and a torrent of rain pelted down upon the city: large drops that fell hard and cold like little stones. Within moments, Kata was drenched. Streams of water ran along the tram tracks, and in the gutters. The long heat of summer had broken.

Now the seditionist army had the upper hand and the House forces fled. On and on the seditionists surged, back up Via Persine toward the Technis Complex. Still the House thaumaturgists were nowhere to be seen. Kata killed again. Again she was lost in the clamor of battle, the jostle of arms and legs and steel, the screams. Twice she slipped on the wet cobblestones and found streams of water running over her hands. Yet still she fought, with citizens beside her. And then they were at the square in front of the Technis Complex. The remaining guards retreated inside and the vast doors closed behind them. The crowd did not call out in joy, but looked wet and weary.

Word came that Marin was holed up in its palace. Its guards had not appeared on the streets. But there was bitter fighting in the Arantine around the Arbor Palace. Rumors came that the Arbor Palace had been overrun, then that the seditionists had been defeated and Arbor's thaumaturgists were marching at that very moment toward them. No one seemed to be sure of anything. Everything was confusion.

Jostled as she stood watching, Kata looked at the huge man next to her. It was not in fact a man but a minotaur, powerful.

"Dexion," she said.

"Ah, to see this," he said. "Something new!"

His voice snapped Kata from her reverie. "Soon the House will release their creatures upon us, their thaumaturgists will come out and crush us."

Dexion looked at her, his great eyes twinkling. His hide was wet, but he clearly didn't care.

She found herself smiling back at him. "But at least we'll die doing something."

"At least you will," he said.

Kata nodded and looked at the sealed gates: great black doors covered by a portcullis.

Already the crowd was building barricades or carts, furniture, planks of wood. Soon a great wall mirrored the complex's walls.

Whispers rumbled among the crowd. "Will the thaumaturgists come?" Where are the Furies?" The crude barricades, made of broken carts, torn fences, rocks dug up from the road, would be slight protection against their powers.

Again Kata imagined Director Autec up in the complex, his cronies around him, working out his plans scientifically: so many guards to recapture this section of the city, this number of murders of seditionists required, this number of arrests, the ratio of torture exactly one to every twenty citizens. He was always so certain of himself, so decisive and cruel. A rush of thoughts ran through her head. Did she dare hope that the Houses could be conquered? What arms did the citizens possess? Homemade weapons. A few bolt-throwers. The weapons of the philosopher-assassins that had come over to the seditionists' side—and certainly this did not number all the philosopher-assassins in the city. Was Maximilian right, after all? The Houses possessed thaumaturgy, and what could withstand that?

Maximilian—the thought of him struck at her like a knife. Maximilian—he was somewhere underneath the complex there. Right at this moment his limbs were probably being burned and broken, his skin stripped like that of an animal as he watched. Dare she hope that they could save him?

"Come, let's help." Dexion took her wrist in his mighty hand and led her to the barricades, which formed a semicircle around the front gate.

All the time the whispers came from the crowd: "Where are the thaumaturgists? When will they come for us?"

Around them blew a cool breeze.

FORTY-FIVE

Alone on the balcony of House Technis, Boris looked over the city where only a day ago he had been the highest power. The storm had raged with frightening intensity but passed quickly, leaving a cold wind blowing. Now campfires burned in the dark squares and a seditionist militia patrolled the night streets, meting out whatever justice they desired. There was no order to it, he imagined, just bands of brigands and fools, their hearts filled with bloody vengeance. He had known, in his deepest recesses, that this would happen. He had once been a tramworker and had once known the very men and women who were encamped out there in a show of strength. These formed the backbone of these rebels, misled by outsiders like that Ejan.

At first the officiates and subofficiates had come scurrying in, warning of a immense crowd gathering. Their eyes were filled with doubt. That was always the way in times of crisis: The strong kept their heads, the others vacillated. The world seemed to them incomprehensible, as if gravity had reversed and objects had begun to fall up to the sky. Boris had sent an order for the thaumaturgists to summon the Furies and join the House guards. But they had not obeyed. Boris had prepared himself to face Alfadi, the bald prefect of the thaumaturgists. But he continued to put off the confrontation. The reports kept coming: The crowd in Market Square was prodigious; seditionism was openly being advocated from stages in the square; they had marched toward the complex and been beaten back. Rather than confront Alfadi, Boris sent the instruction that the apprentices, who had been summoned from the university, should march forth. Then the terrible report, given by a trembling subofficiate: The philosopher-assassins had thrown themselves into the battle; the guards had been routed and the complex was surrounded.

The only officiate who had any presence of mind was Armand. As usual he was unflappable, calmly walking in and out of the office. Boris sent him to ensure that the guards, rattled from their grievous losses in the street battles, were ready to strike once more. The rest of the officiates and intendants he waved away. He then retreated to his balcony. There he looked out over Caeli-Amur, the city that had made him the man he was.

A little while later, Armand returned and leaned against the balcony rail next to him. In one hand he held several scrolls. His voice remained calm as ever. "I have copied the maps of the tunnels beneath the city, in case we need to send them to Varenis." He held them toward him.

Boris clasped his hands together, released them and rubbed his face. "It's like a volcano."

Armand turned Boris by the shoulder. "I think it may be time to meet Alfadi, don't you?" He stepped back, his eyes wide. "Director—what has happened to your face? It's such a strange color."

The words barely registered. Instead, Boris looked at Armand. "You'll never understand the citizens, will you? You're like a spearbird flying high above the land. The rest of us seem far below to you, don't they?"

Armand's face remained unmoved. "I come from a long line of House officials. I belong here, Director. I had hoped that you did, too, but I see that you were not raised for this position."

Boris looked at the younger man. "It is true. I'm not. I never was."

Boris walked away. He felt ill, as if something were sitting in his stomach. Images of Mathias came to him. In his mind he spoke to his old tramworker friend. "See, Mathias, see what strikes and actions bring us to." But the Mathias in his mind did not agree. Boris angrily pushed the picture away. He felt like crying. He couldn't think. He tried to locate the feeling inside him, swirling like a mist. Annihilation: that was the name for it. Look how far I have fallen, he thought. There is no way out.

He would need to press the thaumaturgists into action. But

moments passed and still he put it off. Was it the fact that the thaumaturgists were increasingly intractable? What bargain would he
have to strike in order for them to act? Already Marin had lost
control of theirs. And Arbor—who knew?

Boris made a small keening sound, as if he was about to cry.
Perhaps he was. Then, once more he mustered his fury, for he
knew it was his anger that drove him on, and he stormed from his
office toward the thaumaturgists' hall.

The corridors of the complex were filled with scurrying but silent agents. As he came into view, they lowered their eyes. Embarrassment, fear, confusion—he could read all these in their faces.
He wanted to smash them, break their teeth, have them spit out
the fragments onto the floor.

Boris stormed into the thaumaturgists' hall. Only a few sat at
their desks. Where were the rest of them?

Prefect Alfadi watched them from his platform across the room.
"It was only a matter of time."

"Before what?" Boris apprioached.

"Before you arrived to force our hand." Alfadi's white pupils
bore into Boris.

"It's time to strike. It's time, now, in the middle of the night,
to bring down the wrath of the House onto these seditionists.
Loose them—the Furies. I command you."

The thaumaturgist pursed his lips and looked at the side of
Boris's face. A puzzled expression passed briefly across his features before he settled back into impassivity. "They won't."

"What?"

"For years they have served the House, and for what? Yes, they
learn; yes, they have some level of power—but don't you understand, these things are not enough. They want something more.
We all do. Meaning, give them that. Purpose."

"You're the prefect. Convince them."

"*I* won't."

Somewhere lurking inside him, Boris had known that this
would be the case. His life seemed like one revelation after another;
time after time a veil was ripped from his eyes. Boris felt sick once

more. What did he feel now? Desperation, self-pity? His voice shook. "What can I offer you?"

The thaumaturgist chief smiled. "What can you?"

"Anything you want." Boris dropped to his knees. He wanted to be away from all of this. He wanted someone else to be in his stead. "Everything."

The thaumaturgist smiled. "Director, you are on your knees."

Boris put his head in his hands.

Alfadi stood up, stepped from behind his desk, took several steps away, and turned back to Boris. "It's too late Director. I warned you, but you would not listen. There's change in the air."

Boris staggered through the Palace in a haze. The corridors seemed to tilt and sway. Faces loomed toward him and fell away again. Here a pair of eyes, massive and accusing, there a shadowed figure who refused to look at him. People—who were all these people?

He tried to imagine ways he could sway the thaumaturgists. There was only one option: He would have to face the Elo-Talern, who thought that he had everything under control. A feeling of shame washed over him. A failure—that's what he was. He had wanted to make things better for everyone, and now this.

He came to the throne room disheveled, but she was not there. He continued on, down the long corridor and into the never-ending bacchanalian feast of the Elo-Talern. He stood at the door to the vast chamber and there looked on at the scene. From a group that sat along the wall sucking smoke from pipes attached to the wall, she came to him, swaying like a drunkard—Elo-Drusa.

"Look at you." She creaked her way toward him and took his hand. She pulled his elongated arm up. It looked like the great forearm of an insect, thick blue veins glowing under the skin. "It's reached your face and soon will touch your brain. The ascension has begun."

"I've failed." Boris hung his head.

"No. Look at you. You're magnificent. You're on the path to even greater magnificence." She lifted his head with her free hand and looked down on him.

"The city. We've lost control of the city."

"I know," said the Elo-Talern.

"How? How do you know?"

"I know everything," she said. "I've always known. I never needed your information Boris. It was all to test you, Boris. To see if you're the right one."

"But the Elo-Talern—you're the powers behind the city."

She gestured at the orgy of eating and drinking before her. "You think they care? Look at them, Boris. The world could burn and they would not notice. No, the Elo-Talern have not cared for hundreds of years. When you live between the two universes, you lose connection to both. You become dissociated, uncaring and unfeeling. Life itself loses its luster. The Magi understood this, for that was the fate that awaited them. That's why I need you—I need you to keep me alive."

"We'll never be alive again," said Boris.

"Yes, we will, my love. You are filled with everything that's human: love and grief and hope and despair. We'll be more alive than anyone! Together!" Her face flashed into its deathly skull. "I've only ever wanted you."

"No," Boris sobbed.

"Yes. You are becoming one of us, Boris. In just the same way we changed all those years ago. But you're not like all of these old ones. You're a new generation of Elo-Talern!"

"You were once human," Boris said to himself, looking down at the ground.

"We were the Aediles," said the Elo-Talern. "We spent our time ensuring the smooth working of the world. We measured the seas, we tested the air, we ensured that we lived in a world where each was given what they needed. Others played, but we worked for the greater good. After the cataclysm, we protected what we could. We saved lives, we preserved knowledge where we could, we placed what we could find in the Great Library of Caeli-Enis. But it was a losing battle. Entropy—there's nothing you can do to resist it. And when Caeli-Enis descended beneath the sea, we sank with it, such was our grief. Nothing was left of our beautiful world, and so, we sought to save the last thing we could—ourselves. If our carefully designed world was broken, then we would save it in our memories, we would be the living enbodiment of our lost utopia. But then this . . ." She looked around at the other Elo-Talern.

Boris looked up at her, "Can I be killed?"

"Not by age."

"Just by violence?"

"Or accident."

The despair was black inside Boris. "Then I'm more alive than I've ever been."

"Your transformation is not yet complete. But it will be soon, my love. And here—" She led him to the pillar that stood near to the great door. There sat the prism that Boris had noticed when he first entered the Undercity. Elo-Drusa reached up, took it from its resting place.

"Do you know what this is?" Elo-Drusa asked.

Boris stood speechless.

"The Prism of Alerion." She looked around at the other Elo-Talern. Some watched her with distant curiosity. A couple seemed to whisper to each other. But then they turned back to their abandoned revelry, lost to the world of the living.

Elo-Drusa held the hexagonal-shaped crystal prism in her hands. Unlike the scrying ball, at its center was not some mechanical device but instead a misty swirl of fog, occasionally billowing into shapes that suggested something alive. "Alerion's essence itself was encased in here and it possesses the knowledge of the Magi. It is the only object known to stop the thaumaturgical illness, to stop the warping of body and mind. Use it to bribe the thaumaturgists, to win them over."

Boris fancied he saw a stern and frightening face looking out from the prism. Then the mist billowed back into a cloudy ball. Boris looked up blankly at Elo-Drusa. He had to escape this charnel-pit, for he did not have much time before his transformation would be complete. He took the prism, perhaps the most valuable item in Caeli-Amur, in his hands. It was cold and did not warm with his touch. "Thank you, my love. I must go and quell those rebels."

"When you return to me, I will show you the wonders of the world. Such beauty."

"Such beauty." Boris looked up into her horselike skull-face.

FORTY-SIX

Back in his office, Boris sobbed uncontrollably. He punched his fist against the wall again and again. Despair churned and ate away inside him. He stopped sobbing, leaned his head against the wall, breathed deeply, began moaning and punching the wall again. The prism sat before him and again the face seemed to emerge inside, to look at him grimly. He was sure of it: it was a terrible and sinister face, and yet he found himself gazing intently as the form dissolved mesmerizingly back into shifting mist.

Stopping suddenly, he pulled himself together, straightened his clothes. There were some final things to do. First: Varenis. He uncovered the great scrying ball. He pulled the lever, and the great tower of the Sortileges projected into view around him.

A man Boris had never seen sat at a desk, which, since the last time he spoke to the Director, had been placed in front of the sister scrying ball. On the balcony overlooking Varenis, Boris could just make out an eerie green smudge on the edge of the image. Whatever it was, the ball could not focus on that region of space. Fear shot momentarily into Boris. There was something wrong with that smudge, something eerie and unnerving.

The man at the desk looked up: "Ah, Director Autec. What has occurred in Caeli-Amur? We've heard rumors."

Boris looked blankly at the man. "Who are you?"

"I'm the Director of Varenis, of course."

Boris blinked a little: the *new* Director. It made sense, for the Directorship of Varenis was a keenly contested position. While in Caeli-Amur, the feuding had become mostly between the Houses, in Varenis it came within the Directorate. Stories abounded about the vicious struggles for the position, the sudden ascents and the precipitous falls of each Director.

"I warned you," said Boris, "the rule of the Houses is over."

The green smudge moved. Boris started: now he could just make the smudge on the balcony out as a frighteningly tall figure, just on the edge of the scrying ball's range. The figure turned to face him. A strange luminescent darkness shone around it—that same light that Boris had seen previously. The image unraveled and distorted—freezing in a coagulation of pixels—so that Boris could barely see the shape. He looked away, frightened. "Damn you. Damn you all to the land of darkness."

He looked up to see the figure had moved inside the tower, but now the ball could not capture its outline at all. A great seven-foot fuzzing whiteness blotted out the room.

Boris spoke bitterly. "Leave Caeli-Amur alone. Let it find its own path out of these troubles."

Boris heard a voice, deep and loud. The ball cracked and popped, as if struggling to reproduce the sound. But beneath the distortion, the voice was ancient and full of menace. The Sortilege said, "No, Autec, we will not. We will come to your city, and when we arrive, we will scourge the place of seditionists. We will take it for our own, strip it of all its wealth and glory. And when we are done, we will take you and show you what real pain is like."

The picture flickered for a second and shrank in size back into the scrying ball, until it became a point of light and disappeared.

Boris was filled with all the grief and horror of his life, like a blocked sewer that spewed back its contents. He looked back on the mistakes he had made. He thought of his long-dead wife, Remmie. What would she have said? Her heart would have broken, to see what he had become. Why, all those years ago, did she have to die? *That* had been the moment everything went wrong, when he had lost his family. If she had been there, beside him, she would have helped him choose a better path. She would have cocked her head, the way she did when she told him off, and said, "Boris!" That's all she had to say, and he would have seen the implications, known the steps to take. Now there was no chance of making things right—he had done too much damage. There was no hope for him, but he would do what little he could. Remmie was dead, but Saidra was still alive. He needed to see her, one last time, though he knew that she would spit in his face, strike out at him with words if not fists. He still had hope for the last member of his family.

He looked up to see Paxaea standing at the doors to his private quarters.

"Paxaea," he said.

"Director Autec."

He stumbled toward her. "I'm sorry. I'm sorry. I'm sorry. I'm sorry." He repeated the words again and again, mechanically. "I'm sorry, I'm sorry . . ." He was crying now, and his hand was on her arm. But she stood upright and impassive. "It was always like this with you. You never opened yourself to me. You were always impossible to penetrate, like a labyrinth."

"You cannot force someone to open herself to you."

He nodded, crying. "How else . . . how else?"

"Some things are just beyond the reach of some of us."

Boris felt nauseated now. All around shadows were shifting and swirling. He could see the Other Side clearly, the dark lands superimposed onto the one in which he sat, the death lands, where as an Elo-Talern he would spend half his pitiful existence. In the shadows of that world Paxaea now seemed brighter and more alive than ever, like an emblem of a domain where things had meaning. She gleamed now, and from his place in the dark, she seemed farther away than ever.

He sobbed. "I'm sorry." He spoke the words that released the torc from her neck—"Taritia-atas"—and reached up, unfastening it, grasping it in his hand.

Still she stood motionless, as if she were weighing her possibilities.

Boris let go of her arm and took a step backwards.

Paxaea threw back her arms and her head, as if stretching. She took several steps and looked at the door into the office.

A fierce inhuman look came over the Siren's face. Intensity burned in her eyes, like those of a wild animal. She opened her mouth wide, and the jaws dropped lower than any human's. Like a great cat's mouth it gaped. She screamed: two powerful notes vibrating together. The windows to the balcony shattered; the door bust from its hinges. Cracks ran like spiderwebs down the walls.

Boris was thrown back and everything went black.

When he came to, Boris lay on the floor still stunned by the force of Paxaea's cry. He blinked rapidly, though everything seemed silent. Something ran down his throat and there was a metallic taste in his mouth. Above him a deep lightning-shaped crack ran across the ceiling.

Boris sat up and surveyed his empty room. Something itched on his upper lip. He touched it and pulled his hand away: his nose was bleeding. He sat there, alone, holding his nose as blood trickled onto his hand.

He stood unsteadily, walked to his desk and froze. The Prism of Alerion was gone. So, too, were the copies of the maps Caeli-Amur's subterranean tunnels. He put his hands on his head. He could scarcely breathe. He had hoped to give the prism to Saidra. But now Paxaea had taken it, and the maps also—a final betrayal.

There was no time to lose. There was nothing to do but to find the original maps in his drawers. He examined them once more, outlining the hidden ways beneath the city. He threw on a cloak, pulled up the hood, and took an elevator deep into the ground. From there a passageway led into a series of caves, tunnels, some sandy steps leading up, and he emerged, finally on the side of one of the cliffs, not far from Via Persine.

Dawn was breaking now over the water, and Boris approached the Opera. The city was as he imagined it. A cool wind blew through the streets, which were filled with refuse. Many of the shops along Via Persine had been looted. Blue-suited workers lay drunk in the gutters. A band of seditionists marched up the street, kicking the drunks in the back. "Get up. Get up." A number of them entered the cellar of a nearby bar and began smashing flagons. A drunk in the gutter cackled. He was missing teeth.

When Boris came to Market Square, he pulled the cloak over his head. He passed through the Opera's entry hall, which had been turned into a makeshift armory. The seditionists seemed to be taking over the building, and they scurried around like rodents building a nest. Above, the globes of light were bouncing up and down in excitement.

He passed by unchecked. There seemed no order to any of it. He considered seeing if Paxaea was in her room, collecting her valuables. But he had other priorities. He arrived at Saidra's room and stood before the closed door, trembling. The corridor here was gloomy. Look at yourself, he thought. Trembling like a frightened animal, before you meet your own daughter. You gave her life, and yet she has so much control over you. He dreaded knocking on the door, dreaded facing Saidra's scorn.

He knocked. The door swung open.

"Father! Father, thank providence you're alive." Saidra's voice shivered. "Come in." She turned back to a half-packed case, clothes folded on the bed next to it. "There's talk of storming the House complexes. I was worried." She turned back to him and gave a little start. "Father. Oh, what has happened to you?"

Boris hung his head. The kindness in her words shocked him. He felt like crying. "I'm ill."

"You're—what are those blue lines spreading up your face? And your limbs: it's almost like you're . . . you're taller. And gaunter." When Boris didn't answer, she added: "Come in. Come in. They're evicting us. They've turned this place into a seditionist center. Father, are you . . . *flickering*?"

Boris took the keys to his apartment from his pocket. "Here are the keys to the house. You should stay there. I must return to the Technis Palace. My destiny lies there."

"No, Father. The Houses are finished. You must escape."

"Saidra, there is no hope for the seditionists. Varenis may well be mobilizing as we speak. If not now, they will eventually. The Sortileges are coming. When they arrive, they will integrate Caeli-Amur into the Empire."

"Oh." Saidra's eyes were wide as she absorbed this information.

"Yes." Boris sat on the side of the bed, next to the case. "Saidra, I'm sorry for everything. I'm sorry I failed as a father. I, I wish I could say it better, stronger, but I'm just a tramworker really. There's so much I'd like to—"

Saidra was crying now, and she stepped forward, as if she wanted to touch him. But they had never been a close family, and touching was not something they had ever done. "No, it's I who should be sorry."

"I'm the father," said Boris.

"Come back to the house with me. We'll get you healthy again."

Boris took the maps from his bag. "These are maps for the tunnels beneath the city. They will help you escape, if you need to. Otherwise, you may want to give them to the seditionists. There's a man called Ejan—perhaps he can use them. There has been too much bloodshed."

"But, Father, you'll return. I'll see you again?"

"Oh, sometime." Boris smiled weakly.

"When?" demanded Saidra.

"As soon as I can set some final things straight."

"Promise me!"

Boris smiled again, and tears were in his eyes. "I promise." It wasn't the first lie he'd told.

The walk back to the Technis Palace was not difficult. Boris knew all his roads led into his office. The dungeons were now emptied and the corridors in the palace itself were chaotic. House agents ran panicked, to and fro. Others seemed to be looting the place, for their arms were filled with sculptures or lamps or coins or other assorted paraphernalia.

Boris shivered feverishly. He felt sweat run down his back, even though cool air blew through the corridors. As he stood surveying the wreckage of his office, which had now apparently been ransacked, Armand entered through the broken doorway. He looked around at the cracks, the broken glass. "Director—" His voice seemed to come from far away. "Director, the thaumaturgists . . ."

Boris nodded. He stood up and walked to the small table in his room where his fruit and dried meats lay. He took the knife, long and sharp and carried it with him to the balcony. There he surveyed the city from the balcony again.

Armand stood behind him. "You've failed."

"We've all failed," said Boris. "Though perhaps I have had some final moments of success. You see, the means are more important than the goal, Armand. The everyday actions: those are the important moments."

Armand stared blankly. "What will we do now? Wait?"

"The Directorate of Varenis will send its legions. They will descend on the city like carrion-birds on dying prey."

Armand placed his hand on his shoulder. "Things won't be saved, though. Things can't go back to normal, can they?"

"Nothing ever will." Boris turned to face Armand.

At the sight of him, Armand took a step backwards. Horror filled his eyes, which quickly roved over Boris. Boris knew that the change was coming over him quickly now. The arteries and veins in his entire body seemed to burn, and he knew the uncanny blueness ran through them.

"Director, why do you have that knife in your hand? Do you fear for your life?" Armand asked.

"I fear for myself."

"Director, you don't look well. Director, you . . . Shall I call the physicians?"

"Send them in an hour."

Armand nodded. He spoke, but there was no conviction in his voice. "You'll be all right, Director. You'll make it through. We all will. Change is a lot harder than anyone can imagine."

When he did not answer, Armand walked away. For the first time, Boris had seen fear in the other man's eyes.

After Armand left, Boris again looked out over the city, which to him had almost worn itself out like an ancient machine. He looked out over the geographies of their lives: the port, where the Xsanthians led their collared lives; the Opera, with its Sirens in rooms with barred windows; the factories where the workers struggled and ground out their lives amid the smoke and soot; the clifftop cafes of Via Gracchia, where philosopher-assassins lounged like dispossessed artists. At least there was life out there, something moving, something changing. He could hear the laughter and the music of the seditionists floating across the air. There was life out there. But here?

Boris clasped the knife tightly. Without hesitation, he dragged it across his throat, cutting deep to the bone.

FORTY-SEVEN

The day after the battle, the House doors remained closed. Kata and Dexion remained behind the barricades, watching the motley collection of seditionists and citizens as they set up camp or drifted through. Nearby houses had been commandeered as organizing loci: seditionists and citizens slept in dark rooms filled with beds; kitchens were turned over to the cooking of tomato and potato soup. Philosopher-assassins—gratificationists, matriarchists, Cajiuns, apocalyptics—drifted through, watching and talking. Ejan spent his time moving between the barricades and the Opera House, which was designated the logistical center for the city. A council had been set up to coordinate the major decisions and would meet that evening, though Kata avoided any participation. She did not deserve to play a part. For her, now, was the role of foot soldier. So she remained on the barricades, watching and waiting, under the pregnant sky. Still the air was humid and hot, and many sought out the shade, though there they found no relief.

In the afternoon, as Kata and Dexion lay on their backs looking at the moody sky, a cry went up. They scrambled to the top of the barricades, weapons drawn. The Technis Complex's portcullis rose smoothly, boomed into place at its zenith. Behind, huge iron gates creaked open and the seditionists on the barricades tensed. Bolt-throwers were aimed, bottles filled with oil held in hand. Kata held her knives in her hands. Next to her, Dexion shifted his massive bulk, a great axe in one hand, a hammer in another.

"So this is it," said Dexion.

Something moved in the darkness beneath the arched gateway. Seditionists shifted nervously. Again a flitter of movement. Kata noticed that she was holding her breath. Her exhalation seemed loud enough for those around to hear.

A tall suited figure emerged from the darkness, followed by another. They came, one by one, unorganized, as if they were just a collection of refugees.

"Thaumaturgists!" someone said.

"Strike now!" a voice shouted.

Bodies shifted once more, readying themselves to unleash their weapons.

"Wait!" Ejan stood on the barricade and turned his back to the thaumaturgists, with no concern for his own safety. He held his hands up to stop the seditionists from attacking.

Yet more thaumaturgists wandered into the square. There was no urgency to their actions. Rather, they appeared to look out at the seditionists, perched behind their barricades, with curiosity.

Ejan turned and stepped down the barricades.

"He'll die," said Kata.

"Watch," said Dexion.

Ejan approached the first figure, a great round man with a bald head. The thaumaturgist's irises were as white as his beard, giving him an alien, inscrutable appearance. They exchanged a few words with the man. He turned and was taking several steps toward the barricades, calling out in a steely voice. "The thaumaturgists will work no longer for the Houses."

A ripple rushed through the barricades, but no one cheered. The world had been turned upside down.

Following the thaumaturgists, a straggle of figures had emerged from the House Technis Complex. The bearded and the broken, many of them insane—they hobbled out, their clothes gray from the hours spent underground. Like rats from a flooded sewer they ventured forth. A man with a withered arm keened quietly. A young woman, perhaps no more than a teenager, held on to her rags as if they were her most precious possessions. Hundreds of them there were, each one as wretched as the others.

Kata rushed among the prisoners. Where was Maximilian? She searched the faces: a toothless man, a young gaunt woman, someone—was it man or woman?—scratching obsessively at their hair. A face she recognised: Aceline.

Aceline stared at Kata blankly.

"Where's Maximilian?" asked Kata.

Aceline staggered on, her eyes haunted.

Kata searched in vain. When she returned to the defensive side of the barricade, Aceline had sat down, her face drawn. Aceline stared glassily at the ground. "It's confusion in there. The House is disorganized. No one seems to know what's happening. I think that's the only reason we got out—there was no one to lock us up again. We hid in the gardens for a while, until we saw the thaumaturgists open the gates."

"They're finished then." The idea seemed impossible to Kata. She spoke like a child uttering new words for the first time. If only Maximilian were here to see it, she thought.

"They won't be finished until the building is razed. They'll hold on as long as they can, hoping to rebuild themselves, to strike back." Rikard sat on the top of the barricades nearby. He swung his legs idly. "Unless we break them now."

In front of the barricades, Ejan mustered a force of seditionists. When they were ready, he turned to the crowd, vast now behind the barricades. "Now is the time to press the advantage. Now is the time to break the House once and for all." He turned and the seditionist force charged forward toward the still-open gates.

Kata followed the hundreds who rushed forward, leaving Dexion with Aceline. Perhaps Max was wounded and lost in the Complex's gardens. Perhaps he was too weak to walk and rested, propped up against one of the Palace's corridors. Along the roadway the seditionists ran, which cut through the gardens and between the buildings. As Kata hurried, she became aware of guards, dropping to their knees and begging for mercy. She passed them by, unaware of whether the crowd offered them compassion or dispatched them coldly.

Through the vast doors of the palace she ran, armed seditionists before her, into the corridors. Through those labyrinthine passages she searched for Max. Others citizens or seditionists were stripping the place of the few valuables that were left.

She climbed up stairs, through the chaos of the place. She passed along corridors where the corpses of guards or House officials lay sprawled. She moved through wide halls that were divided into hundreds of cubicles. Everywhere she looked for a wandering or wounded figure with curly hair. She passed a huge room filled with great cabinets of files. There a seditionist guard stood. "No one allowed in, Ejan's orders."

Finally, Kata came high in the Palace to the vast open office of Director Boris Autec. The glass doors that led to a grand balcony were shattered. Ejan was busy rifling through the drawers, while Rikard examined a scrying ball atop a pillar in one corner.

Sprawled on the balcony lay a corpse and for an instant, Kata's heart tightened. But it was not Max. She approached the body, which lay sprawled on one side, a knife clutched tightly in its skeletal hands. The corpse was gaunt and cadaverous, its jaws clenched in a deathly rictus. The veins of one side of its face were an unnaturally luminescent blue, as if a spidery hand were reaching beneath the skin to the scalp. Across the throat lay a jagged bloody cut, deep to the bone. The eyes stared blankly into space. Kata recognized those eyes, though she could barely recognize the rest of the corpse, for it had changed so profoundly since she had first met Autec. Then he had been an overweight, stub-nosed former tramworker. Now here was a skeletal thing, gaunt and eldritch. So ends the life of Boris Autec, she thought.

Rikard stood beside her and looked down at the corpse. "He took his life before I reached him."

"Are you disappointed?"

Rikard looked out over the city. He has bested me again."

Beyond the balcony lay Caeli-Amur. From this height it did not seem to have changed much at all.

Rikard led a group of four seditionists through the labyrinthine corridors of the palace, and Kata decided to accompany them. As they marched deeper, one of the seditionists hastily drew the corridor on a makeshift map, a squiggle of lines, curves. Two others carried lamps. Great pipes and tubes twisted and coiled along the walls and roof here, in places joining, though they lay silent and dead. Interpersed along them were wheels and levers of unknown function.

A sign read, ZONE RESTRICTED TO OFFICIATES. KEEP OUT. There were no lamps to light the way, so she returned and unhooked one from the wall and then continued on into the darkness.

In an empty corridor, they came to an elevator, and Kata pulled aside the accordion doors. The elevator rattled and groaned as it carried them up to vast and empty hallways leading to desolate ballrooms, lit with natural light from shafts cleverly cut into the ceilings. In alcoves along the walls stood statues of trunk-faced creatures, insect-men and ancient mechanical devices, all lattice-work of metal, cogs, wheels, miniature pistons. The deserted spaces were filled with a ghostly melancholy. All the time, the seditionist sketched his crude maps, moving from one sheet to another as they moved or climbed.

They were now filled with a sense of foreboding. Kata kept fancying that she saw Maximilian's body on the floor, but each time it was only piles of refuse and rags. Great seas of cobwebs coated the walls of some of the rooms, or hung in ropy strands from the roof. A wispy gray mist hovered in the air and everything seemed soft and blurry.

Eventually, they heard a sound echoing through the hallways. At first it seemed like the sound of a broken engine, a relentless arrhythmic coughing, but then it rose high into a whine, a keening backed by a torrential downpour. Kata's skin crawled at the unnatural nature of the sound, for now it seemed to be the wailing of a creature.

Fearfully, the group followed the sound; with each step, it became stronger, more unnerving. Doubt crept into the eyes of Kata's companions. Rikard pressed his lips—the top lightly dusted with hair, he had become a man in these last weeks—together and marched more resolutely forward.

Before them stood a great double door; on its face were pressed ornate, spiraled bands of metal. Spirals and geometric shapes and ideograms seemed to drift off the doors' surface and float in the air.

From behind the door came the terrible cry of an inhuman creature: the cough-cough-cough of a shuddering bawl, then a wail too high to belong to any human, and behind it all, an unnatural sound that to Kata seemed to be that of a waterfall, or perhaps of rustling paper.

Rikard touched the doors, which seemed to moan as they swung themselves open.

Collapsed before a scrying ball in the middle of the marble lay a creature, its insectoid limbs sprawled desolately outward. It's an Elo-Talern, thought Kata in horror. Its inhuman cries ran spikes of ice down Kata's spine; her skin crawled as if spiders ran over her.

The creature turned its horselike head toward them, then flickered out of existence. As it vanished, Kata caught a glimpse of a decaying image somehow *beneath* the form of this one. In an instant the Elo-Talern flashed back into existence.

"I forgot that to be human means to betray," she spat. "Life—I wanted to rejoin the living. I wanted to . . ." But her words—croaking and whispery—trailed off.

The group stood fixed to the spot, overwhelmed by revulsion and fear.

The Elo-Talern attempted to push herself to her feet, collapsed back onto them, and crawled to the throne. Halfway there, she collapsed again, pushed herself up with one arm and looked back at the others. "Now I have to return to the rest of them. They're all dead, lifeless, ruined! It's your fault!" As if drawn up by a cord above her, in an instant she was on her feet, her face twisted and filled with anger. Again she flickered out of existence.

Beside Kata, one of the seditionists fled.

But the Elo-Talern again crumpled in on herself as her anger was exhausted. She turned and walked toward great double doors behind the throne. She touched them, they opened, and shortly afterwards they boomed closed behind her. Something shimmered in the doors and they took on a more solid look, locking the Elo-Talern once again away from the world.

FORTY-EIGHT

Maximilian sat before a great underground lake. Around him, lichen lit the gloom with an eerie glow. How long had he sat here? He couldn't be sure, but he thought it might have been a day or two. It reminded him of fasting on the rocky hill when he was young. Back then—no, that wasn't him. He remembered passing through the dungeons of Technis like a silently gliding spirit. Through the corridors he had walked, accessing some deep knowledge. As if he sensed his way, he knew which turns to take to venture deeper into the dungeon, past the cells and into the ancient tunnels and caves beyond. He had come eventually to this underground lake. It appeared as if once again the way was barred.

He relaxed, breathing in and out. The great skill of the Magi was a discipline almost impossible to achieve—it had taken him almost forty years to master, and even then it was a constant task. First, to learn the formulae and equations, then to allow the conscious mind with its self-centeredness to drop away, to dissolve oneself into the universe. From there, the Art, like any art: creativity and flow and imagination and the use of the equations without self-consciousness. He remembered Iria had been angry with him in those days. She had wanted him to spend more time with her. He had been torn. They had ventured up to one of the satellites orbiting the world. They had even talked of leaving it, of returning back to the Unity, but they were not allowed. That had been part of the condition of staying, of building their very own world the way they wanted it. Hubris—that's what it had been. Looking down on their world, their own Eden, he and Iria had held hands.

"When I'm with you, I'm completely with you," he said. "That's all I can offer."

"But you're not," said Iria. She tossed her head and her hair had hovered in weightlessness. "That's the price of the Art. None of us is now, and none of us will be again. Not properly. The more we use it, the further it drives us apart."

That's how it started, he remembered. They were fighting when they returned and he had left the others, gone across the sea to the great jungles that he loved.

"You can't shut everyone out," they said. "You must come back." They wanted to force themselves together with laws and coercion. He was an embarrassment to their planes.

"Isn't that what we did?" he replied. "Didn't we break away from the Unity? Why can't I break from you?"

Angry, they came for him, and they fought, and war had begun.

Max held his head. Behind his eye the jabbing pain like needles. Ever since his return, he had been blinded by terrible headaches. He felt his mind had been shattered like a glass vessel, and now that it had been reconstructed, there were pieces missing, and the remaining fragments did not sit flush against each other. He squatted to the ground and groaned. Nausea rose within him, and he fell back onto his haunches. Finally, the most severe pain passed, leaving only resonances fluttering from behind his eyes to the back of his neck.

Max stepped into the cold water, first to his knees, then to his waist. The black liquid swirled around him, revealing nothing beneath. On he waded. When he was halfway across the lake, the waters had risen to his chest.

—Aya—he said.—I need the equations again.

Aya lay within him, gathering strength by the hour. Even now Max could feel Aya slipping around, probing his mind, collecting stray memories and knowledge, integrating them. But with each absorption, Max perceived some of Aya's mind drift also into his.

Aya withheld the equations. *I offer you these only because I need this body also.*

The equations drifted again into Max's mind in all their austere beauty.

—This cannot go on forever—said Max.—You and I will have to somehow reach a compromise.

Perhaps you should allow me control of this body. After all, I am Aya.

—What will become of me?—said Max.

I'll absorb you, integrate you.

—You mean destroy,—said Max.

Max dived beneath the silent waters, feeling the coldness rush over his body. In the blackness he swam, reaching out with his mind, roving across the wall to where the aperture lay. As he had done when he escaped from Caeli-Enas, he opened his mouth and took in the water, taking from it the oxygen he needed. It coursed into him uncomfortably; there was a little pain as his body initially rejected it. Yet he continued on, down through the black waters and into the subterranean tunnel. On he swam, until the tunnel rose and he burst through the water into another great empty chamber.

He stepped from the water and found that he was in the ancient pleasure palaces beneath Caeli-Amur. Here travelers had come to spend months in the honeycombed labyrinth, living in great communal worlds generated by their minds. He had been here an aeon ago.

He stepped from the water onto a set of stairs that led to a platform. He collapsed. He was exhausted—from his time beneath the sea, his time in the dungeons. He could not use the Art without great strain. He fell onto the ground and again the pain returned to his head. He lay there, alone in the dark with only the piercing pain for company. He lay there for some time.

Nearby a great round door stood closed. Beneath the closed door ran tracks. Along one wall stood great tanks from which pipes and pumps ran into the wall. This was probably one of the supply rooms for the cells, where nutrients were mixed into the tanks and pumped into the pleasure seekers. But it had all come apart during the cataclysm, and this whole palace had been twisted beneath the ground.

Maximilian started. Above him, hovering some ten feet above the ground, a figure sat in a chair. Over the figure's head a helmet was clamped. But the small man sat as motionless as the skeletons that lay scattered around.

After a while spent staring at the figure, Max stepped to the control bank. He touched the bank and it hummed slowly, little lights glowing in the gloom. He searched for the controls: here was a series of pads to open doors, there a readout for the cells—dead, dead, dead, it read, cataloging the death of the pleasure seekers. But this one: he touched the pad and dragged his finger along it. The chair above him clunked into gear and lowered itself. Max swiveled his fingers across the pad and the helmet opened like an inverted bulb.

The figure fell forward from the seat.

"Omar," said Max.

The little man looked up at Max and smiled gently. "I was having such nice dreams."

Not long afterwards, the two figures, supporting each other like injured soldiers, passed through the hall of machines. Still the machines lay dormant, creatures in the depths of a long hibernation.

My carapaces! said Aya. A burst of excitement rose within Max. *Oh, how we fought Alerion. We danced and struck at his armies on the plain. What we could have achieved! And here they are, waiting for me.*

Maximilian ignored the voice, and they continued on to the seditionist base. Strewn across the floor were the remnants of personal possessions. Black patches of blood stained the floor. Maximilian lay Omar onto the ground, found one of the cooking pots, some dried beans and powdered spices. He cooked up a barely edible paste and the two men ate slowly in silence.

Finally, Max said, "I need to see the city. I need to feel the air on my face."

Omar nodded. "I'll rest here. I'm too weak. But you go ahead. You usually do, anyway."

Maximilian trod the familiar path along the tunnels until he stepped out into the bright morning sun. At first his eyes were blinded by the brilliance of the sun, but slowly his eyes adjusted and the forms of the city appeared before him: a vast sweep from the Factory Quarter along Via Gracchia, with its cafés across to the luxurious Arantine. Below the Arantine, the great Arena and the Lavere nestled in the arms of the Southern Headland. There he could just make out the crisscrossing of the Thousand Stairs. Closer to him lay the Ancient Forum, covered in fog, closer still the cramped Quaedian with its narrow alleyways—his quarter. The Opera towered over the piers, with their steamers and cutters. Finally, the canals nestled in the arms of the Northern Headland, its water palaces gleaming. Fires burned in the city's squares, perhaps because it had been cold, though there seemed to be less smoke billowing from the Factory Quarter. Otherwise it seemed much the same, a busy city, a city filled with life.

Aya's voice was horrified. *Caeli-Amur, my city. What have you done to it? You've ruined it!*

The scent of smoke drifted up to Maximilian. "Caeli-Amur is alive. Full of possibility. I hope it never changes."

Part IV

FUTURES

010101000111001001110101011001010010000001101011011101
110011011110111011101101100011001010110010001100111011101
100101001011000000110100000101001001001011100110011001000
000111010001101111001000000011010110110111001101111011
101110010000000111100101101111011101010101110010001000010
001101001011001110110111100110111101110010011000010110
111001100011011001010010010111000001101000001010010101000
111001001110101011001010010000001110101011011100110011001
000110010101110010011100110110111101000011000010110101110011
001000011010010101101110011001110010110000001101000010101
00100100101011100110010000001110100011011110010000011
101010110111001100100011001010110010011100110011011101001
01100001011011100110010000010000001111100101101110111011
010101110010001000000011000110110111101101011100110011001100
111010101011100110110101001011011110110110011000101110000011
010000101001010100011100100110011101010110010100100000011
010100110101110111100100101100000011010000101001001001
01110011001000000111010001101111001000000110110001100110
0001011101010101100111011010000010000011101000110111111
011001110110110010101110100011010000110010101011100100010101
11000001101000010100101010001110010011101010110010010100
1000000111000001101111011101110110110011001010111001000101101
0000001101000010100100100100101110011001000000011100110101

10100001100001011100100110010101100100001000000011101
11011010010111010001101000001000000110111101110100011
01000011001010111001001110011001011100000011010000101
00100100100100000011000110110111101101101011001010010
00000110100101101110001000000111001101100100101100001
01110010011000110110100000010000001101111011001100010
00000111010001101000011010010110111001100111011100011
00100000010010010010000001101000011000010111011001100110
01010010000001101101011010010101110011011100110110011001010
11001000010110000001101000001010010010110110111001101
11101110111011010010101101110011001110010000000111010001
10100001100001011101000010000000111010001101000001001
01011110010010000000110000101110010011001010010000001
10111001101111011101000001000000111010001101000001001
01001000000011101000011010000011010010110111100110011101
11001100100000010010010010000001110100011100100111101
01011011000111100100100000011100110110010101100101011
01011001011100000110100000101001010011011101010110001
01101000000100000011010010101100110010000001010100011
10000110010100100000010101110110000101111001001000000
01101111011001100010000001110100011011010000110100101100
11100110011101110011001001011100010000000000110100001010

FORTY-NINE
୧ᴥ୨

Kata sat in the rowboat and pulled on the two oars. She insisted this time that *she* row. Like a night not so long ago, the oars creaked against the wooden oarlocks and splashed subtly as they entered the water. Behind her, the child leaned over the prow looking down into the water. Facing her in the boat's rear, the minotaur Dexion sat, looking up at the sky.

"On a night like tonight, you can see the Sunken City," Kata said to them.

Henri stared at her with his great round eyes. Dexion laughed, and said, "No!"

"It's true."

The water was glassy, like the sea so many nights before. The sound of the citizens of Caeli-Amur echoed over the water. As in most of the squares of the city, a great bonfire burned in the center of Market Square. The citizens had come into the streets and now it seemed that they would not leave them. A strange vitality had overcome the city in these last few days. No one was sure of anything, and that meant that everything was questioned, everything discussed. People talked and talked.

History had proved to be more fickle than she thought. Where once history had held her in its iron-tight grasp, clenched and immovable, now it seemed more like floodwaters rushing toward the sea: it found hidden channels and swept all things up in its tide. At places it was a deadly torrent, in others as gentle as a lake. Before long it would take them all into the vast ocean of the future. And was that future ocean a blue green idyll or did monsters lurk beneath its surfaces? What it all meant, Kata could not be sure. A million pathways seemed to open up before her. And yet, up there in the dark recesses of the mountain, the Elo-Talern waited. For now, she was content to breathe in the crystal air, to bathe in the gleaming stars above, to close her eyes and feel her heart beating, steady.

"You can see it! You can see it!" Henri said.

Kata pulled the oars into the boat and looked down into the water. Beneath them, Caeli-Enas glittered in the water. White marble spires shifting and twisting. Its splintered beauty struck Kata. She thought of Maximilian. Where was he? She still held on to hope that she might find him, somewhere, alive. Hope—she had no right to it, and yet there it was, hope, beating within her for the future.

"The city sank before I was born," said Dexion, looking down. "But the older minotaurs speak of it. The old world, gone now." He sighed. "The perfect world, they used to call it, where each gave what they could, and each took what they needed. Would we ever be able to build that again?"

Kata looked at the minotaur: his great hulking frame, his rippling body. "Who can say what is possible," she said. She looked back at the child, who dipped his hand in the water. He tasted it, stuck his tongue out, and grimaced. Kata smiled and looked up at the sky.

Above her, the wind whipped the clouds away, as if they were pulling back a great sheet. The unwrapped sky was littered with stars of diamond-white brilliance. In between them, patches of jet black, the vast reaches of the universe. In that moment, everything was bathed in the clear light. When they finally returned to the city, the same brilliance seemed to embrace everything. The corners of the buildings were sharp and crisp, water in the gutters shone like rivers of silver, the world seemed once more a place of potential, as if possibility had been set free, just like the unwrapped sky above.

FIFTY

About halfway up the mountain face behind Caeli-Amur, a figure stepped out of the darkness. It was wrapped in a cloak and a hood, and appeared to emerge from the very rock, the soft glow of a lantern in hand. Its other hand held the stirrups of a horse. Hidden from view was an opening in the mountain's rocky face, a tunnel that led through the labyrinthine passages all the way through the mountain, past the catacombs and the strange ancient city, past underground streams and dams, close to the Undercity of the Elo-Talern. The figure dropped a heavy bag onto the ground and, turning a knob on the lamp, killed its flame.

Armand stretched in the cool of the early morning. He was born for just this moment. The times demanded a certain sort of individual—his sort of person. Not like Director Autec, who was nothing but a tramworker. It was true, Autec had understood certain realities: There would need to be change in Caeli-Amur, change in order that things could remain the same. A Forum perhaps, laws and rules, regulations, an overarching power higher than the Houses. A paramount authority, like the Directorate in Varenis: it was Armand's destiny to become such a force. When he returned to Caeli-Amur there would be war. Order required force, and he could foresee a brutal struggle to crush all forms of sedition. But in his mind, he pictured a new Caeli-Amur, a Caeli-Amur returned to its days of glory. All things would find their proper place.

Armand strapped the bag onto the side of the horse. Inside was everything he had taken from Technis: the subterranean maps, lists of seditionists, lists of officiates, plans of the city, and wrapped in a silk overlay, the most valuable of possessions—the Prism of Alerion. He had carefully informed his contacts, mobilized his supporters to be ready for his return. Then he had taken a horse from the Technis stables and used the copies of the maps to pass through the hidden passageways to the other side of the mountain.

When the bag was fixed, he swung up onto the saddle. The pathway was steep and possibly dangerous, but he was anxious to be well on the road to Varenis by the time the sun rose over the sea to the east.

With this he led the horse slowly down the side of the mountain. By the time he reached the flat of the valley, the sky to the east was lightening. Before long, he was on the wide cobblestoned road that led northwest toward Varenis. He broke into a gallop, feeling the wind in his hair, the powerful rhythm of the horse beneath him. Finally, when he was surrounded by the foothills, the sun broke over the horizon behind him. Although the road was still shaded, the hills to his west lit up with golden light, the gray stony surfaces brought into sharp focus. North, he thought, to Varenis, the greatest city in the world. There his fate awaited him, and the fate of Caeli-Amur itself.

FIFTY-ONE
✦✧✦

At the edge of a high cliff on the island stood a figure. The wind blew her raven black hair from her face. Her skin was clear and fresh, her eyes huge and green. She looked over the sea, which was unusually aqua colored as it coursed around the dangerous shoals and channels of the Taritian Archipelago. From where she stood, she could see the sunken wrecks of ships that had tried to navigate those treacherous straits, which were impossible to map. Even now she could perceive the islands shifting slightly, moving around each other so that soon they would find a whole new configuration and her view would be different and fresh. The thought filled her with joy. A new configuration, she thought to herself.

She breathed in the cool salt air and the wind felt cool on her skin. I am free, Paxaea thought. The time in Caeli-Amur was now a distant memory. Even the pain of it no longer burned her as it once had. She touched her neck, where the torc had once been clamped. Boris Autec had been a curious man, so filled with contradiction. He had been alien to her, not just his strange beady eyes, his round fleshy face, but his odd emotions, his desire for—for what? She couldn't tell. She could not feel sorry for him, and yet, of all the people in Caeli-Amur, he had freed her. She had left the House Complex with a long straggle of others: prisoners, thaumaturgists, lower officials. She had bought passage on a clipper headed for Numeria. The sailors were filled with radical ideas. They sailed as close to Taritia as was safe and gave her one of the small rowboats to take her the rest of the way. It had been dangerous, but she knew the shoals and reefs well. Finally, she came home to her island, her very own island, free of anyone else.

Now, standing on the edge of the cliff, she threw her head back and cried out. Her voice carried powerfully over the islands and out over the ocean, in the direction of the city she had left. From another island another cry merged with hers. And then yet another carried from another island, and yet another, until the archipelago rang with the sounds of these cries, beautiful and terrible and seductive. The figure stopped her call and listened to the Sirens' chorus. And then she opened her throat and called out again. She *was* free.